THE BOOK OF SECRETS

THE BOOK OF SECRETS

ANNA MAZZOLA

ORION

First published in Great Britain in 2024 by Orion Fiction,
an imprint of the Orion Publishing Group Ltd
Carmelite House, 50 Victoria Embankment
London EC4Y 0DZ

An Hachette UK Company

1 3 5 7 9 10 8 6 4 2

A CIP catalogue record for this book
is available from the British Library.

ISBN (Hardback) 978 1 3987 1430 4
ISBN (Trade Paperback) 978 1 3987 1431 1
ISBN (eBook) 978 1 3987 1433 5
ISBN (Audio) 978 1 3987 1434 2

Typeset by Deltatype Ltd, Birkenhead, Merseyside

Printed in Great Britain by Clays Ltd, Elcograf S.p.A.

MIX
Paper from
responsible sources
FSC www.fsc.org FSC® C104740

www.orionbooks.co.uk

To all the women who know.

I

Rome, 1659

Girolama

The angels stare, stone-eyed, at the casket. Their chiselled faces are smooth and untroubled, as they are throughout the many funerals, marriages and baptisms that take place beneath them every day. Mostly, this past year, it has been funerals, for the plague has swept through Rome and the mosaic of states that make up Italy. Now, though, the plague is silent, having burnt itself out. It is not plague that killed this man.

On the floor of Santa Maria del Popolo, Girolama watches the mourners as they walk past the body laid out for burial, bowing their heads, murmuring. Some touch the arm or gloved hand of the willow-tall young woman who stands near her dead husband's casket, her face shrouded in a black veil. Behind her waits another woman: older, broader, but with a similar bearing. This, Girolama, thinks, must be the widow's mother, for her protective gaze doesn't leave her daughter.

There are two young men by the casket now. They're peering too closely, speaking in a manner not suited to a funeral, to the death of a man who died at just thirty years of age. Death might have ravaged Rome, the plague carrying off the good and the evil and the young and the old, but it has, in Girolama's experience, not inured people to it. They still grieve as deeply as they ever did, each loss a puncture to the soul. These two young men, though, seem untouched by grief or pity. They might be visiting the waxworks at a fair. She hears one say, 'What rosy cheeks! He looks better in death than he did in life. I'd say it rather suited him.'

Under her breath she curses them, wishes them down to the devil. They know nothing. They understand nothing because they're young, confident males and haven't experienced what she has, nor what these women have. They have little idea what it takes to survive in a city made by, and for, men. She wishes that the earth would swallow them up, but there's only one man who's going into the ground today, and he is long past caring.

Once the people have paid their respects, the church workers begin pushing their pikes into the black and white rosettes that bloom on the flagstone floor. The smell is immediate – the noxious breath of death released as the floor is raised, for this is the lid to the common grave. The ground beneath the church is divided into a honeycomb of coffins and corpses: a whole house of the dead lying beneath the living. Even if the women had wanted to, they couldn't have buried him elsewhere. The chapels and tombs are the preserve of the rich. Most of Rome's dead reside in this subterranean city.

The priest and the chaplains have withdrawn, as have the mourners. Only the workers and the women remain, and the perfect Madonna, robed in crimson, her arms open wide as if to comfort them. As Girolama watches the body being lowered by ropes into the pit beneath, she wonders what secrets the man takes with him to his grave, for in life there are secrets we write down in books, others we pass on, and yet others we carry with us to our deaths.

She crosses herself, then leaves the church. Outside, the sky is a pale, scrubbed blue.

2

Stefano

It is, Stefano thinks, a moment of unalloyed joy. All these
people, together again, celebrating the intertwining of two
families, a union that will bring new life and light to Rome.
Above the bright music of the quartet, they hear the clop of
hooves, and his little sister arrives in the palazzo courtyard on
a white horse, the scarlet silk of her gown stark against its pale
flanks. Fioralisa's new husband, the son of an ambassador, steps
forward to greet her, his face flushed pink above the black
velvet doublet. She bows her head, the picture of Roman
womanhood: beautiful, blossoming, biddable. Fioralisa's hair is
garlanded with flowers, and the girls that follow her throw dried
petals and crushed lavender, so that the air is sweet-scented and
filled with the laughter and chatter of the guests. How different
it is to the pestilence and desolation that the plague wrought
these past two years: the empty streets, the whispers, the fear.

Stefano watches as his brothers walk forward to help their
little sister from the horse and, for a moment, his happiness
dips, knowing why he hasn't been chosen for this role. But he

has no time to dwell on it for the players strike up a new song and the bridal couple begin their dance, weaving before the ornate tapestries that have been hung from the walls, their eyes only on each other.

Stefano catches sight of Lucia, his older sister. She is watching Fioralisa with what, he thinks, is a trace of sadness. But then of course she is alone: there is no husband at her side, no children clutching at her skirts. At thirty-six, she is a widow, returned to the authority and home of their father, not something Stefano would wish on anyone. For Lucia, this wedding must be a bittersweet event. She could, Stefano thinks, remarry if she set her mind to it, for she is still handsome, and clever into the bargain, but she has shown little desire to find another husband. Perhaps she considers herself too old, for in Italy, women are compared to roses: sweetest when they've just bloomed. Perhaps it is the dowry, or lack of a decent one, for all the money has gone on their little sister's portion and her marriage *cassone*; on the rented tapestries, sparkling wines and lavish entertainments that surround them. Now, Stefano thinks, if he were to advance himself, improve his position, he could afford to be more generous with her. She senses him staring at her, turns, meets his eye. He gives her a smile but it is a moment before she returns it.

There is a feast to follow the ceremony, the many dishes laid out on long trestle tables in the courtyard: roast capons and baked eels, dove breasts in white wine and pears in sweet liquor, sea bass ornamented with pomegranate, and roasted hares covered in juniper. His father holds court amid the many courses and the numerous guests, two cardinals and the Governor of Rome among them. A senior prosecutor, a man with a large beard and an even larger opinion of himself, is seated to Stefano's right and absolves Stefano from the duty of making conversation by talking without cease of his cases and the importance of severity in punishing criminals. Stefano himself is but a junior magistrate and, though he is young to have reached such a role, it galls him that he is still a small fish in the great pool of the Papal Court. True, he is not yet three and thirty, but God knows there are many who die before that time. So many of his colleagues have succumbed these past few years that Stefano knows he is lucky to be here at all. The smell of pestilence has gone from the streets, but the reminders of death and mortality are everywhere: in the faces that are missing from this wedding banquet, in the names removed from the plaque on the entrance to the court. The sand falls through the glass with every minute that passes. He must succeed, and quickly, or what will he have achieved in life?

As for Stefano's younger sister (now seated at the table and pink-cheeked with wine), she must breed and quickly, for that is what women do. Already she has been taking potions to ensure her fertility, or so he has gleaned from snatches of overheard conversation. Women have all sorts of means for encouraging their wombs; indeed they have potions for almost everything. He is not sure what these remedies are, only that they are shared and traded between women and referred to as 'secrets' and written down in *libri di segreti*: glorified recipe books.

Stefano's oldest brother, Vincenzo, a cardinal's secretary, leans over the table towards him. 'And when will it be your turn, Stefanino?' he teases him. 'When will you choose one of the lucky daughters of Rome?'

'When the time is right, Vincenzo,' Stefano says, washing his hands in a bowl of scented water. When he has made a name for himself and is allowed to select his own bride. He wants to find someone to match his brother's wife in beauty and wit, someone to raise their family's status. He glances across the room at a woman called Sulpizia: skin white as a sugar loaf, hair dark as a raven. But Sulpizia is of noble birth. As things stand, he doesn't stand a chance. Though they have money, he and his siblings are still the children of a cloth merchant in a city where the undisputed elite are some thirty noble families who vie for supremacy and whose oft-spilled blood marks them out as better – the Colonna and Orsini, the Aldobrandini, the Borghese, Barberini and Chigi.

As the youngest son, Stefano will inherit the least, and he does not delude himself that he has sufficient looks or charm to offset this lack of wealth. He is well enough looking with a clear complexion, a full head of dark hair, and an almost full set of teeth, but he is shorter than his brothers, and slighter, and he has not their easy confidence, nor their father's commanding manner. His eyes are hazel, not the rich brown of his siblings and father. With his dark lashes and beardless chin (he has tried, but it does not grow), he worries that he has a feminine aspect about him. No, if he is to raise himself in stature, then it will require something more.

'Well, don't leave it too long, Stefanino,' Bruno says, 'or you'll end up having to marry your horse!'

'Yes, very good, brother.' This is Bruno's idea of humour. He and Vincenzo have always mocked Stefano for his love of horses, as they have mocked him for many things. Stefano wishes he would grow immune to it, as Mithridates grew immune to poison by taking a little a day, or as men build up a tolerance to liquors. Still, however, his brothers' taunting stings, the alcohol notwithstanding. He must grow a thicker skin. Perhaps the women have a potion for it.

After the feast and the sugar sculptures come the entertainments. There are dancers on stilts and breathers of fire spitting pillars of flame into the air. A dozen acrobats dance across a new-made stage and begin to climb one atop the other, the crowd urging them on. As the final performer takes his place at the pinnacle of this pyramid, Stefano feels a hand on his shoulder. He turns to see the immense form of Francesco Baranzone, the *Governatore di Roma* himself. 'A word?'

'Of course.' Stefano feels a pulse of alarm. Baranzone, both bishop and governor, has been their father's friend for years and Stefano has never felt comfortable with him. He is too broad, too impressive and self-assured, much like the man Stefano wishes himself to be. In his presence, Stefano always feels like a minnow.

'This way,' Baranzone says as confident in Stefano's father's house as he might be in his own. He enters the *saletta*, where a fire is burning and where more food and wine have been laid out. He pulls the curtain that divides the rooms, then turns back to Stefano.

'Your father says you are already being tasked with some of the most complex cases.'

Stefano shifts from one foot to the other like a schoolboy. He is mildly surprised his father has said anything positive about him, but then everything the man says is calculated to impress. 'I have been fortunate in that regard, yes.' Fortune, in fact, has little to do with it. He works harder than most.

'I may have a role for you.' Baranzone is scrutinising him with his small, dark eyes. 'But it requires a man of some mettle. Some ... stomach.'

Stefano meets his gaze. 'I don't shirk from difficult matters.' In his time as an advocate, he's seen a variety of humanity's horrors, a decent amount of gore. After all, this is Rome, a city founded on Romulus's murder of Remus. Its male-heavy population is preoccupied with honour, status and vendetta; most men carry knives or swords and know how to use them. The conflicts of French and Spanish factions, rival artists, warring beggars, and gangs of thugs and thieves regularly spill over into nose cutting, face-slashing, death. 'I have dealt with the most serious crimes.'

'Indeed.' Baranzone gives a half-smile. 'I'm sure you have, but this isn't just about dealing with the dirt. It is about keeping going, and holding firm.'

Stefano holds his gaze. *And?* He might be small, but he is tenacious. He has had to be, growing up in the house he has.

'Come. Sit.' Baranzone takes a seat at a small table on which cups are set out, and he pours wine from a flask into two of them. When Stefano has joined him, he says, 'Here it is: word has come to me of a dyer recently released from prison, struck down with some sickness and dead from it, leaving a grieving widow. So far, so normal.'

Stefano waits, drinks. From the next room he can hear laughter and conversation. Why is Baranzone talking to him about this here, now, at his sister's wedding?

'Only,' Baranzone says, 'the corpse does not decay as it should.' He raises his eyebrows. 'It's said that the man remained ruddy and healthy looking for days after his death; that, even when he was buried, there was no scent of decay.'

Stefano frowns. He has heard all this before, in tales of saints whose bodies do not decompose and who remain as beautiful in death as their spirits were in life, preserved by some celestial magic. This, though, is no saint, but a common man, a prisoner. 'You did not see the body yourself?'

'No, but I'll come to that. You see, Stefano,' – and here Baranzone glances around to check they are still alone – 'there are rumours. Rumours that are dangerous at times such as these. Specifically, there are rumours that, despite the thankful passing of the plague, men continue to die in unnatural numbers.'

Stefano feels the hairs on his arms rise. 'Is there any truth to these rumours?'

'Well, that is where you come in, if you are up to the task. It

9

may well be that these are just baseless whispers, no more than the chitter-chatter of market women. Or it may be that there is something to them.' Baranzone nods. 'This Dyer at the Elm, as he was known: his is not the first story that has come to me of a body that is strangely preserved after death.'

'Who——?'

The Governor cuts him off. 'There are no names, no specifics. I am merely telling you of the rumours. It will be for you to investigate, if you think yourself capable.'

'Investigate the dyer's death?'

'The dyer's death, the death of any other common man which seems to you to be linked. Carry out an *inquisitio*. It may be, as I say, that this is women's talk with nothing to it save for a need to pass the time and titillate. Let us hope it's that. But it would pay to be sure and to carry out a proper inquisitorial inquiry, secretly. Rome is on the rise. We're clawing ourselves back from pestilence and reshaping ourselves as the centre of the Catholic world. The Pope wishes Rome to exemplify the new order, and this hardly fits with the brief.'

'The Pope is aware of all this?'

'Of course. It is done on his orders, my boy. This will be a Papal inquiry, a holy inquiry. You would be appointed inquisitor on his behalf.'

Stefano swallows. Alexander VII himself, centre of all of Rome, spiritual head of Christendom reigning across all the territories of the Church. 'Then of course I will do it. Indeed, I am honoured to be asked.'

Baranzone takes another sip of wine and smiles. 'Good man. But, and I'm sure you don't need me to tell you this, you must proceed with the utmost caution. The utmost discretion. It would not do to alarm people. They've suffered enough these past years and are only now beginning to prosper again. If they think there is some possible new epidemic, then the public mood will be dangerous. This *inquisitio* must be kept from the public gaze. You may tell those closest to you, but no more.'

'Of course. I will be discreet.'

'Very well. For there is a second reason for such an approach: if there is any truth to these rumours, and if it is human hand rather than the hand of God behind the deaths, then it's vital that the person or persons responsible are not alerted to your investigation.'

'I understand.' Not just rumours, then. They must think there is something to it. Why else order an *inquisitio*? Why else proceed so very quietly? Stefano feels his heart thumping. '*Some possible new epidemic*', the Governor said. Please God, let it not be so. 'This would be my first appointment as sole investigating magistrate in such a matter. Not, of course' – he hurries to say – 'that I think I'm unable to carry out the task, merely that I may need some assistance.'

'And assistance you shall have. I've already appointed a doctor, a man whose mind is as keen as his blade.'

'Excellent.' But that was not what Stefano meant. He has only recently been appointed a judge. Complex cases he has considered, yes, but he's never played the role of inquisitor investigating a suspicious death.

Baranzone says, 'You'll forgive me for raising this on such an auspicious occasion, but the body, you see, is on its way up.'

'I'm sorry?'

'They're exhuming the dyer's body tomorrow, before decay can set in, so you'll need to get started at once.'

Stefano stares at him. He thinks of the other cases he has said he will take. There is no choice, however, but to accept. He cannot refuse. This is the Governor asking him, the Pope's man in the courts, and, really, he is not asking him, he is order-ing him.

Baranzone gets up. 'We must return to the fray. There

is celebrating to be done. Although' – and here he nods at Stefano's glass – 'you may wish to curtail your drinking if you're to keep your stomach contents in the morgue tomorrow.'

Stefano smiles, for he must oblige the man. 'I said I had the stomach for it, and I do.' He pauses. 'Does my father know of this?'

'Well, I did not seek his permission before asking you. You are hardly some blushing bride.' Baranzone's eyes are hard. 'But yes, I told him I had a project for you. He assured me you wouldn't disappoint me.'

As Stefano leaves the chamber and makes for the central courtyard, a tall woman turns towards him. Lucia. She waits until Baranzone is some distance away. 'What did he want?'

'Why do you assume he wanted something?'

'Because he always does. That's the sort of man Baranzone is. It's why he's got where he has.' She folds her arms. 'Well?'

'Well, sister, I have a new and important role. One which I must carry out with some subtlety.'

She frowns. 'What is this role?'

Stefano considers. Baranzone had said he might speak of it to those closest to him, and Lucia, surely, is the closest. There are few others, truth be told, for he does not find it easy to make friends. 'This is not to go outside the household, but I will tell you.' And he does, with some excitement. He watches her frown deepen as he reaches the part about the exhumation of the body.

'I am not sure that you should accept this commission, Stefano.'

Anger flares within him. He should have known not to have told her. He should have known she would only pour cold water on his joy. 'I've already accepted it, Lucia. It would have been unwise for me to do otherwise, and, in any event, this is an opportunity.'

She chews her lip. 'But if it is indeed some new epidemic, then you are putting yourself at the forefront of it, and your health—'

'I will be careful, I promise you. I am not a sickly little boy anymore, Lucia. You really don't need to fuss.'

She shakes her head. 'I don't like it.'

Stefano snaps. 'For goodness' sake, Lucia, why cannot you simply be happy for me? Why must you always regard life as a glass half empty?'

His sister turns away from him and Stefano feels a moment of regret, but it is true what he says. These past few years she has often seemed cast down, peevish.

'I am trying to help you, *fratellino*, as I always am. I don't trust Baranzone and I don't trust his motives. Why has he given this commission to you? You are only newly a judge.'

'Maybe, Lucia, he thinks me capable. Had you considered that? Maybe he has heard I have a quick mind and thinks I will do a good job.'

'Or maybe he thinks he can manipulate you,' she says quietly.

That cuts him to the quick. He has always been the little brother, the runt of the family, the weakest. 'God's blood, I am not going to let the man push me around. Would it hurt you to have a little confidence in me, Lucia?'

'It isn't that. It's him.'

He doesn't believe her. 'If that's the case, I don't understand why you're so against the man. He's obtained his position through hard work and the tireless pursuit of justice, and he's been a friend of Father's for years. Or do you doubt Father's judgement now too?'

She turns back to Stefano and regards him, her dark eyes still. 'I am a good judge of men these days, I think.'

'No, Lucia, you are bitter. Jealous of your sister and now jealous of me.' Maybe he should not say such things but the wine and the anger combined make him rash. 'I'm going back to the celebrations. This is Fioralisa's marriage day, remember? It is supposed to be a day of joy.'

'Supposed to be, yes,' she says quietly.

'Meaning what?'

'Meaning one cannot assume happiness, Stefano. One cannot assume anything. It is all more complex than that.' She has turned away from him again and is looking out of the window.

'One can hope, though, Lucia. One can hope and make merry and wish the best for those you love. You've just chosen not to do those things.' He leaves her and returns to the laughter and dancing outside. Despite the Governor's warning, he takes another glass of wine and drains it to take away the taste of her bitterness. He will not let Lucia ruin his moment. He is entitled to some happiness.

As if in echo of his thoughts, fireworks shoot all at once into the sky like comets: astonishing, sparkling jets of silver and gold making a river of gold across the darkness. The coos of the guests mix with the delighted screeches of the children and Stefano thinks yes, this is the moment.

Everything is about to change.

3

Anna

Have mercy on us, O Lord.

The banging on the door is so loud that Anna can feel it right inside her head, and she knows that if her husband gets in, the fists will be pounding not her eardrums but her body, her skull, her swelling stomach. Fear has lived within her for so long that it should be a familiar thing, grown rounded and numb. Still, though, its edges are sharp as a knife.

'In God's name, let me in, you witch, or I'll kill you!'

He doesn't seem to see that there is no logic in what he says, but then he is drunk and furious. There is no point attempting to reason with him. Anna discovered that months ago, after weeks of pleading and begging. It's best, she's deduced, to remain entirely silent while he rages, and hope that he'll tire himself out, or pass out, before he manages to break down the door. And so she stands, back against the wall, one hand over the unborn child in her belly, quietly praying, in that small and darkened room.

Next to her stands her maid, Benedetta, also silent, also terrified. Philippe has never hurt Benedetta, but Anna doesn't doubt that he'd knock her out of the way were she ever to get between them. It's why she's told Benedetta to keep back and stay quiet when the rages come. 'There's nothing you can do for me. You must protect yourself.'

It is enough to know Benedetta is there with her in the darkness. That she is not alone. The woman came to her only a month ago and immediately she saw how it was between them. From what her maid has said, Anna understands that she too has had much difficulty in marriage, and though Benedetta says that her husband died, Anna suspects she ran away from him, or that she was deserted.

More banging, this time with something harder than a fist. He must be using a chair leg, or some other implement. She fears that the door will begin to crack. 'I am your husband,' Philippe is shouting. 'I am lawfully entitled to punish you, and punish you I will!' Another violent thwack against the door.

Anna can feel the sweat trickling down her neck and prays that the babe in her stomach – over six months now if she has calculated right – cannot sense any of her anxiety, nor hear his father's anger.

'You must do something,' Benedetta whispers. 'It can't go on, it can't.'

Anna takes her hand from her stomach and reaches out to Benedetta, as much to comfort herself as her maid. Do something, yes, but what? Where can she go? Who can she ask, other than God, who does not seem to hear her prayers? It's a question she has asked herself over and over. She has begged her mother, even showed her the bruises on her thighs, but her mother only pulled down her dress and said sharply, 'He is your husband. It is his right. He is of an artistic temperament. It is your duty to soothe him and to forebear. It is all of our duties, Anna. This is the world in which we live.'

Maybe if her father were still alive, her father who promised

Anna to Philippe in the first place ('a rising artist', he had claimed. 'A man of great promise'), then he would do something, but her father died shortly after her marriage, and never got to see its true misery, never realised what he had done.

So no, not her family, not the law, certainly, for she knows the police and courts won't help her. What her husband does is lawful, mostly, and the things that aren't? Those are things she can't talk of, even to God. In Rome, a husband may kill his wife in some circumstances, if his action is passionate and swift. That is how much value is placed on a woman's life. No, the law will not help her. Though she might in theory apply for an annulment of her marriage, she has no money to pay the lawyers and, even if she had, Philippe would surely kill her as soon as the papers were served. Who, then? Who? How can she find a way out?

She sees a flash of light through the door. The wood is giving way. It is seconds until he is here.

4

Stefano

When Stefano opens the door out onto the street, a line of sightless mendicants are passing, hand in hand, the man at the front holding out a basket for money. The blind leading the blind. Stefano gives them a handful of copper *baiocchi* and hopes this is not an omen as to how his investigation will proceed. He has sometimes seen Lady Justice depicted wearing a blindfold, though it's unclear to Stefano whether this is to suggest she is blind to the iniquities carried out before her, or anxious to ensure she is not swayed by wealth and status. He will ensure that, in his court at least, it is the latter version of justice that presides.

He walks to the church of Santa Maria in Trastevere where he dips his fingers in the holy water of the font, crosses himself, genuflects, then kneels and prays for divine guidance. He offers thankfulness to the Holy Spirit for his new commission and asks for his assistance in finding the truth, in ensuring he does not disappoint his father, his family, or himself. He also prays for protection, for Lucia was surely right in that regard: this case of the dead Dyer might mark some new disease, some new scourge come to taunt them after the plague's departure. That would account for why Baranzone wanted it dealt with quickly and quietly and perhaps why he has chosen him for the task, rather than some aged judge. For the first time in some months, Stefano has lined his pockets with taffeta pouches of sandalwood, cinnamon, camphor and musk: a protection against disease. He has also taken a dose of theriac to guard against the plague. He regrets his harsh words to his sister at the wedding. Lucia has always considered it her duty to look out for him, as their mother died when he was still young and their nurse was a curious woman, full of frightening tales and peculiar superstitions. It was churlish of him to accuse Lucia of trying to ruin his happiness. She was trying to protect him, as she always is. He will apologise to his sister, take her a small gift. Some sugared fruits to sweeten her.

Stefano crosses the grey-green Tiber at the Ponte Sisto and makes his way south, past a cackle of women beating their laundry against the stones of the riverbank, past the grand Palazzo of the Orsini, and through a piazza where dust-covered workers are still constructing a church. So much of Rome has been a building site for so long that Stefano has given up on expecting things ever to be finished. For his entire life, popes have been pouring money into the capital, redesigning it, trying to reshape it into a model that will compel faith and crush dissent. New layers are being added to the old; an army of architects, artists and urban planners have been tasked with turning Rome into the image of Catholic majesty and triumph. For now, though, it is a city swathed in scaffolding and sheeting: churches without domes, buildings without roofs. This doesn't deter the pilgrims. They still come in their thousands, more to see the crumbling relics and touch the shrines to martyred saints, than to view the ambitious architecture and astonishing art. Even this late in the year, a swarm of them sleep on the steps of Saint Peter's Basilica, rolled in their dark cloaks like moths in cocoons.

As Stefano reaches L'Ospedale del Uomini Feriti, a patient is being hurried in on a stretcher, his cries piercing the air. The stretcher-bearers move too quickly for Stefano to understand exactly what he sees, but there is enough blood for him to appreciate their urgency. That man, at least, is alive. Where Stefano is bound, there lie only the dead. A nurse directs him along a corridor and down some steps. He knows he is in the right place because, even outside the mortuary door, the smell of the air is putrid. Dottor Marcello, for he assumes it is he, sits on a stone seat, waiting. He is a dark-complexioned man and as he stands, Stefano sees he is not much taller than he is himself, but stockier, better formed. 'Dottor Marcello?'

'Signore Bracchi, a pleasure.' The man has a wide, mischievous smile. 'Your first time at the morgue?'

'It is,' Stefano concedes. 'Not yours, of course.'

'No. This place and I are old friends.' He has warm brown eyes that seem to twinkle. Stefano cannot tell if he's laughing at him. Perhaps he is merely good-humoured, but it seems a strange thing to be good-humoured around the dead. 'They've had me in here before examining a variety of things that have been dragged out of the Tiber: a two-headed calf most recently.'

'An omen?'

The man shrugs. 'The Governor feared so. He suspected sorcery, but strange things happen in nature with no need for human hand.'

'You ... like this particular work?'

'I am paid for it.' Another smile. 'And yes, I find it interesting. Our bodies give up secrets after death that we've maintained during life. They are like books that we learn to read. We will have to hope this fellow has some answers for us today.'

'You've seen the body?'

'Only from the outside. Baranzone instructed me to wait until you arrived.'

'Very good.' Stefano follows Marcello into a room and towards the table on which the man lies, his body covered by a sheet. The smell is overwhelming, despite the herb pomanders that have been hung from the ceiling. Stefano is reminded of the odour that wafted from the plague pits every morning when they began the incinerations: the sweet, sickening stench of death. He hasn't missed it, that's for sure.

Marcello looks at Stefano. 'Given that we don't yet know for sure what caused this man's death, it is sensible to be cautious, I think. I would suggest you stay away from the body.'

Stefano swallows and steps back, grateful for the excuse to do so. 'You think, then, that it might be some new disease? You think that is why Baranzone has tasked us with investigating?'

'Perhaps. Truly, I don't know.' Marcello is putting on a pair of gloves. 'I understand that the physician who saw the man while he was still alive didn't think so, but we will know better when we've examined the body. You've not seen a post mortem before, I take it?'

'No, but I've read much of them.'

A small smile. Marcello draws back the sheet to reveal the dead man's mottled face and Stefano, though he has vowed he will appear untouched, struggles to keep his own face expressionless. This is no flush-faced saint preserved from decay. This is a man whose skin has begun to bloat with corruption, his lips as thick as worms.

'Yes,' Marcello says, 'not exactly perfectly preserved and full of health, is he? But then he has been in the ground a week at least.'

'What is this, on his hands?' The man's palms and fingers are discoloured – streaked with deep red like a birthmark.

'The mark of his trade,' Marcello says, rolling up his sleeves. 'You can't dye gloves or hides without some rubbing off on your own skin.'

Of course. Stefano feels a fool. 'Could it be the dye that killed him?'

'Unlikely. It would have to be some very potent substance and this is a man who'd been a dyer for years, I believe. Let's see what the insides show.' He takes a knife to begin his work.

Stefano realises he is holding his breath.

'We open the chest first,' Marcello explains. He makes the first incision along the collarbone and down the man's side, lifting the skin to expose the breastbone and lungs, then the unpleasantly meat-like heart. He then begins to work at the ribs with a handsaw. The sound is disconcerting.

Stefano listens and watches carefully, wanting to miss nothing. The smell is worse than he anticipated and he is grateful that his breakfast was plain and that he stopped drinking before ten o'clock at night. Even Marcello, who must be used to such things, occasionally refreshes himself with a perfumed handkerchief. As he cuts and saws, he explains what he finds: heart and lungs normal, liver consistent with cholera.

'Nothing unusual so far?'

Marcello shakes his head. 'Not really. It all fits with a man who's been sick with cholera. The liver and spleen congested with blood, the intestines much diseased. The decay is, admittedly, less pronounced than one might expect of a body this age, but then his corpse is severely dehydrated as is often the case with cholera. There's nothing to suggest assault. Nothing that I can see that might suggest contamination or poison, for there are no blackened nails, no spots on the skin, no corrosions in the oesophagus or stomach. His stomach is perhaps redder than I would have expected, but then it may just have been

22

particularly inflamed by the disease. So far as I can see, there is nothing to suggest some mysterious new illness.'

'Then he died just as his family claim?'

'Perhaps, but, as I say, the decay is not as advanced as I would have expected in a corpse that has been in the autumn earth for a week.'

They both regard the body.

Stefano says: 'Assuming that the people who viewed his corpse at the funeral were right and his flesh did at that time seem ruddy and healthy, what might have caused that?'

Marcello licks his lips. 'Honestly? I don't know. Certainly he's far from ruddy now, but rather has the bluish grey complexion I'd expect. I've been reading what literature I can put my hands on and have found nothing to provide an explanation. It could of course have been that the people who made up the man's face did a particularly good job, but Baranzone was told he was not painted at all.'

'How do you know him? Baranzone, I mean?' Stefano curses himself for this clarification. It's obvious how he knows the other man. He has just dissected him.

'I've worked for him several times before, on various cases. We met some years ago when I gave evidence on an instance of alleged witchcraft.'

'And was it?' Stefano asks sharply. 'Witchcraft?'

'It could not be proven,' Marcello says vaguely.

Stefano realises that the doctor may be one of those new men who do not believe in witchcraft at all. He wishes he had his certainty.

They both look back at the dead man. 'Could it be some medical trick?' Stefano asks. 'Something administered to slow the decomposition of the body?'

Marcello slowly shakes his head. 'I cannot identify what that would be. If it is a poison, it has left no trace. Clearly he hasn't been dried or mummified or pickled like a herring. I don't see how it could have been done with potions or ointments, and what other solution is there?'

Sorcery, Stefano thinks. *Maleficia*. Magic swirls about the streets and alleyways of Rome: tales of people cured or killed by incantations and curses, people brought back from the dead by healers. This is a new age, the age of the Reformation, and they are not supposed to believe in such miracles unless they're those sanctioned by the Church, but still, people do, just as they pray to saints, create wax statues, and wear amulets for luck.

Stefano says: 'The Governor suggested that there were stories of another man so preserved.'

'Yes, he did. We must find out more of these stories, see if there is any truth to them, speak to any doctors who treated the deceased.' Marcello puts up his hands. 'Forgive me: I am not telling you how to do your job. You are the investigating judge here.'

Stefano's instinct is to be annoyed, but he realises that in fact he needs all the help he can get. 'I welcome your suggestions, Dottor Marcello. Indeed, if we are to succeed we must work together.'

Marcello glances at his gloves, which are coated in gore. 'I would give you my hand, but you may not wish to shake it.'

Stefano smiles. 'Do the man's family know that he has been exhumed?'

'In theory they should have been informed,' Marcello says, 'but based on my work with Baranzone before? I very much doubt he's told them. These are poor people, after all.'

Stefano is grateful for Marcello's ease and good humour. He often struggles with initial meetings, feeling himself awkward, but this one has proceeded well. They agree to visit the dyer's widow, Teresa, at once. She lives not far from the Pantheon, behind the church of Santo Stefano del Cacco. The Pantheon area is the heart of the city, full of craftsmen and workshops, art merchants and pastry shops. Teresa lives in the poorest part. Here the city retains its old dark, narrow and dank streets, winding and crooked, many still unpaved and muddy, their gutters filled with refuse. The widow's apartment is in a crumbling building that reeks of decay. The woman who comes to the door, however, is beautiful, quite strikingly so: tall and slender with skin like porcelain against the black of her rough woollen dress. Yes, she says, surprised, she is indeed Teresa Verzellina, wife of the Dyer at the Elm. Stefano introduces himself and Marcello and explains that he has heard about the sad demise of her husband, and has been tasked with conducting some enquiries. He does not say what those enquiries are, nor who has tasked him with them.

The woman stares at Stefano, her white brow slightly furrowed. 'You're with the police?'

'No, indeed,' he smiles. The police – the *sbirri* – are ruffians and scoundrels, in general, renowned for their corruption and greed. He does not wish to be mistaken for one. 'I am a magistrate – a judge. My friend here is a doctor. We are here with the authority of the Governor of Rome, but you mustn't concern yourself. We are merely doing as we do in all such cases and making sure all is well.' This is a patent lie. If the Governor investigated all deaths, then he would have no time to do anything else, even piss, for scores die in Rome each day.

Teresa is polite, however, invites them in and introduces them to her younger sister who sits sewing by the window. Stefano is struck by the poverty of the rooms: the flaking walls, the meagre furnishings (two beds, two chairs, irons for the fireplace, and an aged wooden trunk). A third woman, older, emerges from a back room. She wears a black dress with slit sleeves over a dark grey underdress, and worn black slippers on her feet. Teresa introduces the woman as her mother, Cecilia. She is handsome enough with still rich dark hair, but she does not have her daughter's graceful beauty. Nor, it seems, does she have her naivety. This woman is warier than Teresa, and wishes to know what his purpose is. 'The Governor sent you, you say? But why?'

Stefano takes the drink Teresa hands him, glances at Marcello, and decides he must tell them some of it. 'There were some concerns raised about the state of Signore Beltrammi's body. No doubt it was your good work in preparing it, but he appeared, it was said, not to have decayed.'

There is a flicker of alarm in the older woman's eyes. 'If someone has been suggesting some sorcery, some trick…!'

'No, no,' he hastens to reassure her, 'no such thing is claimed.' Though in Rome such suggestions are frequent. This is the city of saints and relics, of potions and portents, where a flight of red butterflies might be seen to augur death. 'Tell me,' he says. 'When did Signore Beltrammi grow ill? I understand he'd been in prison.'

'Only for his debts,' Teresa says quickly. 'He wasn't a criminal.'

'Of course,' Stefano agrees, though he doesn't yet know if that's true. Certainly it is plausible. A good part of Rome has spent time in prison for debt.

'It was there he grew sick,' Cecilia tells them. 'Only a few days after he was arrested. Tell me how that makes any sense: to imprison a man because he can't pay his creditors, then keep him in such conditions that he sickens and dies and can never pay them at all?'

'He was kept poorly, then?' Stefano asks.

Cecilia looks at him with, he thinks, a hint of scorn. 'It is, Signore, one thing to be rich in Rome and to be imprisoned, quite another to be locked up with nothing. We took him what food and blankets we could, but he was sleeping in a damp cell on the stone floor.'

Marcello leans forward. 'And this illness: what was it? What symptoms did he show?'

'It was a persistent fever,' Teresa says. 'He complained first of a burning in his throat, but then the pains went to his chest and stomach and he became so weak that he couldn't stand.' She is tugging at the fabric of her dress.

'Do you know what malady it was?' Marcello asks.

'We didn't then. They wouldn't let us take our own doctor to him.' Tears are now running down Teresa's cheeks.

'Why not?'

Cecilia has her arm round her daughter. 'The prison governor said it wasn't permitted. That only their own doctor could see him, but he was some old quack who saw hundreds of prisoners a day and cared nothing for any of them.'

Stefano nods. This is interesting. He will have to talk to the prison governor. 'Was it because of his health that Beltrammi was released?'

'No, the creditor dropped the suit,' Teresa said, wiping her eyes.

'Because you paid them?'

'No, because I begged them. It made no difference, though, for by the time we got him home it was too late. We couldn't save him.'

'You nursed him yourself?' Marcello asks.

'We did. Our doctor said it was cholera and prescribed medicines and purges, but nothing we tried made any improvement. He only worsened.' Her voice is choked. Stefano cannot doubt that her distress is genuine.

'Can you give us the name of the doctor you saw?' Marcello asks.

27

'Of course, Signore. It was Dottor Corsilli who lives near Sant'Ignazio.'

'What medicines did you use?'

'At first an emetic with acid of sulphur. It made him vomit so badly that he said it felt as if the roof had fallen on his chest. We didn't try it again.' Teresa looks at her hands.

'Anything else?'

Cecilia takes the lead: 'An infusion of ginger, and a draught of sal volatile and poppy. Mint and vinegar for the fever.'

'Also the Saint's oil,' the younger sister says.

Cecilia glances at her daughter. 'Yes, that too.'

'You'll forgive me for asking,' Marcello says, 'but how long between him first becoming ill and his sad passing?'

The women look at one another and Teresa says: 'He grew sick within four days of his arrest, which was just before the festival of the Assumption.'

'And he died on the sabbath after the day of the Madonna in September,' her mother concludes.

Stefano calculates. 'So, three weeks.' It is a fairly standard period of time in which to die. If you do not rally within the first week, you will succumb over the next two. 'Did anyone else at the prison grow sick, that you know of?'

Teresa shakes her head. 'The prison said that others were ailing, but none so sick as he. Certainly no one else died, so far as I'm aware.'

Stefano nods, but he is thinking. 'I'm so sorry to have troubled you with these questions, but we want to be sure, you see, that there is nothing strange in the manner of your husband's death.'

Teresa merely frowns, as though not understanding. A tendril of hair has escaped her bun and winds its way down her delicate neck. Stefano can imagine her husband would have been protective of her, jealous even. 'What sort of man was he, your husband?'

'A good man, Signore. A strong one.'

'Did he have enemies?'

'Not more than any man.'

Yes, then. 'Anyone in particular?'

'There were some brothers he'd fallen out with over of some supplies they were supposed to have got for him. But really, it was not the sort of dispute that would have caused them to harm him, I think. It was a trivial thing.'

Stefano nods. Men in Rome kill each other every day over apparently trivial matters: swords are drawn over honour besmirched, the wrong look, the wrong gesture. 'Who are these brothers?'

'Rinaldi is their name. In the Prati district. They sell flowers and lichens. For the dyes. Madder and vermilion and such. There was some disagreement, I think, over payment.'

'I see. Were there any other quarrels with anyone else? Had anyone threatened him?'

'Oh, no. They wouldn't have dared.'

Stefano scrutinises Teresa. He has a sense she is holding something back, but maybe she is simply nervous in their presence. 'Did he have any trouble in prison? Any fights, disagreements?'

'If he did, the prison didn't tell me.'

'But, Signore,' Cecilia, her mother, says with a touch of impatience. 'Even if someone wanted to harm him, you can't intentionally kill a man with cholera, can you?'

Stefano glances at Marcello.

'No, Donna Cecilia,' the doctor says. 'You cannot. You must not worry yourselves.'

Cecilia nods. 'Well, if that is all? You can see my daughter is distressed. It has been a difficult time for her. For all of us.'

'Of course,' Stefano says. 'We will take our leave.'

They make towards the flimsy door.

★

'Is that true?' Stefano asks Marcello once they are back in the street. 'That you can't infect someone with cholera?'

'I suppose it may be possible to do so,' Marcello says. 'I've heard of the disease being passed on with clothing or blankets. There were tales too of Caterina Sforza trying to infect Alexander, the Borgia Pope, with plague, and in Naples there were riots against alleged purveyors of powders spreading the contagion. But, Stefano, I don't believe this was cholera. If it were cholera and he contracted it in jail, other prisoners would most likely have died of it.'

'Unless the prison are lying?'

'That's possible,' Marcello says. 'We'll have to speak to the prison governor.'

'Yes, and the physician the women spoke of. Those brothers too.' Stefano pauses. 'What did you think? Of the women? Of what they told us?'

Marcello shakes his head. 'The insides of people's bodies: those I can tell you about. The contents of their minds? Less so. After all, do we even know our minds? Often not, I'd say. I thought the mother seemed defensive, but perhaps that isn't surprising. People like that only come in contact with authority when there's some calamity or crime, and she wishes to protect her daughter. To them, you with your black lawyer's suit must seem like a harbinger of doom.' He gives Stefano a toothy grin.

5

To deliver a child in danger:
Take a date stone, beat it into powder, let the woman drink it with
wine, then take polipody fern and emplaster it to her feet, and the
child will come whether it be quick or dead; then take centaury,
green or dry, give it the woman to drink in wine, give her also the
milk of another woman.

Girolama

The woman is screaming. This is good. It's worse when they're
too exhausted to scream, when they turn their faces to the
wall. Girolama puts her hand to the woman's chest, which
is damp with sweat, the pulse fairly strong. 'How long's the
labour been?' she asks Vanna.

'It started after the Ave Maria bell.'

Some twelve hours, then, poor *putta*. During a pause in
screaming, she mops the woman's forehead. 'And little movement?'

'It's the wrong way about,' Vanna says. 'That's what the
midwife said.'

'Where's the midwife?'

'Gone home. Tired, she said, but she stank of wine.'

And who could blame her? 'At least she sent for you.'

They're not midwives nor doctors as such, but they and their
circle know a few things. Many things, in fact, Girolama in

particular: secrets that have been passed to her, closely guarded. At forty-three, she's been written off by most of society as worthless or worse, but Girolama knows her value. So do the women who assist her, and the women they assist. She's no gem, perhaps, but she's as unbreakable as the hardened magma of Etna. She's saved a few lives in her time, one way or another, and she's attended enough births to know this woman doesn't have that long. If they're to act, it must be now.

'Please, help me,' the woman begs as another wave of pain begins, and it's not clear if she's speaking to Girolama or God or the devils that torment her body.

'Yes, *cara*,' Girolama answers. 'We'll help you, all right, but you're going to have to be strong.'

She doesn't have to instruct Vanna on what to do. They've worked together for many years, and before that Vanna assisted Girolama's stepmother, Giulia. They remove the woman from the birthing chair with its grips and straps and bolts.

'Look at it,' Vanna mutters. 'Like something the Inquisition would use to torture a woman.'

'Well, you would know.' Vanna escaped the Holy Inquisition not so long go, denying claims she was a healer. You wouldn't guess it by looking at those gnarled old hands, but they've achieved things no doctor could. The Church doesn't wish to see power of any kind in a woman's hands, least of all power that threatens its own. They wish to hold the monopoly on miracles and have demonised all other rituals and magic.

Once they've got the woman onto the bed, Vanna begins to massage the woman's body with scented oils: verlain and nutmeg to draw the womb downward, madonna lily, chamomile and mallow. Girolama takes a little of the draught of belladonna and henbane and pours it down her throat. It's forbidden, this soother of pain, but then in this city, laws are made by men who believe that all women are the descendants of Eve and should suffer as she did, though their knees would buckle at only a fraction of such agony. Girolama's seen them cry over their riding injuries and gouty toes. She's seen them weep for the loss of a tooth. In any event, Girolama has little interest in the legalities of the matter. She wants only to ensure that this woman doesn't continue to suffer as she has for the past twelve hours. She wants only to stop her screaming.

'Fetch Maria,' Girolama tells Vanna after a time. 'Tell her we may need to cut.'

Vanna's face is a frown, her grey eyes narrowed. 'We don't need her.'

'We do. Whatever you think of the woman, she has the skill of a surgeon.'

'A butcher, more like.'

'*Dio e tutt'i santi*, I'm not interested in your disagreements,' Girolama snaps. 'Just get her.' Girolama has four key women who help her and, though they are largely fast friends, sometimes tempers flare. For the past few weeks, Vanna and Maria have been at each other's throats, each thinking that the other is trying to oust her from her position and deprive her of her proper cut of the money. It's like dealing with squabbling children, fighting over some toy, though both women are long past fifty. 'First, though, bring me clean linen and hot water. Once the pain has lessened I'll try to pull the baby out.'

Half an hour passes, however, and Girolama makes little progress. For all her unguents and oils and prayers to Saint Margaret, it seems she can't help the woman, nor the babe. She begins to fear that she will lose both, and though Girolama has spent her lifetime thickening her skin, the woman's screams still rattle her. A memory; a flash of red in the darkness. She sees herself, smaller, younger, writhing on a wooden floor, no midwife, no friend. No one. Pain beyond anything he'd done to her, and that was saying something. She'd been fifteen summers old.

She doesn't try to stem her rage, for it's anger that drives her, anger that fuels her: anger at what's been done to her, done to others like her, for generations before her. Anger at the injustices she sees every day. It keeps her mind sharp and her household running, it provides a living to a host of others. Giulia, her stepmother, had that flame of anger too. It didn't burn as strong as hers, for she was softer, Giulia. She'd experienced good times as well as bad, but it was Giulia who taught her that, in a world in which women are granted little room, they're entitled to use a few tricks.

Girolama stares at the pregnant woman who is now lying, exhausted, half-asleep, half-dead, her lips pale, the skin around her eyes were tinged grey. She decides she will try something else, something for which the Holy Office of the Inquisition, were they to hear of it, would have her arraigned before the tribunal by dawn. '*Maleficia*' they'd call it, but why should they decide what's evil and what's good? In nature, nothing is wholly good. Nothing is wholly evil.

She dips her fingers in scented water, then lights a candle and turns her face to it, so that she is recreated as a dark, shuddering figure cast across the wall.

'Good evening,' she whispers. 'My shadow, my sister. I call upon you to help us.'

6

Stefano

The prison governor is the sort of person Stefano seeks to avoid in everyday life, but today he must try to charm him and extract the truth about the dyer's death. The governor is a broad, coarse-faced man with a nose deepened to red by wine and a temperament embittered by years of working in the pit that is the Curia Savelli.

'I don't see why you're asking me, Signore,' he tells Stefano and Marcello. 'It wasn't here that he died.'

'No,' Stefano says, 'but I believe it was here that he first became ill and I need to try to establish what happened. Tell me: what sort of man was the dyer? On what charges was he held?'

'He was a *puzzola*, a stinking, bad-tempered rogue, much like the rest of the scum we keep within these walls, locked up here for debts he couldn't pay because he drank too much to earn his keep.'

From the looks of the governor's nose, Stefano suspects this to be a touch hypocritical. 'What do you mean by bad-tempered? Had he any fights here?'

'Oh, there were a few scuffles. There always are. He certainly wasn't liked, by either the guards or the other prisoners.'

'Any particular enemies?'

'None that I know of. Nor any particular friends. As I say, he was an unlikeable character. A dour-tempered brute, so far as I could tell.'

Stefano nods. 'That's not what his family say.'

'Well, it wouldn't be, would it?' the governor answers. 'Not now he's in the ground. They can pretend he was all sugar and spices.'

'Perhaps.' And yet, Stefano thinks, his widow's distress had seemed genuine. 'Had other prisoners been sick?'

'Plenty. They come in here riddled with worms and pox and spread it to one another. Then there's gaol fever, though there hasn't been much of that of late.'

Marcello steps forward. 'But was there anyone else with symptoms such as Beltrammi complained of? His wife said he'd had pains in his throat, that spread to his chest and gut.'

The man lifts his hands. 'Go to our hospital now and you'll find men complaining of pains to the gut, head, feet, every part. Men sicken and die in Rome every day, Signore.'

'They do,' Stefano says. In apparently increasing numbers. Was that true? 'But today we are asking you about this man and we do so on the orders of the Governor of Rome.' Stefano retains the smile but it has become slightly fixed.

'Look, Signore,' the governor says. 'The man may have grown sickly here, but Beltrammi was well enough to sit and talk with the other prisoners and to play dice. When he left this prison he walked from it, unaided. Indeed, he said he'd been feeling better the few days before he went. You can check the doctor's book.'

And he would, Stefano thought. 'Yet, two weeks later he was in the grave.'

A shrug. 'Then the care he received at home was less than the care he received in here. What can I say? It's not my responsibility.'

'I do not say that is, Signore. It may not be anyone's fault.'

'Then why investigate?'

Stefano hesitates, glances at Marcello. 'Because of an anomaly that was reported on his burial.'

'A what?'

Stefano decides he will have to tell him. 'His body looked healthy, his face rosy. At least that's what was claimed by some observers.'

For the first time since Stefano entered the room, the governor looks interested in what he is saying. 'Still ruddy? Like in life, you mean?'

'Yes, exactly. You know something?'

'I heard it said of an innkeeper a while back – that he'd gone into the grave looking as though death hadn't touched him.'

Stefano's heart rate quickens. 'When did this happen? Of what did he die?'

The governor shakes his head. 'I don't know. My wife told it to me and she had it from other women, I suppose.'

'Can you ask her where she got it from?'

'I can ask her, but I doubt I'll get much of a reply. She died in childbed just before Christmas.'

Stefano is chastened. 'I'm sorry, Signore, for your loss.'

The man waves away his pity. 'She was a nag. She'd have hounded me to my death had she not died first.' He is standing up.

'Do you recall anything else your wife said about this innkeeper? Where he lived? Who he was?'

The governor opens the door to hurry Stefano and Marcello out. 'L'Osteria della Segna de Trè Rè. That's the name of the inn at which the dead man worked. My wife claimed it was a mark of sorcery, his body looking fresh like that in the grave, but then she was always full of wind, that woman, right up until the end.'

7

Anna

Anna is healed enough now that she can walk, but the pain in her ribs is exquisite and every few minutes she must put her hand on Benedetta's arm to steady herself. She rarely leaves the house, as Philippe does not like her to be seen in public, but she is permitted occasionally to go to mass, to church, and today they are going to Trinità dei Monti. Anna has resolved to speak to the priest to whom she normally confesses. He knows, from what she's told him before, of some of the beatings and brutalities, but today she will ask him to help. She knows it's contrary to the workings of Catholicism, but she cannot see any other option, and the priest is a human being who must see how she suffers. Surely he cannot turn her away.

Together, she and Benedetta climb the steep Pincian Hill, the wind in their faces, until the pain is too much and Anna must pause and gather her strength. She looks back over the Piazza di Spagna and can see the streets radiating out from it, the amber and ochre buildings spreading into the distance, the pale domes of churches rising among them. She can do this. She must.

The church is colder than outside, the air laced with frankincense. Though Anna sees a few men and women she knows, she keeps her head down, her shawl over her face. She cannot bear to interact with these people, to see their consternation or discomfort at her injuries. They will assume, rightly, that she has displeased her husband and she does not want their disapproval or pity. Instead, she makes her slow way to the confession box and waits with Benedetta for the people in front of her to confess their sins and be given absolution. Mostly she keeps her head down, but occasionally Anna peeks up at the vast portrait of the Coronation of the Virgin: Mary – immaculate, perfect womanhood – being crowned as Queen of Heaven, a flock of angels about her.

At last it is her turn, and Anna's heart pulses with fear at what she is about to do and say. Inside the confession box, the air is thick with the smell of its previous occupant: tobacco smoke and musk. She can hear the rustling of the priest's vestments in the adjoining box. Then comes a rattling as the priest draws back the curtain over the grille. 'Yes, my child?'

It takes Anna several moments before she can summon the courage to speak. 'Father, I have come to you today to beg for your help.'

'You have come to confess?'

'To confess, yes, but also to ask for any assistance you might be able to give me.' Her voice breaks. 'I don't know who else to turn to.'

A hesitation. 'Tell me.'

Anna summons her strength and speaks. Of the jibes and insults, the threats, the fists, the boots, the pains that spread across her body, of her fear not just that he will kill her, but that he will kill their unborn child. 'He wishes us dead, I think. He hates me, though I don't know why.' She has wondered often but there is no real answer. She has not done anything to incur his wrath. He seems merely to hate her for existing. He has a pool of bitterness and venom in his soul and it is onto her that he chooses to pour it, at least for the time being. She has little doubt that others have suffered before her. There is a reason his sisters do not visit.

Finally, the priest answers. 'You must not say these things.' The voice is flustered, not the confident tone for which she had hoped. 'Rather, you must ask yourself: have you maintained a close union with your husband, suffering his shortcomings with patience and charity? Have you been sufficiently obliging towards him?'

Her heart falls. 'I do everything I can, everything I should. None of it makes any difference. What, then, can I do?'

'You can bend yourself to his will.'

'But—'

Now the priest's voice comes quickly, as though he is assuring himself, not her. 'It is the role of the wife to succumb to the will of her husband. If he beats you, it is because you are sinful, because you displease him. You must soothe him, see to his needs. You must pray, pray upon your knees, for harmony between your husband and yourself. You must do the following things.'

Anna feels herself plummeting, feels all hope draining away from her. She cannot bring herself to feel anger towards this man, for what else, truly, could she have expected? This is the doctrine she has been taught all her life, the words her own parents have recited: acceptance, forbearance, resignation. Yet, to find such a lack of compassion in the centre of what is supposed to be good? It is difficult not to feel despair. In the darkness, she focuses on the pinpricks of light from the other side of the grille. The priest is still talking but she does not listen to what he is saying. She pulls herself up and leaves the musty little room, staggering into the light.

She feels a hand on her arm. It is Benedetta. 'Come, mistress. This way.'

It is not until they've descended almost all the way to the piazza that Benedetta stops and speaks. 'I have an idea.'

Anna turns to look at her maid, such a pretty woman, but her face already lined, her dark eyes serious. 'Yes?'

A pause. 'I wouldn't suggest it if I thought you had any other option, but if the church will not help, or the police, nor your family…'

'Yes?' Anna says again.

Benedetta glances about to check the street is empty. Very quietly, she says: 'I know of a woman who says she can reconcile couples.'

Anna stares at her maid. She knows what Benedetta means: she means a woman who creates love philtres and reads fortunes and makes matches. All of this is illegal in Rome, where any such activity is seen as devilish and against the workings of the Church. But then the Church, it seems, has forsaken her. 'What she does,' Anna says, 'does it work?'

Benedetta shrugs. 'I don't know, mistress. I can promise you nothing. But I can think of nothing else to try.'

8

Stefano

The lead ball whooshes through the air and Stefano hurls himself forward to hit it.

They are at a *pallacorda* court in the Campo Marzio area. It has become a ritual that the brothers must meet here every fortnight to play and sweat and fight. It is, Stefano supposes, a mild improvement on the actual fighting in which they engaged when they were boys, but not hugely different, in that Bruno and Vincenzo often combine forces against him and he usually comes away with some form of injury. At least this game he sometimes wins, however, for he is quicker and nimbler than his brothers.

A cord is strung across the court. The aim of the game is to hit the ball – a lead pellet wrapped in wool and leather – over the cord to one's opponent and to avoid being hit squarely in the face by the returning ball. For some reason this sport has become hugely popular in Rome, where there's a whole street devoted to the game. Some run about playing while others watch from the steps, placing bets on who will win. For those of the middling order or nobility, some private courts now exist, often palazzo courtyards that have been modified for the purpose. So it is with this one, which is owned by a lawyer friend of Bruno's.

'Come on, Stefano. Put your spine into it.'

Their father sits to one side advising them as to tactics, or complaining of their apparent lack of effort. But it isn't that Stefano is lazy – far from it. It is that, having had one of his lungs blighted by scrofula as a child, he sometimes grows out of breath. His father has conveniently forgotten that, and Stefano has no wish to remind him. Rather, he runs faster and knocks the ball harder, so that Bruno is unable to defend it.

'Bravo!' Vincenzo, his eldest brother shouts, laughing as Bruno grimaces.

'Bruno, you grow fat and lazy,' their father tells him. 'You need to stint on the meats and wine.'

Stefano feels a flash of pride, then dismisses it. He shouldn't fall in with this game of his father. It is how it was when they were younger, playing at fencing or wrestling, their father pitting them against each other. To him, it is a form of sport. Stefano rarely won. He was always smaller and, after his initial illness, always weaker, often sick. Perhaps this is why his father regarded him little, but it is too painful a question to probe.

'How does your new investigation progress?' Vincenzo asks, handing Stefano a linen cloth.

Stefano sits, wipes the sweat from his face. 'It's a strange business.' He does not want to say too much.

'Strange it may be,' his father says, 'but it's surely something that can be solved in good time. I assured Baranzone it would be so.'

Stefano feels a spark of anger. How could his father, with no knowledge of the case nor the law, have provided any such assurance? 'I am working to the best of my ability, Signore.'

His father surveys him. 'Good. Important that you don't let us down on this one, Stefano. There are important people watching. It *could* be the making of you.'

Or the breaking. The doubt that clouds his father's words is palpable, but perhaps Stefano is misreading. It's natural his father should be anxious.

'Strange in what way?' Bruno asks Stefano, taking a seat beside them, a salty sweat rising from his body.

Stefano hesitates. He thinks of the unnaturally preserved corpses, Cecilia's fear of sorcery, and the cholera which did not spread. 'There are elements of the case that don't appear to have any natural explanation.'

Bruno takes a swig from a waterskin. 'That, little brother, is our old nurse talking, with her superstitions and cures and nonsense.'

'God's bread, that woman was a nuisance,' Vincenzo recalls. 'Those tales she used to tell us of the long-armed witch! How she'd drag us down her well if we misbehaved. Poor Stefano didn't sleep for weeks!' They all laugh as though this is a joyful memory, but Vincenzo underestimates: it was not for mere weeks that the tale stayed with him.

'An effective method, I suppose,' he says. 'I rarely misbehaved after that. Even took her wretched medicines.' Spoonfuls of bitter herbs and oils that she claimed would keep him well. Lord knows what was in them.

'Less effective on us, though,' Bruno says, truthfully. 'We still left toads in her bed.'

The brothers laugh, their father tuts. 'You were irreverent then, and you are irreverent now.' He stands up. 'I must get back to my work.' Work, work, always work. From his meticulously organised *scrittoio* their father runs a small empire of trade: velvet from Venice, indigo from India, cochineal from the insects of the Americas.

45

'Stefano, there will be some practical and straightforward solution to your case, I have no doubt. You simply need to be methodical. That is how I have always worked. The solution is always found.'

Stefano and Vincenzo exchange a glance. Stefano refrains from pointing out that investigating mysterious deaths is hardly the same as finding the correct dye for any particular fabric. Although their father has always pushed them to achieve, he does not like to be reminded that he himself is a tradesman.

'I will bear that in mind, Father,' is all Stefano says, and after all, he is right that it is by being analytical that he may find the answers. He just suspects that the task ahead will require more than mere method.

Stefano walks from the court to l'Osteria della Segna de Trè Rè, the taverna whose previous owner is now in his grave. The place is near Castel Sant'Angelo, in Vicolo degli Ombrellari, a small lane where the shops of the umbrella-makers cluster together. The air reeks with the smell of oiled silk and, once inside the inn, this mixes with the smoke of pipes and stale wine. The customers seem none too bothered by the stink. They are a cheerful bunch, mostly workmen in overalls, sitting at rough wooden tables or at the bar, where a man and a woman are serving.

Stefano takes a seat in a corner and watches, trying to determine whom he should approach. At the table next to him, a group of men are finishing a game of Tarocco, using a set of worn but beautiful cards. One of the men thumps the table with his fist and shouts '*batto!*' meaning he holds the highest trump card. The others jeer and laugh.

After Stefano has been sitting there a few minutes, the woman comes to his table to ask whether he wishes her to bring him a cup of wine. She is young, no more than nineteen, he thinks, with a sweet face. Can she be the innkeeper's widow? If so, she's surprisingly young. As she returns to the bar, she greets one of the Tarocco players: a man in a green cap. He makes some joke at which she laughs. Assessing this man as a regular, Stefano moves over to him and asks for a recommendation for a local eatery. Once the man has answered him, with much gesticulating, Stefano moves on to asking him his real questions.

'A decent place, this?'

'Oh, it is. They're honest folk that run it. No watered-down wine here, I can tell you.'

'You've been coming here for some time, then?'

'Many years, many years.'

'Did you know the previous innkeeper?'

'Borelli? *Ahi*, yes, I knew him well, poor bastard.'

'He died, I heard.'

'He did. In the year of the plague.'

'*Of* the plague?'

'Well, there's those that say yes, and there's those that say no.'

The woman approaches with Stefano's cup of wine. He thanks her, noticing as she puts down the cup that there is a deep scar running around her wrist. Perhaps she has been a slave, or a prisoner.

Once she has gone, Stefano asks the man, 'What was it, then, if not the plague?'

'I'm not a medical man, I couldn't tell you, but he had terrible sickness, terrible pains, I heard. His brother-in-law nursed him. Tomaso. He's a barber.'

Stefano nods. Barbers often act as a doctor of sorts, for those that cannot pay for physicians. 'Fortunate to have someone in the family to help.'

'Didn't save him, though, did he?' The man shakes his head. 'Left Camilla there to manage the inn on her own, *poveretta*.'

47

Stefano looks again at the young woman who served him his wine. 'That's the innkeeper's wife, Camilla, then?' She must have been married very young.

'Was, yes. She's Camilla Capella now. Wed again soon enough, though, to Marco here, but you can't blame her for that. She couldn't have run the place on her own.'

'No, indeed.' Stefano's eyes move to the man at the bar, who he assumes is Marco, a young, hearty-looking fellow. He wants to ask the man with the pipe more: about the innkeeper's body and the rumours it didn't decay, but he fears he will give himself away. Instead, he thanks him for his help, returns to his table and finishes his wine, which he's fairly sure is watered down.

Stefano watches the pair at the bar. At one point the young innkeeper leans close to Camilla Capella and says something that makes her laugh. She gives him a quick kiss on the cheek and for a moment Stefano feels a pang of sadness, or perhaps it is jealousy.

He resolves to find this barber, Tomaso. He will take Marcello with him.

It is not difficult to find the barber. He runs a small shop in an alley not far from the taverna, its entrance marked by the sign of a bleeding foot. The interior is dingy, the air a mixture of soap and blood. Stefano wonders if he might die here. Nevertheless, he takes the barber's chair first, loosening his collar so that the man, Tomaso, may set to work.

He looks nothing like his sister, the innkeeper's wife, for she is a pleasant-looking woman with large eyes and light-brown hair. The barber, meanwhile, is a dour-looking individual with a large forehead that gives him the look of a bad-tempered ape. His conversation is limited and Stefano waits until the man has fully soaped his face before he starts asking his questions.

'You're the brother of Camilla Capella at the Three Kings, aren't you?'

'Yes. What of it?'

'It was you, then, who tended to her first husband in his illness.'

'It was.'

The man has now got out his blade. Stefano is keen not to annoy him. He glances at Marcello, signalling he should take over.

'Tell me, Signore,' Marcello says, 'What symptoms did Borelli exhibit during his sickness?'

The man shifts his gaze from Stefano's face to Marcello's. 'Why are you asking me this?'

'We're making enquiries,' Marcello says quietly, 'on behalf of the Governor of Rome. Nothing serious, nothing official as yet. Just enquiries. We wanted to know what it was that he died from.'

Tomaso continues with his work, but Stefano can see from his face that his mind is working on other things. Eventually he says: 'It was a strange illness that came and went.'

'How do you mean?' Marcello asks.

'I mean, I would give him purges and syrups from the apothecary, and he would seem to get better, and then two days later, he would worsen again.'

'Worsen in what way?'

'Vomiting, shitting, pains, fever, terrible thirsts.' He turns Stefano's face slightly so that he may shave the other cheek. 'I almost pitied the bastard.'

Marcello and Stefano exchange a glance. 'You didn't like him?' Stefano asks.

'He wasn't exactly likeable.' The man wipes his blade and looks at Stefano's face to survey his handiwork, then moves to shave his neck.

49

'But you treated him, nonetheless.'

'Family is family,' Tomaso says. And yes, in Rome, it is. 'Camilla asked for my help.'

'You said he had pains,' Marcello says. 'Where?'

'He complained of pains in his stomach and guts. Writhed with them like an eel.'

Similar, then, to the dyer. Stefano's heart rate has begun to quicken. 'When did he die?'

The man takes a cloth to wipe Stefano's face. 'A few days after Whitsun. By then he was vomiting so that I thought he'd turn himself inside out. We called a priest to administer the sacraments.'

Stefano makes himself ask the question: 'I heard that his body seemed unnaturally preserved before he went to his grave.'

Something flickers in Tomaso's eye. 'Yes, that's what people said: that he seemed rosy-cheeked during his laying out. But if you ask me, he looked dead enough before they put him in the box. The thing that was odd about him was that he didn't seem to go rigid like men normally do after death, but remained eel-like even then.'

'What do you mean?'

'I mean he was supple even a few hours after he died. You could bend his limbs. I've seen enough men die to know that isn't the normal way of things.'

'You treat men here, in your shop?' Stefano asks.

'Men, women, children, dogs. Whoever they bring to me I do my best, for most can't afford a doctor. Sawed a few limbs off on this very table.' He is wiping his hands. 'Your friend next, is it?'

Marcello, however, is standing up, remarkably quickly. 'In fact, we are running short on time today, but thank you.'

Tomaso shrugs.

Stefano looks him straight in the eye. 'You said Borelli was an unlikeable man. Had anyone reason to want him dead?'

Tomaso's gaze assumes a blankness. 'A fair few, I'd guess, though I couldn't give you names.'

You won't now, Stefano thinks, *but I might make you.* He will leave it until the man doesn't have a blade in his hand. 'Did he know a dyer called Beltrammi?'

'Not that I'm aware, but then we weren't fast friends. There was a dyer that drank at the Three Kings, but I never knew his name. Tall man.'

'He doesn't go there anymore?'

'I've not seen him for some months.'

No, Stefano thinks. You wouldn't have. That is because he is in the ground.

9

For a burning fever:
Take half an ounce of Endive-water; of Sorrel and Rose-water, of
each half a pint; of Water-lillies and Scabio's, of each six ounces;
Cinnamon-water, two ounces; Syrup of Violets or Roses, half a
pound; Juice of Lemons, two ounces; mix them, and add Spirit
of Vitriol so much as to give it a grateful acidity. It is an excellent
Remedy in a burning Fever, in a spotted, purple, malignant fever,
and all other malignant Distempers.

Girolama

Mint, musk, cloves, wormwood. These are what Girolama
needs to make the poultice for the new mother, plus sorrel for
the woman's fever. In her herb garden off the Via della Lungara,
she uses her pruning scissors to cut the plants, then hands them
to Cecca – faithful, grey-haired Cecca who's worked for her
and her family for more years than Girolama can remember,
coming with them when they fled Palermo and set up again in
Rome, never questioning anything. Giulia planted this garden
shortly after they reached the city, when Girolama was only a
girl, and it is now filled with fresh curative herbs enclosed between hedges of sage and rosemary, their odours scenting the
air. Giulia Mangiardi, *mia Madregna*. No evil stepmother from
a fairytale, but a woman who took Girolama under her wing
when she was a girl and taught her what it took to survive in a

world which is paved for men. Girolama's Uncle Lorestino also taught her much: how to control minds, read faces and palms, how to interpret the stars. But it's thanks to Giulia that she can read and write; thanks to her that she knows how to tend the garden, harvest its plants, and use them to help other women. Though Giulia died eight years before, Girolama still feels her presence in this place, among the pennyroyal and costmary. Though she is dead, she's still weaving her magic.

Girolama will stew the plants and strain their juices, then mix them with the dried ingredients. The woman they helped last week rallied after the birth and the child too survived, but now the mother has lapsed into a fever, as so many mothers do. Plenty of those women die. This one must not.

'Will they pay?' Cecca asks.

'They'll pay what they can,' Girolama answers. 'And no, it won't be enough, but there are others that can pay a deal more, so don't fuss. It will even out.'

Cecca purses her mouth but doesn't say anything further. It's she who manages the house's finances as concerns food and sundries and she sees it as her role to ensure that Girolama doesn't give away her treatments and remedies too cheaply. But Girolama is the boss, and Girolama is no fool. She knows her own worth and knows the value of each customer and how much to charge them. When the situation requires it, she will help a woman for free, but such situations are not frequent. She is not running a charity, but a business. She has to. Her second husband fled his debts and her some years ago, taking with him Girolama's last shred of hope that she'd find happiness with a man. Word came last year that the plague had taken him and she felt a strange numbness down to her soul. It's all on her now: to make a living for the other women, to assist her two sons, now near full grown, and her adopted daughter, just turned fourteen. She can't afford to be sentimental, and in any event, it's not in her nature, or at least not the nature that has grown upon her.

'Mother!' Angelica has appeared at the end of the garden. 'There's a carriage here – a grand one!'

Girolama makes her way towards Angelica, whose young face is flushed with excitement, and whose hair is still damp from washing. She braided it for her so that it would keep the wave. *Dio*, how she loves this girl. Angelica is hers not by her own blood but by that of her mother who shed so much it killed her, leaving her an orphan, as her father had died the month before. Girolama, responsible for the birth and thus for the babe, began to care for the girl, meaning to pass her on to some other woman. She found, however, that she couldn't. She has not had cause to regret it. Angelica is one of the main things in life that bring her joy. But it will not do to be soft with her. Not given the duties she'll inherit, and the world in which they live. 'Sweet Mary and the Saints,' she says, 'what are you? The town crier? You needn't shout it to the rooftops, Angelica, though I'm sure the neighbours have seen in any event.' The neighbours are a nosy lot, forever peeking through shutter slats to see who's at their door and, in fairness, their clientele are an interesting and varied set.

'It's inlaid with gold, Mother, and it bears a coat of arms.'

Nobility, then. This isn't so unusual. Girolama's second husband gave her a higher status name, if nothing else, that's helped her to infiltrate all circles of society, selling them her face waters and secrets. In Rome, youth is prized and old age is despised, so most of a woman's life is spent trying to hold back time, with silver sublimate and powdered porcelain, and Girolama is only too happy to supply them. Usually, however, they'd send a messenger to her. This must be something urgent. 'Hurry, and find out who it is, and for pity's sakes cover your hair, or you will catch cold!'

Girolama walks quickly into the house where she peels off her gloves and washes her hands in a bowl of rosewater. She removes her apron to reveal her black dress beneath, the skirt stitched with tiny eagles. Her only ornament is the *clavacuore* about her waist, hung with keys, and little scissors. She doesn't want her customers to think her a pauper, but nor does she wish to appear fanciful.

Angelica returns a minute or so later: 'It's the Duchessa di Aldobrandini,' she whispers. 'She wants to see you at once.'

'Very well. Bring her up to the *sala*. Make sure the curtains are drawn. We don't want the neighbours spying.'

The Duchessa. She hasn't seen her for months. As Girolama climbs the stairs to the *piano mobile*, she thinks back to their last meeting, to the questions she managed to evade.

'What does the woman want now, eh?' she asks the cat who is curled in the sunshine on the couch.

The cat yawns as if to say 'Who cares?' and stretches his back and paws. Not for the first time, Girolama wishes her life had the simplicity of a cat's: no ties, no obligations, no memories that grab you by the throat, no legacy to pass down the line. She's just finished plumping the cushions when the Duchessa enters the room with a rustle of velvet and silk. About her neck, a string of pearls as fat as butter beans.

'How are you, Signora?' Girolama asks her, bowing slightly.

The woman clutches at her pearls, looking about her nervously. She has evidently forgotten what it's like outside the enclaves of the nobility. 'I am ... I am worried, Girolama. I had a dream.'

Ah, the dreams of the rich. They're always a lucrative business. 'Please, sit. Tell me.'

The Duchessa lifts her heavy satin skirts and perches on the very edge of the sofa, as though afraid it is teeming with lice. Yet Girolama knows her quarters are far more salubrious than most of the houses of Rome. If the lady had visited only the next street rather than this one, she'd have rats running about her feet, never mind the occasional flea. But Girolama keeps her irritation trapped behind a smile. She waits for the woman to speak.

'I dreamt,' she begins, 'that my daughter was underground. That danger was near – a darkness. It was coming after her and she was unaware. I tried and tried to warn her, but she couldn't hear me.' She wrings her hands in her lap. 'It has made me concerned, deeply concerned. I wish for you to carry out your divinations and see what the future holds. I cannot bear the worry and anticipation. I need to know if my daughter will be well.'

Girolama nods. Fortune telling. That is essentially what she does, taught years ago by her uncle Lorestino, a master of the art, as he was of many things: astrology, chiromancy, physiognomy. The nobles like to call it 'divination' as if that makes it more religious and respectable. In fact, the practice is outlawed, no matter what term you use, as no one but God is supposed to know what the future has in store for us. Girolama, however, doesn't believe that fortune telling should be restricted to the Church. It's one of their ways of trying to control the poor: claiming theirs is the only true path to the divine, theirs the only allowable rituals. It's why they penned the Jews in the ghetto and banned all manner of books, it's why the Pope began the Holy Inquisition: all means of trying to prevent the common folk from having any power or control over their destinies; of keeping them in their place. 'Of course, Duchessa. I'll fetch my looking glass.' To Angelica, who's standing in the doorway, she says: 'Fetch three candles. The good ones. And bring me a handful of henbane seeds.'

Girolama keeps the glass in a locked box in the *camera*, her bedroom. It once belonged to Giulia, who in turn inherited it from her mother. Trapped within the silver glass is believed to be a spirit, a dark force, who must never be allowed to leave. It's with this spirit that Girolama must now try to communicate. To do so, she must enter a trance-like state and hope that the visions come. They don't always. Sometimes she makes them up, for otherwise the people won't pay. She carries the wooden box back to the *sala*, unwraps the mirror from its protective cloth, and props it up on the table. For a moment, she studies her own face within the looking glass, noting how her features are sharper than they once were, her dark eyes more hooded, the bones at her neck more pronounced. Well, such is the passage of time. Although Girolama does her best to stop it in such women that ask her, for herself the veil of age is useful: it helps make her almost invisible; hidden in plain sight. Angelica returns with three beeswax candles and uses a taper to light them. Girolama takes the taper to the henbane seeds so that the smoke passes over the mirror and over her face. She inhales it deeply and mutters to herself, words that Giulia taught her, words that soothe and cleanse, words that connect her with the spirit within. Her breathing is deep and rhythmic, the henbane is strong in the air.

'*With the veil of Lady Saint Mary I am well veiled so that I can go well and return well.*

By water, by land, by sea, by ship, by all the ways, both means and path . . .'

Gradually, shapes begin to form, though whether they are in the filmy darkness of the mirror or of her mind, Girolama is not sure. She believes, though, that they are true. She sees movement: it is a bird, she thinks, trapped. She sees the shudder and flutter of wings against a cage. Then, behind the bars, different shapes slide into focus: a man sitting at a table, a book in his hands. A woman seated before him, cowering. Is it herself, she sees? Is she remembering the past rather than seeing the future? For a moment she is once again a frightened young woman, her heart in her mouth, waiting for the violence to come. But no, this is no young woman, but an old one, bowed and terrified. Girolama shuts her eyes against it, draws herself back into the moment. She doesn't wish to see any more.

'Well?' the Duchessa is saying. 'What did you see? What is it?'

Girolama forces herself to smile. 'Your daughter is well,' she tells the lady, which is what she has come to hear. 'But change is on its way.'

'What change?'

Girolama shakes her head. 'It isn't clear, but whatever it is, I don't think it will hurt your daughter. She is protected.' By wealth and privilege, by the walls of the cloister, however much she may wish to escape them. 'You have no need to worry.' Is that true? She isn't sure, but few people have been helped by worrying, and few will pay to be told what they fear.

'Thank goodness,' the Duchessa says, breathing out. 'I've been so worried. She's always been so flighty, you see. So regardless of danger, and where she is I cannot protect her.' A pause. 'There is no need, then, you think, to bring her back?'

Girolama considers the woman's face. What answer does she truly want? Does she want to summon her daughter home, or is she relieved to have dispensed with her? Girolama will play her cards close. 'As I say, Duchessa, she is not in danger, though the fact she came to you in your dream may be a sign that she's unhappy; that she misses her mother's company.'

The Duchessa nods. 'Perhaps I should pay her a visit at the convent sooner than I'd planned.'

Girolama smiles. 'Very good.' The woman doesn't want her troublesome daughter back home; she just wanted her own conscience soothed. It's how many women treat their daughters. It is not how Giulia treated her, though, nor how she treats Angelica, who she notes is eyeing the Duchessa with something approaching contempt.

As they watch the coach leave, Girolama allows the smile she had pinned on to fade. She feels lightheaded, drained.

'What did you really see?' Angelica asks quietly. The girl has more perception than most.

'A man. A book. A cage.'

'What does it mean?'

Girolama glances at Angelica, feeling a sudden pang of fear for her, this child who is reliant on her, on whose shoulders the mantle must fall. 'I've no idea, girl, nor have I time to ponder it. We've much work to do.'

For a moment she thinks that maybe the Church is right. Maybe it is better not to know the future.

IO

Stefano

There must, Stefano thinks, be a link between the two men. Both drank at the same taverna, were of a similar age, and seemingly of a similar disposition. But what is that link?

As he rubs a rosemary-soaked cloth over his teeth and prepares himself for the day, Stefano thinks over what he and Marcello have learnt during the first few days of the investigation. They have spoken again with Teresa, the dyer's widow, but she could say only that yes, her husband did sometimes go to l'Osteria della Segna de Trè Rè. She knew of no particular friendship with the innkeeper, and said that the dyer never mentioned him. They have spoken too to Camilla, the sweet-faced innkeeper's wife, and though she said that she remembered the dyer as an occasional customer, she claimed her then husband had no particular friendship nor connection with him.

'You would have known?' Stefano asked her.

'Yes, Signore, I believe so. I was rarely apart from my husband.'

'You had no secrets?'

'No, Signore. I learnt to read my husband well.'

Stefano felt a needle of sadness as she said this. What it would be to have someone who knew you completely.

'Is there anything else, Donna Camilla, that you think we ought to know? Any enemies or disputes of which we should be aware? If you knew your husband entirely then you are the person to tell us.'

The young woman shook her head. 'Truly, Signore, I have thought and thought and I can tell you nothing else.'

Is she hiding something? Stefano does not know. She seemed genuine, but he is not convinced he is good at reading women and their emotions. After all, they are taught from childhood to shroud them. What he knows of women comes from his sisters, and the way they behave, especially Lucia, doesn't always chime with what the Church and the law have told him to think of women. He still has much to learn.

Stefano wonders if both men were involved in some trade or business that fell outside the law. Smuggling, perhaps, could that be it? Or something even darker?

There comes the sound of knocking on the front door and Stefano moves to the window so that he can see the street below. It is Marcello, lively Marcello whom he is growing increasingly to like, realising his manner is not mocking (such as is Stefano's brothers'), but full of wry humour: he laughs at life, including at himself. Stefano wipes his face and makes his way downstairs, to find that the maid has admitted the doctor into the front room and now stands waiting on them both.

'I bring good news,' Marcello says. His voice is excited, his face animated.

'You have? What?'

'I have found us another corpse.'

Stefano glances at the maid, a bold girl of sixteen years who often makes him uneasy. 'Thank you, Concetta. That will be all.'

She appraises both men, clearly annoyed to be dismissed, and gives a swift bow of the head.

Once she has gone, Stefano says: 'You call this good news?'

'I do,' Marcello says, 'because it is another ruddy-faced corpse, a man whose death was apparently preceded by pains and vomiting. Only this time, a man cut from rather different cloth.' Marcello pauses for effect. 'The Duca di Ceri.'

Stefano blinks. The Duke died over a year ago. His father had known him. 'Are you sure?'

'Well, it was told to me by another doctor, one with whom I studied anatomy some years ago. I may have told him a little of our mission—'

'Marcello!' Stefano admonishes him.

'He is a man of discretion. I'd trust him with my life. In fact, I did once. I let him carry out an experiment on me, but that's for another time.' He winces. 'Claudio says he was told by Ceri's physician that there were peculiar things about the body. That rigor mortis lasted far longer than other patients.'

'But that is the opposite of what the barber told us.'

'It is, but there may be a connection. And then, and here's the most interesting thing: the inside of the stomach was scarlet red, just like with our unfortunate dyer, only more pronounced.'

'Well, well,' Stefano says, his earlier worries forgotten. 'Do you know the name of Ceri's physician?'

'Not only do I know his name, but I know where he works, where he lives,' Marcello says. 'I say we go there at once.'

'Bravo, man. Bravo!' Stefano's excitement, though, is touched by a tinge of unease. 'We must proceed carefully, however. This is a nobleman we're talking about, a very rich family. They won't want their affairs aired in public.'

'We won't air them to anybody,' Marcello says. 'We'll merely ask a few well-chosen questions.'

They smile at one another. Maybe they are getting somewhere.

'You've eaten?' Marcello asks.

'No, not yet.'

'Then we'll go via Piazza Farnese, take some of their excellent pastries, and formulate what we're going to ask the esteemed Dottor Venici.'

As they walk, past cassocked priests and children leading dogs on ropes, Stefano asks Marcello about his training and how he came to be a dissecter of corpses.

'I studied medicine at Padua and became an anatomist's assistant to make the money I needed to last the course. I'm not from a rich family, and the fees were considerable.'

'But your family supported you?'

'So far as they could. My mother always had ambitions for me, though perhaps not the ambition that I should become, as you put it, a dissecter of corpses!'

'Forgive me,' Stefano says, cursing himself.

'That is indeed my job and I find it fascinating. My wife has no issue with what I do, but I tell my mother I'm a doctor of anatomy. This makes it sound more palatable over the dinner table. Your parents: they know you're hired for this task?'

'My mother is long dead,' Stefano says. 'As for my my father – he knew of my appointment before I did. Baranzone is a friend of his.'

'Ah. Your father is also a lawyer?'

'No. A cloth merchant. Therefore he has ambitions for me, just as your mother did for you.' Is ambition the right word? 'He's told me in clear terms not to disappoint.'

'Oh, we can never entirely please our parents, Stefano. It's more important that we work out what we want for ourselves, I'd say. In any event, hopefully Dottor Venici is about to give us some useful answers.'

They have reached the physician's palazzo, a three-storeyed building of rose-coloured stone. They are shown through a series of chambered rooms to the office where Dottor Venici works. It is a far cry from Tomaso's crude cutting table: upholstered chairs, gleaming walnut surfaces, rows of medical books bound in gold-tooled leather, and a fire crackling away in the grate. The reception they receive, though, is frosty.

'You've approached the Ceri family, have you?'

'Not yet,' Stefano says. 'We didn't wish to distress them unnecessarily. We merely wished to ask you a few questions.'

The physician stares at him. He is a large, pudding-faced man with small eyes pressed in like currants. 'It is most untypical,' he says, 'to come here without appointment and without warning. I am a busy man.'

'I'm sure your skills are much in demand,' Stefano says soothingly, 'and we will only take a few minutes of your time. We ask merely that you confirm how you believe the Duca died and what symptoms he exhibited before his death.'

The man frowns. 'As I wrote in my medical report at the time, it was a malignant fever: sudden, painful, fatal. Killed him within a week despite my many remedies and methods, which I assure you, usually work.'

Marcello says: 'And his symptoms?'

'His symptoms, young man, were what you would expect with a malignant fever: pains of the stomach and gut, great thirst due to the fever, much production of vomitus and excrementum.'

Stefano notices that man's hands are like raw hams. He would not fancy being under his knife. 'Was there any discolouration of the skin? Any marks?'

'No.'

A lie. 'And you were confident that there could be no other cause for his malady?'

'Yes.'

'You did not conduct an autopsy?' Marcello asks him.

'Certainly not.' Bright spots of anger have appeared on the man's cheeks. 'The family had no reason to doubt my diagnosis, nor to suspect any foul play.'

'Of course,' Stefano assures him, but he and Marcello exchange a glance. Why mention foul play at all?

'The very fact that you are asking me these questions suggests you have little understanding of how such illnesses progress, or indeed of how polite society functions.' Venici stands up, his jowls quivering. 'You cannot simply come in here and interrogate my methods.' He glares at Stefano. 'I am surprised any authority has been invested in one so young and apparently ignorant.'

Stefano tenses, tries not to let his anger show in his face. 'It is as you say: appearances are not always everything.' He bows. 'We are sorry to have troubled you. Good day, Signore. We will show ourselves out.'

I I

Anna

Anna has been praying for a sign, a hint from God as to what she should do, but there has been nothing. Perhaps she is to take meaning from the angel carved into the cornicing above the woman's door, but it is so caked in dirt that it does not seem a very auspicious omen. It looks more like a fallen angel, but she will not allow herself to follow that thought. The building is on a narrow, sunless street on the Via Veneto and, when Laura shows her and Benedetta up to her apartment, Anna sees that it is a single, barely furnished room with a strange smell to it: of medicines and foulness and damp.

Laura herself is a thin, haggard-looking woman who could be forty or could be sixty. Her ankles protrude from her gown like sticks.

'Benedetta tells me that you know of ways to reconcile husbands and wives, when things have gone rather' – she hesitates – 'awry.'

The woman watches her with narrowed eyes. 'From the looks of you, I'd say they were more than a little awry.'

Anna swallows, a painful act in a throat as swollen as hers.

Last night wasn't the first time he has throttled her, but it's the first time she has blacked out. It has frightened her.

'How often does he beat you?' the woman asks.

Anna glances at Benedetta. She had expected help, not an interrogation. 'I don't see why that's relevant. I'm asking if you know a way to assist me with gaining my husband's love.'

The woman scoffs. 'Gaining, not regaining? As bad as that?'

'Yes, as bad as that,' she says tightly. Clearly it was a mistake to come here. 'Can you help me, or not?'

'I can't make him change his temperament. No woman can.'

Anna feels a pulse of pain. She knew this, really, but still part of her held out hope that there would be someone who could make it all right. 'So, you can't help me?' She tries to stand up, but Benedetta puts her hand on her arm.

'I didn't say that,' Laura says, a little more gently. She surveys both Benedetta and Anna. She lowers her voice. 'I know a woman who can do things, make things. I know a woman who can save you.'

'How?' Anna knows her tone is desperate.

'It'll cost you. You have money, I take it.'

'Some.' Not much. Upon their marriage, all her fortune had been transferred into Philippe's name and he grants her only a few *baiocchi* at a time, for food or a piece of clothing. It is another means of control.

'Well, you'll need a fair amount, so get together what you can and I'll talk to her.'

'About a different remedy?'

'Oh yes, a strong remedy.'

'To reconcile us?'

Without warning, the woman reaches out a hand to touch Anna's neck. She flinches away from her.

'He'll kill you soon enough, you know that, don't you? That's why you're really here.'

Anna is horrified. She cannot think of anything to say.

'So, you get there first,' Laura says. 'That's how it works. Come back next week with fifty *scudi*. Then we'll solve your problem.'

Anna walks away from the house in a daze. She can't quite believe she heard the woman correctly. Has she misunderstood? Benedetta keeps her head down and refuses to meet Anna's eye. Did her maid know, when she brought her here, what this woman was, and what she was really selling?

After a few minutes, once she has gathered her wits, Anna confronts her: 'I will pray for you, Benedetta. I will pray for both of us. For forgiveness and Divine guidance.'

Her maid looks at her levelly. 'Eye for eye, tooth for tooth, hand for hand, foot for foot. Is that not what the Bible says?'

Anna finds that her throat is once again choked, but this time with tears. 'Do you really think so little of me that you think I'd resort to such means?'

Benedetta does not respond. Her mouth is set in a line.

Anna walks ahead of her. There is a way, another way. There must be.

12

Stefano

Damigella, Stefano's chestnut-brown mare, is waiting for him in his father's stables. She snuffles to him in greeting as he approaches. When he reaches her, she rests her head on his shoulder and he strokes her velvety ears. For a moment, he is calm and content, breathing in the familiar scent of horses, hay, leather and dung. He knows he is lucky to have a horse with such a temperament, but it is also, he thinks, to do with how one treats them. His father's horse, a black stallion, is a much angrier beast, but then he had the spirit beaten out of him when he was a colt. It's little wonder he is not the nuzzling kind.

The tread of boots on straw. 'Bracchi.'

Stefano turns to see Baranzone, and he can tell from the flash of his eyes, the tightness of his jaw, that this is not a social call. He is in trouble.

'I have just received a visit from a very displeased ambassador. He tells me that you've been interrogating the physicians of noblemen.'

Stefano swallows. 'Not interrogating, we merely asked some questions of the doctor who treated the Duca di Ceri—'

'God's teeth, Stefano,' and his own teeth are clenched. 'Are there any brains in your head at all, or is it stuffed with the hay you feed your horses? You know what the rules are in this city. You know how these things work. If we start investigating the nobility then the little power we have will be taken from us.'

'But the symptoms Ceri suffered—'

'You are taking the wrong path, Stefano. I told you to investigate subtly, carefully, not to go running to the physicians of well-known families and subjecting them to your cross-examinations! It is no wonder that the family send their physician complaining to ambassadors.'

Stefano feels the fire of shame in his cheeks. 'Monsignore, my apologies. I didn't fully think through the repercussions.'

'No, you didn't. I expected more of you, Stefano. I handed you this chance because I thought you would prove yourself, not that you would embarrass yourself and me into the bargain.'

'I will do better, I promise you.' Stefano knows his voice sounds thin.

'I don't want your assurances. I want your actions and your discretion.' Baranzone's tone is clipped and cold. 'You must do a better job of keeping this inquiry under wraps, or you will drive the culprits, if culprits there are, underground. And the last thing we want is to cause panic in Rome.'

'Of course.'

Baranzone regards him coolly. 'You had better start applying your mind properly to this task, or you will find that your career stalls, that no further appointments come your way. Do you understand?'

A cold fist closes around his heart. 'Yes.'

Baranzone breathes out. 'Very well.' He begins to walk away, saying over his shoulder, 'The next thing I want to hear from you, Stefano, is that you've made progress. I don't want to hear anything from anyone else. Get on with it.'

After the Governor has gone, Stefano stands motionless for a time, his cheeks still burning, his stomach full of bile. He has acted without properly considering, carried along with the excitement of the chase. There is an unspoken rule in Rome that the nobility are above inquisitions by the likes of him, and yet he approached the physician directly, without even trying to conceal his purpose, so excited was he to find the truth. If they had approached it differently, they might not have been shut off. He feels a warmth in his ear. It is Damigella, nuzzling him, her breath hot against his skin. Horses know when things are wrong, when to comfort. Stefano would never dare say this aloud but he feels it. He touches the horse's head.

A short time later, Lucia appears. She must have heard some of Baranzone's words, or at least the sound of a raised voice, but she does not question Stefano, and for that he is grateful. She says only, 'I've made you *minestra*. Come. Eat.'

Stefano follows. He has no appetite but Lucia sits in the *sala* and watches as he spoons the soup into his mouth, not tasting it.

Only after he has eaten a decent amount does she say, 'You are a better man than him, Stefano. Better ten times over.'

'No, Lucia, I am a fool.'

She shakes her head. 'You've simply not yet learnt the duplicitous ways of the courtier.'

He regards her, this older sister of his, who has often acted as a mother. What Stefano remembers of his real mother is merely a shadow, though he's unsure whether she was like that in life, or has dwindled to a spectre with the passage of time. 'You don't think, then, that I should let it lie?'

'I didn't say that.'

71

'You say very little these days, it seems.'

'I'm a childless widow, *fratellino*. I'm not expected to have an opinion. I'm expected to stay quiet and obedient and not take up space.' She stands and moves to the credenza where she begins to reorder the majolica dining set. 'Just as you're expected to toe the line. Perhaps it would be wise to do so.'

'Perhaps.' Stefano chews the bread without tasting it. He is thinking. The physician could not have run to an ambassador without the approval of the family. Why are they so keen to keep him from their door?

Without turning, his sister says, 'You could excuse yourself from this investigation, Stefano. I worry that it will not end well.'

More of Lucia's glass half full. 'Sister, I will follow this to the end, and I will make a success of it.'

She remains silent.

Stefano is still thinking. 'What do you know about the Duca di Ceri, Lucia? He was a friend of Father's, wasn't he?'

She glances at him. 'More an acquaintance, I think. I know little of him.'

'Did you meet his wife: Agnese Aldobrandini?'

'Only a handful of times. A vain, pretty woman, half her husband's age. I suppose we had that in common,' Lucia smiles. 'But the Aldobrandini family are of course rather a step above us.'

'Several steps,' Stefano says. 'They produced a pope not fifty years ago.'

Lucia says: 'You must have seen the Duca and his wife yourself. They attended Bruno's wedding – she in a gown of blue lace and pearls that far outshone the bride's.'

Stefano thinks back. Yes, he can picture her: an elegant, fair-haired woman. 'She was with Sulpizia,' he says. Sulpizia he remembers well: her dark hair, her porcelain skin.

'Yes. They're fast friends, those two. Neither has a brain in their head so far as I can deduce.'

'And Agnese danced with Father.' He remembers a whirling form in blue.

'That's right. The Duca himself was too ridden with gout.'

'Him I don't recall.'

'You wouldn't, perhaps. He remained seated all evening talking about his collection of relics. I remember him saying he'd paid one hundred *scudi* for one of Saint Christopher's toes.' She gives a wry smile and turns back to the sink.

Relics. Could there be something there? Stefano wonders. The relic trade in Rome continues to boom, but it's a grubby, questionable business that relies on the perpetual pilfering of graves and ancient monuments for saints' fingernails and such. Could this somehow link the Duca to the dyer and the inn-keeper? 'Lucia, where did the Duca obtain his relics?'

'I've no idea. I assume he bought them at auction.'

'Yes,' Stefano says. He is thinking about l'Osteria della Segna de Trè Rè, imagining the tradesmen and the Duca meeting in the gloom, discussing terms.

Lucia can evidently tell he is ruminating, as she says: 'This is only one case, little brother. Do not let it consume you.'

One case, yes, but what a case. Stefano had wanted to cut his teeth on something complex and significant, but now he begins to fear this snake that uncoils before him. He thinks back to the physician's defensiveness. The man has run straight to the authorities to try to shut down this line of inquiry. It is possible that he's merely angry at the breach of protocol, but Stefano does not think it is that. He must speak to Marcello today.

When Stefano arrives at the doctor's house, he finds him sitting down for dinner with his wife.

'You must stay and eat with us,' Mirtilla insists. She is a lively, chestnut-haired woman. She doesn't give Stefano the opportunity to decline, but pulls up a third chair and fetches another bowl.

'*Dimmi*, Stefano,' Marcello says as his wife ladles out a serving of rabbit stew. 'Tell me.' Seeing Stefano hesitate, he says: 'Mirtilla is well used to revolting tales from my work. I doubt you'll be able to shock her.'

'It's true,' Mirtilla says, pushing the bowl towards him. 'Guts and gore are our usual fare. Give me your very worst.'

Stefano duly relates Baranzone's tirade and the physician's complaint about their unannounced visit.

Marcello tears off a piece of bread. 'That bloated wineskin. He complained on behalf of the family?'

'Apparently so, yes.'

'Then it is the Ceri family, and not just their fat physician, who are concealing the true means of death.'

'That's what I've been thinking,' Stefano says. 'And why would they do so? Families will often conceal a suicide, but I don't believe that's what we're dealing with.'

'No,' Marcello says. 'It's something else.'

'Something that would damage the family's reputation,' Mirtilla suggests. 'Roman families are all obsessed with honour and appearance.'

Stefano nods. 'You may well be right. I've encountered several cases where witnesses have refused to give evidence that would damage a family's public image.' For in Rome, image and status is everything, much more important than the truth. It is why rich women paint their faces with cerusa, though they know the lead will one day rot the skin.

Marcello wipes his bowl with his bread. 'And of course that's all the more likely to be the case where the family concerned is noble.'

74

'But this is precisely why we can go nowhere near it!' Stefano frets. 'If we continue on this route, then Baranzone will remove us from the investigation and probably destroy our careers to boot.'

'I don't say we must pursue this openly,' Marcello says, more quietly. 'But we must get to the bottom of it as it may well lead us to what killed the other men, and that, remember, is the task we were set.'

Stefano exhales. 'That is true.' More than that, he cannot let it go. He knows there is something here.

'Let us think this through,' Marcello says. 'Let's assume that it is indeed this desire to protect the family which is incentivising the Ceri clan. The physician knows what has killed the Duca but he obscures it from us, and indeed from the world, in order to safeguard someone, or perhaps because the means of death is considered shameful. However, he can't conceal everything, because we have the reports of the people who saw the body laid out. We know that the body didn't decay as it should have. We know too that at least some of the symptoms he described were real, as they were corroborated by one of the servants.'

Stefano looks at him sharply. 'How do you know that?'

'Because, Stefano, I asked him.'

'When?'

'Shortly after we spoke to the physician,' Marcello says calmly. 'The opportunity arose.'

'"The opportunity arose"? Dear God, no wonder the physician has run crying to the Governor. You have been interrogating his staff!'

Mirtilla gives a rich laugh. '*Ragazzaccio!* Naughty Marcello!'

'Oh, I doubt the physician knows,' Marcello says. 'I paid the fellow with whom I spoke, but he assured me that, from what he'd heard, the Duca had suffered from terrible pains in the throat and stomach, terrible thirst, copious vomiting.'

75

'The same symptoms as the innkeeper and the dyer.' Stefano's heart is racing.

'The very same. Plus of course the ruddiness of the face that others saw at the funeral. So I've been poring over my books and I've been thinking: what could produce all these symptoms? Is it truly some sickness? Some new epidemic? But I can find nothing to suggest that it is so.'

'Nor,' Stefano says, 'does it fit with the reaction of the family, for surely if they feared some new disease they would make it known.'

'Exactly. Of course, you might well be ashamed to have a relative die of the French pox, but that isn't what these men had. Nor was it any other venereal disease of which I know. No, to me, the symptoms described – the coming and going of the pains, the resistance to treatment – suggest something else.'

'A poison,' Stefano whispers.

Marcello smiles. 'A poison.'

Though Stefano has many reasons not to do so, he smiles back, because this is what he too has decided. It would explain the family's subterfuge, for poison – *veleno* – is considered devilish, occult, heretical. It has a long history in Italy stretching from mass poisonings of the ancients, through the plotting of Nero and Agrippina, to the machinations of the Borgias and the Medicis. He can understand why the Ceri family would have wished to conceal that this is how the Duca really died. 'What is it, this poison, do you think, Marcello? Evidently it's one that leaves no real trace.'

'I've reached no firm conclusion, but come.' Marcello kisses his wife on the cheek. '*Mia tesora*, you must forgive us.'

She waves him away: 'Go. Talk about poisons.'

Marcello walks to his bureau and takes a book from the top of a pile, opening it at the beginning. 'There are numerous poisons that can be used and are used to harm. Venoms from animals: snakes, scorpions, toads, salamanders and fish, poison from blister beetles. Next come the plants' – he turns the page – 'belladonna, oleander, aconite, nux vomica, black nightshade, white hellebore. Then there are mineral and alchemical poisons such as arsenic, gypsum, and the mercury salt called solimato. But most of these have particular characteristics that would leave a trace of some kind. Strychnine causes a facial 'death mask' or rictus that none of our victims have had; many others cause hallucinations or marks. In that way I have narrowed it down.'

'To what?'

Marcello shows Stefano a piece of parchment covered with his scribblings. 'From what I can deduce, poisoning from arsenic, foxglove, and death cap mushrooms causes symptoms that might match those of our dead men: stomach pains, vomiting, confusion, dehydration. I think arsenic is our most likely culprit, but it has an odour like garlic that surely the victims would have noticed, or which we would have noticed during the autopsy.'

'Unless it was cleverly disguised.'

'Perhaps. Or it was some rare, clever potion that is not listed in my books, nor widely known.'

'You think such a thing exists?'

'Possibly. There are legends that the Borgias had a secret poison called cantarella: a brilliant white, slow-acting venom, that was pleasant to the taste and which penetrated the victim's veins, with insidious, deadly effect.'

'You do not know what was in this canterella?'

'No.' Marcello has turned to a different book. 'It may have been a myth, invented by the Borgias to frighten their enemies. If it was real, its recipe is not printed in any book, or at least not one that's been found, but of course not all recipes are written down. And that isn't the only secret poison of which I've read. The Council of Ten are said to have hired botanists at the University of Padua to create new and undetectable poisons. Who is to say it wasn't one of those?'

Stefano takes the book from Marcello and flicks back to the opening pages to see the various poisons listed: hellebore, hemlock, henbane, mandrake. He shivers as he recalls his nurse talking of how witches brewed poisons using those very same plants. 'So, if it is a poison, it is a very clever poison. Who's making it, and how? Why are they using it to kill these men?'

'That's our next step: to find the poison maker, or the poison seller.'

'No doubt he won't advertise himself as such, but the maker must be someone skilled. An apothecary?' Stefano turns the page and finds an illustration of water hemlock. It looks so innocent – much like Cow Parsley – yet one root could kill a cow.

'An apothecary, or a *speziala,* selling botanical remedies: they are the people most likely to have the knowledge,' Marcello agrees. 'And, certainly, they wouldn't advertise their wares widely, but there must be places where they spread word of their skills.'

'But which places would those be?'

Mirtilla has returned with a plate of fruits and nuts which she sets down before them. 'Dark places,' she says. 'Underground ones. I think I know where you should begin.'

13

For him that hath his head swollen with a fall:
Take one ounce of bay salt, raw honey three ounces, turpentine two
ounces, intermingle all this well upon the fire, then lay it abroad
upon a linen cloth, and thereof make a plaster, the which you shall
lay hot to his head, and it will altogether assuage the swelling, and
heal it perfectly.

Girolama

'You call this fresh, do you?' Girolama says to the market trader
who's offering her some lettuces. 'I wouldn't use these leaves
to wipe my fundament. You must have better than this kept
back. Stop trying to sell me your day-old rubbish.'

The trader scowls, but brings out the fresh produce that he's
been keeping at the back of the stall.

Angelica has turned beetroot with embarrassment. 'Did you
have to mention your backside, Mother?'

Girolama laughs, selects what she needs, passes a few copper *giulii* to the trader, and moves on to buy some cheeses:
pecorino, parmigiano, Montèbore. They're at the market at the
Campo de' Fiori where various traders have set up their tents
and are weighing, slicing and packing their wares: the spaghetti
vendor, the salami-maker, fresh ricotta-sellers, herb dealers and
fruit sellers and flower sellers, who've brought their produce
from the countryside. Others move among the crowd: a snow

vendor, an orange vendor, a vinegar seller, pedlars with baskets of buttons and fans, bird sellers with wire cages of canaries, finches and nightingales.

As they pass a bird seller, Girolama thinks of the bird she saw in her mirror, the flutter of its wings against the bars. She thinks too of the young man, holding a book, and the woman cowering before him. The images have remained in her mind, though she's tried her best to scrub them from it. They were a warning, she thinks, and a reminder that she must begin teaching Angelica before too long. She can't yet face the task, however, for she knows what she's asking of her adopted daughter, who is still in the full flush of youth and whose nature is sweet as honeysuckle. She knows the danger with which it'll coat her.

Another kind of cage hangs nearby, used to display not birds, but criminals. There are stocks too, and a whipping post. On execution days the gallows is constructed or, worse, a fire is built, for heretics or other subversives. That's the fate of those who challenge the Papacy: burnt to death in the very same place that people buy their suppers.

A crash, then raised voices. Girolama turns. At a fruit stall, a trader is shouting at a woman, presumably his wife. A tray of apples lies on the ground.

'Stupida donna! Stupida!'

There is a smack as he hits his wife's face, open handed, hard, and for a moment time is suspended, the crowd quiet, watching.

The woman falls badly, awkwardly, her shoulder hitting the flagstones. You can almost hear the crunch of bone.

People gawp, then look away. After all, a man is allowed – even required – to discipline his wife, isn't he? As the saying goes, 'A woman is like an egg. The more she's beaten, one way or another, the better she becomes.' The hum of conversation starts up again, the sound of knives chopping and of

80

blacksmiths striking metal. A woman holding a flapping fowl gives its neck a sudden, savage twist.

Girolama, though, does not move on. She stands stone-still, silent, watching the woman try to crawl back to her knees. There is blood on the woman's face, around her nose and mouth. Her cheeks are flushed with shame and distress. As Girolama stares, the wall of the present gives way and the past flows in. She is in that moment her younger, softer self, sick with fear, trying to haul herself up despite the protesting of her body, trying to get herself somewhere else, somewhere safe, but knowing there's no such place. Flames lick within her belly, rise through her chest, and propel her forwards, across the flagstones.

Ignoring the trader's cold gaze, Girolama moves closer to the woman. She holds out her hand. 'Please. Let me help you.'

14

'Who is there who would deny that in all good things poison also resides? Everyone must acknowledge this. This being the case, the question I ask is: must one then not separate the poison from what is good, taking the good and leaving what is bad? Of course one must.'

Paracelsus, The Paragranum

Stefano

The Ave Maria bells sound the beginning of curfew for all citizens. This is the time when the good people of Rome return to their homes and their beds and pinch out their candles, while young, quarrelsome painters, prostitutes and thieves spread out into the night like ink. The lowering darkness is punctured only by the *lampioncini* that burn beside the many Madonna statues that gaze from corners and alleyways.

Stefano and Marcello pass from the darkening streets to the Forum and the shadowy remnants of ancient Rome. They pass the ruined arch of Septimius Severus, beneath which goats are sheltering, then past the broken apse of Maxentius's basilica, the Arch of Titus where it sits embedded in a wall. Before them looms the enormity of the Colosseum, its broken-toothed ring of arcades rising like a devil's castle. But this is no deserted ruin, occupied only by bats. The interior of the Colosseum, a labyrinthine series of tunnels, ruined walls and collapsed columns, has become a warren for buyers and sellers of objects and services that cannot be sold by day. In the fragmented darkness, the magical criminal underworld of Rome is at work.

Like many of the denizens of this secret city, Stefano and Marcello do not show their true selves, but are disguised as something else. They have bought coarse clothing from a second-hand clothes seller and are pretending tonight that they are not magistrate and doctor, but disreputable characters on a mission to find something they suspect is sold here: poison. They do not seek just any poison, however, but one which leaves no trace. One which, like that which they suspect has been used on the three dead men, will allow the poisoner to escape scot free.

The darkness makes it impossible to see anything clearly. They can distinguish only whatever is open to the sky and the pale light of the moon, or what is lit by occasional candles or lanterns. As they walk, Stefano takes in what he sees with a mix of wonder and horror. Everything, it seems, is on sale here, fleshly and other-worldly. The alcoves and crevices of the Colosseum are peopled by shady apothecaries, supposed wise women selling fortunes, back-street abortionists, fakers of documents, and clerics freelancing as black magicians. It is the apothecaries they try first. A crooked man selling twists of herbs whispers to them that he knows of a plant that can make them feel as though they are flying through the air. But he cannot tell them of a poison that will leave no trace. Nor can a dirty-faced woman hawking love potions, nor a man with one eye who claims their mission is pointless. 'There's no such poison,' he tells them. 'If there was, it would be well known in this place.'

The Colosseum smells of incense, smoke and the unwashed, and in some crevices it is almost entirely dark. Though Stefano tells himself not to be foolish, he finds it difficult not to feel that there is something evil about this twisting city. For years it has been considered an enclave of demons and devils and, now that he's here, he can understand why. There is a sickness to it, a deathliness. Everything in his body is telling him to leave. It is not a feeling he has ever had before. They cannot leave, however. They have a job to do. At the urging of the one-eyed man, Stefano and Marcello wind their way even deeper into the depths of the Colosseum to find a woman who he says is called Bettina. If anyone knows of such a potion, he says, it will be her. 'She knows magic,' the man tells them in a whisper.

Stefano and Marcello glance at one another. No natural magician would abide in a place such as this. If the woman indeed knows magic, it must be black magic, sorcery, the sort that the Inquisition have been investigating since the last century and for which men and women have been tortured, hanged and burnt. And though Stefano tells himself he cannot be harmed by such magic, he knows too many people who have claimed that it was witchcraft, and not some regular illness, that tormented and killed their loved ones. He knows a man who brought a legal suit against a local woman who'd cursed his pregnant wife so that when her child was born, it was gnarly and twisted as a root.

Eventually, after many false turns, they find the woman the man has spoken of. Stefano had envisaged some bow-backed old hag, but she can be no more than thirty. If she was not so malnourished, she might be handsome, or at least so Stefano imagines in the semi-darkness. And if she is a witch, which is what Stefano fears, then she does not reveal herself to them as such. Indeed, she is reticent to speak to them at all and when she does speak, her voice is reedy and thin. 'I know nothing of such a poison,' she insists. 'I don't know why that man might have said that of me.'

Perhaps, Stefano thinks, she has deduced that he and Marcello are not what they pretend to be, or perhaps, in this age of inquisition and accusation, she is simply careful to whom she speaks.

'But we are in much need of a remedy,' Marcello insists. 'We can pay. We have heard that you may know of someone who can help us. That you may know of a man who makes a slow-acting ... solution.'

The woman shakes her head. 'No, not me. You're confusing me with someone else.'

She is, Stefano thinks, afraid. He will use this to their advantage. 'I don't think so. I think you just won't admit what you are. With whom could we possibly be confusing you?'

The woman stares at him for a moment with her dark eyes. 'There's talk of a woman called La Strolaga,' she whispers. An astrologer, she must mean. 'Of how she can do such things, make such things. That she deals with demons in the centre of the earth. I've no idea if it's true.'

Stefano is reminded of the tale his nurse used to tell him, of a witch who dwelt in wells and who used her pale arms to grab at little children. La Manalonga, the long-armed one. Even all these years later, the thought makes his skin shrink.

'Where is she, this La Strolaga?' he asks.

'I don't know. Not here.'

'In Rome?'

'Maybe.' She turns away from them.

'I think you know more than you let on,' Stefano says.

'I think you misrepresent what you are,' the woman cuts back, turning suddenly to face him. 'You are no tradesman, Ser,' she lisps. 'Nor is your friend. We are poor people, but we aren't blind, nor stupid. We see many things you don't.'

There is something cat-like, demonic, about this woman, but Stefano refuses to step away from her, refuses to be cowed. 'If you know where this La Strolaga is, or who exactly she is, then you would do well to tell us. We can pay you.'

The woman hisses at him then, right in his face, baring her teeth, and he can smell her fetid breath.

'Let's get away from here,' Marcello mutters, grabbing him by the arm, and Stefano is only too glad to leave the woman's dark den and stumble back towards the entrance.

They have only gone a few metres, however, before another woman stops them. 'You'll pay for information, will you?' Her voice is throaty and dry.

'For good information, yes,' Stefano responds, wary. This woman is older than the first, with hair dyed straw-yellow and her scant bosom pushed up in her dress. A prostitute, Stefano assumes, for they are so numerous in Rome that they outflank the clerics. Largely, though, they are confined to the prostitutes' quarter, known as *L'Ortaccio* – the garden of evil, (just as the Jews are penned into their ghetto). 'You know of this woman, La Strolaga?'

'I've heard of a woman called La Profetessa who reads the stars. Perhaps they're one and the same. They say,' she whispers, 'that she trafficks with demons to predict fortunes.'

Astrology is illegal. It is seen as the right only of God. This is why in Dante's Inferno, the soothsayers' heads are twisted backwards, so that the tears streaming from their eyes wet their buttocks.

'But is she a seller of poisons?' Stefano says.

'She's a seller of all sorts, so far as I know.'

'Where is she?'

'I don't know. But I can find out.'

Is she bluffing? The woman has pustules on her face, he sees, about her mouth. 'It's specifically a poison seller we're looking for. One who produces a poison that leaves no trace.'

'I'll keep my ear to the ground for you, gentlemen, should you wish to give me a means of contacting you, and a little retainer for my troubles.'

Stefano glances at Marcello. Is this a trap? He has no intention of giving the woman his address, so he says, 'If you have good information you can contact me at l'Osteria della Torretta. You can say the message is for Signore Scricciolo.' This is the name his brothers called him when they were younger: little shrimp.

'Very well. My name is Flavia.'

Stefano knows this name is no truer than the one he has given her.

'And the coin?' she says.

Stefano is reluctant to take out his purse in a place such as this. He imagines it could be magicked away in the darkness easy enough. Marcello, however, has produced some *scudi*.

'Is that all?' the woman says, surveying the coins. 'I'd make that in an hour's work.'

'If you can bring us the information we need,' Marcello says, 'then we will pay you handsomely, and I can provide you with medicines to treat your condition.'

The woman stares at him and Stefano fears this one will hiss at them too, but instead she says, 'You'd best be true to your word, Ser, or there's people here who'll put a curse on you for lies told to a friend.'

'He's telling you the truth,' Stefano says, unnerved by her talk of curses. 'You can choose to believe it, or not.'

Flavia secretes the money in her bodice. 'I'll find you your poison seller, don't you worry.'

As soon as they have escaped from the Colosseum and are back in the cool night air, Stefano regrets having told the woman anything. Who is to say she won't find out who he is and seek to hurt him in some way? 'What was the condition she had?' he asks Marcello. 'The pox?'

'I would guess so,' the doctor answers. 'It's common enough among her profession.'

The flesh-eating plague. The '*mal Francese*', the Italians call it, 'The Neapolitan disease' say the French, for it began, it's thought, in Naples, and has spread like wildfire through the Italian states.

'Can you cure it?'

Marcello shrugs. 'Maybe. For a time.'

Stefano shudders. 'Good, because I don't fancy her curses.'

'Do you believe in curses, Stefano?'

Stefano hesitates. Many do believe, of course; most, perhaps, despite the Church's attempts to squash such beliefs. His own nurse taught him rhymes to counter curses, and talked of people palsied by an evil touch. It is difficult to shift such beliefs, when fed them very young. 'I confess I'm undecided,' he says. 'And you? Presumably, as a medical man, you have some scepticism of black magic and witchcraft.'

'I'm not sure that I believe in witches,' Marcello says.

'Yet they have been fought and imprisoned across Europe.'

'Many women have, yes, and some men, but I think witches the creation of frightened men who wish to provide a solution to questions of evil and ill fate. It's not so simple as all that.'

'How then do you explain how a man or child may grow ill after being cursed?' Stefano asks. He will not say so, but when his mother grew suddenly sick he, then seven years old, was convinced that it was a witch's curse that caused the slicing pains in her chest, the draining away of her energy. It was what his nurse told him often enough, and who was he to doubt her?

'I believe that if a man believes he's cursed, then he will suffer,' Marcello says. 'It's a peculiarity of the mind. But yes, best we don't test out this woman's curses. If she comes to us, I'll give her the mercury treatment.'

They have reached the Forum now. The moon has slid from behind the clouds to bleach the ancient remnants, and the

88

columns of the Temple of Castor and Pollux rise, ghostly, before them. The dead are all around you in Rome, Stefano thinks. A constant memento mori. It is difficult, in such a place, to believe that only the living direct our fates, or that witchcraft is a mere invention.

15

Anna

Philippe has gone to visit a cardinal to attempt to persuade him
to take his paintings, as he has sold little this past month and
is fast burning through the money Anna's father left her. She
knows this because it is she who keeps the household accounts,
being far better with figures than her husband, though he does
not acknowledge it. Anna does not anticipate his trip will be
successful. Rome is a honeypot for artists all over Italy, all over
the world, and Philippe's is, by Anna's reckoning, a rather indif-
ferent talent. This is the city of Caravaggio and Michelangelo,
Borromini and Bernini – it has little need for French artists of
reasonable ability. No doubt this is partly what feeds Philippe's
bitterness, though the seed was planted long before he came to
Rome, perhaps as soon as it entered his mother's womb. He
only ever speaks with enmity of his parents, claiming they did
not value him, did not love him, did not care.

Anna waits at home (because she is not, of course, allowed to
leave) praying that he takes at least a few of his works. If they
do not, it is she who will suffer his outrage. Benedetta paces,

fretting, which makes Anna even more nervous. She wishes Benedetta would stop and sit down but she doesn't chide her, for her maid has shown her a possible way out, and Anna has not only rejected it but criticised her for suggesting it. So they both wait, barely speaking, too afraid to eat. Anna is knitting little boots for the baby. The only sound is the click of her wooden needles, the rustle of the fire.

Half an hour after the Ave Maria bells comes the noise of the door unlocking, opening. Anna freezes, trying to gauge from his step how drunk he is, how angry. His footsteps are soft and, when Philippe enters the room, he has a strange smile on his face. She knows, however, that it is not a true smile and sees that his skin is clammy and pallid. He says nothing, merely sits down. Anna does not recognise this mood and she fears it. At least when he is shouting and drunk she knows what's to come and how she may attempt to dodge him. This is something else. She doesn't dare ask Philippe what happened but begins to fix his supper. All the while that Anna is working, he remains silent, merely tapping his foot on the floor. It makes her sick with nervousness. When she is done cooking she puts the plate and cutlery before him together with a cup and flask.

She is about to pour the wine when, quick as lightning, Philippe grabs the fork and stabs into the back of her hand. The shock hits before the pain, and for a moment she stares at her hand, the fork, the blood that flows, without feeling anything.

'Why?' she finds herself asking him. 'Why?'

'Three thousand *scudi*, that's what he promised me, the lying pig.'

'Who? Who promised you?'

The pain kicks in and it is so intense that she drops to her knees, and struggles to stay conscious, but through it all Anna can hear him still talking.

'Your verminous father, that's who.' Philippe is drunker than she'd realised; or perhaps he has taken some drug. 'He told me your inheritance would be ten thousand when he died, and all we got was a paltry one thousand.' He gives a mirthless laugh. 'He tricked me.'

Anna clutches her hand, the fork still within it. Is this true? Did her father lie about how much money she would inherit in order to marry her off? It is not as though she was a terrible prospect: she is good-looking, healthy (or was), of a respectable family. Why would her father need to lie?

'You misunderstood,' she says. 'You must have.'

'No, dearest wife, it is you who misunderstood because he lied to you just the same.'

'I don't believe you.' She is crying now, gasping.

'Did you really think I'd have taken you with such a small dowry if I didn't think there would be more money shortly to follow? But no, decrepit as he seemed, he lived on and on, months and months, until I changed his medicine.'

Despite the pain and the distress, Anna's mind is suddenly very clear. 'What do you mean?'

He laughs again. 'I mean nothing, little wife. Nothing at all.'

Anna stares up at her husband, at his flabby face, his reddened drunkard's eyes. She thinks of her father as he was in his final days, racked with excruciating pain, crying out for her and her mother. *Until I changed his medicine.* She looks at her hand, covered in blood, as though it belongs to someone else.

A sudden clarity, blinding white. *Then thou shalt give life for life, eye for eye, tooth for tooth, hand for hand.*

This is it, Anna thinks. This is the sign she's been waiting for, her own epiphany. The blood drips from her palm.

She will avenge her father and save her child, and if she hangs for it, then so be it, because if she stays here she will be killed sooner or later. That was what the woman, Laura, had said: that she must get there first. And, by God, she will.

★

They go to her the following day, though Anna is still weak with pain.

The woman almost sneers when they enter the room. 'I knew I'd see you again. You have the money?'

'I have everything I could collect: thirty *scudi*.'

'Not enough.'

'It's all I have,' Anna says. Benedetta obtained the coins from selling Anna's pearls, the only jewellery she had left.

Laura shakes her head. 'There are other ways of making money.'

But Anna will not have this. She will not be trampled any longer. 'I'm with child, as you can plainly see. I cannot sell myself without fear of harming him. Have some pity or at least some common sense. If your remedy works as you claim it does, then it will be easy enough for me to obtain the rest.' She knows Philippe has some gold secreted away, but she does not dare to touch it while he lives. 'Thirty now. Twenty later.'

The woman strokes her chin. 'It's not my decision to make,' she claims. 'It's another woman who makes the Aqua.'

The Aqua. The water. 'Who is she?'

'A clever woman who lives across the river in a house marked by a lily, and with a garden full of herbs. She guards her book of secrets, and her money, carefully.'

'Then I beg you to ask her. Explain to her my circumstances. You yourself said it: if I leave it much longer, I will be dead, my babe too, and then neither you nor your friend will get anything. This way, we all shall win.'

Laura looks her up and down, running her eyes over the

bandaged hand, the bruised skin, as though measuring her worth, calculating how long she has to live. What she sees there must satisfy her, as she says: 'I'll ask her, but I can make no promises. She's a businesswoman before she's a good soul, with two sons to feed and two husbands dead, so it is all on her to earn.'

Anna swallows. 'What is in it, this water, that makes it so expensive?' And so deadly.

Laura gives a thin smile. 'If I knew, I'd assure you I'd be making it myself. But, whatever it is, it works.'

16

Stefano

Supper at the palazzo of the cardinal for whom Stefano's brother, Vincenzo, works. It is an expensive, impressive property surrounded by vineyards and overlooking the city. As the guests are seated, the sun begins to set, deep orange behind the twisted black vines. The dishes (anchovies in olive oil, redwings in bacon) are of the finest quality. Not so the conversation, for Stefano has been seated with his brothers who have heard of Baranzone's displeasure regarding the physician and are using the opportunity to goad him.

'Please tell me,' Vincenzo says, 'that you have a few other paths you may pursue in investigating this business, and haven't thrown all your chances to the wind.' He is dressed in a black silk cape and cap which, with his thin face, give him the air of a plague doctor.

'Rest assured, brother, that I am pursuing several lines of inquiry.'

'I hope so,' Vincenzo says, attacking his chicken with some gusto. 'Father is unhappy, of course.'

'Of course,' Stefano says lightly, glancing over at their father, who sits on a table nearby. 'That is my role in this family: to be the son who disappoints.'

'Now, that is not true.'

Yet it is, and Vincenzo knows it. Their father has always favoured Stefano the least. Perhaps it is because, with his pale skin and dark lashes, Stefano most resembles their mother. Perhaps it is because he is small. Stefano has pondered it many times and never reached a conclusion.

'But it would not do to let the Governor down on this one,' Vincenzo continues. 'He's not a man prone to leniency.'

'Oh, I don't know,' Bruno chimes in. 'He's always been a good friend of the family, and I asked him to go a little easy on you, Stefanino. Allow the occasional mistake.'

Stefano feels his face tighten. He does not wish for his brother to make excuses for him. He wants to succeed on his own merits. 'I will not make any further mistake,' he says quietly. 'I merely got carried away with the task, with trying to find the truth.'

'Ah, but that's typical of you, isn't it?' Vincenzo says, beckoning over one of the servants to refill their goblets. 'I'm reminded of the time you questioned that poor child with a purple stain over his face on how it had come about. Little wonder the lad gave you a beating.' Both brothers chuckle.

'Yes, very well, Vincenzo.' Stefano has no wish to recall the incident: one of his many missteps as a child, one of the many examples of how he didn't connect with others. He hadn't wished to upset the boy, merely to understand what had caused the livid marking that covered his face and neck. He should have guessed that the explanation he'd been given was the one supplied for all things unexplained: it was the work of the devil.

'This was about the Duca di Ceri, is that right?' Bruno asks. 'You cross-examined his physician!'

'Not cross-examined, no,' Stefano mutters. 'I merely asked a few questions.'

'God's blood, you don't think the good doctor hastened his end, do you?' Bruno says, voice low, eyes glinting.

Stefano meets his gaze. 'I assume nothing, Bruno. I've been told not to go there, and, as discussed, I intend not to make further mistakes.'

'But it was the Tertian fever, wasn't it?' Vincenzo says. 'That's what I heard.'

Stefano presses his lips together.

'Ah, our brother is being a good boy and not talking,' Bruno says. 'But surely, Stefano, you can talk to us.' He picks up a redwing and, through mouthfuls, says: 'You're saying he didn't die of natural causes?'

'That would have to mean the Duca had enemies,' Stefano says carefully.

His brothers look at one another.

'Did he?' Stefano asks. He cannot help himself.

'Stefano,' Bruno says quietly, 'the man was a sanctimonious old goat with a collection of saints' body parts. No one liked him. But did anyone dislike him enough to kill him?'

Vincenzo smiles. 'Now, there's the question. Who'd have a motive?'

'Maybe someone who wanted a piece of that luscious wife of his,' Bruno suggests.

'Agnese Aldobrandini,' Stefano says, remembering the woman in blue.

'That's her. Ripe as a low-hanging fruit.' Bruno takes a peach from the bowl of fruit in the centre of the table and bites into it, grinning. 'That'll be why they've shut her up in a convent, no doubt.'

'No doubt,' Stefano echoes, trying to give the air of

97

insouciance, but his mind is running and running. They are a rich family. Why have they put their daughter in a nunnery?

'And what of your woman?' Vincenzo asks Stefano.

'What woman?'

'Ha! Well, there is our answer!' Bruno slaps him on the back. 'You need to get yourself a piece of flesh, little brother, or your *cazzo* will wither and die.'

'*Per carità!*' Vincenzo says, feigning horror, though Stefano guesses several of the girls who serve them food have given him more besides. 'But I suppose Bruno's right that it's only healthy, a young man such as yourself. You don't want people to start thinking you're impotent.' He lowers his voice. 'Or worse.'

Stefano feels a flutter of fear. This is something that his brothers have often taunted him with, claiming he has the look of a catamite, but really it is no teasing matter. Sodomites, as they call them, are still burnt in Rome, though it's rarely those of the higher orders who are condemned. He has no wish to be suspected of such things (and in truth he often feels a deep loneliness, a need for human contact) but also he has little urge to find some young woman and make a harlot of her, which is what would happen were he not to marry her. Wife, nun, whore: these are the three categories of women in Italian society. No, he needs to find a wife, but to do that, he must succeed. 'My focus at the moment must be entirely on my work,' he says truthfully.

'Did you know,' Bruno says, 'that the lovely Sulpizia is to marry again? To a son of the Chigi family, no less.'

Stefano thinks of the young woman in green at the wedding, her milk-white skin, her long lashes, and feels a pang of regret.

'You rather took a fancy to her, didn't you, little brother?' Bruno asks with a glint of spite.

'I barely remember her. Now, tell me: Ceri's wife, this

Agnese. What kind of woman is she, do you know? Lucia described her as pretty and vain.'

'Our sister thinks that of all women who are younger and prettier than her,' Vincenzo says. 'Which is to say a good number of them.'

'That's a little unfair,' Stefano says.

'A little, perhaps, but not a great deal. In any event, Ceri's widow is indeed very pretty, and dances remarkably well, but as to her character? I couldn't say.'

'I could,' Bruno says, 'and I'd say she was a *civetta*.' A slut.

'You know this from any real source, or is this merely your guesswork, brother?'

'Oh, I'm good at sniffing them out,' Bruno says, wrinkling his nose. 'She has a way of regarding a man that makes him know just what she's after.'

'Bruno, you'll forgive me for saying that you seem to think all women are desirous of your person. This hardly marks her out.'

Vincenzo guffaws at that, for Bruno has always had excessive confidence for a man with squashed features and a dark frizz of hair. To Stefano he says: 'You're right, *fratellino*, he does, but in this case I suspect Bruno may be right. She has that look about her.'

Stefano has heard his brothers' views on women many times before: a woman is either an angel, or a whore. There is no in-between. He would like to think his own views are more nuanced. Nevertheless, a pretty, vibrant woman married to a dislikeable old man, then shut up in a convent? Now that is an interesting tale. 'Had you heard of any scandal, Bruno? Any whiff of an affair?'

Bruno is still scowling at Stefano's jibe. 'Stefanino,' he says acidly, 'did you not say that you weren't going to make any further mistakes? That you were going to pursue other avenues? Not disappoint our dearest father?'

Stefano swallows. 'I did, and so I shall.'

'I doubt you have the mettle for the task, little brother. You can't win a game of *calcio*, never mind succeed in a murder case.'

Stefano looks away, weary of the constant animosity and competition that exists between the three of them. He gazes at their father on the other side of the room, seated at the cardinal's table. It is a competition that he has stoked since they were little, and it is one Stefano has almost always lost. Well, he will not lose this time. He will show them of what he is made.

It is almost eleven by the time Stefano reaches home. As he approaches his house, a figure steps from the shadows. A woman. Stefano catches his breath. It is Flavia, the straw-haired prostitute they recruited in the Colosseum. Clearly she's worked out who he is.

'What are you doing here?' he whispers hoarsely.

'I've got the information you wanted.'

Stefano is caught between anger and curiosity. He looks about him. A fur-collared couple are descending their carriage, watching, plainly wondering why a woman of this type is in their neighbourhood. 'We cannot talk here. I told you to communicate with me via the taverna.'

Flavia pulls a face. 'I thought you'd want this information fast, and it wasn't too difficult to find you.' She smiles, showing pale brown teeth. 'I thought you'd appreciate my talents.'

Stefano glances again about him, then gestures for the woman to follow him down a side street. He prays that no neighbour will pass them and think he's resorted to alleyway encounters with whores. 'What is it, then, this information that you believed I'd want to know at once? Have you found this woman they call La Strolaga?'

'Not yet. But listen to what I do have: I've been doing some asking about, like we discussed, and at first I got nowhere, though there are plenty enough men in this city will say they'll do a fellow in for you, if you pay them half a crown.'

'I don't doubt it. But none claimed they had poison?'

'No,' Flavia says. 'Not until I spoke to a woman I know who lives near Santa Maria Maggiore. I told her I was having problems with Sandro, the man who gets customers for me.' A pimp, she must mean, Stefano thinks. A go-between. 'And that's not untrue, though I'm some way from killing the bastard. Anyway, she tells me she's heard of a woman called Vanna, who attends the church at Santa Pudenzia and sells a poison that can't be detected.'

Here we are. 'Who is this woman?'

'Some old crone with decent secrets, it seems. Melissa said she tried to sell it to a woman to give to her brother who was causing her grief.'

'And it killed him?'

Flavia shrugs, as if this is neither here nor there. 'I don't know. I only heard she offered to sell it to the sister, to end her misery.'

'Where is she, this Vanna? Where does she live?'

'She has lodgings in an apartment downhill from San Lorenzo in Panisperna. I found her at the church and followed her home.' The woman nods, pleased with herself. She is evidently good at trailing people.

Stefano considers. He could ferret this Vanna woman out in her dingy apartment and ask her directly about the poison, but she would simply deny any knowledge, just as the woman in the Colosseum did. No, he needs something better than that, and faster.

'So you'll pay me, yes?' Flavia says. 'And your doctor friend, he'll treat me?'

Stefano regards her. 'Yes, I'll pay you. Marcello will give you medicine, just as he said he would. However, I may have a further task for you before then.'

'You want me to find someone else?'

'No.' Stefano is still thinking. She is wily, this Flavia. She found Vanna. She found him. Is she good enough to play the part he intends for her? He decides he will have to risk it.

17

A preservative against envy:

If it be the witchcraft of envy, you may know it thus. The infected loseth his colour, hardly openeth his eyes, always hangeth his head down, sighs often, his heart is ready to break, and sheddeth salt and bitter tears, without any occasion or sign of evil. To disencharm him, because the air is corrupted and infected, burn sweet perfume to purify the air again, and sprinkle him with waters sweetened with cinnamon, cloves, cypress, lignum aloes, musk, and amber.

Girolama

Of all of Girolama's circle, Laura is the one she likes least. 'Lauraccia' some of the others call her: evil Laura. Girolama doesn't believe there's anything so simple as an evil person, but there is a toxicity to Laura as powerful as white snakeroot or oleander. She was abandoned by both her husband and her daughter years before and curses the rest of the world for it, but Girolama suspects the woman was born bitter and life has just soured her further. If Vanna is honey, Laura is vinegar. But she is useful. Unlike Vanna, who is too slow and too kind, Graziosa who is mischievous, and La Sorda who is too talkative, Laura gets things done. She is a good seller, if not a good person, and Girolama's continued success depends not just on the milk of human kindness, but on cold, hard coin.

'I can't give you the usual commission on it,' Laura says after she's explained the situation, 'as this Anna woman claims she can only scrape together thirty *scudi*.'

Girolama eyes Laura carefully, taking in her thin frame and skeletal face. Lord knows, the woman could afford to eat well if she wanted to, but perhaps her insides are as bitter as her tongue and turn all food to acid. 'You'll take your normal fraction, Laura. If the overall sum is less, then your portion is smaller too. You know very well how it works.'

The woman scowls. 'I have bills to pay. Not all of us live so comfortably as you.' She looks around the room, jealously regarding the wall hangings and ornaments, the polished walnut credenza.

'Why can this Anna not pay more?' Girolama asks, ignoring her complaint. She knows Laura lives well enough, or could if she wished to. 'You said she was the daughter of a merchant.'

'A dead merchant. She says her husband has squandered all her money, and her father's money, and left her with nothing.'

Girolama nods. 'A familiar tale.' She thinks of the man Giulia married after Girolama's father died – a man whose apparent charm concealed a soul as empty as his pockets. Ranchetti. He thought everything belonged to him, including Girolama, though she was then but a child. Her skin recoils at the memory. He took not only her body but her dowry. For an instant she sees Ranchetti again, holding a knife to Giulia's throat, demanding that she give him the money. She sees the thin trickle of blood as the knife pierces her skin: the shock of red against white. That was the point at which everything changed. That was the point she met Tofania.

'Would you say her case was pressing?' Girolama asks Laura.

'I'd say she'll be dead by Carnival time if she doesn't act,' Laura says casually. 'This painter is clearly one that likes to use his fists and boots, and that even though she's with child.'

Girolama feels it as a pain in her own stomach: a muscle

memory, perhaps. 'One of those, is he? Then we'll help her. I'll mix up the Aqua now. Wait for me in the garden.'

Laura's face acquires a sly look. 'I could assist you.'

'No, Laura. I work alone. I've told you this before.'

Girolama leaves Laura and secretes herself in what she calls her 'kitchen', though really it's more akin to an apothecary's workshop with cauldrons, copper weighing scales, alembics and pans, and bundles of herbs hanging from the ceiling. She keeps the room locked, as there are many treasures and dangers here: glass vials and majolica jars full of the ingredients for her face waters and potions and pills. Here she makes face waters and balsamic creams to clear the skin and remove blemishes, face masks of lead to whiten the flesh, drops of belladonna to make eyes sparkle, tooth powder with pumice to scour off stains. She can make dark hair pale and blistered skin smooth. She can make the sleepless sleep with syrups of poppy, and she can make the anxious calm as a lake. But she also makes other things: potions to stop babies forming in the womb, *il remedio di restringere* to remake virgins, a cream to guard against the French pox. Potions made from the hearts of animals that will besot the drinker with love. Solutions that – said with the right incantation – will cast a curse upon the subject.

Many of the recipes were developed by Giulia, and, before her, by Aunt Tofania. She wasn't really Girolama's aunt, but she was close and similar enough to Giulia that the two might have been sisters: smart, witty, tough. As Giulia explained the story to Girolama, Tofania had been married to a *speziale* who not only cured but harmed, who created not only medicines but misery. Tofania, though, was clever, much cleverer than him, and she learnt as much as she could, even taught herself to read. After many years of torment, she turned the tables on her husband by concocting her own potion to kill him, using the skills he himself had taught her, and that she had taught herself. Other poisons had names that sang out what they were: wolfsbane, deadly nightshade, the destroying angel. Tofania, however, called her poison 'Aqua'. Water. It was odourless, colourless, clear.

The recipe was too good, too powerful, for Tofania to keep to herself. At first, she gave the Aqua only to a few friends, or friends of friends, who had suffered for many years, or were at real risk of being killed. Then word began to spread, whispered between women, and they would come to her door, begging for her help. That was why she decided she would expand her business and help other women in need while making the money she needed to keep herself afloat. When Giulia came to her, Tofania saw a woman who not only needed her assistance, but who had a quickness similar to her own. After Giulia disposed of Ranchetti, Tofania took both her and Girolama in. She trained Giulia to make not only the Aqua and other, better-known poisons, but remedies that would help women: herbs to prevent pregnancy, herbs to encourage it, poultices to ease the pain of monthly bleeding and to help heal after birthing, draughts to stem the pain of childbirth and to help with the changes that come later in life. All of these were written in her lambskin-bound *libro di segreti,* book of secrets, which she kept under lock and key.

Girolama spent many years in that house, among the warmth and wisdom of those women, helping them in the workshop, tending to the herb garden, learning the craft of the apothecary. But it wasn't until she was eighteen years old (until she'd been married to a man who showed her very clearly why the Aqua was necessary) that Giulia taught her the recipe that she makes now. Crush or be crushed. Strike or be struck. That's what life has taught Girolama. That's how she justifies what she does.

She puts on her chicken-skin gloves and gathers together the ingredients she needs. She begins to grind them together in a mortar. There isn't a chance in hell that she'll teach Lauraccia this recipe, though she knows that's what the woman is angling for. She doesn't trust Laura not to sell it to anyone who asks, without thought or scruple. She's heard tales of children poisoned, whole families. Though she's hardly conducting a careful judging process, Girolama thinks the men she helps send to their graves are, by and large, ones who deserve to go there. Often, they're men who are fit for the fiery pit of hell and she's only too pleased to help speed their slippery descent. Such things she's seen and heard in her time. Such cruelties and barbarities. Not always purely physical but cruelties of the mind that can be worse than any cut: that can eat away at a woman until she's corroded inside, a shell of a human being. They, often, are the ones she can't help. They're the ones that wither and die like plants without sunshine, believing they've lost the power to fight back. She almost went there herself, what seems like a lifetime ago, so can recognise the signs. Sometimes she reaches those women, or her circle of women do. Several times Vanna, Maria or La Sorda have seen a woman at church or at market and known, have whispered to her that there's a way. It's a risk, this strategy. Sometimes these women are horrified by their words, and threaten to report them. But sometimes, as happened in the Campo de' Fiori, the women grab hold of what she offers like a branch held out to a drowning man.

Often it isn't themselves they wish to save, so much as their children, who suffer too. Girolama pounds away with the mortar. That she cannot abide. When she looks upon the faces of her own sons, full grown now, when she looks at the sweet face of Angelica, she can't understand how anyone could wish to damage their own kin. Yet they do, often enough. This Anna Conti, Laura said, has a child in her belly. Perhaps that's what has spurred her to seek a way to escape a husband who beats her senseless. Or perhaps it's something else. Often the things that act as the final straw seem small in relationships of barbarity and bitterness – a further infidelity, a niggardly action, a nose broken for the third time. Girolama thinks for an instant of her first husband: a man with a black hole within him so deep that it sucked in all the light. She transfers the powdered ingredients to the pan and blinks the memory away.

Poison, she's heard priests say in their sermons, is the worst of evils because it's insidious, creeping, silent. And her poison is the slowest and most silent of them all. But what are these women supposed to do? Surprise their brutish husbands with a sword? Attack them with their bare hands? It isn't a fair fight, not on any level. This is a man's world and the laws and the norms of the land favour him. Often there's no other way out. So yes, creeping, creeping in the night. Is what she does evil? Girolama isn't sure she believes in evil at all. There are different kinds of human nature, some approaching good, some bad, just as there are different plants in her garden for different needs. Some plants are healing, some are toxic. So it is with humans. If she has caused some people excruciating pain and death, then there are others she has saved. Many would say that this is the role of God, not of some uneducated woman from Palermo, and that by taking his role she acts as the devil. But that is a God written by men for men and she has little time for it. In any event, she must make a living, and this is what she does, just as Giulia did before her, and Tofania. Girolama doesn't poison these people herself. She simply provides the means for those who need it. Is that any worse than selling knives or swords to men? They, after all, kill people every day in the streets. It isn't something on which she dwells too often. She doesn't have time for such thoughts.

The mixture begins to simmer.

At some point she will have to show Angelica the recipe, for they can't afford to let it die out. For many, it's a lifeline: a small bottle of hope, a small bottle of power. But Girolama can't yet bring herself to teach her. She's too young, too carefree. It's a burden to shoulder such responsibility, to hold so many lives in the palm of ones hand. No, let her live a little more, untainted.

Girolama takes a spoon and stirs. The crystals begin to dissolve.

18

Stefano

The bells sound for midday. It is the agreed time for Flavia to produce the poisoner. The air beneath the bed is thick with dust and, in the darkness, Stefano imagines spiders and scorpions crawling about him. He is reminded of when, as a child, he would hide from his father to escape another beating. He has an unbearable urge to sneeze. He must, however, remain entirely still, as he can hear footsteps on the stairs. Is it Flavia? Is she alone or has she managed to net her prey and drag her bag to her lair? The plan to trap the poison seller had felt ludicrous, but there must be a witness to what follows, and what better witness than himself?

His heart beats faster as he hears female voices growing louder. Then comes the noise of the latch rising, the door opening. Stefano presses his finger to his septum, trying to stop the sneeze.

'You must forgive the poverty of my quarters.' Flavia's voice, cloying.

'You've nothing to apologise for.' The second woman's

voice is quieter, humbler. 'I'm a poor woman myself, as are most of my customers. We do what we can to get by, eh?' He prays that this is Vanna, the woman who is rumoured to sell poison.

'We do, we do,' Flavia responds. Stefano can hear her moving about the room, getting down what must be cups and pouring some liquid into them. 'You'll take a drink with me?'

'That's kind of you, thank you.'

There is a settling sound from above him, and Stefano realises that one of the women, Flavia presumably, is sitting on the bed. She is ensuring he can hear their conversation.

'So,' Flavia says, 'I'll tell you the truth of the matter, which is that I'm in a dire position and need your help.'

'What help would that be?' the other woman asks blandly.

Flavia coughs. 'My so-called protector. He mistreats me.'

'I'm sorry to hear this.'

'But you can help me?' Flavia asks.

'I'm not sure what you mean, Signora.'

Beneath the bed, Stefano hears something scuttle past him.

'I need help getting rid of him,' Flavia whispers, loudly.

A long silence. 'I don't know why you think I can help you,' Vanna says.

Is she holding back, Stefano wonders? Has she deduced that Flavia is not to be trusted? Or is this rumour of poison-selling all a nonsense? Is he hiding beneath this filthy bed for no point whatsoever?

'Please,' Flavia says, her voice breaking rather convincingly (but then of course she is used to faking feeling). 'Such things he does to me, and I've no one to turn to, no other place to go. There's no one will take me in, no one to hide me.' A creaking of the mattress as Flavia leans forward. 'He says he'll kill me often enough that I fear one day he will. I've heard you can brew a mixture that will put such people away.'

A long pause. 'There may be something I can do.'

'Yes?' Flavia's tone is urgent.

Vanna lowers her voice so that Stefano must strain to pick up what she says. 'I can get you a liquid from someone I know.'

In the darkness, Stefano tenses. Then it is true. It exists.

'A poison, you mean?' Flavia says and Stefano breathes in quickly. She has surely gone too far.

'Not anything you've heard of before,' the woman says. 'But it will do the job, if you're sure that's really what you want. If you're sure that there's no other option.'

'I wouldn't be asking if there were another way. Is it costly, this liquid?'

'Twenty *scudi* would be all I ask, as I see you're not a rich woman, and as you tell me your need is real.'

'*Dio vi benedica*,' Flavia says, though Stefano thinks it unlikely God will be blessing this woman. 'When? When can you get me this liquid? How soon does it act?'

'The Aqua is slow acting. That's the trick of it. You must give it a little at a time.'

'But will he not know that he is poisoned? Will others not find me out?'

'This water that I will give you is subtle. I have seen it work before, many times. It will take me a few days to get some. You can find the money?'

'I'll do my best. I'll have to.'

Stefano hears the sound of the other woman's feet on the floor. She is standing up. This is his cue. He must do it now. 'Stop!' he says, dragging himself up. '*Agenti!*'

Two *sbirri* officers rush into the room to assist him, but really it does not need more than one of them. The woman, Vanna, is smaller and older than he'd anticipated: a husk of a woman with light eyes, hair faded to an eggshell colour, and widow's weeds turned slightly green from too many washings. She makes no attempt to run, but stands, pale-faced, with her back against the wall, staring at them.

'Have you nothing to say?' Stefano asks her, but she appears merely stunned. One of the *sbirri* takes out the handcuffs. It seems foolish to restrain her, but procedure is procedure and this woman has apparently just agreed to sell a poison that will kill a man. Stomach and tenacity, that's what Baranzone expects of him; it is what he expects of himself.

One officer cuffs Vanna's wrists behind her back. The other empties her purse, which yields up only a few keys, coloured powders wrapped in paper, and a number of pawn tickets. 'You're to come with us, and quietly.'

The men hustle Vanna downstairs and into a waiting black carriage. Though Stefano has told them to leave with as little noise as possible, without causing alarm, the neighbours – ever alert to any intrigue – have come to stand in their doorways, or lean from the windows, watching closely. 'Where are you taking her?' a woman demands.

Stefano ignores her, and climbs aboard a second carriage which will follow the prisoner to her place of detention. Though he will not tell this to the waiting public, they are bound for the Tor di Nona: that infamous and ancient prison has been reopened at the Governor's command, ready for the arrests Stefano has promised he will make, for the witnesses he has vowed he will find. This woman, though a thin scrap of a human, is the first piece of the jigsaw; the first step towards creating the whole picture. As Stefano watches the prison cart move off, he feels a swell of pride in his chest.

Within half an hour, they are at the Tor di Nona. A row of apparently normal city buildings, three to five storeys tall, mask the prison within. No one peers at them from the barred windows. No one stands to greet them. The place is abandoned, the prisoners having been moved to the Carceri Nuove some months before. The courtyard is eerily quiet and the gate, as they push at it, creaks. No matter, Stefano thinks: this is his domain now. This is where he will make his name. This is where he will find the truth.

19

Anna

In the kitchen, Anna slices the endive and lettuce for the soup. Benedetta silently watches her. The recipe is what Laura has recommended: the endive is bitter in any event, so if Philippe detects any note of sourness he won't question it. Or at least that is what Laura claims. Please God, let her be right. Earlier that day, she passed Anna the small glass vial, saying, 'Don't worry. The solution is almost tasteless and, as you see, as clear as the cleanest water from the deepest well.'

Now, in the kitchen, Anna holds it up to the light and yes, it is transparent. She lifts the bottle to her nose and smells. Nothing. She does not dare taste it. How is she to know that it is not, in fact, just plain water for which she has paid everything she has? She can only add a little to his soup and hope that it does its job. That is what she does, unstoppering the vial and letting the liquid drip, drip, drip into the bowl. As she stirs, her hands begin to shake.

'Hold your nerve and he'll suspect nothing,' Laura had insisted, but that is easier said than done. Anna knows that if

Philippe gets any whiff of what she's about, then he'll break her neck, or maybe not make it so quick. Does she really dare to do this? She feels a kick within her stomach. Yes, it seems she must. For her child, if not for herself, and also for her father. She continues to stir, then removes the saucepan from the fire, and begins to slice a loaf of bread.

Before Anna leaves the kitchen with the tray of food, Benedetta holds her gaze and she feels her maid is giving strength for what she knows she has to do. She reminds herself: an eye for an eye, a hand for a hand.

Nevertheless, by the time she enters the room where they eat, Anna's hands are trembling so severely that she has to put the tray down fast on the table before he notices. The liquid jumps lightly in the bowl and Philippe lifts his eyes from his book to give her an icy glare. He does not question what he is given, though. He continues reading the book, then picks up a piece of bread.

Anna stands in the doorway, hands folded, and watches as he dips his bread into the broth and eats. She feels that she cannot breathe, her chest is so tight, and her heart thumps loud in her ears. Philippe makes no comment, however. No compliment, certainly, but no criticism either. He behaves as if she is not there at all. As though, like the poison she has slipped into his food, she is as clear as glass.

Hours pass. Anna waits. She prays, though quite what she is praying for she is not sure. Not for forgiveness, not yet, for though she has sinned, she also wants the poison to work. Or does she? Can she really desire something so terrible? *You shall not murder; and whoever murders will be liable to judgment.* As the hours go by and nothing happens she feels a mixture of fear and relief. Perhaps the woman has indeed sold her a lie. Or perhaps God has intervened. By the time they go to bed, Anna has concluded that nothing is going to happen.

However, in the middle of the night, Philippe begins to thrash in the bed beside her. His throat, he says, is burning. She must get water for him and fast. Anna's heart begins to race. She hurries to the kitchen. She brings him water and he drinks, grumbles, returns to sleep. She, however, lies rigid beside him, watching the night lighten into dawn.

In the morning, Philippe seems better. He takes his coffee and pastry without complaining (or at least no more than is usual) and tells her he is spending the day in his studio. Anna watches him carefully but can see no sign of sickness. Was the pain in his throat nothing to do with her? Perhaps. She is not sure she believes it. This poison is like a snake.

Sure enough, in the middle of the day while she and Benedetta are sorting the washing, the door slams open. Philippe has returned, eyes strangely bright, saying he has a fever. He blames Anna, just as he blames her in everything: for not having kept the shutters closed against the sickness, for not ensuring that his constitution remained firm. 'You are a useless wife, just as you're a useless woman. For godssakes get me some water, for I have a terrible thirst again.'

She regards him. His pudgy face is flushed and clammy.

'Well?' he demands. 'Get on with it!'

'You must go to bed,' she tells him calmly. 'I will bring you water and broth.' And so she will, the special water, mixed into his soup. His insults make her stronger. Now that she's begun on this course, she will complete it. She doesn't deserve his hatred or his slander, any of it. In the kitchen, as she opens the little glass vial again and holds it to the light, she thinks of how she used to think that she must be at fault, that there must be a reason why he hated her. She knows now that there is no reason, or at least no reason that is anything to do with her.

He is a man drowning in his own bitterness, and that is how he will die.

She heats the soup upon the stove. She adds a few precious drops.

20

A water to make your face beautiful:
Pulverised silver litharge, two soldi's worth, very strong white vinegar, milk, orange juice, oil of tartar. Put the silver litharge in a carafe with the vinegar and boil until reduced by two thirds and keep. Add milk, orange juice and oil of tartar. Mix all together.

Girolama

A loud, pounding noise. Someone is hammering on Girolama's front door. It ceases for a few moments and starts up again, more urgent. Girolama, who's been distilling a face water with Cecca, meets the older woman's eye. This doesn't bode well, not at this hour of day, for the Ave Maria has only just sounded. 'Look through the aperture, Cecca. See who it is. If we need to, we can leave by the other exit.'

Cecca hurries as fast as her aged knees can manage to the hallway and peers through the small glass window that lets them check the identity of visitors. 'It's Maria,' she says, turning back to Girolama.

'Well then, for goodness' sakes let her in!' Girolama's sharpness comes from fear. Maria is not a woman prone to panic. It's why, of all Girolama's circle, Maria is the one she values the most. They met many years before when Girolama heard her speaking Sicilian and knew her at once to be from Palermo:

another woman who'd fled the poverty of the south. She was tough as elder bark then. She is even tougher now.

A moment later Maria stands before them, leaning on her stick, wheezing, one eye brown, one eye white: capable of seeing everything. Vanna is a healer, but she, among other things, is a seer.

'Maria, what is it? Come in.' Girolama takes her age-speckled hand as Cecca closes the door behind them.

'It's Vanna,' Maria breathes. 'She's been locked up in the Tor di Nona.'

The breath stops in her throat. 'By who? For what?'

'I don't know yet,' Maria whispers. 'But, Girolama, I fear we're undone.'

Girolama feels a sinking sensation, but she stops it in her breast. Despair will get her nowhere. She has always known that this day might come: that one of her ring would be caught. That doesn't mean it's all over, not by any means. Indeed, it cannot be over, for she owes it to Giulia, to Tofania, to the many women with no way out, to ensure the line continues. She has already made her plans. 'We mustn't be afraid, Maria. We must stand together. We must trust in Vanna.' For though the woman looks like a gust of wind would blow her down, Vanna has weathered many storms. 'We've known her for many years, you and I, and she has always been loyal, hasn't she?'

'To you, yes.' Maria turns away.

'Maria,' Girolama says, more firmly. 'We don't know why they've arrested her. Even if it's for what we fear, there's no reason to believe she'll buckle.' At least not for some time. There are methods for extracting information from prisoners, methods on which she doesn't wish to dwell. 'Who told you of this?'

'One of her neighbours. She said another woman saw Vanna

arriving at the Tor di Nona last night with two men dressed in black.'

'But the Tower is closed.' Girolama is speaking mainly to herself.

'Then they have opened it up again,' Maria says.

A wash of cold terror sluices through Girolama. You don't reopen a jail for one arrest. But she won't allow her thoughts to run ahead. 'On whose orders was she arrested?'

'I don't know, but we'll deal with them, whoever they are,' Maria says quietly.

'Yes, *mia amica*, we will.' She turns to Cecca. 'We must take good food to Vanna today, and blankets. We must comfort her in every way we can.'

'Yes, *padrona*,' Cecca says. 'I'll start cooking at once.'

'Very well,' Girolama says. They'll keep her body as strong as they can, and remind her to whom she owes fidelity. As for her spirit and her mind, Girolama will have to go to work with her own methods. 'Maria, you must hurry to La Sorda and Graziosa. Get them to help you with informing all of the others.' As well as her key circle, Girolama has a network of lesser sellers, selling her wares throughout Rome and its out-skirts. Many of these women don't even know her name. She is simply La Strolaga or La Profetessa, a shadowy and dangerous figure. She has kept it so, maintaining her distance, across the Tiber, screened by others. Meanwhile the man who bought the main ingredient grows cold in his grave. Laura, though. She may be a problem. 'Let me deal with Lauraccia. She'll require special treatment.' She would warn her that if the woman gave up her name, then Girolama would make sure she suffered.

'What do I tell our women?' Maria asks.

'Tell them they're not to flee Rome. That will help no one. Nor are they to panic or squawk their concerns to anyone else. This may have nothing to do with our business. If it has, we can manage it, and we will.' She considers. 'Assure them that we'll protect them as best we can. It's what we've always done. If we hold the line it will be difficult for any man to break it.' Though she doesn't yet know what kind of men they are dealing with. She will make it her business to find out, and to hide anything that might help them. 'And you must remind the women, Maria, that it is us who have protected them all these years, who have provided them with a living. Those who know my name will not utter it, nor give any clue as to my whereabouts. If they do, they'll come to regret it.' They know what powers she has.

Maria no longer pants with exertion, and her wrinkled face is still. 'I'll tell them.'

'Good. Take a few moments here to gather yourself. Sit here. Cecca will get you some spiced wine.'

She shakes her head. 'I should go at once to Graziosa. She's faster on her feet than I and can spread the word to the others.'

'You're a good woman, Maria. Thank you for coming to me.'

They embrace for a moment and Girolama feels the woman's thin, sinewy body, smells her earthy scent. How long have they known one another? Fifteen years? More? Together they have developed an empire. But will it now hold?

21

Stefano

Stefano was not prepared for the Tor di Nona, though he's heard of it spoken often enough: it was here that Benvenuto Cellini was held as well as Giordano Bruno, the friar and philosopher who was burnt alive on a pyre at the Campo de' Fiori. Before it was a prison, the Tor – a square-fronted, forbidding building – was a fortification, where hundreds of people perished. Have their screams been swallowed into the walls? Stefano's old nurse used to tell him that bricks and timber soaked up terrible events, stored what they had witnessed, and released them as ghostly echoes. Is that why the Tower seems so repellent? The whole place gives off a distinct reek of dereliction and menace. The rooms, most of which have been closed off for months, some for years, are cold and damp. One cell is entirely flooded, and there the rats have bred. He and Marcello can hear them scurrying and squeaking, the only other inhabitants (aside from a morose guard) of this dark and decaying place. He will have to talk to Baranzone about making the cells more habitable, or at least less deathly.

They need to secure some kind of heating. The only room with a fire is the room in which he and Marcello now sit, a stark square chamber with a shallow balcony overlooking the grey waters of the Tiber. Next to them is a smaller room with a heavy rope dangling from a pulley.

Stefano hears the drag of footsteps on stone: the guard finally bringing Vanna up from Le Segrete – 'the secret places' – the solitary confinement cells. The woman looks considerably worse than when she was arrested, her face bone-white, her faded hair unbrushed, and her clothing marked with dirt. He feels a splinter of unease at this, but then he does not want her to be comfortable. He wants for her to talk. They have searched her house, and the things they found there have disturbed him: a box full of teeth and a small wooden horse, its hindquarters bound together with string.

The notary, a pale, scrawny young man called Lodovico whom Baranzone has appointed, opens the large, leather-bound book of evidence in which he is to record everything that takes place in this room. In a toneless voice, he begins to speak (in Latin as custom requires) to record the woman's name, the time, the date. He does not set out the purpose of the interrogation, as it is a requirement of Roman law that the prisoner should not be told of the charges against them. Stefano directs the woman to sit in the chair opposite his table. There are others who would leave their subjects to stand for long questioning, but he is not that sort of man. He wants, though, for Vanna to believe that, if needs be, he will resort to other means of extracting the truth. That is why he has left open the door to the adjoining room, so that she might see the shackles and whip that hang on the wall, rusting. He does not believe he will ever resort to such things (he has rarely used a whip on a horse, never mind a woman), but she need not know his thoughts.

Once she has sworn on the Holy Scriptures, Stefano says:

'Vanna de Grandis, do you have anything to say about why you have been arrested?'

'It's not for me to say why you've chosen to bring me here,' she says, and though her tone is neutral enough, Stefano feels it as an accusation. She is saying, 'I am a poor old woman and you've locked me in a rotting cell.' But he is not going to be tricked by this woman, no matter how weak she may appear. He knows that the Holy Office of the Inquisition imprisoned her not long ago on suspicion of occult practices, specifically magical healing and selling love philtres. Both are considered by the Papal court to be forms of sorcery, though much lower on the scale of criminality than poisoning.

'Vanna, I heard you in plain terms agree to sell poison to another woman.'

'No, Signore.' She shakes her head. 'You did not hear that. I did not agree to sell her poison.'

And Vanna is right that she did not explicitly say it was poison. Her wording was careful. 'What then, is this powerful liquid of which you spoke? This Aqua?'

'It's a face water, Signore, that can remove stains and scars from the skin.'

'Ah.' He pauses. 'In that case, why would you sell it to a woman who told you she wished to rid herself of a man who was causing her woe?'

'That's not what I was selling it to her for.'

Stefano gives a tight smile. After many years of being treated by his elder brothers like the village imbecile, he does not like being taken for a fool. 'Vanna, you seem to forget that I was in that very room and heard all that was said. I do not believe what you now tell me. I warn you to speak the truth.'

The woman doesn't respond, doesn't flinch. It's possible she understands that, unless they have a full confession, or two eyewitnesses, it's unlikely they can secure a conviction. Such is the Roman criminal law. Who, though, would have explained it to her?

Marcello speaks now: 'What is in this 'face water' that you sell, Signora? What do you say it contains?'

'It is a distillation of fennel, betony, endive, roses, and white wine mixed with argento vivo.'

Stefano glances at Marcello who says, 'Yes, that might whiten flesh soon. It would not, however, kill. Not unless drunk in large quantities.'

'I didn't say that it would, Signore,' the woman says.

'Where is this recipe? In a book?'

'It is in my head, Signore.'

How convenient. 'But you wrote your name in the registration book here, Vanna. You can read and write.'

'A little, Signore. I had some education.'

'Your surname: De Grandis. It is a noble surname, is it not?'

'Yes, Signore. It is my maiden name, but I have fallen upon harder times. My first husband died, and, after I raised my daughter alone, she too passed. I married again, more recently, but he too succumbed, and his children, all dead from the plague.'

It is a grim story, but common enough. 'How have you subsisted since then?'

'Through taking in washing, mainly, removing stains, and in selling face waters and lotions. Sometimes I've been reduced to begging.'

Stefano scrutinises her: her pale eyes and faded hair. She certainly has the look of a woman who's lived a hard life, drained by sickness and grief. Her apartment, though, which he visited last night, is not as mean a place as that of the dyer's widow, Teresa. Vanna has another set of black clothing, and another pair of shoes, in a city where shoes are a luxury. By the bed, he found a tortoiseshell brush and a small mirror. Such things are not common among the poor. Then there are the powders they found in her pockets and the strange items they found in her old walnut chest: a little box filled with teeth, a jar of dried toads. Marcello thought these might be ingredients for love philtres, though Stefano struggles to see how they'd inspire devotion. She must have yet other things stored elsewhere, for the keys they found when they arrested her did not fit the chest, nor anything else in the room.

'You are some way from penury now though, aren't you, Vanna? It is a decent enough apartment that you own and the dress you wear now, though worn, is of good wool, I think.' Grubby now, of course, and far from fine, but not patched or ragged as is the clothing of many of those he sees in the streets.

'I do not complain, Signore.'

'I don't say that you do. I fear, however, that you lie.' He pauses. 'You do not make your money simply from taking in laundry and selling face waters.'

'Yes, Signore, I do.' The woman will not meet his gaze.

'And you use toads, do you, in your laundry, Vanna? Is that why you had a jar of them in your rooms?'

'The toads, Signore, are for toothache.'

'I see. You must suffer considerably to warrant that many toads.'

A silence.

'What about the box of teeth? How do you explain those?'

She has prepared an answer for this: 'They were my children's. I kept them as they lost them over the years. There's no crime in that.'

'No, Vanna, but perjuring yourself is a crime, and you speak on the Holy Bible.' When she doesn't reply, he says, 'I understand that you own a vineyard outside Porta Portese. You bought that with the proceeds of your laundry work, did you?'

'That property, I was given by a friend.'

'That is some friend.'

'Yes, Signore. But it is now laden with debts. I make no money from it. I am a poor widow. I make money in whatever way I can.'

'Then I can see that making a little money from selling poisons would be useful to you.'

'No, Signore. That is not what I do. As I say, it is face water for bleaching stains from the skin.' Vanna speaks as someone reciting lines. She has been told exactly what to say.

'But I have been to your dwellings, Vanna. You have no proper kitchen, no equipment. Where do you make these face waters?'

'I keep my things at a friend's house.'

'Who is this friend? Where does she live?'

The woman bites at her lip.

'Vanna, if you cannot tell us who this person is then we will have to assume you are lying. We will have to move on to other means.' Stefano does not intend to use such means, but she cannot know that.

She looks at him through narrowed grey eyes. 'I would not wish my friend to come to any trouble. She's an old woman. She's only been looking after some things for me.'

'What is her name? What is her address?'

No answer.

'Vanna, you know there are methods we can use to extract this information from you.'

The woman seems to shrink into herself. She glances at the next room, at the whip and the rope and pulley and Stefano feels a twinge of shame, but this is the job he has been employed to do. This is the inquisitor's role. 'What is her name?' he says loudly.

Still nothing.

'She has a workshop, this woman?'

'No, but she has a fire.'

Stefano meets Marcello's eye. He thinks of their discussions, of how this poison must be clever; carefully prepared by someone who has been trained. 'Vanna, I think you obtain what it is you sell from someone else.'

'No.' Her eyes dart to the side.

'Do you think this person will protect you, Vanna? Because they won't. They will leave you here.'

A silence, which he feels to be full of malice.

'Well?'

'As I said, Signore, I make the face water myself from a recipe I learnt some years ago.'

Outside, the light is fading. He will not, he thinks, get anything from this woman today, at least not without force, but he has begun the process of instilling fear. That is part of his job. 'Well, Vanna, I have little time for riddles, nor for travelling in circles. I have my investigation to continue. It will be interesting to hear what the other witnesses say of you.'

She darts a look at him. Yes, that's got through to her. Clearly there are indeed others who may speak.

'*Guardia!*' he calls. 'You may take her away.'

The sole guard that they've been allotted moves forward. He is a large, ageless, hairless man with a face like a lump of clay.

'But Signore,' the woman says as the guard reaches her, 'it is cold in the cells. It is very damp. I am an old woman.'

All this is true, but it is important, Stefano thinks, not to show her words affect him. 'Then, Donna Vanna, you would do well to hurry up and tell me the truth, or your stay will be much longer. Think on that this evening.'

Once the guard has taken Vanna away, he turns to Marcello. 'Will she succumb to illness down there?' he asks quietly.

'Quite possibly,' Marcello says, 'though I'll do what I can do improve the conditions. This prison is a breeding ground for disease. It's part of the reason they shut it down. We must speak to Baranzone. It's not in his interests to have the prisoner die before she's coughed up the truth, though I fear the place is a death trap regardless.'

Stefano considers. 'It's what we have to do, though, isn't it? For if she has no fear, then she will stick to her story, which has clearly been carefully prepared. We must find this friend that she refuses to name – the one who has her things. There must be neighbours with whom we can speak. First, though, I must speak with Baranzone and update him on our progress.'

He glances at Lodovico, who is still scribbling in the book of evidence, his long white fingers clasped around the quill. Stefano suspects the notary has also been tasked with updating the Governor. He must be careful what he says.

Stefano decides he will risk going straight to the Palazzo Nardini without arranging a meeting. He has important information to impart to Baranzone. Before Vanna's arrest, he informed him of the possibility of poison and received the reaction he anticipated: excited talk of how *veneficia* is the same as *maleficia*, not poison so much as bewitchment, the work not just of chymicals, but demons. Stefano is remembering all this as he rides his horse through a high archway into a vast, arcaded courtyard. There he is greeted by a servant in livery who directs him through another archway and to a stall where he may feed and tether Damigella. Stefano is then led to an anteroom while his arrival is announced.

The palazzo is as rich and imposing as its owner: Turkish carpets, vases from the Orient, a row of swords, classical cornices and statues. Pomades of burning herbs lend the air a strong, slightly nauseating smell. Baranzone descends a wide stairway to meet him. He is dressed in a dark green brocade jacket, reminding Stefano of one of Vanna's bottled toads.

'Ah, Stefano!' His manner is far friendlier than during their meeting in the stables. He could be a different man entirely.

'Forgive the imposition, Monsignore, but I thought you would wish to be updated.'

'Of course, of course. Come up to my study.'

He leads Stefano up the staircase and past numerous devotional paintings to a large room with velvet curtains and floor-to-ceiling windows, a walnut writing desk and several calfskin chairs. A huge fire burns in the hearth.

'Tell me. What news? You made the arrest last night, I hear.'

'Yes, all went according to plan. I questioned the woman this morning, though at the moment she refuses to accept that she was selling poison, nor tell us from where she obtained it. I will interrogate her more harshly in due course.'

'Good, good. That is the way. Let her sweat for a few hours and then go back in stronger. Who is she acquiring the poison from, then, do you think? Some apothecary, some necromancer? Well, we will find the whoreson.'

The comment helps the theory crystallise in Stefano's mind. 'In fact,' he says tentatively, 'I wonder if it is not a man who provides her with the poison, but a woman.'

'A woman poison-maker?'

'Yes, perhaps.' This Vanna appears to feel a great loyalty to whomever she is protecting. And if they are disguising the poison as a face water, is it not more likely to be a woman than a man who's concocting it? He remembers his own mother creating simple beautification liquids: egg yolks and vinegar. There are also the whispers of La Strologa or La Profetessa: the woman who cavorts with the devil. 'It isn't so uncommon for women to have some training as apothecaries, or perhaps she's learnt her skills in some other way.'

'Lord have mercy, is this really what we're dealing with? A

female conspiracy to poison men?' Baranzone is staring at him, his pupils very large.

'I could be wrong,' Stefano says quickly, alarmed by the Governor's response, but it is too late. Baranzone is up and pacing the room.

'This is something dark, Stefano. Something deeply dark. A lower class woman assuming the knowledge of learned men in order to poison them silently.'

'As I said, it is merely a theory—'

'It is a theory that holds, Stefano. Poison: it has always been a woman's instrument. Think of the notorious Locusta who assisted Agrippina. Think of Elisabetta Gonzaga of Urbino, Isabella d'Aragona of Naples, Ippolita Sforza of Calabria, Caterina Sforza of Forli! Caterina de' Medici and her cabinet of poisons!'

'Yes, Monsignore, but, as I say, we don't yet know in this case whose hand is at work.'

Baranzone is not listening. He is now plunging the poker into the fire, releasing an angry shower of sparks. 'We should feel no surprise that it is a woman at the black heart of this thing. It is well known that women are more predisposed to doing the devil's deeds than men. That was the conclusion of the *Malleus Malificarum* and it's been confirmed again and again in the witch trials.'

'Most of those women were not convicted, though, were they?' Stefano says, unsurely.

'In Rome, no, because our inquisitors and judges were too lax. Because they believed the lies they were told. Elsewhere, however, in Germania in particular, many were brought to justice for their evil-doing and poisoning was one of the evils they perpetrated: poisoned apples, poisoned cakes. Ointments rubbed on skin that sent the subject insane. We have seen all this before. I don't know why it didn't occur to me sooner.'

Stefano feels a pinprick of unease at the Governor's excitement. 'Well, my investigation will uncover the truth of it.'

'It must, Stefano. It must. You cannot let up. You cannot let these women's feminine wiles dissuade you from doing what is required.'

'Of course.' Men were forever talking of feminine wiles. Stefano would hardly describe his own sisters as wily and they are the only women he really knows.

Baranzone points the poker at him as though it were a sword. 'I tell you, Stefano, they can be like vipers, these women. You are a young man, you don't know, but believe nothing they say unless they say it under torture.'

Stefano swallows. 'If that is what is necessary,' he says quietly, but he will try to accomplish confessions without such things. He is not a brute.

'Assuming that you are right,' Baranzone says, 'and this Vanna woman is being supplied with poison by another woman, then how many other women are also receiving and selling on her wares? How many others are drinking it? How many men have succumbed to their evil?'

'We will find out.' This, it seems to Stefano, is a good moment to ask for the resources he needs. 'I will work as quickly as I can, Governor, but I will need more men. More men in the prison, possibly more men to help with the arrests.'

'Yes, yes.' Baranzone is stroking his chin, thinking.

'And we will need to improve the conditions of the cells.'

'What?'

'They are exceedingly damp. In some places, flooded.'

The Governor gives a gesture of confusion. 'We are not operating a hostelry, Stefano.'

'No, indeed, but we need the witnesses and suspects to survive long enough to confess and implicate others, Governor. If it is indeed women who are involved, then they are of a weaker constitution. There needs at least to be some heating. It is winter.'

'Very well. Make basic arrangements and we will meet the cost. But no communication between them. I will not have the opening up of the cells. Nor will I have them housed in the Largo, where they may speak together. We know how it is when women talk.'

Do they? Stefano finds he is beginning to feel sorry for Baranzone's wife. 'Yes, Governor.' Whatever it took to get the funds and manpower he needed.

'I need you to keep me regularly updated. Any key development, I want to know of it.'

'Of course.'

Baranzone looks at Stefano. 'By God, Stefano, if you're right about this, then it may be the vilest conspiracy to have penetrated Rome for many years. They have used the evil of the plague to cloak their even deeper evil.'

'Quite possibly, yes.' For how many would question another dead body amidst the many piled up in pits?

'You must make this Vanna woman talk. We must see the shape of this thing.'

Stefano begins to fear that it will have no clear shape, but be a thing that reaches all places. He says: 'My lord, I will.'

★

Vanna's neighbours have proved talkative. In response to the *sbirri* officer's questions, they spoke of a tiny, red-haired friend whose house Vanna often visits. Stefano and Marcello are now on their way to Santa Maria ai Monti to try to find this friend, one Graziosa Farina. The area is a labyrinth of narrow, tortuous alleyways, almost all of them unpaved, many strung with greying laundry. They pass hens and geese pecking at heaps of

134

rubbish and reach a small square where street sellers stir huge cauldrons of pasta and dish out fried fish to waiting labourers. By talking to one of these sweaty-faced food sellers, Marcello ascertains that Graziosa lives in an apartment close by.

The building, when they find it, is piss-stinking and gloomy. This is surely not the place for an apothecary. Indeed, when Stefano knocks on the door and the woman answers, he understands that this is not their poison seller, nor their devil's workshop. The woman, Graziosa, is older than Vanna, and even smaller, with badly dyed red hair, a washed-out black dress and a mouth without a single tooth. She says nothing and makes little attempt to stop them, only stands with her back against the wall so that Stefano and Marcello may enter. It is a dim and spartan chamber no bigger than the dyer's widow's, the only furniture a walnut kneeler, a narrow bed, and a large, battered chest.

'We've come for Vanna's possessions. She left them with you, didn't she?'

The woman stares at him, rubbing her gums together, but does not answer.

'Where are they?' Stefano says, more loudly. 'Where are her things?'

Still nothing. Have they frightened her into dumbness? Or is this woman lacking her wits?

Frustrated, Stefano pulls open the chest, seeing only old spoons and plates, a worn pair of shoes, containers of flour and other foodstuffs, a doll made of sacking. Then he spies, at the very bottom, a wooden box. He feels a thrill of excitement. 'That must be it.'

'You have the keys?' Marcello asks, following his gaze.

'I do.' Stefano lifts out the box and draws from his cloak the tiny keys that they had found on Vanna when she was arrested. It takes him several attempts, but at last the lid opens.

'Well, well,' Marcello says.

The box is full of square glass bottles. Some have a picture of a man on one side. In a compartment, Stefano finds several pawn tickets, in another a pair of black silk slippers. There are also some bottles of dried substances, which Marcello sniffs. 'This one is rosemary. This nutmeg.' He sniffs a third and wrinkles his nose. 'Some kind of animal droppings, I think. These won't poison anyone, but they might well be sold as love philtres, to bind one person to another. As I said, that might well also explain the teeth we found in Vanna's rooms, and the unfortunate toads.'

The only other item in the box is a small black book, much worn. Written on its well-thumbed pages are numbers and dates: '10th September: 5. 2nd October: 3.'

'What does this mean, do you think?' Stefano asks Marcello as he flicks through it. There is no writing, save on the last page, where he can make out a sentence, which he reads aloud: 'Maria owes 5 *scudi*.'

'Show me,' Marcello says, putting his hand out for the book.

'Graziosa, who is Maria?' Stefano asks, standing up from the box, searching for the red-haired woman. 'Graziosa!' he shouts, but the only answer is the sound of hurried footsteps on the stairs.

'The devil take her!' Marcello shouts, and runs after Graziosa.

Stefano pockets the book and two of the bottles and follows through the doorway. He catches up with Marcello just outside the building.

'She could have gone anywhere.' Marcello gestures at the different alleyways.

'Not fast, though. Not at her age.'

'That way!' shouts a small boy. 'If you're looking for the red-haired hag.'

They take the passage at which he points and race as quickly

136

as they can over the heaps of dung and rubbish, and old chairs left out to moulder. A man yells abuse at them as they upend a cart, a group of children begin to chase after them. A cat leaps from a wall and shoots before Stefano's legs, a woman shrieks a curse. Stefano's lungs begin to scream out against the exertion, but he cannot let her get away. Round another wall and past an old woman milking a goat, then down a back street and sudden quiet: the backs of houses, the smell of garlic, the sound of a girl singing. When they emerge onto a piazza, they are once again surrounded by people, children playing *calcio*, women washing clothing at a fountain, but of Graziosa there is no sign.

Stefano has to stop, bend over, rest his hands on his knees. He feels darkness cloud his vision.

'This is futile,' he hears Marcello say. 'She could be any-where.'

Stefano waits for the breath to return to his lungs before he stands upright. He cannot believe he's been outwitted by a woman he thought a witless crone.

Slowly, they return to Graziosa's apartment. The door is still hanging open, but the box inside is gone.

Well, Stefano has found his wily women. Perhaps the Governor was right on that score. His task is now to hunt them all down before they can flee from Rome. 'We will need more men,' he tells Marcello. 'We must arrest any suspects before they can leave the city.'

As they leave the wretched building, he can hear a child's laughter.

22

Anna

Anna opens the wooden shutters to a dawn that spreads like a golden gauze drawn across the sky. It is the third day since she began the poisoning. Philippe has grown far worse during the night. Anna has been up, mopping his brow, feeding him sips of water, clenching her teeth every time Philippe shouts at her to tell her she's done something wrong. But his continuing vileness towards her is helpful. Had the sickness made him simpering and sweet, then she might have struggled to do what she had to do. As it is, the drops come thicker and faster, for she can't bear to nurse him for much longer, this man who murdered her father and who, if she lets him live, will kill her and her child too. Laura advised her to take things slowly, but Anna finds that, now that she has set upon the course, she wants it over as soon as possible.

'A doctor,' he coughs. 'Get me a doctor. A French physician. This sickness, whatever it is, is killing me.'

For the amount I paid, I should hope so, Anna thinks. 'I will go this morning, but, oh, we will struggle to pay, won't we? You told me you had spent it all.'

Philippe emits a growl. His breath is putrid, as though something inside him has already begun to rot. 'I'll pay. Just do as I tell you, and fast. You should have got someone for me last night. Go to Docteur Durand in the Strada Paolina.'

Anna leaves the bedroom, relieved to escape the sticky sickbed air, and gathers her cape and hat. Benedetta follows her to the door. Women may not walk alone in Rome, even on errands of mercy.

Once they are outside, Benedetta says: 'Must we do as he asks?'

'I cannot see that we have any choice. If we refuse to fetch a doctor, he will suspect what we are about, and then Lord knows what he'll do.' Anna takes her maid's arm. In truth, she is relieved to be able to leave the confines of the house. 'But please God this doctor will not see the true cause of his illness.'

They walk to the Piazza di Spagna where the foreign artists congregate and where a shepherd is driving a herd of sheep past the Fontana della Barcaccia. A shoemaker is beating out strips of leather against the edge. Anna stops to look at the fountain – a half-sunken boat — and the jets of water that flow from it. She is in no hurry to find a doctor who may reverse all her good work, or deduce what she is about.

When they return some time later with the physician, Philippe is practically spitting with anger. 'What in God's name took you so long? Get me something to drink!' His face has taken on a bloated aspect and red blotches mottle his skin.

Benedetta fetches water while the doctor, an aged man with rheumy eyes, takes Philippe's pulse and feels his brow. Anna's chest constricts as she watches the man frown and prod at Philippe's stomach, noting his discomfort. Might this doctor, decrepit as he seems, detect the truth of the matter?

'What's wrong with me, doctor?' Philippe growls at him.

'Can you cure it? By the blood of Christ, hurry up! My innards are agony, I tell you. It is like rats gnawing at my entrails.' Philippe writhes upon the bed and Anna's mind returns briefly to her father's sickbed scene, to his strangled cries in the darkness that pulled at her own insides.

The doctor looks at Anna and for a moment she fears he has read her thoughts. To Philippe, he says: 'You've had problems with your liver before, I recall.'

'Yes, but nothing like this, man.'

'Perhaps not, but I think this is some more severe inflammation of the liver. I will give you a purgative and some poppy and mandragora to numb the pain.'

Once they are further away from the bed, the doctor says to Anna: 'Signora, I fear that your husband is in an advanced state of disease. He drinks?'

'Heavily.'

'Yes, I thought so from the yellowish colour of his skin. I fear the liver is near destroyed. Perhaps if I had been called sooner I might have been able to do something, but I think that his organs are much corrupted. That is the cause of all this bile.'

Anna stares at the doctor's grey-tinged face, which does not seem to her to be unkind. She would like to tell him that she's been the victim of her husband's bitter bile for many months. She knows it is expected of her to put on a show of distress but she finds that she cannot. She is too tired. 'How long?' is all she says.

'I would guess only a few weeks, maybe even days,' the doctor replies, 'but I will do what I can to ease your husband's suffering.'

She nods. 'Thank you, doctor. I will pray for my husband. That his suffering will soon end.'

He looks at her distended stomach. 'Eight months? More?'

'I am near the time, I think.'

'Then I am sorry.'

'No, Dottore. Do not be sorry. I'm lucky to have carried the child this far.'

His gaze moves to her face.

For a long moment there is silence and Anna feels her heart pulsing in her chest like a moth trying to escape. Has she said too much?

But no, he reaches out to touch her hand. 'Signora, you are very brave.'

23

To make Rosolio:
Collect roses when they are still not full open and pluck the petals.
Take the white of the petals and mix them with sugar. Put the rose
sugar in a jar together with zest of lemon and spirit and leave for ten
days. Add water and more sugar. Leave for a further seven days,
shaking it now and again. After a week, filter through muslin and
bottle.

Girolama

What a group they make, Girolama thinks, as she watches her women around the fire. If the Holy Inquisition were to come upon them now, they would take them for a coven of witches, with their black widow's weeds and wrinkled faces, wreathed in the smoke from Maria's pipe and from the fire in the hearth. There is a line between a poisoner and a witch, but, in the eyes of the public and the Papacy, it is a fine one. People believe that to create poison you must call upon the devil, and though Girolama gets little practical help from him in her potion-making, she knows there are many who'd consider her a witch. *Magia* is often elided into *stregeria*: witchcraft. She, however, prefers to think of herself as a physician who sees to the ills that normal doctors ignore. A pill to get rid of your monthly pains, a poison to get rid of your husband.

Girolama has gathered together her key women: Maria,

Graziosa, Laura, and La Sorda, so named because she's almost deaf. All her circle are there save for Vanna, who remains under lock and key.

'The men knew only that I was keeping some of her possessions,' Graziosa tells them. 'Lord knows why she'd felt it necessary to name me, though. Couldn't she have led them some merry dance?'

Girolama pours out little glasses of rose liquor that she herself makes. 'We don't know for sure that it was her who gave them your name, and we don't know what methods they're using. We don't know what they've threatened her with, nor what state she's in.' Vanna was already in middling health before they threw her into a cell.

'They didn't seem the torturing types,' Graziosa says, adjusting her false teeth. 'The judge couldn't have been more than thirty, and he's small with it. His face is pretty and fine-boned like a girl's. The other man was some young doctor. They spoke like gentlemen, or at least they did till I gave them the slip.' Graziosa smiles, the purloined teeth now like a straight line of pearls.

'The fact a man speaks like a gentleman is no indicator as to what lies within,' Girolama says, and she's seen enough supposed gentlemen to know. 'I've heard this Stefano Bracchi is an ambitious man: a merchant's son who's worked his way up the ranks and who's no doubt keen to make his name.' She hasn't been idle. She's been gathering information wherever she can. Only some of it will she pass on.

'He knows my name now too,' Maria says, downing her cup of liquor (the woman can drink the stuff as if it's water). 'Foolish Vanna. Why didn't she hide the book better, or write what she needed in code? I've had to leave my apartment and beg a place at l'Ospedale.'

La Sorda laughs: a laugh as large and generous as she is. 'He only knows that there's a Maria. A Maria! In Rome! That's as good as a needle in a stack of hay!' Again she laughs her raucous laugh and the other women begin to chuckle. For yes, this is the city of the Madonna, where Marias cover church walls and teem through markets. One wouldn't wish to be sorting through Marias.

'Still, we can't afford to be complacent,' Girolama says. 'He's acted quickly and he has a whole tower to fill with prisoners if he chooses. We don't know what other information Vanna's given him, nor who else he might've spoken with. Maria, you're right to keep from your home. We should hide anything that might give us away, and we should all make ready to flee if the word comes.'

'Easy for you to say,' Laura complains. 'To where can I flee? And what with?'

'That's why I've brought you here, Laura,' Girolama says tartly. 'So that we might make a plan. In any event, Laura, you've enough saved up to buy a carriage, never mind hire a cart to take you from Rome.'

Laura begins to grumble but Girolama cuts her short: 'We're all of us at risk. You know what the punishment is for poisoning.' It is death. Her mind flies to her aunt Tofania, to the vile way she was killed. She will not tell them of that. 'Only if we stand together will we protect ourselves and the Aqua with us.'

This chastens the women. La Sorda crosses herself and Graziosa mutters. Maria pours herself another glass and tips it down her throat.

'Graziosa, tell me more of this Stefano Bracchi character,' Girolama says. 'He was well-spoken, but what else? What else did he and the doctor say? They took some of the glass bottles, did they?'

This was Tofania's trick: to put the Aqua in bottles marked

Manna of St Nicholas, an oil sold to pilgrims. No one would suspect that a poison was hidden in the bottle of a saint.

'They did, but the bottles were empty. They said that the herbs in the box wouldn't poison anyone, only be sold as love philtres, which is true enough. They disregarded me, as most men do. I'd guess they think they're looking for some learned apothecary or doctor, not a bunch of old women like us.'

'Most likely,' Girolama says. 'So much the better.' Nobles always assume that a clever poison can only be made by someone of their class, not an unlearned woman from the poverty of Palermo. It's how Giulia escaped evasion. It's how a potion formulated many years ago is still saving the lives of many women. That is now, however, at risk.

'As for what kind of man he is,' Graziosa says, 'I reckon he's clever enough, and determined, as you say, but beyond that I couldn't tell you.'

Maria taps the ash from her pipe onto the table. As she presses in a new pinch of tobacco, she says: 'We should find him, watch him. We can better plan in that way. Work out how to hurt him.'

Girolama nods. 'We can do better than just watch.' She'll collect his hair, his nail clippings, if she can. She'll use everything she can against this man, everything Giulia and Tofania and her Uncle Lorestino taught her. She can't let the Papacy destroy everything she's worked for, everything Giulia and Tofania built. 'We'll mislead him. Confuse him. Make him search for things that don't exist, and miss the things that do.'

'And you should show us your book of secrets,' Laura says, cloying sweet. 'Just in case, Heaven forfend, something terrible should happen to you. You wouldn't want the recipes to be lost.'

Maria laughs her hoarse laugh. 'A good attempt, Laura, but she'll be showing you precisely nothing.' Maria turns her gaze to Girolama. 'Laura's right, though, that you must make sure the secrets survive.'

Girolama scrapes at some hardened candle wax on the table. She doesn't like to be told what to do. 'I know that perfectly well.'

24

Stefano

In the interview room, Stefano sets down one of the glass
bottles on the table before Vanna. There is a long crack running along its side.

'We found several of these amongst your possessions, Vanna.
All empty.'

The woman blinks. Her eyes are red and crusted. In the few
days she has spent in this prison, she seems to have aged several
years. Stefano does not like this, but he also needs for her to stop
lying to him. He needs to stop the poisoning. 'Yes, Signore,'
she says. 'They are old bottles that I bought at market.'

A line, he thinks, written by someone else, that she has been
taught to recite. 'What does this mean? The man depicted on
the side?' He taps the bottle with his fingernail.

'That is Saint Nicholas, Signore. The bottles must've con-
tained the manna from his tomb.'

Stefano glances at Marcello who sits to his right. Their eyes
meet. Is Marcello remembering, as he is, what the family of
the dyer said?

'Donna Vanna, at the very least, these show you are guilty of fraud, of selling some substance which you pretend is from the bones of a saint. But, in fact, I think these bottles usually contain something far more dangerous than that.'

Vanna keeps her lips pressed together.

'I think this,' Stefano continues, 'because Teresa Verzellina treated her husband, the Dyer at the Elm, with the supposed oil of a saint, and the Dyer at the Elm is now dead.'

Vanna's mouth begins to work. He can see she is terrified, and so she should be.

'Did you hear me?' He raises his voice. 'An innocent man is dead! How many more are being poisoned this very day?'

'I didn't kill the dyer,' she blurts out.

So, she knew he was dead. Stefano lets the silence grow between them, then pushes the glass bottle further towards her. 'Vanna, I have you agreeing to sell a liquid to a woman that will get rid of her pimp. I have the bottles in which you keep the liquid. That alone may be enough for me to secure a conviction, but I'm giving you an opportunity to reduce the severity of your sentence. I am giving you a chance to save your life. You do not work in this enterprise alone.'

'Yes, I do. I do,' she mutters.

'You confess, then? You confess that you are a poisoner?'

Vanna gazes at him, shocked. She knows she's made a dreadful mistake. 'No! I've never poisoned anyone,' she says quickly, twisting her hands together. 'I have never done that.'

Stefano nods. He says, calmly, 'But you sell the poison to others.'

'No. I— No.'

'Does your daughter help you?'

'What? No! She isn't even in Rome.'

'No, she's in Ferrara, isn't she?' Stefano says, for he's done his research. 'But for all I know, she is selling your poisons there. I could have her arrested.' He does not like having to play this trick, but he needs for the woman to speak.

Vanna is trembling. She looks as though she might retch. 'No, you mustn't. You can't. Not my daughter.'

'Then you must tell me, Donna Vanna. You sell poison to others.'

Vanna clutches her head as though she might somehow contain the fog that whirls within it. 'Sometimes, yes, but only where their need is real. Only where they are suffering terribly. Where there is no other way out.'

There it is. He has her. 'Who provides you with this poison, the liquid that you put in the bottles?'

She stares at him. 'I make it myself.'

Stefano nods again. 'Ah. And what does it contain?'

Vanna swallows and it is so quiet that he can hear the saliva in her throat. 'It is ... it is quicksilver, just as I use to whiten the ladies' skin, with viper's venom mixed in.'

Stefano looks at Marcello, who gives a very slight shake of the head.

'What symptoms does it cause, Vanna? How does it affect the victim?'

This Vanna can answer and she jumps at it, as though the words will save her. 'I have never seen it work myself, but I've been told of how it acts: slowly and surely, first causing a dryness and hotness in the throat and stomach, then causing terrible pains and vomiting and soiling until they die with it.' She says again, 'But I have never killed anyone myself.'

'Who else sells the poison?'

'I ... it is only me.'

A lie. 'Odd, then, that your little friend Graziosa was so quick to run from us. Why flee if she had nothing to hide?'

The woman's face falls as she realises her accomplice has been identified. In a low voice she says: 'When you're of our status, Signore, you have reason to fear the law, even if you've done nothing wrong.'

Stefano allows a pause. 'What about Maria?'

'Who told you about Maria?' The words seem to shoot out of her mouth before she can stop them.

'Vanna, we have not been sitting twiddling our thumbs. We have been speaking to all sorts of people.'

'To Maria?' The name is full of bitterness in her mouth.

'Maria sells poison too, does she not? Does she make it too?'

Vanna stares at him, horrified.

He gives a half-smile. 'Vanna, the liquid you sell is a very clever poison that has been undetected for some time. It is not lead and venom.'

'Yes, yes, it is.'

Stefano looks again at Marcello. 'Dottore, would such a poison kill in the way that the men we know of have died?'

'No,' Marcello says softly. 'It would not.'

Stefano returns his gaze to Vanna. Now he speaks more quickly: 'You are not an apothecary. You are not a learned woman. You have no equipment or recipe books in your house, nor are there any in Graziosa's house. You do not make the poison. Is it Maria who makes it?'

'Maria is no cleverer or more educated than I am,' she spits, 'though she might think herself so.'

'Then she does not make it either, but sells it. Where does she live?'

Vanna swallows again, looks at the ground.

'Vanna,' Stefano says, 'if you do not tell me, then the responsibility will all lie with you, and it would be wrong, I think, if you were to take the blame for the work of a number of people.'

Her eyes remain on the floor. Stefano knows he will need more leverage to get the information. He doesn't much like the idea of causing distress to this old woman, but she is, he reminds himself, a poison seller. The poison she sells has killed and will kill yet more if he fails to track the poisoners down.

He stands. 'In that case, I have no choice but to send to Ferrara. If you will not talk, maybe your daughter will. Guard, take her away.'

'No!' Vanna is standing too, her legs trembling. 'Please! I will tell you.' Stefano watches her form the words several times before she can make herself speak. At last she says: 'Maria lives near Santa Maria ai Monti. By a butcher's shop. But she does not make the poison.'

'Then who does?'

Vanna shakes her head. 'I told you. I do.'

Marcello leans forward. 'Vanna, the truth will come out. This poison, it is killing. It is still killing. How do you know it will not be given to a child? How do you know it is only used for good?'

'No, no,' Vanna says quickly. 'Never on a child. Never.' She is shaking, her teeth rattling.

'Who is La Strolaga?' Stefano says. 'Is it she who makes the poison? Who is she?'

Vanna sinks back to her chair, clutching at her head. 'I don't know, I don't know. There is no such person. Please. Let me be.'

For a long moment there is silence, just the crackling of the fire, the distant buzz of the city. Stefano is convinced now that La Strolaga exists. In his mind, he begins to imagine her: tall, twisted, pale, poring over her book of poisons.

Stefano cannot face destroying this woman further today. He calls for the guard. He will have to let her deteriorate a little further in her cell before he tries again. As she leaves the room, he says: 'We will find her, Vanna, and the more that you tell us, the better it will be for you.'

Once their footsteps have died out, Stefano stands up. To Marcello he says: 'I must speak to the dyer's widow today, and I'll instruct Maffeo to find this Maria at once.'

Baranzone has allocated Stefano two officers to assist with further suspects, Maffeo and Bertuccio. They seem rough characters whom Stefano would not himself have chosen, one with a face ornamented by scars, the other with shoulders so muscular and malformed that Stefano suspects he has been a galley slave.

'I'll go with him,' Marcello says, standing also. 'I can't say I trust our new *sbirri* friends to conduct the arrests with discretion.'

'No, but we must work with what we have and they've arrived in good time, at least. We must move with all speed.'

Stopping only to take a drink of water, Stefano leaves the Tower for Teresa's house, taking with him the scar-faced Bertuccio. Despite the man's menacing appearance, Stefano finds he is entertaining company as they make their way across Rome, their cloaks held close about their necks to keep out the icy wind. He has a black sense of humour, this Bertuccio, forged perhaps from a need to find some levity in a job which gains him little love and takes him to the darkest pits of hell: squalid dwellings and stinking slums where danger and evil abound.

As they pass a boy sweeping refuse away from a shop door, Bertuccio says, 'I sometimes think that more respect is granted to poor bastards like him who sweep the shit from the streets than to the *sbirri* that sweep the criminals from their lairs.' He has, like some of the other police officers, adopted the offensive term 'sbirri' as his own. In his mouth it becomes something amusing – a comedy character in a play. But if this is a play, then it is a tragicomedy, for many of the tales Bertuccio tells

Stefano make his blood curdle: gangs of thieves circling like wolves, leaving their victims without property or pulse, a man crucified upside down in the manner of Saint Peter.

When Bertuccio realises that the woman they are to arrest is the wife of the Dyer at the Elm, he nods. 'I knew him well enough. Big fellow. Brought in a few times for fighting, for belting his wife, once for threatening to slash a woman's face with a knife.'

Stefano looks at him sharply. 'Which woman? His wife?' He is thinking of Teresa's beautiful face, imagining a blade slashing across it.

'Maybe, though it's usually whores whose faces they cut,' he says, his tone still conversational. 'Definitely knocked his wife about, though, and more than the usual. We wouldn't have got involved otherwise. Is this the street, then, Maestro?'

'Not this one, but I believe it's nearby,' Stefano answers. He is thinking of Teresa's claim that her husband was a good man. He is thinking too of the innkeeper's widow and the scar about her wrist. His stomach is tight with apprehension. He begins to fear he has made a mistake: he has been thinking that there was some criminal connection between the dead men, but now he thinks perhaps the link is nothing to do with the men. Perhaps it's about their wives.

The alleys are growing narrower and fouler. Small black pigs root in the refuse, along with two, near-naked boys. They cannot be more than seven years old and their eyes are dull in their bony faces. How does God allow such things, Stefano wonders. It is a vision of hell on earth. He quickens his pace, wanting to get to Teresa's house as soon as possible, wanting to calm the panic that worms through his gut.

When they arrive, they find that the windows are boarded shut. Stefano feels his stomach drop.

'This is definitely it?' Bertuccio asks.

Stefano looks about him, taking in the crooked buildings and flaking doors. He thinks of Teresa's porcelain skin, her apparently artless manner. 'Yes, this is the building, all right.'

Bertuccio glances at the doorway and then, without warning, throws his whole body at the door so that it buckles. Once inside, they see that the apartment is empty, not a stick of furniture remaining.

Stefano closes his eyes against the scene for a moment, then kicks the doorframe with all his might. *Stupido!* Isn't the role of the inquisitor to suspect all, no matter how genuine they might appear? He should have doubted these women from the first!

'Long gone, I reckon,' Bertuccio says, rubbing his hands against his arms. 'This place is cold as a tomb.'

Stefano breathes out and bends down to pick up a scrap of paper from the floor. It is a receipt from a pawn shop. 'Not so long gone. This is dated only from last week. With their resources, they can't have gone far. We will find them.' He twists his mouth into a smile. 'I suppose I should thank them for teaching me a lesson.'

He cannot give such women the benefit of the doubt again, nor allow his softer nature to dictate his actions. Every person whom he has any reason to suspect will be taken to the Tower, young or old, beautiful or ugly. There they will remain until the case is solved, and the matter prosecuted. Only then will he allow himself to rest.

25

Anna

Her husband is dead and her baby is coming. It is quite a lot
to take in.

'Here,' the woman says and tips a cup of bitter liquid down
Anna's throat.

Anna doesn't ask what it is. She doesn't care. She only hopes
it will do something to numb both her mind and her body.

She's removed Philippe's paintings from the walls, but his
face still appears in her mind: pallid and blotched and angry.
He didn't go to his grave quietly. No, he died as he lived,
raging and screaming and vowing vengeance against the world.
At one point near the end, Anna thought she heard him say,
'Your medicines have cost me dearly.' Did he realise, then, that
he had underestimated her, that she'd poisoned him just as he
had poisoned her father? Perhaps he recognised the symptoms.
Or perhaps this was merely the dying talk of a man who in life
blamed his wife and others for everything, whether or not he
had cause to do so. Either way, Anna decided to up his dose
and speed him to his end so that no one else might hear his

accusations. Within a day and a half he was dead. She felt no sorrow, nor any guilt, not at that stage. Merely a vast sense of relief that the pain and suffering were over and that her child might stand a chance. She could not rest, though, for she needed to ensure the burial was prompt and unquestioned. She couldn't sleep until he was in the ground. After the funeral, she fell asleep on top of the coverlet in her mourning dress. She slept and slept and when she awoke, she felt that the baby had moved further down in her body. This evening, the labour began. She knows it is too early.

Benedetta ran to Laura who it seems deals in bringing life into the world as well as taking it, for she brought them a midwife almost at once: a tall, dark-haired woman with a sharp chin and quick, ebony eyes who seems a different species to Laura. It isn't just the woman's clothing, which though widow's black, is of fine quality, with little eagles stiched into the skirt. It is her bearing and demeanour. Her manner is stern, but Anna senses that there is warmth behind it, even fire. Her movements are quick and assured. She knows what to do and how to calm Anna, she knows how to carry her through the pain when it seems almost impossible. She's brought with her a case of salves and potions which she uses to smooth over Anna's skin and dull the torment of the contractions. The smells are distinct and strange. Is she just a midwife, or something else? She's nothing like the pudding-shaped women who attended her mother's many births and brought her little relief.

For a time the dark-haired woman goes into the next room to speak to Benedetta and Anna does not know what they are saying. What is it they aren't telling her? Do they fear that the baby, born too soon, will die? Do they think there is something wrong with her? Anna would ask, but another wave of pain hits and it fills her mind entirely. She wants to call for the woman, but she realises she can't remember her name, or perhaps was never told it. 'Benedetta!' she calls instead, and her maid is beside her in an instant.

'You can do this, mistress.'

'But I can't. I'm so tired.'

'Nonsense.' The dark-haired woman is on her other side. 'You're strong enough for several women. Now, let's get this little girl out of you, since she's decided it's her time to be born.'

Anna stares up at the women's faces. Benedetta's is pale and frightened, but the midwife's expression is determined, hard. It's on her that she'll focus. She will not think of Philippe at all.

26

Stefano

Half an hour's riding from Rome, the road plunges into an area of muddy wasteland. They are in the countryside, on their way to visit a physician with great expertise in poisons: a Dottor Morosini. Stefano breathes in the cold, damp air, the scent of rotting leaves and manure. It is a relief to be out, a relief to be riding. His lungs have felt clogged and constricted in the damp, cold air of the jail. He and Marcello pass the ruined walls of a convent, fragments of medieval towers visible through the gaps. Sheep graze about the land, around the remains of out-houses and dilapidated stables. Crows perch on broken beams, watching the horses pass.

As they ride, they discuss the events of the past two days. The women Vanna named – Maria and Graziosa – remain hidden in their lairs, but the *sbirri* have arrested three sisters, all of whose husbands died within a year, and whose neighbours are now pointing fingers. Marcello, though, is nervous. 'Word is spreading of the investigation, meaning accusations will be made, not all of them valid. That is what happened with the witchcraft inquisitions,' he warns. 'People accused those they had reason to dislike or fear. We must be careful. After all, many have died of the plague, not of poison, and so it may be with the husbands of these sisters.'

'Of course,' Stefano says. 'We will be rigorous.' He cannot, though, help feel a pulse of excitement as this inquisition gathers pace. 'But the pestilence provided perfect cover for those wishing to end life. We must consider that too. How many unnatural deaths have been concealed within the charnel house that Rome has been these past years?'

'It's a good question,' Marcello concedes. 'No doctor, myself included, will have been closely examining a body if it was thought to be full of the contagion. They will just have had them shovelled into the earth.'

When they reach Frascati, they stop at an inn to feed their horses and seek directions to the physician's house. It is a fine, sandstone villa surrounded by vineyards.

Dottor Morosini greets them in his office: a large, dark-wood-panelled room lined with rows and rows of bookshelves. On the wall hangs a painting of a group of courtiers sitting at table, eating. To their right, a skeleton offers a carafe of wine. Seeing Stefano looking at it, Morosini smiles. '*Death Comes to the Banquet Table*. But in your case, I understand there are no banquets.'

'No, indeed. There is no obvious case of a poisoned meal or drink that precipitated these deaths. Whatever it is, it works slowly and quietly.'

The man nods. 'Tell me everything you know.'

Between them, Stefano and Marcello explain about the investigation so far, the women they have arrested, what they have learnt from the autopsy of the dyer, and of the symptoms experienced by the men.

Morosini opens one of the little drawers in his bureau and brings out a small velvet box. When he lifts the lid, they see a chunk of silver mineral about the size of a walnut. 'Arsenicum.'

Stefano takes the box and peers closely. 'You are sure? This is our poison?'

'I'm not certain, no, but many of the symptoms you describe – the burning throat and stomach, the terrible thirst – these are symptoms of arsenic poisoning.'

'That is what we have been thinking,' Marcello says, 'but it doesn't explain all of the torments these men suffered.'

'Then the poison may not be entirely arsenic,' Morosini says. 'It may well have other components. Lead, perhaps. Nevertheless, many of the symptoms you describe fit with poisonings that I've encountered.' He pauses. 'In fact, one case in particular is strangely similar. It is almost as if history repeats itself.'

'Which case?' Stefano asks quickly.

Morosini pours himself some of the wine which a servant has brought. 'Many years ago, in Sicily, there were a series of poisonings. The circumstances were very similar to those that you have just related.'

Stefano is now very alert. 'Dottore, what were the circumstances?'

'I do not recall the precise details. However, I do remember that a notorious woman was hanged in Palermo for brewing and selling poison. For killing her husband and other men.' He considers. 'La Tofania, that's what they called her. She was accused of selling a liquid that came to be known as Aqua di Palermo, or Aqua Tofania. There were other women too, hanged as poisoners, though their names I don't recall.'

'How many women?' Stefano's heart is racing.

Morosini shakes his head. 'It's so long ago. I don't remember. It was much discussed at the time in my circles, but this is over twenty years ago now, maybe closer to thirty. There was a man too, I think, accused of using poison in Sicily. A whole host of them went to the gallows.'

'What was the poison? What was this Aqua di Palermo?'

Morosini takes a fig from a plate. 'I'm not sure that they ever knew the precise recipe, but its key ingredient was arsenic. This Tofania had found a way to dissolve and distil it such that it could be administered without arousing suspicion.'

'Well, well,' Marcello says.

Stefano meets his eye. He feels the blood beating in his brain, for surely it is impossible that there is not a connection between these two cases. 'Dottor Morosini: would arsenic explain the ruddiness of the corpses? Would it explain why the victims seemed not to decay?'

The man finishes chewing. 'It might explain the prolonged rigor mortis and the drying of the body. And I suppose if a body does not begin the decaying process then the body will look unnaturally preserved, if not flushed.'

Stefano's gaze returns to the shining silver piece of mineral. 'What became of those women in Sicily? They were hanged?'

'I think all that were caught were put to death, but who's to say that they caught everybody, or that the recipe did not make its way into other hands? As I recall, this Tofania had a book of secrets that was never found.'

Stefano imagines the book, wrapped in cloth, passing from hand to hand. It has crossed the water to mainland Italy, and then reached Papal Rome.

'This Tofania,' Marcello says. 'She had training?'

'She did, though quite what, exactly, and how she obtained it, I do not know. I've known of poorer women, some within convents, working as quasi-apothecaries, mixing medicines and beauty treatments from recipes in *libri di segreti*. Like those women, La Tofania must have obtained training from someone so as to set up her own workshop.'

'And she passed that learning on,' Stefano concludes.

'Yes, if it is indeed the same poison.' Morosini pauses. 'One wonders for how many years it has been circulating in Rome.'

'Who would know more about this book and these cases in Sicily? With whom should I speak, Dottore?'

'As I say, it was so long ago that most of the men involved at that time are no more. De Ribera, Viceroy of Sicily at the time, died only a few years after Tofania. But there must be records of the investigation and prosecution. They will survive even if the doctors and lawyers do not.'

'Yes,' Stefano says. He will write to the Viceroy of Palermo this very night, see if he can tell them anything that may take them further. 'Dottor Morosini, are you aware of any other spates of similar poisonings save for those in Sicily?'

'Well, we all know that it is often women who revert to poison, for want of other methods. However, aside from the Tofania matter, I cannot think of any other case involving a group of lower class women selling poison to one another. And it's such a scandalous matter that surely any such case would be known.'

'Indeed,' Stefano says. He is thinking of Agnese, the Duca di Ceri's widow. Hardly lower class, though of course she may be entirely innocent. 'Dottore, we know that the poison sellers we've arrested so far are all humble women. But it's possible that some of those *buying* the poison in Rome were of a different status.' He pauses. 'Needless to say, if that were the case, we would not be permitted to investigate them.'

The man nods slowly. 'Yes, I see that.'

'If it was women of all classes purchasing the poison, does that change, do you think, who we're looking for? Does it help us narrow the field?'

Morosini raises an eyebrow. 'Well, it means you are looking for someone who has access to all levels of society. Perhaps someone who has been married to a noble, or assumed an upper class name. Perhaps someone who has initially entered the houses of these women purveying other wares: cosmetics, perhaps. That might explain how they procured the arsenic, for it is used often enough to whiten the skin.' He considers. 'Then again, she might be a midwife.'

27

Anna

Anna has only really one thought, and it is that she must protect her baby daughter. Because yes, the dark-haired midwife was right and it is a girl, not a boy, and though society values male babies higher than female, to Anna she is a constant miracle: her tiny fingernails, her unblinking gaze, the mere fact of her existence. Aurelia, she has called her: the golden one. She looks nothing like her dark-haired father.

For a day and a night they feared that this small bundle of creation would not survive. But she has clung on to life as strongly as she now suckles at Anna's breast, and seems unlikely to leave it. Her daughter, she has decided, is a survivor. Indeed, that is what the midwife said. She survived Philippe's kickings in the womb and his wishes for her death, she survived a long and arduous labour that exceeded in pain anything that Anna could have imagined, despite the midwife's draughts. Now, every time Anna awakes, she is awed all over again at the sight of this small, breathing human whom she has brought into the world, whose head is a whorl of spun-gold hair and whose scent, of milk and musk, is the best thing she has ever smelt.

A knock on the door, which Benedetta answers. It is the midwife come to check on her progress. Anna recognises her voice, the Sicilian accent. She can hear the two women talking in the hallway, but she cannot hear what they say.

The woman enters her room and lays down fresh linen. Once she's looked over Aurelia's lovely limbs and swaddled her, she says to Anna: 'Are you recovering your strength?'

'A little.' In truth, Anna is still very weak after the birth, exhausted right down to her bones not just by the labour but by the months of fear and pain that had preceded it. Her mind is largely a fog.

'The bleeding has stopped?'

'Not completely.'

The woman takes from her case a small bottle. 'This will help speed your recovery. You must take it three times every day.' She hesitates, glances at Benedetta. 'You have told her nothing?'

'No, not yet.' Benedetta flushes. 'I didn't want to worry my mistress so soon after the birth.'

'Worry me with what?' Anna sits up straighter. All at once she is very alert.

The midwife licks her lips. 'A young magistrate is taking women into the Tor di Nona, accusing them of poisoning.'

That cuts through Anna's exhaustion: a cold knife to her heart. Does this woman know what she did? But of course she does. Laura has told her. Or, it is more than that.

'Now, there's nothing,' the woman says, 'to suggest that he knows anything about you, but it's right that you should be told that certain women Laura and I know are now in the confinement cells.' She frowns. 'Signora, you mustn't squeeze your daughter so tight.'

Anna realises she is clutching Aurelia to her. She has begun to whine. 'What must I do?'

The woman takes the baby from Anna and settles her in the wicker cradle. She rocks it with her foot. At last she says quietly: 'You must recover, then you must decide what you think is best, as each of us must do. It isn't safe for you to travel yet, not given the amount of blood you've lost, not given how small the child is. But with my remedies and a good diet hopefully it will not be too long.'

Anna glances at Benedetta. Her face is parchment white. In her crib, Aurelia is quiet.

'Thank you,' Anna says to the midwife. 'Thank you for everything you've done. You must forgive me, but I cannot remember your name.'

The woman gives her a half-smile. 'It's best that you do not know it.'

When the midwife has gone, Anna sinks back on the bed. 'Benedetta, sit down.'

Her maid takes the chair by her side. For a long moment, the two women are silent. In the cradle the baby now sleeps. If only, Anna thinks, this moment could just stretch out and none of them would have to move. She is so very, very tired.

'We should go,' Benedetta whispers. 'As soon as we can. The neighbours. They may talk.'

Yes, Anna thinks. They might. They surely heard enough of what happened within her house to know she would have wanted her husband gone. They might have noticed how quickly he died, and also how speedy the burial. 'I'm not sure I have it in me, Benedetta.' She is thinking of a journey anywhere, of how much her body hurts.

'I think you do, mistress. Not at once, but as soon as the bleeding has stopped, as soon as you feel a little stronger.'

'Where on earth would we go?'

'Not to your mother?'

'Lord no, not my mother. She would turn us in soon enough.'

Benedetta is silent for a moment. 'Maybe we could go to Venice. I have some family there. You can convalesce. We have money now and can survive for a time, until we think of another plan.'

Anna smiles weakly at this brave woman who has been keeping her fears a secret so that Anna might recover; who has stayed by her side throughout, though she could by now have fled Rome. 'Very well. We will do it. We will arrange the carriage and pack the clothing. We will leave as soon as I am a little stronger.' Anna eases herself out of bed, looking at the napkins and swaddling clothes scattered next to the bed. 'But Benedetta, if the worst should happen and I am taken to the Tower, like the other women. If I do not come back, will you promise me ...?' She cannot say it.

Benedetta nods, knowing immediately what is being asked of her. 'Yes, mistress. I will care for Aurelia.'

28

Stefano

It spreads like the cold winter mist rising from the Tiber and swirling through the morning air. From mouth to ear, from house to house, from street to street, the word seeps and creeps. A conspiracy of poisoners has been detected in Rome and now witnesses and suspects are being dragged from their abodes at dawn or dusk and rehoused in the darkness of Le Segrete beneath the Tor di Nona. There are at least ten prisoners in there now, or a hundred according to other reports, their presence expanding in the darkness like the rats that inhabit the place, clawing fruitlessly at the bars. The prisoners are all women poisoners according to some of the claims, or a mixture according to others, of witches, sorcerers and evil clerics: all part of some vast poisoning empire whose evil-doings are being dragged into the light.

In the marketplace of the Piazza Navona, wives talk of how incubi suck on the souls of these women, and how many others have been led into evil, still others are being primed. It is said, they tell each other, that hundreds upon hundreds have been poisoned – a veritable plague of poison. Others mutter that this *inquisitio* is more a malaise of the authorities than a sickness of the people; that it speaks of the sort of moral panic that prompted the Holy Inquisition. Though the Italian courts have not equalled in cruelty those elsewhere in Europe, they haven't stinted from prosecuting and punishing any man or woman deemed to have committed sorcery or witchcraft, any person who has challenged the teachings of the Church: heretics, magicians, healers, witches. Nobody is safe from suspicion, especially not those who cling to the outskirts of society, and those people who crawl in its shadows. Fear therefore stalks many streets, mainly the darker, poorer ones, and the screams and shouts that are always heard in the city of Rome at night now take on a more frightening aspect, for they may no longer be simply the shouts of the victims of a robbery or the loser in a fight, but of innocent people dragged to the cells.

In Le Segrete the fear is almost palpable and the air is not far above freezing. The women are kept separate in small, cold cells and cannot see one another. Indeed, they can rarely see their own hands before their own faces, so dark is it in this place for much of the time. But they can hear. They can hear others crying and praying, they can hear the clank of heavy doors and the clip of boots as women are led up the stone stairs to the interrogation room, then back again, their tread slower. They can sense the rats scurrying, and the water dripping, and the murmur of men's voices planning things they cannot detect, the occasional angry shout of a guard. They can smell too, smell the tang of urine, the scent of unwashed bodies, the growing sense of fear.

The guard, though, is a drunk, and on some nights, when he's insensible, they can talk to one another over the walls of their cells without being told their tongues will be cut from their mouths. Sometimes they even sing. Several of these women know each other and know how to comfort, how to plan. They have not yet given up hope.

★

In the large stone room above Le Segrete, Stefano is doing his best to grow into his role and into the sort of man he's decided he should be. Lodovico sits at a small table to the side of him, sharpening his quills with a small knife. Stefano knows he is not yet at the heart of the conspiracy, but he is creeping closer. He now has two women who are accused of selling poison and several possible buyers, including the three sisters, the widow of a butcher, and Camilla Capella, the innkeeper's wife, whom he's decided he must pull in. There are also a handful of witnesses in the cells, people who may be able to give him further names and firmer evidence. With each witness he interviews, Stefano feels he is becoming more expert in the techniques of wheeling the truth out of the reluctant and wily. The secret to it, he thinks, lies in determining what sort of person he is dealing with before he commences the interview, planning a line of attack. Marcello helps him in this, carrying out a physical examination of each prisoner and reporting back to him on any peculiarities, any distinctive features.

This morning, Stefano is to interview Maria Spinola, the woman whose name was written in Vanna's black book. It took the police a few days to find her, for she had gone to ground like little Graziosa: a clear sign of guilt.

'She looks much older than her sixty years,' Marcello told him earlier. 'A stooped and wrinkled woman. One eye is almost blind with cataracts. But she still has her wits about her. Indeed, she seems less frightened than some of the other women. I wouldn't assume that she'll be an easy witness.'

Stefano has established that, like the devil, this woman has many names. Some call her La Guercia, the squint-eyed one. For reasons that are less clear to him, others call her La Secca, the dry one. Most interestingly, she is also known as Maria Palermitana as she came to Rome from Palermo many years before. Could she have brought the recipe for the Aqua with her? It seems unlikely, though, that she is their key poisoner. Stefano has been to the rooms she rents with her husband. There is a fireplace with grill, tripod, and spit but there is nowhere to create or store poisons. There is none of the equipment of the apothecary.

When the woman is brought before him, Stefano thinks that perhaps it is her wrinkled, dark-complexioned face that gives her the name 'La Secca'. But perhaps it is her wit, for when he asks her if she knows why she has been brought here, she says wryly, 'I could not say, Signore. Perhaps the Lord is trying my faith with new ordeals.'

Her pearl-like right eye disturbs Stefano, for it is white like rancid milk.

'Maria Spinola,' Stefano says, the Latin preliminaries having been completed, 'you make your living by telling fortunes and selling "secrets".' Her neighbours speak of her as a sort of wise woman, knowledgeable about secrets and remedies, adept at resolving marital problems and in helping prostitutes keep their clients.

'I make a scant living by weaving and by helping other women, Signore.'

'Yes, in a variety of ways, I understand.' He looks down at notes. 'Charms, ointments, spells, divination. All sorts of things that are in fact proscribed by law.'

She gives a slight shrug. 'I do nothing harmful, Ser. On the contrary, I prevent harm.'

'That is not what our witness says.'

She regards him with her white eye and her good eye. 'People will say all sorts of things, Signore, to do down a woman who looks as I do.' She smiles. 'I did not choose to look like a witch, but fortune has decided it should be so.'

Stefano has no answer to this. She is right, of course, that people are prejudiced against those whose appearance or character is slightly different, and, as Marcello says, there are many wagging tongues in Italy who would accuse a neighbour of witchcraft out of spite. Here, however, the claims fit. 'There is a witness who says you sell poison.'

'No.'

'No? Well, our witness is clear: that you sell a slow-acting poison, kept in glass bottles.'

'Perhaps this witness of yours wants to settle a score with me. Perhaps your witness is a woman called Vanna who's using your legal process to get at those she thinks have slighted her down rather than telling you the truth.'

Stefano regards this small, shrivelled woman. Marcello was right that she is keen-witted. 'Was it you who brought the recipe over from Sicily? Was it taught to you by Tofania?'

'I don't know what you mean.' He can tell nothing from her expression, nor the tone of her voice.

'You don't make the poison though, do you, Maria?'

'There is no poison, Signore.'

Stefano has been led this dance by Vanna and will not have it. 'From whom do you buy the ointments and balms that you sell? You have very little equipment in your house. You do not make these things yourself.'

'Yes, I make them myself from herbs that I pick.'

Stefano regards her. 'You would like to buy your freedom, I think.'

'I have my freedom, Signore. It is in here.' Maria taps her head.

Stefano has some respect for this, for the mind can be its

172

own vast expanse, just as it can be its own prison. He gives her a half-smile. 'Nevertheless, you would, I suspect, prefer to sleep in your own bed rather than on a pallet on a stone floor.'

She gives a slight shrug.

'Tell me: who is La Strolaga?'

'I don't know what you mean.'

'Oh, I think you do. A woman who makes and sells a variety of remedies, including a slow-acting poison such as you yourself sell.' Stefano has continued to imagine this woman, his guesses melding with the well-dwelling witch of his youth so that the figure he now pictures is somewhere between a human and an amphibian, ghostly white.

'As I said, Signore, there is no poison.'

Stefano tries not let his annoyance show. 'It says in the police reports that you were arrested five years ago for arranging accommodation for another woman in a house that was not her husband's.' It has crossed his mind that she may be a procuress.

'Yes, I did that.'

'Why?'

'Because I knew that otherwise, Signore, her husband would kill her, the way things were going. So I secured lodging for her, temporarily, in the house of an old neighbour of mine. Only, the husband went to the *sbirri* and demanded that they arrest me and bring her back.'

Stefano is still. 'Did they? Bring her back?'

'Yes, Signore, they did.' A small, sparkling silence. 'And yes, Signore, he killed her in the end, as she knew he would. As the *sbirri* knew he would.' Another smile. 'There's only one of us who has a police record for the matter, and it isn't the husband. But that's the law for you, isn't it, my lord? That's the system of which you're a part.'

Stefano feels a twinge of discomfort. 'I'm not part of that system, Maria Spinola. I am merely enforcing the rules.'

'Is there a difference?'

A flash of anger. 'It is you who is the suspect in this case, Donna Maria, and a key suspect at that. It is for me to ask questions of you. Tell me who makes the poison.'

'As I said, Signore, there is no poison to be seen.'

He breathes out. 'Maria,' he says more softly, 'if you can tell me who makes the Aqua, I can ask that you receive Papal immunity. Your future would be safe. You could return to your husband. Live out the rest of your life in peace.'

The woman's one good eye is bright and he thinks maybe he has some hope of persuading her to name the central poisoner. Indeed, she begins to smile. 'I think, Messer Bracchi, that you could have a family of your own if things go well for you. Two girls and a boy.'

Stefano flinches. 'What?'

'Yes.' She is nodding. 'A strong boy. But you must guard your own mind, your own freedom.'

'Stop this!' Stefano says abruptly. 'I do not wish to hear your nonsense.'

Again, a slight shrug. 'I am merely saying what I am seeing, Signore. You must watch that you are not led into evil.'

'Donna Maria, it is not I who is sitting here charged with procuring poison. You can save your false-biblical pronouncements for your friends.' He gestures to the slab-faced guard to take her away. 'You would do well to think on what I have offered you,' Stefano says coldly, 'or you will not see freedom again.'

Maria still appears unperturbed. 'And you would do well to look to yourself, Messer Bracchi, or the way will grow a deal darker.'

Stefano says to the guard: 'Take her back to the cells.' He refuses to look at Maria as she stands and limps from the room, though he can hear her stick on the floor.

Once she has left, Stefano glances at Lodovico. He is still scribbling in his book. 'What on earth was that about?' he says, attempting lightness.

Lodovico looks up and stares at him with his pale grey eyes. 'I couldn't say, Signore. They have strange ways, some of these women.'

'Yes.' Stefano gives a short laugh but he is disconcerted. What did she mean, look to himself? He is not the one on trial here. He needs to get out of this place.

Stefano finds Marcello measuring out powders and insists that he join him for luncheon. They leave the confines of the Tor di Nona and make for an *osteria* on the Strada del Orso. Stefano has a sense of being watched, but when he glances back, there is only a decrepit beggar woman bent over her stick, and a group of young men, laughing and talking among themselves.

It is a relief to be out of the dark, damp tower and the place Stefano chooses is lively with a strong fire, making for a fug of warmth and smoke. They order cutlets and olives and chew on bread to curb their appetites.

'For how many years, Marcello, do you think that this poisoning network has been at work? These women are advanced in years and Tofania was hanged more than twenty years ago. They've been at this evil for a long time.'

Marcello is quiet. 'What is it, Marcello? You've barely said a word since we left the prison.'

He drums his fingers on the table. 'This morning I have been examining the inn-keeper's wife, Camilla Capella.'

Stefano had her arrested the previous day from the inn where she works. 'Very good.'

'No, Stefano. Not good.'

He feels a pang of unease. 'In what way, not good?'

'Her body ...' Marcello grimaces. 'It is covered with scars.'

Stefano frowns, remembering the deep scar to her wrist. 'What sort of scars?'

'Of abuse, I think, Stefano. Many, many beatings, burns, cuts.'

'Cuts?'

'Yes. All over her body.'

Stefano envisions her skin. The meal arrives, but he finds he has lost his appetite for his lamb. 'Who does she say caused her these injuries?'

'She does not. She does not speak at all, but we know, don't we, Stefano? We know who caused those scars. Officer Bertuccio says he has come across this Camilla Capella before. The *sbirri* have been called to her house several times after complaints made by neighbours. Her husband was known to beat her just as was the case with the dyer's wife, Teresa. Indeed, she sought refuge in a convent but the police brought her back home. After that, the records are silent.'

Stefano takes a sip of his wine. It tastes sour in his mouth.

Marcello leans forward. 'It would make sense, wouldn't it, Stefano? Why else would she poison her husband: a young woman like that? A woman who's never been in trouble with the law?'

To escape him. To save herself. That is what Marcello is saying and, though Stefano has considered that it might be the husbands' brutality which links their deaths, it is another matter to have that brutality set out quite so clearly, written on skin. The thought makes the wine curdle in Stefano's gut. 'I will have to find out as much as I can before I question this Camilla. I too will speak with the police. Perhaps I will speak again with the barber.'

'Yes,' Marcello says, still looking at the grain of the table. 'But what if all of these women ... what if that is what the poison was for? To get rid of men who would otherwise have killed them?'

He hesitates only for a moment. 'Then it was still against the law, Marcello. It was still murder.' Stefano speaks with more confidence than he feels.

The doctor nods. 'All the same, it has rattled me, seeing such signs of harm. It makes me doubt our purpose.'

Stefano grips tighter to his knife. 'Our purpose remains the same. It has to, surely. One cannot excuse murder, no matter what the cause. Even if this Camilla Capella was horribly abused, she should have sought another remedy.'

'Yes, and perhaps she did,' Marcello says lightly. 'Perhaps there was no other remedy.'

Their eyes meet. Stefano fears he is right. Because what remedy would there be, for a poor woman, against a man who beat her black and blue, who tormented her day and night, if that is indeed what they are dealing with? He has heard that in Venice and Verona, the courts give women some leeway to leave bad marriages. In this city of God, however, marriage is indissoluble, divorce almost unheard of. *Quod Deus conjunxit homo non separet.* It is clear from what Bertuccio has told them that men who beat their wives more than is deemed acceptable are rarely arrested for long. 'I have read,' Stefano says, 'of judges granting beaten wives shelter in convents.'

'Yes,' Marcello agrees. 'But to get to such a judge, you would have to be able to pay a lawyer, would you not?'

'Ah, yes. Lawyers. Whatever society's ills, it is somehow always our fault.' Stefano smiles. 'But yes, you would need to pay and I fear that even those wives who can pay for such separations are eventually returned to their homes.' For God has joined them, and they cannot be put asunder. He thinks of Maria's story of the woman whom the police returned to her husband, only for him to kill her. Till death do us part. 'But Marcello, all this is no excuse for, nor defence to, murder.'

'Perhaps not. But she also has a little boy,' Marcello says. 'What if . . .?' He does not complete the sentence.

Stefano takes a bite of cutlet. He does not wish to think of such things. 'We will keep this under consideration. We must continue as we have to date, but your examinations of the prisoners could perhaps become more thorough.'

'You mean to look for marks of severe beatings and torments? Many will have faded by now, Stefano. And there are other types of injury that leave no scar, except inside the mind.'

'Yes, Marcello, I know that, but I'm asking you to establish what you can. I don't say that it will change the way we operate, but it's always best to be armed with all the facts.'

Marcello pushes his food about his plate. 'She has burn marks, that I think are the marks of his pipe, all over her body. What kind of man would do that to a woman?' he asks.

'One whose soul is as black as tar, I would guess,' Stefano says quietly. He imagines this innkeeper and his wretched pipe and remembers Camilla's lovely face. 'But even if the need for vengeance or escape was extreme, is it really for us, mere men, to decide to excuse the taking of another human life?'

'Is that a rhetorical question, or a real one, Stefano?'

'It's mainly a question I'm asking myself,' he says honestly. 'After all, it is I who have been given this role of investigator.' For the first time he thinks that maybe Lucia was right to have warned him at the outset – that perhaps this commission is a poisoned chalice. Stefano checks himself. He must not let himself think that way. It is not how he will advance. Men do not become great by shirking from responsibility, nor from allowing their emotions to take over. 'But we jump ahead of ourselves, Marcello. There are many others who have bought poison. We do not yet know their motives.'

'Agreed,' Marcello says. 'Let us hope that the others wanted their victims dead for less compelling reasons.'

'What else do we know about the Duca di Ceri's widow, Agnese?'

Marcello raises an eyebrow. 'The Governor was clear we weren't to go there, wasn't he?'

'The Governor was clear we were not to rile the nobility. That doesn't mean we can't find out whether the circumstances of that case fit with the facts of others.'

'You mean: did Ceri abuse his wife?'

'Yes. Or was there some other strong cause.'

'For her to poison him?' Marcello asks.

'Exactly.'

'We could, I suppose, begin making discreet enquiries, but it is dangerous, and even if we were to find anything, then ...?' He spreads his hands.

'It may nevertheless help us identify the players.'

Marcello nods slowly. 'It might. But it would be wrong if the only players to be placed on the board were those without a title.'

'I don't go there yet. I merely say we must work out whether Ceri's widow fits the pattern. As I understand it, she is in a convent and did not go willingly.'

'There is, sadly, nothing unusual in that, Stefano.'

'No, indeed.' Many daughters of Italy's nobles are coerced into convents. 'But this is a family with money. They didn't need to use the convent as a cheaper alternative to a dowry. Indeed, as a widow, she could have returned to her family, just as my sister did.' Not that Lucia relished such an option. 'Maybe they wanted her out of the way to conceal some whiff of scandal. We return to the business of families wishing to protect their reputations.' He pauses. 'We need someone from within the Ceri house. Someone who knows what passes within it.'

Marcello folds his arms. 'Surely, Stefano, you are suggesting that I speak with the servants? If I recall correctly, you reprimanded me for the time I spoke to the physician's man.' Marcello's eyes are twinkling.

179

'It would be entirely wrong of me to suggest such a thing.' Stefano suppresses a smile.

29

Experiments upon enemies may be performed in several ways, but, whether with waxen images or some other instrument, the particulars of each must be diligently and faithfully observed. Should the day and hour fail thee, proceed as already laid down, and prepare the image or instrument proper to this effect in the order and manner thereof. Fumigate with the proper perfumes, and if writing be required on the image, let it be done with the needle or stylet of the art, as aforesaid.

Girolama

'You must leave Rome, Mother.'

'Must I?' Girolama says mildly. She is checking the laurel for frost damage and the hellebore for leaf spot. Plants to heal, plants to hurt.

'You know you must!' Angelica says, stamping her foot. 'They have Maria now, and they're seeking Graziosa. It's only a matter of time until they come here, knocking on our door, taking you to that wretched tower.'

'Well, if they come, I will go, and I will tell them nothing.'

'But why not flee now?'

'You know why. Because my life is here. My plants and herbs are here who need my tending. My workshop is here.' (Albeit the important items are now hidden away.) 'My women are here who need my help. I can't just abandon them.' They have been taking provisions to the prison every day. 'If I run, it will suggest that I've done something wrong. At the moment, they have nothing.'

'You don't know that. You don't know what people are saying in there – what they're making them say.'

Fear curdles in Girolama's stomach, but she will not run like a rat from everything she's created, from the women who've supported her for so long. She must stay here and help them with what powers she has. 'Angelica, if the judge had something – anything – to lead him to me, he would already have had me arrested. Maria will hold firm.'

'For how long, though? This man: he won't give up, you know.'

'I wouldn't be so sure of that.' She has been watching this investigating magistrate, this Stefano Bracchi. She waited outside the Tower, then followed him to his home, listening to his conversation with his doctor friend, watching everything he did. She'd guess that he's perhaps five and thirty, a slightly built man with quick, bright eyes that seem to see everything. He is, she thinks, a young man lacking in confidence, a man in thrall to the opinions of others, desperate to succeed. He has an energy about him that could quite easily become mania. She's seen enough men in her time to know. To Angelica, she says: 'The law is such that they may only convict where they have a confession.' Girolama has made it her business to learn the law so far as it relates to her and her women. She cuts another stalk. 'I do not plan to confess.'

Angelica exhales, frustrated. 'You know what things they can do to extract confessions.'

She does: she's seen them at their work. Men hauled up by the strappado and left there to hang until their shoulders dislocate, women whose hands have been crushed into misshapen purple lumps. They won't do that to her, though, surely. She's considered an old woman. At most they'll break her fingers, but she doesn't believe it will come to that. She has her own ways of causing pain and torment. She clips the dead head off another plant. 'Angelica, I'll keep things under consideration, but you aren't going to change my mind on this now. You would do better to help me.'

'Help you with what?'

Girolama smiles. 'With preparing a supply.' If she's to be put out of business for a time, then she must stockpile her wares and make up her plants into produce.

'You must teach me,' the girl says. She has said it many times before.

Girolama glances at Angelica, at the freckles that sprinkle her nose, and for a moment her heart squeezes. It isn't so long since the girl was playing with her dolls: simple things Girolama made her. If she herself is taken, what will become of Angelica? She supposes she will have to grow up and survive, just as she, Girolama, did, but she doesn't want that life for her daughter. She wants something better, kinder, more nurturing. She can't bear for the world to crush her. Nor can she bring herself to saddle the girl with such heavy responsibility when she's only fourteen years old. 'I will teach you soon enough. For now, we have more pressing matters. You must help me with some lozenges. I will fetch the book.'

She knows, though, that Angelica is right. She can't delay the lesson for much longer, for though she hopes her powers and her forbearance will ensure her survival, she can't be sure of it. Nor does she know yet what this judge might be capable of. From what she's been able to glean, he is a man who plays by the rules, but to have got so far so young he must also be a man of great ambition, and she's seen ambition corrode the soul of a man until he remakes the rules in his shape.

Tomorrow. She will start the teaching tomorrow. Today she has other things to do.

While Angelica is heating the molasses for the lozenges, Girolama visits the little room in which she keeps the wax. It's a ritual that her Uncle Lorestino showed her when she was younger. 'It works better than you might think,' he had said. You must infuse it with the blood of toads. Then you must warm it over a fire of ebony. Sprinkle it with amber and myrrh, and mould it until it takes the form you desire, be that a person, an animal, a body part, a spirit. It is in this way that the wax will emulate the real person.

It is in this way that you may control them.

30

Stefano

Wolves have been seen in the Vatican gardens. They've made their way over the city walls, starving in the freezing weather, searching for something to eat. Meanwhile in Naples, the police search for the Dyer's wife, Teresa, and her mother, Cecilia, for they've learnt that it's to Naples they've fled.

As for Stefano, he searches for a speedy resolution to this matter, for the spider at the centre of the web. He needs to conclude this case, and fast, for word is now out of his activities and he knows that suspects will, like Teresa, be fleeing Rome and concealing their traces as best they can. He knows too that if this thing is as murky as he fears, then he must finish it before his courage fails him. He sleeps poorly, twisted in his sheets, his mind still teeming with names and images and yes, sometimes with doubts. There is nothing so comforting, however, as a list, so he is writing lists of the known and suspected poison sellers, and of the known and suspected buyers. He is working out how they interconnect. He sits in his study – a small, ordered room full of his law books and the scent of ink and sweet tobacco. He has moved his desk close by the window to gather the last of the light. Although it is only four o'clock the sky has darkened to a steel grey.

There is, it seems, a central ring of poison sellers that includes Vanna, Maria and the tiny, red-haired Graziosa, who has finally been found. In the Tower, she has reverted to the guise of a confused old, toothless lady and pretends she does not understand what he asks her, but Stefano is not deceived. She is a seller, just as the others are. They disturb him, these women, Maria in particular. Stefano has tried interviewing her again, as he senses that she knows more than the others, but she gives him nothing. Indeed, she seems to gather more information about him than he does about her. During the last interrogation, she said: 'You wake, don't you, every night before first light, and nothing you do can ease your mind?' Stefano has said nothing of this to anyone, not even Marcello, and although he supposes his ringed eyes give him away, he has the uncomfortable sense that she knows more than she should. It has even occurred to him that it may be her who keeps him from sleep, for these women are not far off witches and he does not have Marcello's confidence that witchcraft is a creation of the state.

These women's backgrounds are similar – little education, hard lives. These are not skilled apothecaries or magic-makers. They are sellers of someone else's wares. He does not even think all these women know exactly what poison they have been selling, though they know, for certain, that it works. That is what they have told their customers again and again: that this is a slow-acting poison that will leave no trace and is as clear as water. It is the same poison, he is almost certain, as killed many men in Palermo. He has written to the Justices there and sent a rider to carry it direct to Sicily, but it is too early to expect a reply.

How many others are there in this strange circle, and who is at the centre? The women deny that there is such a person as La Strolaga or La Profetessa, or that there is any poison-maker at all. They are lying to him. Stefano understands that these women serve someone else, someone whose identity they are protecting regardless as to the threats to them. That must mean either an incredible loyalty, or fear. Or both. What power is this person exerting that she can keep them from speaking out? When Stefano tries to picture the poisoner what comes to his mind is the vile witch of his youth: La Manalonga with her white hand stretching from a well to grab at him, her arm impossibly long. But perhaps Stefano has been confused by this idea of a mysterious woman, influenced by his own childish fears. Possibly the central poisoner is not a woman at all, but a man, and one with considerable power. That would explain how the poisoner is able to acquire arsenic in what must be considerable quantities.

As for the list of poison-buyers, Stefano includes Agnese Aldobrandini in tentative brackets. Marcello has determined from a former servant of the Ceri household that she was rumoured to have a lover, and thus perhaps a reason to murder her husband. He knows, though, that such rumours often surround beautiful women, particularly those who do not hide their loveliness. Asides from Agnese, the buyers are largely lower class women: the wives of butchers, shopkeepers, market traders, fishmongers. They buy the Aqua without knowing what it contains, or who makes it. They are told only that it will work, and, time after time, it does. They are are using the lethal liquid to rid themselves mainly of husbands, but also of brothers and fathers. This is where the matter grows more difficult and where the lists do not help Stefano at all. A few of these men are inconvenient. Some are highly unpleasant. Others, however – indeed, the majority of them – are deeply, troublingly, abusive. They have threatened to kill. They have violated and maimed. They have made the lives of their wives or children unbearable and unliveable.

Vanna has told Stefano of several of the women to whom she has sold poison, and their stories eat away at his mind: a wife whose husband harmed both her and their child in ways he cannot contemplate; a sister who dispensed with a brother who had abused her since her childhood; a young woman who'd entered a convent for the ill-married – the *malmaritate* – but whose husband had tracked her down.

Stefano has also interviewed Camilla, the innkeeper's widow whose body is covered with the marks of cruelty. She refused to speak of what happened once she was married, aged sixteen, his little sister, Fioralisa, in Camilla's place. Perhaps that's why he said to her: 'Donna Camilla, for some people who help this investigation, we will ask the Pope for immunity. If you tell me who sold you the Aqua then I may be able to ensure that you are not prosecuted for the wrong you have done.'

Camilla, though, just stared at him calmly. 'I have not done anything wrong, Signore.'

Does she believe that? Has she convinced herself that what she did was justified?

★

When Lucia arrives to visit him, Stefano finds himself explaining much of it to her: the sellers, the buyers, the irksome stories, the women's refusal to give up the name of their leader. Perhaps he should not tell his sister all these things, but he feels a need to unburden himself.

For most of this, Lucia sits quietly, eyes on the floor, but when he talks of Camilla Capella, she interrupts: 'Surely there's no interest in prosecuting such a woman. You would be leaving a child without a mother, and for what?'

The sharpness in her voice surprises him. 'Lucia, it isn't for me to decide who is and who isn't prosecuted. I'm just supposed to investigate: to root out the evil in this city and ensure that no further people come to harm.'

She stares at him for a long moment. 'Evil. Is that what you're dealing with? Evil?'

'Lucia, we are talking about murder. Cold-blooded, premeditated murder.'

'Well, could it have been anything else but pre-meditated? Women may not kill in passion as men do. They have not the strength. If they wish to escape, they must plan. And yet for that, there is no defence, regardless as to their circumstances.'

He frowns at her. 'I hadn't realised you were so well acquainted with the law, sister.'

'I do sometimes listen to what you tell me, you know, and you've talked of defences to murder before.' She pauses. 'I'm right, aren't I?'

'Yes. You are right. For such women, there is no defence. In the most sympathetic cases, however, there may be clemency.'

'But surely there's no interest in even prosecuting the worst cases, Stefano. Surely it will just make the state look cruel and wasteful. Think of how people still speak of Beatrice Cenci and what was done to her.'

Beatrice Cenci. A young woman – a girl, really – who was executed many years before. Stefano has seen the girl's face, beatific, heart-breaking, in the portrait by Reni. Her face, and her story, have remained with him as they have with many other people, for it is a tale of depravity and horror. Her father, the sadistic Count Francesco, made her life and those of her family a living hell. After many years of Francesco's abuse (against his wife, sons, but predominantly Beatrice), and the refusal of the Papal authorities to take action, the family

189

decided they must find their own solution. They bludgeoned him to death and threw the body from a balcony in an attempt to make it look like an accident. The plot, however, was uncovered and Beatrice and her relatives were sentenced to death. Despite pleas and protests, Pope Clement refused any clemency. Rather, he decided to use the Cencis as an example. All were executed, publicly and horribly, save for Beatrice's twelve-year-old brother, who was made to watch his family die.

'In the minds of many,' Lucia continues, 'Beatrice should have been spared. The public thought so back then and they think it now, for she'd suffered appallingly and with no other way out. What, then, will the people make of a judge who pursues women who poisoned their husbands only to save themselves?'

'Lucia, sometimes I think you should have been the advocate, rather than I.' Stefano smiles at her. 'You present the case most convincingly, but I cannot see that Baranzone would agree with you. He will say that it isn't for me, a mere junior magistrate, to decide who is and who is not prosecuted.'

She gives a little shrug. 'Shouldn't you nevertheless try? Didn't you tell me you weren't going to let him push you around?'

He regards her. 'You're right. I should speak with him.'

For why should this decision, this doubt and guilt, fall upon his shoulders only? He will go to the Governor the following morning.

'You should visit your little sister too, busy though you are. She is in a new house with people who are largely strangers to her. She would welcome your company.'

Stefano knows he is being reprimanded. 'How is Fioralisa?'

'She is already pregnant.'

'So quickly! Well, that is good, isn't it?'

Lucia shrugs. 'It is what is expected of her. She has done better than me.'

Stefano cringes. They have never discussed this outright: Lucia's failure to produce children during her marriage (and yes, it is always considered the woman's failure, not the man's). Is that why she does not remarry, Stefano wonders: for fear that she is barren? 'Lucia, you have much else to offer.'

She laughs. 'None of that matters, as you well know.' She stands. 'I will leave you to your lists.'

Stefano stands also and, as he does so, he feels a short, sharp pain in his chest.

Seeing him wince, Lucia says: 'You are unwell?'

'Not at all. I suspect I gobbled my luncheon too quickly.'

31

Stefano

Monday morning. The sounds of shutters being opened and steps being swept, buckets being emptied into the street, the calls of market traders and hawkers beginning their day, the inevitable ringing of bells. At the palace, Stefano finds Baranzone already at his desk, signing documents. A clerk stands at his side passing him pieces of parchments and sealing the letters when they are done.

'Ah,' the Governor smiles to see Stefano, though he does not get up to take his hand. 'Our investigator. Tell me, how do things progress at the Tower?'

'We make good progress, Monsignore,' Stefano says. 'We have made new arrests and found fresh witnesses. We begin to see the skeleton of the thing.'

'Excellent, excellent.' Baranzone is still signing his signature.

'Yes. Except that ...' Stefano struggles to find the right words.

'Except that what, Stefano?' Baranzone looks up. 'You need more resources, is that it? More men?'

'Not at present, no. It is something rather more complicated than that.' Stefano glances at the clerk.

Baranzone understands. 'Laurenzio, leave us for a few minutes.'

The clerk, a tall young man with a sallow face, gives a short bow and departs, but not without shooting Stefano a cold look.

'Well?' Baranzone sits up in his leather-backed chair.

Stefano, who has not been invited to sit, does his best to appear confident, and not to fidget. 'There is a certain moral complexity that has arisen.' He explains about the scars to Camilla Capella's body, about the stories other women have told him, about Vanna's account of the women who came to her in fear of their lives; the terrible stories they told.

The Governor is frowning. 'And?'

'And, your Lordship, I wish to check with you how to proceed in such cases. Because, if it transpires that many of these women have been severely abused, the public may not be with us in their prosecution.' He pauses. The Governor says nothing. Stefano continues: 'I was thinking of Beatrice Cenci. You will remember how her execution inflamed the public order situation in Rome.'

A sigh. 'Do you not see, Stefano, that you are falling into their trap?'

'Their trap?'

Baranzone opens a silver box and takes a pinch of snuff. 'Yes. These women have been slowly poisoning their lawful husbands. Others have been selling that poison for profit. You have found them out. You are locking them up, wrenching the truth from them. How else do you expect them to defend themselves but with their forked tongues? They are telling you the story that they think you need to hear in order to let them go.'

'But the scars, Monsignore. They are real enough. Dottor Marcello examined the woman.'

The Governor shrugs. 'Scars can be made by many things. You have no proof that it was this woman's husband who caused them. Nor, I suspect, do you have any proof that any of the other victims did anything more than displease their wives or sisters or daughters in some way. No, no, do not fall into that net, Stefano. These are no Beatrice Cencis we are dealing with here, but a network of evil women who are attempting to destroy Rome's authority through insipid and secret means.'

Stefano is not convinced. 'All the same, there may be some who were fighting for their survival. Or for that of their children. In those circumstances, are we to proceed as we would for the others?' He is thinking of Camilla Capella's little boy.

'Stefano, if the evidence and the circumstances warrant it, no doubt His Excellency the Pope will grant clemency to those women most grossly abused. But it is not for you, or indeed for me, to determine who should and should not be tried. If the crime is made out, then you pursue the case, no matter what these wily women may try to make you believe. That, after all, is the law.'

Stefano nods. His mind churns.

'Tell me: this young woman who says she was much abused by her father, does she have others who validate her story? Does she have witnesses to what she claims happened?'

'I confess I do not know. This is one of the cases related to me by our key witness, Vanna de Grandis.' But then there would not be witnesses, would there, to such private and heinous acts? Even if there were, they would not speak.

'Well, then,' Baranzone says as though that answers his question. 'Then it is a story, invented to pull at your heartstrings. I am surprised you didn't identify it as such.'

Stefano thinks of Vanna recounting to him the details of the people to whom she'd sold poison. Was she lying? He didn't think so at the time, but then he failed to identify Teresa, the dyer's wife, as a liar and in that way allowed her to escape. And of course Vanna would attempt to present herself as a saviour rather than a murderer.

'Remember,' Baranzone says, 'that God does not excuse vengeance, no matter what the cause. Romans 12:19. "Do not take revenge, my dear friends, but leave room for God's wrath, for it is written: 'It is mine to avenge; I will repay,' says the Lord." When they hurled their insults at Christ, "he did not retaliate; when he suffered, he made no threats. Instead, he entrusted himself to him who judges justly." So must we all, Stefano. So must we all.'

'Yes, Monsignore.' But did Camilla kill from vengeance, or from self-preservation?

'Therefore, if there is to be any clemency it cannot be us, mere mortals, who grant it. It is for the Pope, God's emissary on earth.'

'Yes,' Stefano says, although he is thinking of Beatrice Cenci. He is thinking of the Pope who refused to pardon her. From what he knows of Pope Alexander, he is a milder, more intellectual character. Surely he will be more clement.

Baranzone surveys him. 'I had not thought you a weak man, Stefano.'

He is stung. 'Nor am I.'

'I hope not,' the Governor says slowly. 'Your brother, Bruno, warned me that you could be a little soft, but I assumed that was a little playful sibling rivalry.'

Stefano feels the fire of anger flare up within him. 'My brother will always see me as the younger, smaller brother, but, Governor Baranzone, I am far from weak. Indeed, in many ways I am made of stronger stuff than he. I was merely confirming how to proceed. I assure you I will do what is required.'

Baranzone smiles. 'Good, good. Then we will not talk of this again. You'll keep me informed, though, of any key developments, anything of which I should know?'

Stefano bows. 'Of course, Monsignore. Thank you for making the time to see me.'

Leaving the room, Stefano comes face to face with the clerk he ousted. It is clear from the man's expression – a slight smirk – that he has been listening. He twitches his lips into a smile and gives a mocking bow.

When he arrives back at the Tower, Bertuccio informs Stefano wryly that he has a special visitor.

Opening the door to the waiting room, Stefano sees that it is Flavia, the prostitute, her hair freshly dyed, the pustules on her mouth much improved. She stands up as he enters the room.

'You have news?' he asks her. 'Of La Strolaga? The poisoner?'

'Not of her, but of another woman, one whose husband is lately in the ground.' Flavia smiles. Her gums are black from the mercury treatment.

'And?' Stefano asks.

'And her neighbours say that he died awful quick, and that she had much reason to want him gone.'

Stefano is about to ask what the reason might be but he decides he already knows it, and he does not want to have it confirmed. 'Who is this woman? Where does she live?'

Flavia walks closer to him and he can smell the wine on her breath. 'She is a woman of good family with a fine house in Via della Croce. Her name is Anna Conti.'

32

Malediction:
I conjure thee, thou spirit, and that by him that did make the world
to shake, and by him that made the stones rent, the graves open,
and dead bodies to rise up, and by him that entered the lowest parts
and dispossessed devils forth of men, that this fire of hell may burn
thee, that thou may now feel thyself to burn and be pained, and
that in thine own person, eternally.

Girolama

It is raining. It seems never to have not been raining. Girolama
can hear water from the roof gushing out in streams onto the
flagstones of the courtyard. A few more days like this and the
Tiber will burst its banks as it has many times before, sending a
vast wave of water through the city, taking with it the contents
of cellars and graveyards. It might well flood the Tor di Nona,
as it has in years gone by, and then her women will not be
just imprisoned, but drowned. Girolama can't bear to think of
them locked up in those rotting cells. She can envisage Vanna
and Graziosa shivering in the darkness and it tears at her insides,
for really it's her fault that they're there. She should have been
more careful. She should've instructed all her women to make
sure no buyer allowed an open casket at the men's funerals.
Maybe, though she won't quite allow herself to go there, she
shouldn't have sold the poison quite so freely.

'Wretched saints and devils,' she curses as she collects a handful of pins. She is making another preparation. A stronger, darker one. She needs something to stop him, to stop all of them. She needs something into which to pour her anger.

'How is it,' she asks the cat, who sits curled beside her, 'that the Governor of Rome has no time at all to deal with husbands who beat their wives to death or within an inch of it, or with men who take the honour of young girls, and yet, as soon as one man is discovered dead, there must be a great *inquisitio* with an army of officers and a whole prison given over to the suspects? Why does one man's life count for more than a cartload of women's?'

The cat has no reply. Cecca, who is bustling about the workshop tidying, says, 'It's the way of the world, and there's not much that can be done to alter it.'

'I do not accept that, Cecca, and nor should you.' Where things are bad, they must be changed or dealt with, through fair means or foul, and Girolama seems to be out of fair means entirely. So it was with her first husband. How long did she live with him in Sardinia? A year and a half? It felt a lifetime, a lifetime in which she began to think that others had been right and that there was no point in fighting back against what was decided, little point in pushing against rules and patterns etched into society by years of practice and forbearance. She started to accept that she would die in that house and that it would be a mercy. But some small spark in her stayed alive beneath the blackness, and from a spark a fire may grow. That fire burns still.

She stands up. There is nothing for it. She must do as Tofania did, as Giulia did, and pass her learning on.

She finds her daughter in her *camera,* throwing beans. For a time she watches her: her slender shoulders, her long, dark plait. She looks younger even than her years. Will Angelica grow to become as she herself has, as she ages: hardened and hollowed by anger, skin tough as old leather boots to defend herself from being kicked? Girolama hopes that, despite being saddled with this role, she'll retain the brightness that now defines her, but she doesn't know. She doesn't know if what she is doing is right. She would like to discuss it with someone – with Vanna, or Maria – but they've both been locked away.

'Angelica, what are you doing?'

The girl turns, looks up. 'Magic beans, like Nonna Giulia used to do, remember?'

'I remember.' Girolama sits down on the bed.

Some grandmothers teach their grandchildren games. Giulia taught hers divination.

Angelica throws again. 'I'm working out who's spoken against you, and who remains firm.'

Enterprising. 'And?'

Angelica points at the bean furthest away from her. 'Maria remains silent. She gives them nothing.'

Girolama smiles. 'As I would expect.'

Angelica moves to kneel by the smallest bean. 'Graziosa's said nothing either. She gives them the runaround.'

At that Girolama laughs. 'Of course she has.'

Angelica picks up the bean closest to her. 'But Vanna is all but broken.' She cradles the bean in her palm.

Girolama's face falls. 'I feared as much.' How much longer until Vanna names her? She feels a sudden ache in her bones, an enormous weariness. Her whole life she has been running and running, dodging blows. She's not sure she has the strength for it anymore.

Angelica sits next to her on the bed and puts her hand over hers. For a time there is no sound other than the rise and fall of their breath and the rushing of the water outside. Girolama can smell Angelica's sweet, appley scent. The chamomile in her hair.

'I should learn now, shouldn't I, Mama?'

'I think so, *mia cara*.'

The girl nods. 'Good. I'm ready.'

She pats her knee. 'No, you're not, but I fear we're running out of time.'

33

Anna

Anna is still weak, but they have decided they must fly now, before it is too late. She and Benedetta have spent the past few days pawning goods, gathering provisions, and packing everything up as tight as they can, for they must give the appearance that they are only on a brief trip out of Rome, not intending to flee for their lives.

She fears from the way her neighbours regard her – the backward glances, the whispers – that they suspect her of some wrongdoing. Rome is alive with talk of poisoners and necromancers, and those busybodies who noted her every injury, heard her cries, but never offered to help may be eager to place her in the growing ring of supposed witches and cunning women brewing up their evil wares. In truth, she would happily poison the lot of them at this stage, but she doesn't have the time, nor energy. She only wants to save her child. She only wants to get out.

Benedetta has decided it is best to leave today, on the day when the whole of Rome is celebrating the feast of St

Anthony. There will be a torrent of people flowing back and forth through the city gates and the guards will have little time to check everyone. Though Aurelia has been up since the first dawn light, there is no time for sluggishness or second thoughts. They complete their preparations in silence, broken only by the baby's gurgling. Both women are frightened and there is no use in talking of it. They can only hope and pray.

Anna feels a dull sickness as she takes one last look at this house: the house where she has been prisoner and mother and murderer. Will something of her distress be left in the walls, or will the new occupant have an entirely blank slate to make their life afresh? Anna hopes so. She would not want anyone else to endure what she has.

'We must go now, mistress,' Benedetta says. 'Before the neighbours are up and at their windows. Here: I'll carry that.'

The streets of Rome glisten from the rains. Sunlight glimmers on puddles; even the muck shines like diamonds. Anna wonders vaguely when she will see her city again – this place where she was born and raised; the soil in which she has grown. Within an hour, they are approaching the customs gate, and Anna's heart is almost in her throat. The baby is clutched to her breast and she feels clammy with sweat and fear. Beside her in the carriage Benedetta's body is tense, her jaw tight. They have their papers all in order, and their story lined up: Anna is travelling to Ferrara to see her mother and show her the new child. She takes with her a basket of sugared plums as a gift and only a small case of clothing and goods: not the belongings of someone intending to leave Rome for good. In fact, all the money from her pawned belongings is sewn into her cloak, and Benedetta is weighed down with silver.

In front of them in the queue, a woman is arguing with the customs officials about some leather hides that she insists she is taking out of Rome as a gift, but which they say must be intended for sale. Anna prays that the woman will hurry up and pay the bribe the men clearly expect her to give them in order to pass. With the raised voices, Aurelia begins to cry and there is little she can do to comfort her, as she is so anxious herself. Benedetta takes the child from her and walks her up and down, up and down, to try to stop the crying, but Benedetta is frightened too. Behind them, men are beginning to shout and complain that they are being kept so long waiting. 'Please, God,' Anna thinks. 'Please. Let us just pass through this gate without issue.' Her crystal rosary beads are in her hand and she prays and prays, to Mary, to Saint Philomena, to Saint Margaret.

When, finally, it is their turn to pass over their papers, Anna feels sure that the guards will know at once who she is and what she has done. She might as well have it emblazoned across her chest. The guards, however, take the parchment and glance at it without interest. She is through. She can feel the sweat trickling down her hair and down her back. 'All glory and praise are yours, Father,' she mutters. 'All glory and praise are yours.'

Next is Benedetta. Her maid stands before the guard, her face averted, the baby clutched to her. And then there is something, a flash in the man's eye. He has moved from bored to alert and Anna feels the blood drain away from her face. Dear God, no. The man has his hand on Benedetta's arm. He is shouting to his comrade. 'Stop them! This one!'

The horse rears up and whinnies, kicking its legs into the air, the dust rising around them, and Anna knows everything is lost.

34

Stefano

Stefano's day does not begin well. He wakes with a strange pain in his chest and is then denied his breakfast.

On his way to the Tower he has stopped at the baker's to which he has been going for months to collect some of his fresh, warm loaves. The doughy scent of them fills the air. The demeanour of the baker's wife, however, is decidedly less enticing.

'It's you, isn't it,' she says to Stefano, 'who's locking up all those women? It's you who's locking them in the Tor di Nona?'

Stefano is so hungry that for an instant he considers denying he is that man, claiming it is some other individual. 'I'm prosecuting a very serious matter,' he says. 'Rest assured I am not locking women up for the pleasure of it.'

Her face is as hard as day-old crust. 'And *I* am not selling our wares to men who go around arresting luckless old women.' She looks past Stefano, to the young woman who stands behind him. 'Yes, Signorina, can I help you?'

Stefano opens his mouth. Is this what people think of him now? That he is some beast who drags innocent women from the streets? They are poisoners, he wishes to tell the baker's wife, and this is my job. I am a judge, an inquisitor. I am merely doing as the law requires. I am working to the best of my ability. He sees, however, that there is little point. He will have to seek his breakfast elsewhere.

It isn't only the baker's wife who is out to thwart him, but his first interviewee of the day, La Sorda, who has been accused by a neighbour of being a seller of poison. She is a stout woman with a snub-nose who puts him in mind of a pig. Pigs, however, are reputed to be intelligent, and this woman is certainly no fool. Indeed, she nearly succeeds in making one of him. She claims to be deaf (hence La Sorda) and his attempts to get her to understand his questions move from the awkward to the farcical. He finds himself miming death by poison before realising that this woman must be able to lip-read. She is merely making things difficult for him.

'Donna La Sorda, you understand what I am asking you, and I'm asking you again what you say to the accusations that you have sold poison to other women. I am losing patience.'

'Messer Judge,' she says in her sing-song voice, 'I am a plain laundrywoman, as I've told you. I'm not in the business of selling any such thing. Whoever told you that has confused me with someone else.'

'Then there are others who sell poison? Who are these women?'

'Oh, Signore, I couldn't possibly say. I've never heard of such a thing.'

Stefano sits back and breathes out. 'You're telling me you've never heard of poison being sold in Rome?'

'It may well be sold, Signore, and indeed I've heard of

certain women buying it, but I wouldn't have any idea who from. You see, us laundresses are a close set and we keep our conversation to our own lot and to the soaps and such that we use for our trade and the clients for whom we work.' She prattles on.

Stefano interrupts: 'Which women, Donna La Sorda?'

'I've only heard rumours, Signore, and what with my ears, I might have heard them wrong. There've been many times when—'

'Nevertheless, you will tell me what the rumours are.'

'Well, let me think. I was at market when I heard the story. There was a woman called Marguerita who I've known for many years, on account of her son knowing my son, and we were talking of this and that, and—'

'Donna La Sorda, please get to the point. What rumours?'

She makes as if she has not heard him and continues with her extended reminiscences of this day in the market, so that Stefano must wave his hand before her face and say: 'Donna La Sorda, I have limited time. Tell me the rumours regarding these women.'

She pretends to be mildly affronted. 'I was getting there, Messer Judge. Marguerita, you see, she had heard from another friend of hers – a weaver – that a Duchessa had done away with her husband due to his bad breath, having been introduced to a poisoner by a noble friend. And I said to her, "Can it truly have been so bad that she murdered the man?" and Marguerita said yes, that it was like air from a sepulchre and that nothing the doctors could do made any difference.'

'A Duchessa. Which Duchessa?' Stefano thinks he knows, of course, but he wants it confirmed.

'Now, her name I don't know, but the name of the husband, it's on the tip of my tongue. I want to say that it was Cella, but I don't think that's right. It may be that I'm confusing it with another story I heard of a woman who fled her husband because of his noxious gases.'

Stefano closes his eyes. A headache is building behind them. After a minute of further prattling from La Sorda, he says: 'Ceri. Was the name Ceri?'

'Ah, yes, that's it, Signore. Well done. I didn't know that you were already aware.'

Stefano can tell from the sly look she gives him that this was a trick to ascertain what he knew.

'What else did you learn of the Duca di Ceri and his wife? Who was this friend who introduced her to a poisoner?'

'Oh, that is all I know. It sounds, Signore, as though you may know more about it than me. But then of course, you couldn't be arresting the duchessas and ladies, could you? It would only be us poor folk who you could lock up.' For the first time since she has entered the interrogation room, La Sorda permits a moment's silence.

Stefano gives a thin smile. 'For a plain laundrywoman, you know a lot about the law, Donna La Sorda.'

'Not really, Signore, though I've picked up a few things in my time. What I know about is life and its fairnesses and unfairnesses and rights and wrongs.'

'I see. And is it right, Donna La Sorda, that a woman has been cooking up poison from her book of secrets and selling lethal doses of that poison to other women so that they may do away with their husbands, brothers and fathers?'

'I'd guess, Messer Judge, that there were probably women who made it and sold it because they believed they were doing right and believed they were saving lives and stopping terrible cruelties against both women and children. Do you not have sisters of your own? Can you not imagine them in a life of intolerable cruelty, with no way out, nothing at all? Can you imagine if the secrets didn't exist because ignorant men had crushed them? But I'm a mere washerwoman and wouldn't dare comment on whether it was right or wrong according to the law or God almighty. I suppose that would be for you to determine, what with your learning and knowledge and all.'

She is sneering at him, this woman, Stefano thinks. She is saying she thinks him foolish and misguided. Worse than that, she knows about him. She knows he has sisters. What else does she know? He has had enough of this interview. He tells the guard to take her away.

★

That evening, returning from the Tower to his house, Stefano finds his staff, such as they are, waiting for him in a state of silent distress. Concetta, the maid, is white-faced, and the cook has evidently been crying. He has an awful presentiment that someone has died. He fears it is Lucia. 'What is it?' he says to them, and then, when he receives no reply, 'For God's sakes, out with it!'

The girls stare at one another and eventually Concetta says, 'Signore, you'd best see for yourself.'

She leads him to the back step and points at a wooden box. 'We put it in there. Well, the gardener did. I couldn't bring myself to touch it. It was out the front we found it. We thought ... well, we thought you wouldn't want the neighbours to see.'

Stefano stares, confused, at the box. What on earth are they talking about? His annoyance is tinged with relief, however, for at least this is not a death, nor some terrible piece of news. It is something which fits into a small box. When Concetta makes no move to open it, he removes the lid himself. What he sees inside makes him draw back as though scorched, though he tells himself not to be so foolish.

208

'What the devil is this?' It appears to be a mess of organs and metal. After a moment, his mind configures the pieces: it is some kind of bird, skinned, with needles protruding from its head and tail. Neither girl will say anything, but he knows what they are thinking: that this is a curse, a death wish, a piece of black magic left by someone who wishes him ill. Indeed, he's heard of witches skinning birds backwards in order to summon the devil.

He forces a bark of laughter. 'Oh, really! You mustn't be scared by this, you know. It's merely a trick. It means nothing. It is old women's nonsense. I'll get rid of it, if it alarms you, but truly it is nothing.' He smiles at them but their faces are still pale with fear. He knows he must pick up the box but he finds that he cannot. 'Go back to your work. Give it not another thought. I'll dispose of it shortly.'

At first, Stefano cannot bring himself to move the box, but he has a stern word with himself and picks it up with both hands, carrying it out into the garden, where he removes the bird from the box to determine if there is some clue as to who left it there. It is someone demented, that is for sure, as the poor creature is punctured like a pin cushion: a long nail protrudes from its chest and, around that, a series of smaller pins, piercing, he assumes, its heart and internal organs. He remembers the hissing woman in the cavernous dark of the Colosseum. He remembers the prostitute's claim that 'there's people here who'll put a curse on you for lies told to a friend'. It could have been sent by a friend or relative of any one of the women now locked in Le Segrete. Or it could be her: La Strolaga, La Profetessa, if indeed she exists at all.

He feels a pulse of anger. They have made a mistake leaving this for him here, in his home. Perhaps it is as Baranzone says: they are seeking to wind him in and dupe him, these women, first with lies, and now with threats. He closes the box on the creature. He will not be frightened by such tricks, nor distracted from his purpose. If anything, this must make him stronger, more determined to get to the rotten heart of this black and putrid thing.

He will go to mass this evening and pray for the Lord's protection. These women may have their curses and charms, but he has something which is surely stronger. He will call on the Holy Spirit to help him find his way through this darkness, and destroy the works of the devil.

35

'The leader should know how to enter into evil when necessity commands.'

Niccolo Machiavelli

Signore Stefano Bracchi
Le Carceri di Tor di Nona
Roma

Most Illustrious Signore,

I write to furnish you with such information as I can regarding the Aqua Tofania poisonings in Palermo. This was of course some time before my tenure as interim Viceroy, but I have gleaned what I can from the legal documents, and spoken to one of the officials who was involved with the case at the time.

It was, in summary, a vile criminal enterprise headed by one Tofania d'Adamo, who became known as La Tofania. Tofania created a slow-acting poison with which to kill her husband, Francesco d'Adamo. She then employed several women to distribute her so-called Aqua di Palermo to others who wished to carry out similar cruelties. It appears from our records that the poison was used predominantly to dispose of husbands and other men who had caused problems to the women involved. During the 'inquisitio', various claims were made of abuse, neglect and hardship, though such might be expected from criminals trying to mitigate their sentences.

Once detected, the poison was purged from the city with speed and severity. In February 1633, Francesca Rapisardi (known as La Sarda) was beheaded as one of the main poisoners. Regrettably, as the execution took place, the whole of the stage collapsed, taking with it the hundreds of people standing upon it, who fell into the huge crowd below. Some people were crushed underfoot; others were killed in the stampede that followed. Given that La Sarda had vowed vengeance on those around her, this gave rise to much talk of the poisoners having devilish powers, though of course the disaster could have had perfectly natural causes.

La Sarda's accomplice, Pietro Placido Marco, confessed under torture, but stated that the real creator of the poison was neither himself nor La Sarda but Tofania. In June 1633, Marco was executed by being quartered in four parts in the Spanish fashion. Tofania herself was executed on 12 July 1633, for killing her husband and trafficking in lethal poison. As an example to the people, she was bound and tied in a canvas sack, then dropped from the roof of the bishop's palace.

Regarding the ingredients of the Aqua, unfortunately the book of secrets you mention was never located, though several witnesses swore to Tofania owning such a book. The exact recipe is therefore not known. However, it is believed that the Aqua di Palermo was a devilish compound of arsenic, antimony and lead, distilled through some means to make it clear as communion water. It was transferred to glass bottles labelled Manna of St Nicholas which the women then sold to other women, shrouding their evil-doing with the cover of a saint.

As to any who may have escaped prosecution, the sweep of the scourge was wide and thorough. However, the former clerk recalls that Tofania was rumoured to have had an accomplice who left the city some time before the arrests – a younger woman with whom La Tofania was fast friends. It is not known to where this woman fled, nor what became of her.

I wish you fortune and strength in your fight against the evil that now courses through Rome.

With all courtesies,
Pedro Rubeo, Viceroy of Palermo

36

Anna

Anna has never been so frightened, and she thought she'd grown well acquainted with fear.

At the city gates, she and Benedetta are pushed into a black carriage, then the horses are whipped to a trot, taking them at speed through the unpaved streets. 'Tell them nothing,' she whispers in her maid's ear as the carriage jolts over stones. 'Nothing at all. I'll find a way to get us out.' Will she?

When the carriage door is opened, Anna sees the Tor di Nona rising before them, its small, dark windows like deadened eyes. Aurelia, by now, is wailing and Anna can do nothing to calm her baby, or herself. As they enter the prison she feels panic swelling in her chest like a scream. Two *sbirri* officers – immense men with the faces of gargoyles – hustle them down a vaulted passage and towards a heavy, wooden portcullis. In the room beyond this, they must sign the prison register, hands shaking, and wait, Aurelia still bawling, as a clerk lists their belongings and consigns them to a chest. How much of her silver and gold will she get back, Anna wonders? Little of it, she suspects, assuming she leaves this place at all.

On, then, through a second portcullis and into a large, eerily quiet prison courtyard. A few pigeons flap about in the wind, but of humans there is no trace. The officers hasten them up a level, then back down a winding flight of stone stairs, the air growing colder and ranker until they are in a vast stone room, barely lit, where Anna can hear the murmurs of women's voices.

A guard emerges from the shadows – his skin pale as the belly of a frog. 'That one in La Monachina,' he says, nodding at Benedetta.

La Monachina. The little nun. What is the man talking about?

The officers begin to drag Benedetta away from her and towards a cell.

'No!' Anna shouts. 'We must be together! Benedetta!' She reaches for her maid's hand, but it is too late. She is being wrenched away from her, and slung into a dark room, the door bolted behind her.

'That one in La Fiorentina,' the guard says, pointing.

The scar-faced officer urges Anna towards a dark doorway. So, all the cells have names. How quaint and incongruous, she thinks.

'But I have a child,' Anna protests. 'It is freezing cold in this place. Please, Sers, surely you must have some mercy!'

It seems, though, that they have none at all, as they bundle her into the cell and close the door behind her.

She is in almost complete darkness, only a crack of light from the tiny window filtering through the gloom.

Anna feeds Aurelia who at last sleeps. She rests her back against the stone wall. Now that the panic has subsided and the sweat dried, Anna is as cold as ice. Her baby is going to die here, she thinks. There is no way a child so young can survive for long

215

in such a place as this. She has nothing with which to clean or warm her and the place must be full of contagion and filth. She would cry, but she is still too shocked.

Then a voice. A woman's voice through the wall. 'Demand to see the doctor,' the voice tells her. 'He's a little softer than the rest. He'll give you extra blankets and rags to change the baby. For now, wrap her in your skirts and keep her right by your skin. You hear me?'

'Yes. I hear you.' Anna moves closer to the spot from which the voice seems to be coming. It must be some chink or hole in the wall. 'How do you know my baby is a girl?'

'You're Anna, the painter's widow, aren't you?'

Anna hesitates, unnerved. 'Yes, but how did you—'

'I thought so from your maid's name, and the baby. I'm Maria. I know your midwife. She's a very old friend of mine. A good friend.'

Anna thinks of the dark-haired woman with her stern face. She realises that, like the midwife, the woman who talks to her now has a Sicilian accent. 'You're a midwife too?'

'Sometimes, yes. I help women in whatever way I can.'

Anna thinks she is beginning to understand what these women are, what they do. 'Thank you, Maria.'

'Tomorrow the charity women will come from the Compagnia di San Gerolamo della Carità. They'll give you some food. Take as much as you can. See if they can give you more clothing. They don't have much, but they may be able to beg more for you, what with the child.'

Anna feels the wall between them. It is damp, crumbling. 'Are we ever let out of these cells?' she asks.

'Twice a day, for a few minutes at a time. Once to empty our slop bucket and to wash. The second to collect what food is given to us. It isn't much, though you, with your money, may be able to buy more. We aren't allowed out of Le Segrete save for when we're interrogated, but he'll be easier on you than he is on us, I'd wager.'

Anna struggles to take this in. Only a few minutes every day out of this dark hole. 'How long have you been here, Maria?'

A long pause. 'Three weeks or so. I'm not that good with counting. Not as long as some of the others.'

Dear God. 'How do you bear it?'

'*Ahi*, how do we bear any of the things we have to bear in this life, Signora? With my will, with prayer and words, and with the support of my friends.'

'They are here, your friends?' Anna asks.

'Many of them, yes.'

'You can speak to them?'

'At night, yes. Sometimes. Often the guard is drunk. Sometimes we can snatch a word or two of conversation when we get our food.'

Maybe, then, Anna will be able to talk to Benedetta. She tries to imagine the woman on the other side of the wall. Maria is old, Anna thinks from her voice, but resilient. She must be to have survived in this place. 'Maria, why are you helping me?'

Maria coughs. 'We must help each other. We have no one else, have we? We stick together in here. We do not name the people who helped us.' A pregnant pause. 'You understand, Signora Anna?'

'Yes, I understand.' Maria is telling her not to talk about Laura, not to talk about the midwife who wouldn't give her name.

But if Anna refuses to speak, is she condemning her own child to death? Is she condemning Benedetta as well? The questions burrow away at her mind like beetles.

Time passes. She rubs the baby's little limbs, but they are so cold. Anna wishes she had her rosary beads. She prays anyway, for guidance, for help. None comes. What, Anna wonders, must she do? She watches the hours creep past in the darkening of the sky outside her high window, she hears them in the chime of the bells.

Night comes. It grows still colder. Anna does not sleep.

37

Stefano

The dead bird remains in Stefano's mind, perching somewhere
in the recesses of his consciousness, a dark reminder. But if
anything, Stefano thinks, it fortifies him, drives him on despite
his exhaustion. Someone, perhaps many people, wish him
ill because of the power he now wields. Well, he will show
them that he is not cowed and that he too can instil fear. His
interview style must grow harsher and more military in its effi-
cacy. He has decided that the witnesses and suspects may now
not sit, but must stand before him, however weak or old they
may be, however tired and pained they may grow, and must
answer his questions or have them repeated, again and again
and again. Stefano is learning how to grind these people down
and how to distil the useful facts from the endless prevarication
and obfuscation. What he obtains from this distillation process
is not a pure and unalloyed substance, but something murky
and unpleasant: further stories of daughters who have sought to
escape violent fathers, sisters who have poisoned cruel brothers.
He continues, however. He has to. As Baranzone has said, it is

not for them to grant clemency where a human life has been taken, it is purely for him to investigate, to extract the truth in whatever way he can, and to do so as quickly as possible. All of Italy now knows of the river of poison that runs through its midst and the Papacy needs to be seen to be acting swiftly: cleansing the city, draining the quagmire. Stefano must therefore squash down any feelings of unease he might have and get on with it. He knows how it will be seen if he fails: he will be the weak little brother with a woman's face and a woman's heart. He can envisage his brothers' taunts, his father's quiet hostility, Baranzone's anger. That will be his career finished, his marriage prospects dashed, his place in society scuppered. No, he must employ the weapons he has – the law, and his mind – to make out the case against these women.

When Teresa, the dyer's widow, is brought before him that morning, her dark eyes already glistening with tears, he refuses to allow her to try to explain herself. She fled Rome just as this Giulia fled Palermo, possibly taking the recipe book with her.

'You must tell me now how it was. I have it on good authority that your husband much abused you, Donna Teresa. That he refused to allow you out. That he beat you severely. That he threatened to slash your mother's face.'

'Who—?'

'It matters little who told me. What matters is that those things gave you a reason to want rid of him. You must speak to me the truth.'

'But I am telling you the truth, Signore. Yes, he beat me. All the time, for the tiniest things, for a look or a word, or for nothing at all. Yes, he refused to let me leave the house, even to go to mass, so that I began to feel that I was going mad, that the four walls of the room in which I stayed were pressing in on me. Yes, he threatened me often enough that he would kill me – accused me of flirting with other men, enticing them, though I could barely see outside the window! But none of this, none of it, led me to consider harming him. Rather, I considered killing myself – though I knew it to be against God – as my life had become unliveable. But I didn't. I prayed and the Lord answered me. My husband was taken into debtors' prison.'

'Then you had some respite,' he suggests.

'Yes. His family still closeted me and shouted at me, but yes, for a time, it was not as bad.'

'And you wished he would not return.'

She stares at him. 'To wish something is not a crime, Signore.'

'No, but to make that wish come true is surely one. You procured poison and, slowly, you killed him.'

'No.'

Stefano bites his lip. 'Then your mother, Cecilia, killed him.'

Her eyes widen. 'No! *Dio*, no!'

It is a pained cry and Stefano does not like having to use this method, but he is running out of time. One of them bought the poison. One or both of them used it. 'Go back to your cell, Donna Teresa. Think about what you are telling me. Think about what repercussions it will have. One of you poisoned the dyer, of that I am sure. If you provide evidence against the other, then you yourself may be saved.'

After she has gone, Stefano realises that Lodovico is staring at him. 'What?' he asks him sharply. 'You can think of some other, fairer, means to extract the truth?'

Lodovico seems to shrink into himself. 'No, Signore Bracchi.'

The notary returns to his writing and Stefano feels a moment of powerful and irrational hatred for the silent scribe who has witnessed everything within this room. He should be thanking Stefano for the education, not questioning him with his gaze.

Stefano could have these women tortured, of course, but the thought vaguely sickens him, for some of the sellers are brittle old women, and some of the buyers (Camilla in particular) have already been tortured physically or emotionally for months, maybe years, of their lives. Moreover, he does not trust the reliability of the information it pulls out of people: he has heard of many false confessions made under extreme pain, then retracted. No, he needs a better strategy to make one of them give him the name of the person who makes the poison. He only needs one to crack, and as the days go by, and the nights remain freezing, surely one will weaken. Indeed, he asks the guards to put less wood on the fires. Some might consider it cruel (and indeed Marcello has disagreed with him on this measure), but surely that is his job as investigating magistrate: to bring the prisoners to their point of greatest weakness and in that way to obtain the truth.

The cold seems to have seeped into his own bones, as there is now a frequent pain in his chest, caused, apparently, by nothing. It meant he could not ride this morning, his one outlet from the stresses of this prosecution. Has he strained himself in some way, or might it be something more serious? He prays God it is not some disease.

There is no time to dwell on this, however, as the guard has already brought him his next suspect – another woman who attempted to flee. This one, however, is, like him, the child of a tradesman: Anna Conti. The police have confirmed that, as with the innkeeper and the dyer, the woman's husband (a painter) was known to them, for his violence to his wife and to various prostitutes. Stefano wishes that the *sbirri* had done a rather better job of curtailing these men's brutality, or they might not be where they are.

Disturbingly, when the woman enters the interrogation room, she has her sleeping baby in her arms. (*Buon Dio*, a baby, in a place such as this!) Well, he must not let this divert him from his course. She is a poisoner as well as a new mother, if

222

what he's been told is true. She does not look, however, like a poisoner. Anna is a broad-faced, handsome woman in a dark red velvet dress. Although her skin is greying with exhaustion, and her hair is greasy with lack of washing, she retains an upright bearing and a certain confidence.

He must get straight to the point. 'We have several witnesses who believe you poisoned your husband.'

The woman looks at him steadily. Her eyes are large, grey, flecked with green.

'Do you acknowledge it?' he asks. 'Will you speak the truth?'

She speaks quietly, but clearly: 'Signore, I wish for a lawyer.'

Stefano frowns. 'You have no entitlement to a lawyer, Signora Conti. Not until the case has been formally brought against you and the papers sent to the judges.' This is how the Roman law works. There is no right to representation for prisoners, even for the monied.

'Well, I am asking you to allow me access to one now so that I may consider my position. I need guidance, and quickly, particularly given the state of my child.'

He shakes his head. 'I cannot permit it. The rules do not provide for it, and if I were to allow it in your case then it might set a precedent, both in this *inquisitio* and in others.' He can see why it might make sense to allow a defendant access to a lawyer now, but were he to agree to it, the Governor would have his scalp.

'Then, Signore, I cannot tell you anything.'

He stares at this woman. Her stomach is still swollen from pregnancy, her breasts engorged. She has bruises beneath her eyes from lack of sleep. Yet she is defiant.

'I can advise you,' he says.

She shakes her head. 'No, you cannot. You are the investigator for the state.'

Stefano swallows. Begins his questions. As he asks Anna

about her relationship with her husband, the police reports that he beat her severely, the speed with which she buried him, she stares into the far distance. 'I will tell you nothing, Signore.'

Stefano finds himself wondering what would have happened had they met at some wedding or banquet. They might have conversed quite happily. He might even have courted her. Here, though, they are enemies, set apart by what she has done and what he is required to do. He says: 'Your maid might tell me, however, and it is to her I'll be speaking next.'

Anna flashes a look at him. 'My maid had no part in anything that you might allege. She is a good and faithful woman.'

'Signora, even the most faithful servants give up evidence ultimately.' Indeed, that was how the Cenci family were undone. Their servant confessed under torture.

Anna holds her baby a little tighter. 'I wish for you to apply for immunity on my behalf, and on behalf of my maid, Benedetta.' It is not a question, it is a statement. He has to admire her gall.

'You know the law, Signora?'

'I know a little, for I have read of it. I know that a prisoner may request Papal immunity and I am doing so, on behalf of myself and my maid.'

'Then you confess?'

'I seek immunity, Signore,' she says firmly, 'and safety for my child. Until it's guaranteed to me, I can give you nothing.'

Stefano regards her. The babe is still sleeping at her breast. 'We already have several women who have admitted to selling poison. We already have several sellers of the poison under arrest. That may include the woman who sold the poison to you. We will find out.'

Anna does not respond.

'So,' he explains, 'I will need something more if I am to convince the Governor to apply for immunity on your behalf.

224

I will need significant information.' He pauses. 'What we need, Signora Anna, is the name of the central poisoner.' Given her status, it is surely possible that Anna has some knowledge of her, even bought the poison from her directly.

Anna considers this for some time. He sees the motion of her face as she grinds her jaw. At length, she says quietly: 'Then you can tell the Governor that, if he promises to grant immunity for myself and my maid, and permission for my baby to be removed from this prison at once and given to a wet nurse, I will give you information that will take you further in your process.'

'What information might that be?'

'Well, that, I cannot tell you, but it may be significant.'

Is she bluffing? Does she really know something that may lead him closer to the poison-maker at the centre? Stefano cannot be sure, but the information he's so far obtained (the possibility she is a midwife, that she is Sicilian, that she must have some skills as an apothecary) has not yet taken him to his quarry.

'I request, Signore, that the Governor grants immediate permission for my child to be cared for by a wet nurse of my choosing outside this prison. It is filthy here, and freezing, and she is not feeding properly.' She holds Stefano's gaze. 'You would not wish to be responsible for the death of a child, I think.'

No, dear Lord, he would not. He has enough on his conscience, never mind that, but he doesn't wish to appear pliant. 'Of your choosing? I think not, but I can certainly ask the Governor that, should you agree to confess everything you know, your child be given into the care of a wet nurse chosen by our doctor.'

Again, the grinding of the jaw.

'Dottor Marcello is a decent man,' he finds himself saying. 'He will ensure your child is looked after.'

'Only if I confess?'

He hesitates. 'Only if you confess.'

She gives a little shake of her head. 'You would wager the life of a child against the success of your investigation?'

Stefano doesn't like that. He is not the villain of this piece. 'My investigation must succeed in order to save the lives of many,' he says, too loudly. 'The poison is still killing, as you know only too well.'

A silence pools between them. He hates that she is seeking to make him feel guilty and responsible. It is why he hasn't visited Lucia recently. He can't bear the weight of her stare.

'Very well, Signore. If you can get the Governor to agree to everything I have asked, and quickly for I fear for my child, I will give you what information I have.'

Stefano nods shortly. 'The Governor Baranzone is not in Rome, but I believe he returns tonight. I will see him as soon as possible.'

Will Baranzone agree? He has no idea. For the sake of the baby and of his own soul, he prays to God that he will.

He goes at once to Marcello, to ask him to do what he can to improve the conditions in the cell.

'I have already done what I can,' Marcello tells him, his tone abrupt. 'Last night I gave her extra blankets and straw, but the child is only a few weeks old and, Lord knows, enough babies die in the best of conditions. I would suggest we stoke the fires, as indeed I've been suggesting for some time.' He looks closely at Stefano. 'You're in pain.'

'Just some discomfort in my chest. It's nothing.'

Marcello exhales. 'When did it begin, this nothing?'

'A few days ago but it has worsened a little. I can't think what might have caused it.'

'No injuries?'

'No, none, though I suppose I could have strained it while riding.'

Marcello stands up. 'Come. I'll take a look at you.'

'Marcello, really, I don't think there's any need for that.'

The doctor points at the table. 'Would you rather I took you to a barber with his blades and leeches and bloodied table?'

Stefano grimaces. 'All right.' He allows himself to be prodded and poked by Marcello. 'Well?'

Marcello shakes his head. 'I can't say. You may, as you say, have strained it in some way. You have no other symptoms?'

'I suppose I've not been feeling particularly well these past few days. Nothing specific. Just a slight malaise.'

'That may well be strain of the mind rather than the body. You must not press yourself too hard, Stefano.'

Stefano scoffs. 'I do not suffer in that regard, my friend. I am merely getting on with the role allotted to me.'

'There's nothing shameful in acknowledging the mental weight of these matters,' Marcello says quietly. 'I too find they press upon my mind. It would be surprising, perhaps, if they did not. Young women, old women. Now a baby. I find it helps to talk to my wife of it all. Perhaps you could talk to Lucia. I would guess you are struggling to sleep.'

Stefano does not wish to dwell on such things. It's true that his dreams have been stranger recently, and that he often wakes in the night, sweating, but he is spending the bulk of his time in a dank prison. Small wonder that his dreams have taken a dark turn. 'But that would not explain a pain in my chest, in any event.'

Marcello gives a slight shrug. 'The mind can do peculiar things.'

'I assure you, man, I am not imagining this.' Stefano grimaces again. 'It is as real as anything I've ever felt. Surely there must be something to treat it.'

'I will make you up a poultice,' Marcello says, 'and I will give you a tincture of liquorice and comfrey – it should help your chest.'

'Good. Thank you.' Stefano breathes out, feeling they are on surer ground with poultices and tinctures, than with stresses of the mind. 'Then I must go to the palazzo and establish when Baranzone is due to return. I need to secure immunity for this Anna Conti and her maid, plus an agreement that the babe may go to a wet nurse. She has promised that, if I do so, she will provide me with some useful information.'

'You believe her? You don't think she's simply trying to save her child?'

'I'm not sure, but I think she may tell me something that will help us grow closer to the spider at the centre of this web.'

Marcello is writing a note to himself in his book. 'Do not let this become an obsession, Stefano. We can only do so much.'

38

To comfort the brains, and to procure sleep:
Take a red rose cake, three spoonfuls of white wine vinegar, the
white of one egg, three spoonfuls of woman's milk, set all these on
a chafing dish of coals, heat them, and lay the rose cake upon the
dish, and let them heat together. Then take one nutmeg and shew
it on the cake, then put it betwixt two clothes, and lay it to your
forehead as warm as you may suffer it.

Girolama

Girolama doesn't know what wakes her, only that she is
suddenly and sharply awake and that the room is washed
in moonlight. Perhaps it was a dream of which she has no
memory, or perhaps it was one of her women, trying to tell
her something. What?

She lies for a long time trying to fathom it, but nothing
comes, only memories she doesn't wish to recollect: Giulia
crying, a letter in her hands. A peculiar thing, for Giulia didn't
cry, not when Girolama's father died, not when Ranchetti
held a knife to her throat, nor when they left Sicily and all
her friends. But in this memory, Giulia is weeping, her whole
body wracked with it, and Girolama is frightened at seeing
this iron-strong woman suddenly splintered. She doesn't go to
Giulia or hug her, but simply watches, awaiting an explanation. None comes. Instead, Giulia locks herself away for a day

and a night. When she returns, her face is dry and the hard exterior has been rebuilt, but she is washed out. 'Your aunt Tofania is dead,' is all she tells Girolama. 'We were right to leave Palermo.'

'How? How did she die?'

'Killed in the square, like a common criminal. But she wasn't common. She was rare.' Giulia is chopping vegetables for a stew as she tells her this. 'It's on us now, Girolama, to continue the work, to keep the business alive. I've been delaying it, with you being so young, but I think now it's time for you to learn.'

Later that day, Giulia began to teach her Tofania's poison recipes, including the Aqua that she has made ever since.

Only months later, through a woman newly arrived from Sicily, did she find out about the full horror of the executions, and learn there was nothing common about Tofania's death. 'It's inhuman is what it was,' the woman told Girolama. 'She was bound in a sack. Imagine it, in the suffocating heat of Palermo? Then, she was hurled from the roof before all the people, to shatter on the street beneath.'

That image has remained with Girolama: a woman in a sack, smashed on the ground like rotten fruit. So yes, Girolama knows what may happen if she is caught and tried. She knows how it will play out. Her real concern, though, is not for herself. It is for Angelica. They're in real danger now, and when Girolama allows herself to think about it for too long the fear swells in her, becoming an uncontrollable, irrational mass. La Sorda is in the Tower, and Vanna, and Maria, and Graziosa, plus various lesser sellers and a host of buyers. Of her circle, only Laura remains at liberty, and perhaps not for much long as Anna Conti has been hauled in now, with the baby that Girolama helped pull out of her. Will she give Stefano Bracchi any information about Laura, or about herself? Will the others? It only needs for one to crumble and Stefano will work out who she is. And yes, she will deny whatever is thrown at her, but what if, under terrible torture, one of her women speaks of Angelica? Although Girolama had vowed that she would not run from Rome, she decides she must now prepare for flight. Everything must be left just so.

Bracing herself against the chill, she climbs out of bed, collects a stub of candle and lights it from the embers of the fire. She pulls her cloak on over her shift and creeps downstairs barefoot. The cat follows her, his fur brushing against her legs. She will miss him, when they go. She is growing sentimental.

In her workshop, she collects the items she needs. Outside, the garden shines silver, the frost-bound plants glistening in the moonlight. With a shovel she sets to work, trying to dent the winter-hard earth beneath the Seville orange tree. It takes some time but she manages at last to dig a hole deep enough for her purpose. Into it she puts her clothbound book and some of the glass vials she's had made, wrapped in an old shawl. As Girolama begins to scoop soil back into the hole, she feels a prickle on the back of her neck as though someone is watching her. The house, though, remains dark and silent.

The earth beneath the tree is not smooth, but it will do.

She stands and sniffs the air. There is snow on its way, she thinks. She is shivering with cold and needs to get back to bed. In the morning, she will put the rest of the plan in motion.

39

Stefano

When Stefano wakes and looks from his window, he sees a fairy-tale land of immaculate white: roofs, trees, streets, all iced with a layer of snow. Is he imagining it? He is so tired, and his existence so strange and harried, that reality seems to dip in and out of focus. He opens the window and puts out his hand. A cold flake touches it and melts in his palm. It is real, then. The snow has come.

Although Stefano has little time for visits, or indeed for anything, he knows he must go to Lucia, if only for a quarter hour. She has sent several messages asking after him. Really, she has no one else. Outside, the streets are oddly quiet, all sound muted by the snow. He rides to his father's house, hoping all the way that his father himself will be away from home but no, he is there, in the reception room as Stefano arrives, putting on his fur-lined cloak.

His father does not like to be taken unawares. He likes everything to be planned and controlled. 'You did not tell me you intended to visit. I am on the point of going out.'

'I merely stopped in on the way to see the Governor, Father, as Lucia has reprimanded me for my absence. You do not need to stay.'

His father frowns. 'Lucia is forever fussing. How goes the investigation? You near its conclusion, I trust?'

'I believe I am closing in.'

His father runs his eyes over his face and frame. 'You are thinner. You aren't sick again, are you, Stefano?'

'No, Father. Merely a little tired.'

'Always sickly,' he says with casual disdain.

Stefano has no answer to this. He hardly asked, as a child, to be laid low so frequently with illnesses, to be constantly coughing, yet his father always blamed him, as though it stemmed from some weakness of his moral fibre. Stefano wonders: why does his father dislike him so? Is it that he looks like his mother? Or is it because he is small and unimpressive-looking? It is certainly not the first time the question has occurred to him, but it is perhaps the first time he has articulated it so clearly to himself.

'I am perfectly well,' he tells his father. 'Don't let me keep you from your work.'

Stefano finds his sister checking on her silkworm eggs. In the spring they will hatch and feed, but for now they are dormant: tiny pearls. Lucia sees immediately how it is with him. He has never been able to hide things from her. It is part of the reason he has stayed away this past week, though he blames his absence on his work.

'Are you still going to mass?' she asks. 'Finding time to speak to God, at least?'

'You needn't worry about me, Lucia.' In fact, he has spent little time in church of late. It seems an incongruous place to be and besides, he is needed elsewhere.

'I do worry, Stefano, whether you want me to or not. You look drained.'

'I was always of a sickly disposition, as you'll recall, but I always recover. With your help.'

'You do.' She half-smiles at him. 'But, Stefano, I know when you're unhappy.'

'Ah, do you now? And what about you, Lucia? Are you happy?'

'I am content enough, brother.'

'Do you not wish to escape our father's house?' It seems such a claustrophobic place to him. Even being there for a few minutes has stifled him more than the prison walls.

'In fact,' Lucia says, 'I am considering taking holy orders.'

'No! A nun! Well, I can see a convent might be more appealing than this house and its inhabitants. But you're not serious? Would you not rather remarry?'

'Yes, Stefano, I think I am serious. I believe I would find peace there, and occupation, and I have no desire to be locked into wedlock and perpetual pregnancy as most women are. But it is you we are talking of now and your own peace of mind. You are in pain?'

She has seen him wince as a strange pulse passes his chest. 'Only a little. An injury, perhaps from horse-riding.' He knows, though, that was not what caused it. The pain seems to come from nothing and to worsen every day. He cannot help but think of the box and its mangled bird.

'Let me get you some liniment.'

'Really, Lucia, there is no need. Marcello has given me a poultice.'

'Does it help?'

'A little.' Not at all.

She stares at him. 'I can't imagine it's easy, knowing that

you're responsible for so many women being under lock and key; knowing that their lives are in your hands.'

'No, it isn't easy.' He thinks of Camilla's tear-streaked face, Anna Conti's baby. 'But then I never thought it would be. You warned me, remember?'

'I merely thought it right to tell you that Baranzone always does what is in his own interests, even if it harms others.'

Stefano considers her. 'Did something happen between you, Lucia?'

She breathes out. At length, she says: 'Many, many years ago, when I was much younger and prettier, he paid me some attention.'

'Oh, indeed? And?'

'And Baranzone was also young at that time, and without the power that he now has. Father wanted a better match for me – someone older, richer, of higher status.' She gives a tight smile. 'So Baranzone was disappointed. He is, as I'm sure you've deduced, not a man who likes to lose, and he blamed me, in part, for the refusal. His words to me then were cruel.'

'What words?' Stefano is instantly furious. 'What did he say to you?'

'Little brother, this is all a very long time ago and I do not tell you so that you may be angry with him. I tell you so that you are clear on what kind of man he is. He is a man, I think, who hates women.'

Stefano sits back in his chair. 'What did he say to you, Lucia?'

Lucia folds her arms. 'He said that I, and my family, would live to regret not having chosen him. That my life would be cold and barren and that ultimately, I would die alone.'

'How dare he—'

'He was right, though, Stefano, wasn't he?' She laughs. 'I am childless and alone.'

'You are not alone.' Stefano puts his hand over hers. 'And you could remarry if you wished to.'

She shakes her head. 'I do not wish to. Nor am I asking for your sympathy. I have a decent life compared to many in this city. But I do not want you to view women as he does.'

'Really, Lucia, do you think so little of me?'

'I think greatly of you, but I also know that you strive too hard to please; that you often think yourself inadequate when in fact you are strong. I am trying to ensure that you don't end up doing things, sanctioning things, that will degrade your moral nature and that you will later come to regret. Did you ask Baranzone about the wisdom of prosecuting these women, when the facts were particularly awful?'

Stefano takes his hand away. 'I did, and he was clear, as I suspected he would be. I am the investigator. I collect the evidence and I pass it to him; he then requests clemency from the Pope in the most egregious cases.'

She scoffs. 'I would not want to be reliant for mercy on that man.'

'Alexander? I thought him generous. Has he not given much money to the poor?'

'Perhaps he has, but from what I hear he has little interest in their lives. No, I would rather be reliant on you for clemency, brother.' She holds his gaze.

'As I say, that is not my role, Lucia. I can only bring forward the evidence for the prosecution.'

Lucia drums her fingers on the table. 'I think we all have to decide what our role in life is, Stefano.' She gets up. 'It's no wonder you do not sleep, little brother, with that on your conscience. I tell you, go to confession. It will make you feel better in yourself. I will pray for you.'

'Lucia, I don't need your prayers.'

'Oh, but you do. I'm sure that there are many summoning

their spirits and saints against you at the moment. Indeed, I heard via the servants that someone had left you a sign of sorcery.'

Stefano silently curses Concetta, his maid. 'They did, and I treated it with the seriousness it deserved. Which is to say I threw it out and thought no more about it. Nor should you. It's old women's nonsense.'

Lucia remains silent. She will know, of course, that he has indeed been thinking of it, because she will remember how credulous he was as a child. She'll remember how he'd mutter protective charms and how the shriek of an owl would frighten him. So much was taught to him by their nursemaid and, however much one may try to talk oneself out of some habits later in life, they stick like the Tiber mud.

All she says, however, is: 'Not all old women are full of nonsense.'

Stefano leaves shortly afterwards, hurrying to the stables and urging Damigella forward with a click of his tongue. He will go fast to the Governor's palazzo in the hope that he has now returned, that he will listen to Stefano's arguments, and grant the requests Anna Conti has made. Given what Lucia has told him, however, he does not have high hopes of success.

40

Anna

During the night, screaming. Anna thinks someone is being murdered in their cell.

Then a woman shouts: 'Camilla! You're dreaming, Camilla! Wake up!'

Hammering on one of the cell walls. 'Camilla!'

After a moment, the screaming stops. There is crying, then scuffling.

'Camilla Capella, he is gone, you hear me?' It is Maria's deep voice from the cell next to Anna's.

Other women begin to speak then, and from the cell on the other side of hers, Anna hears: 'You're all right, girl. You're all right.'

That is Vanna who speaks. Anna has talked with her several times. She is over sixty years old and says she has lost count of how many days she has been in this prison, but that she's been here the longest. 'It's my fault,' she told Anna the previous evening. 'It's my fault Maria is here, and that all the other women are here. If I'd held out and told him nothing, then he'd still have only me, and I'm only skin and bone. He said he'd find my daughter in Ferrara and have her arrested. But maybe that was a lie.'

'Maybe,' Anna replied, 'but you can't be blamed for believing it.' What if, she thinks, with a stab of fear, he is telling each one of them whatever he needs to elicit their innermost thoughts? If that is true, then what of his promise about her baby? Was that an empty claim? Aurelia now sleeps almost all of the time. She is sleeping now, despite the tumult. Anna can feel the baby's chest rising and falling and it seems to her that her heart flutters too quickly.

On the other side of Le Segrete, Camilla has stopped crying. Gradually, the cells return to silence and some of the other women seem to go back to sleep. Anna, though, is too frightened. Camilla's screaming has rattled her. It has made her think of Philippe. She is terrified, too, that Aurelia will die during the night. She sits awake trying to encourage her to feed, thoughts chasing around her head. Even assuming the Governor has returned to Rome and Stefano has managed to see him, Anna is far from certain he will have granted her requests, for she's heard he is an uncompromising individual. 'A mean *mascalzone*', in Maria's words. What, then, will she do? What other recourse does she have?

And what if, in fact, he agrees to what she asks? Will she really leave Aurelia in the hands of some woman she has never met? Will she really give up information about the women who helped her survive? Though she has little affection for Laura, she nonetheless gave Anna the way out in the form of a glass bottle. She may not be likeable, but she is a woman who saved her life. As for the dark-haired midwife, Anna thinks she knows now who she is. She thinks she knows what she is and what she makes. How much of that must Anna give Stefano? How much of it can she hold back and still escape with her life, and that of her maid and child? 'Significant information,' he said. How little can be deemed significant? How small a fragment will lead to Girolama being tracked down? Anna thinks and prays – rounds of Hail Marys and Our Fathers – but, in the depths of this dark and freezing place, it is difficult to believe her prayers are heard. Certainly no answers come. Aurelia seems listless. Still she will not feed.

At last, the silver light of dawn creeps across the cell and the sounds of the morning begin: the sloshing of water in buckets, the barking of a dog. Then the guard's heavy boots on the stone floor outside her cell. He is coming for her again. She tries to steel herself. *Protect us, Lord, under the shadow of your wings.* There comes the sliding of the bolt, the clanking of the door opening, and he is there: the prison guard with deadened eyes, his skin the colour of a grub. 'Get up,' is all he says.

Anna pulls herself to standing, keeping the blanket around her baby. She follows the guard through the open cell door and up the dark, narrow steps, squinting as the way grows lighter. As she goes, she rubs at her face and teeth with the hem of her gown and tries to tidy her hair beneath her cap – to make herself feel more human and to prepare for what is to come.

The guard leads her into the same, large room she saw before: four stone walls, a mouldy tapestry of a knight astride his horse and, thank the Lord, a fire. Stefano is in his wooden chair, straight-backed and tense, just as she was when she first met him. Has he succeeded in speaking to and persuading the Governor? He does not look like a man happy with his achievements, but perhaps he never does. On the other side of the room sits the doctor who has been giving her blankets and syrups for the baby. There is the young clerk too, who stands as she enters the room. There is something sly about him that Anna doesn't like, how his eyes slide over her. Once again he presses a gilt-edged bible into her hands and makes her swear on it. Once again he reads the preliminaries in Latin. All the time, Anna is looking at Stefano and she is thinking: has this man managed what he said he would, and, if he has, what am I to say?

'Signora Anna, are you now ready to speak the truth?' Stefano asks as she takes the seat before him.

Closer up, she sees his eyes are bloodshot, the veins of the skin beneath them showing blue like a bruise. Well, she will not feel any pity for him. He slept on a bed, last night, not in a freezing cell. 'You have spoken with the Governor?'

'I have.' He hesitates. 'I am pleased to say that he is willing to apply to His Excellency Pope Alexander about securing a pardon, providing you give a full confession, including information which will help us find the key poisoner.'

Anna's heart is racing. 'And immunity for my maid, Benedetta?'

'On behalf of her also,' he says.

'You are sure? He made that clear?'

'Yes, that is what Governor Baranzone said. He said that if you provide information that will help us find the key poisoner, then he will apply for immunity for both of you.'

'What about Aurelia?' She is leaning forward, her speech too rapid. 'He will allow her to go to a nursemaid?'

The doctor, Marcello, speaks now. 'I have arranged for her to go to a wet nurse today. A good woman who is known to my wife.'

Anna releases her breath. She had not realised how constricted her chest was, how tense her whole body. 'You promise me? My baby will be safe?'

'We will do what we can,' Marcello says.

'Thank you,' Anna says. Pain and relief wash over her in a wave. She clutches Aurelia closer to her chest and tries very hard not to cry.

Stefano gives Anna only a moment to recover herself, then says: 'And now: your side of the bargain.'

Ah yes, the bargain, which Anna feels she might have done with the devil, for she knows what she will be giving up: the name of the woman who was her route out of hell. She is potentially also getting Stefano closer to the person at the heart of it all: the woman who made the Aqua, who saved her life. How many others like her has Girolama helped? How many women is Anna condemning by helping Stefano bring her to so-called justice? But she must give him something. 'Very well,' she says.

The notary dips his quill in his ink pot.

'Signora Anna, can you tell me how it was?' Stefano says. 'Can you explain to me how you killed your husband, and from whom you bought the poison, how the poison worked?'

He makes it sound so simple. In a way, it is. She tells him. She tells him about the beatings, the stabbing, the constant fear, her desperate attempts to seek help elsewhere. She tells him how she believed Philippe killed her father. Why should she conceal the reason she resorted to poison? Why should it all be her own shame, what he did? It is a strange thing to see her words being re-formed by the pale notary on his piece of parchment: the details of how Philippe would vow that he would kick the baby out of her, how the priest told her that she must forebear and submit, how the police visited, then went away. So many painful stories rewritten in the language of the law. She wonders how many other tales he has in that book, and how many of them are like hers.

'How did you know whom to seek out?' Stefano asks her quietly. His eyes are on the floor. Has her account affected him? If it has, he will not say so. No doubt he thinks that is what makes a man strong.

'My maid, Benedetta, suggested a woman, but she did not

know that she sold poison. Benedetta thought she might be able to reconcile my husband and myself.'

'Who was she, this woman? What was her name? When and where did you meet her?'

'Laura is her name. I don't know her surname.'

'Where does she live? What does she look like?'

Anna pauses for a long time. Then she tells him, because that is part of the devil's bargain. From the interest with which Stefano listens and the speed with which the notary writes, she can tell that they had not been aware of Laura. She has given them another prisoner and the realisation is sharp and painful, but it is a sacrifice she must make.

'You said when we last spoke that you could give me significant information that would take me further in my investigation.' Stefano is looking at her now with his bloodshot eyes. 'What is that information?'

Anna swallows. Is she truly going to help him find this woman?

'Well?' Stefano insists, leaning forward. 'Do you know who she is? Do you know who makes the poison?'

She sees in that moment that his need to know is not rational, nor ordered, but obsessive. It has become a hunt.

'I cannot tell you who your poison-maker is,' she says at last, and she sees Stefano's body sag. 'I can, however, tell you what Laura said to me about her house. She said it was on the other side of the river, that it had a herb garden and, and a sign of a lily.' She hesitates. 'Laura said too that the woman had two sons alive, and two husbands dead.'

'Anything else? What else did she say?'

'She said that the woman who made the poison guarded her book of secrets closely.'

'I'm sure she does,' Stefano says. 'Any other comment or clue as to this woman's identity?'

Anna shakes her head. 'That was all.' Will it be enough, she wonders? For a long moment Stefano is silent and she thinks it won't be, and that he will renege on what he has agreed. Fear flutters like a moth in her chest.

But then he says: 'We will find this Laura, and she shall tell us.' To the doctor, he says: 'I will go this moment to speak with the officers. I myself will find the poisoner.' Stefano stands up and Anna thinks she sees a twinge of pain in his face.

'Signore Bracchi,' – she stands too – 'what will happen now? Will Benedetta and I be moved?'

'No, Signora Conti. Until the investigation is concluded and the *processo* is over, you will both remain in Le Segrete, just like the other prisoners.'

Her heart falls, but what, really, had she been hoping? That they would simply be allowed to go home? 'Please at least let me see Benedetta. Let me tell her that she will not be harmed.' Anna realises she has begun to cry. This was a mistake, for she sees Stefano brace himself, preparing to crush his sympathy and act the stern figure of authority.

'Signora Conti, I will inform Benedetta of the application but I cannot allow the prisoners to speak to one another. Those are my orders. It is how the law operates. I have done everything I can for you.'

Anna swallows. 'And my baby? Her limbs are so cold.'

'I will send for the wet nurse now,' Marcello says. 'She will be with us within the hour. For the time being, you may sit in my room, and I will stoke the fire.' He looks at Stefano as though he expects him to challenge him. He does not.

The doctor takes Anna to his little room, which is neat and clean and warm. He attends to Aurelia and listens to her heartbeat, his face set in a frown. Once he has wrapped the baby in another blanket and dribbled warm water into her mouth, he places her back in Anna's arms and says he will ensure the child leaves the prison as soon as possible. He is going to arrange it now.

Once he has gone, Anna sinks to the floor by the fire, her baby still in her arms, unmoving. She stays like that, her mind a blank, until a bell begins to toll and she realises half an hour has passed and her time with her Aurelia is nearly up.

41

Stefano

Could the poisoner, La Profetessa, have sent the snow to thwart him? Do women have the power to do such things?

The flakes come thick and fast now, and Damigella shakes her mane to rid herself of them. Stefano himself is wrapped in a cloak with his hat pulled down low over his forehead, but his gloves are wet through, and his hands ache with cold.

He and Bertuccio have spent hours riding through streets on the west side of the river, trying to find this house with its sign of a lily. No one seems to know what they are talking about. A house with the sign of a rooster? Yes. A lion, a wolf, weighing scales, a comet? All of these they have been told about, but not a house with a lily. Perhaps this Laura meant real lilies, and of course those would hardly be blooming in the snow. As for her talk of a woman with 'two sons alive and two husbands dead', this too has got them nowhere. Almost everyone to whom they speak knows of someone who has lost a husband to the plague, and another husband who perished of some malady or accident. How weakly the flame of human life flickers. (He thinks again of Anna Conti's baby and prays to God the child will revive.) Numerous people know of women with two sons. Almost everyone knows a woman with a herb garden. It is like sifting through a huge pile of autumn leaves to find one single oak leaf.

'We should turn back,' Bertuccio says. 'We're getting nothing but frostbite. I wonder if this Anna Conti of yours didn't send us on a chase for a wild boar.'

'No, I don't think so.' Stefano is remembering her face, her eyes. She looked as wretched as he feels. Surely she was telling him the truth. Unless this Laura had lied to Anna. 'We just need to find the right person to lead us to her.'

'Maestro, we could search all of the city to the west of the Tiber and not find them, or we find them but they don't tell us the truth.' Bertuccio is already turning his horse back and Stefano feels a spark of annoyance beneath his exhaustion. He is the investigator here. It is for him to say when the search is done. However, Damigella is tired, the sky is darkening, and he knows they will find nothing at this hour. More likely they will run into trouble.

He longs for his bed, but he needs to return to the Tower to see if Maffeo has found Laura, the poison seller. She is the woman who may tell them the answers.

By the time he is back at the Tor di Nona and has rubbed down Damigella with some sacking and fed her, Stefano can barely feel his limbs.

'God's bread, Stefano,' Marcello admonishes him. 'What are you trying to do? Kill yourself?'

Stefano allows Marcello to rub warm lavender oil on his hands. 'I am trying, my friend, to find our poisoner, and I am getting very close.'

'Please let the *sbirri* find her and focus on the witnesses, or I will be obliged to explain to Baranzone why his inquisitor has frozen solid.'

Though his hands are now burning with pain, Stefano laughs, imagining the scene in which the doctor tells the Governor that he's encased in a block of ice. 'He would simply take a torch to me, Marcello. Lord knows, he may do that anyway, if I don't conclude this matter soon enough.'

Marcello raises an eyebrow. 'He is not a man known for his patience, but you can't achieve the impossible. You must slow down, Stefano. Take some hot wine and something to eat. I will send a guard out to an *osteria* for food.'

'There is no need—'

'Yes, there is a need,' Marcello says firmly. 'You've grown thinner these past weeks and you must retain your strength. There will be battles to fight before we reach the end of this thing and, as my mother says, you cannot fight on an empty stomach.'

Stefano smiles. 'Who are we planning to fight? The devil?'

'Oh, I don't think it's quite so simple as that, is it? Nevertheless, you need some sustenance before you interview your next prisoner.'

'My next prisoner?'

'I didn't want to tell you until you'd rested, but Maffeo has found her: this Laura character. Perhaps she'll save you another expedition through the snow.'

Laura Crispoldi, also called Lauraccia: Wicked Laura.

She certainly looks the part, Stefano thinks, as she is led into the room: a scrawny, sour-faced woman, the flesh spread so thin over her bones that Stefano can see her ribs through her dress, and the skin over her cheekbones is like parchment. Her eyes are a wintry grey.

248

'Donna Laura, you sell poison to women who wish to be rid of inconvenient husbands.'

'Whoever told you that will have their tongue ripped out.'

'Oh, I don't think so. I think the punishments will be reserved for those who committed the crimes, unless they are willing to loose their own tongue and speak. Unless they are willing to assist the law with the discovery of the key criminal.'

Something flickers in Laura's eyes, a movement beneath the surface. 'I don't know what you mean, Signore.'

'You know perfectly well. You make your money from selling a slow-acting poison. Unless you tell me who makes it, then it will be your neck that will be stretched. Do you understand?' He has arranged this interview in the room from whose high vaulted ceiling hangs the pulley with a rope where they subject prisoners to the strappado. He doesn't intend to use such torture on this skeleton of a woman, but he wants for her to think he might. He is running out of time and patience.

'I'm a poor old woman, Signore.'

'You are a woman who sells poison, who knows who makes the poison, and who knows where the poison-maker lives.'

'I am merely a laundry woman, I tell you.'

'Ah, the laundry again. It is a miracle how much money may apparently be made in Rome from washing clothes in the filthy Tiber. That is not the only way you make your living, Donna Laura.'

'I sometimes sell second-hand clothing and take in bits of sewing where I can. I make a poor living, Signore.'

'You make a decent living by selling poisons,' he shouts, 'so let us have none of this misery-story of your life.'

Her face seems to shrink into itself when he says this, her eyes narrowed, like a snake eyeing him up as prey. 'You have no idea what my life has been like, Signore. My husband abandoned me. My own daughter left me after I'd given her everything. I have made it through this life alone, with no one, but no one, to support me.'

Small wonder, Stefano thinks. If he was her child, he would have run away as soon as his legs would carry him. 'You have a decent enough house in Rome, and property elsewhere. You make that money from selling a slow-acting poison. What is it? Who makes it? Where does she keep her book of secrets?' He speaks quickly and firmly.

Laura tilts her head slightly. 'But if I were to tell you anything, Signore …?' She spreads her hands.

'If you are concerned about repercussions, I can assure that, certainly while you are in this prison, there is no means by which she can get to you.'

The woman emits a strange wheezing sound, which he realises is laughter. She is laughing at him.

'Something is funny, Donna Laura? Please enlighten me as to what is so humorous.'

She considers him, snake eyes still. 'What you're dealing with, it isn't something that these stone walls will keep out. There's no protection you can offer that would protect me, were I to speak. That's why no other woman speaks either, I'd wager, and I'll guess you've asked a few, have you not?'

Stefano feels a prickle of coldness. He looks at the snow still falling outside. 'We have ways of making you speak.'

Laura glances up, at the rope. She shrugs, as if it were nothing. 'Well, Signore, you may have to try that.'

It is as if she knows. It is as if she cuts through his skull to his mind and sees that he does not have the strength to use these instruments. He says coldly: 'We have two witnesses, Donna Laura, who confirm that you sold them poison. That means we may convict you without your confession. I don't need you to tell me anything for me to have you sent to the hangman. You told Anna Conti, the painter's widow, that the

250

woman who made poison lived on the other side of the river in a house with a garden full of herbs. Where is that house? Where does she keep the book? This is your one and only chance to save yourself.'

Laura lets the silence spread, and Stefano allows it, for he can see she is thinking over her options. At last she begins to whisper. 'I can't tell you where she keeps the book, I've never seen it, but I can tell you something better. I can tell you who—' She begins to cough: an awful, hacking sound. Stefano waits, but it goes on and on. She cannot seem to stop. It reminds him of himself as a child, the blood-flecked phlegm, the cough that would not end.

Stefano glances at Lodovico who is staring at the woman, frowning. They exchange a look as the coughing continues. Is this some ruse to avoid speaking the truth?

The woman puts her hand to her mouth, then holds it before her, aghast. She is no longer coughing. Her hands are stained with blood, and blood drips too from the side of her lips.

Stefano stands, makes to move towards Laura, then backs away again. What is this: a trick?

The woman's eyes though, when they meet his, are not guileful as they were before. They are wide and empty with horror.

42

Stefano

The whinny of a horse, a man's shout. People are arriving in the prison yard. Even before Stefano is at the door to his room, a guard appears, his eyes wide with excitement. Marcello is close behind him.

'The Governor is here, Signore,' the guard says. 'And his men.'

Stefano dully registers an increase in the pain in his chest above the questions screaming in his mind: why is the Governor here? What has he done wrong? 'Then you must bring them up at once.'

'Very good, my lord.'

Stefano and Marcello exchange a look. 'Evidently some development,' Marcello says.

'Or some catastrophe.'

'Not of our making, Stefano. Stay strong.'

Stefano nods and attempts to brace himself. He has done nothing wrong, nor Marcello. He has avoided speaking to the nobles, as he was ordered. He has extracted information and confessions that narrow the gap between them and the key poisoner. He has been working to the best of his abilities.

Any conviction he has managed to summon falls away as Baranzone enters the room, his paunchy face a distressing red. He is followed by two guards, immense men, one with a face pitted by pox.

'Gentlemen,' the Governor says, once he has caught his breath. 'I come direct from a meeting with His Excellency.'

Stefano feels his stomach drop.

'He is much displeased,' Baranzone says, his eye intent on Stefano. 'Word has got abroad of your *inquisitio*. An ambassador writes to him from Spain to tell him it is much spoken of there – a poisoning conspiracy at the heart of the Papal States.' His breath is still laboured and, from across the room, Stefano can smell the sweat on him. 'There is talk too in France, of how Rome is being whipped into a frenzy, with fears of enchant-resses and witches trafficking with the devil. Rome! The centre of Catholic religion! The supposed exemplar to the world.'

'I am sorry to hear that word has carried so far,' Stefano says levelly, though there is a part of him that relishes the idea that his case is talked of elsewhere in Europe. 'We have been working as quickly as we can and doing what we can to avoid such talk.'

'You have not been doing ENOUGH!' Baranzone's words are like a blast of angry rain. 'You have not been acting fast enough, quietly enough. I warned you when you began all this that you were to be discreet.'

'Yes, Monsignore, and we have been doing our best, but we have a prison full of suspects and witnesses. We cannot stop the people of Rome from guessing at what we are about, and I assure you we are very close to detecting the key poisoner. I need only a few weeks—'

'You do not have a few weeks, Bracchi. You have ten days.

Ten days to wrap the whole thing up and get the papers sent over to the *Congregazione Criminale*. His Excellency is clear on that. There can be no more prevaricating or pandering to these women. Rome must be cleansed of sin, and before Lent.'

Stefano feels the flush of anger rise to his face. What does Baranzone think he's been doing all these weeks? Sitting here on his arse? He has barely done anything else, barely slept, while working on this *inquisitio*. It is destroying him. 'Governor,' he says coolly. 'We are very close. We have been working very hard. The truth is unwinding. But ten days? It is simply not possible.'

'Then make it possible. Change your methods. Change your men. We need confessions. We need the ringleader.' He puts up a hand to prevent any further argument. 'These women know, Stefano. These stinking, festering women. They *know*. And it is your job to extract the information and the confessions from them. You told me you had the stomach for it, so in God's name, do it.'

Stefano stares at Baranzone, hating him, hating himself for fearing him and for fearing what he has to do. 'It may be that it cannot be done, Monsignore, no matter what methods we employ.' He is thinking of Laura's mouth full of blood.

'Oh yes, it can be done. Find. A. Way.' Baranzone separates the words so that each is a hammer blow. 'Or you will find that your tenure as investigating magistrate is over.' He glances at Marcello who stands in the shadows, silent. 'You know what your role is in this, Dottore. I will not have you declaring that the prisoners are all too physically weak to be tested.'

'Several of them are old women,' Marcello says quietly. 'Others are decrepit or sick.'

Baranzone shrugs. 'If we lose a few in this process, so be it. It is an evil necessary for the greater good.' He turns to leave. 'Do not disappoint me in this. Rome's reputation depends upon it.'

Once the men have gone and he can hear their footsteps re-treating, Stefano releases a long breath. 'Well, at least he was clear,' he says into the silence.

'Will you do it?' Marcello says. 'What he asks?'

'I don't see that I have much choice in the matter.' Stefano affects levity, though he feels none.

'Yes, you have a choice,' Marcello says. 'You've told me yourself: torture doesn't work. The confessions it extracts are rarely true. That's been shown in the witchcraft inquisitions throughout Europe, but then they were not interested in truth.'

Stefano rubs his eyes. 'Do you have another solution? Another way that we may get the results we need within a little over a week?'

Marcello shakes his head. 'No. What he asks is impossible, or near it.'

'What, then, would you have me do, Marcello? Abandon the inquisition at this point? I cannot, either for my own career, nor for the good of this case. However understandable the motives of some of these women, at its core this is a poisoning ring: a group of women who acted primarily from the desire to make profit. We don't know the central figure as yet, but she's no saint or protector of the weak. She has been the architect of tens, perhaps hundreds, of deaths. If we do not catch and convict her, she will continue. They will continue.'

Marcello folds his arms. 'Even if you do extract the confes-sions, Stefano, even if they do secure convictions, this poison will not die out with its maker, just as it didn't die out in Palermo. Surely you see that. It's not as simple as Baranzone would like to pretend. So long as there is a need for it, then women will try to ensure the Aqua remains in circulation. This demand for a swift finale – it is all a pretence. It's all for show.'

'Nevertheless, it is what we are being asked – no, *instructed*

– to do.' (Stefano hears Bruno's voice again: '*I doubt you have the mettle for the task, little brother.*') 'I told Baranzone I had the stomach for this mission. I can't baulk at it now because the task is unpleasant. This is the process of the law.' He walks from the room to prevent any further argument from Marcello. He must, Stefano thinks, remain focused on his path and on his task, or he will not be able to go through with it, and then he will be the man he always feared he was.

★

Stefano waits until the light begins to fade, then takes the steps down to Le Segrete. It is the first time he has done so since they first arrived at the Tower more than six weeks ago and he is taken aback by the acrid, animal stench of the place, by the deep darkness, and by the sounds that filter between the grilles of despair and pain and fear. It is like descending into hell. The guard at the main door jumps up as he arrives, and Stefano sees at once that the man is drunk. Who can blame him, perhaps, in a place such as this? And yet it is a place that Stefano has created.

'What it is, Ser?' the guard slurs.

'I come to speak to all the prisoners together,' Stefano says.

'You want me to let them out of their cells?'

'Lord, no.' For he cannot stand to see them. 'They must merely be able to hear me.'

The guard takes a bell which he rings three times. Immediately, the moans and whispers cease, leaving in their wake an eerie quiet. The guard looks at Stefano expectantly and for an awful moment Stefano cannot think how to start his speech, or what to call these women collectively. No word seems to fit.

'Prisoners,' he settles on at last. 'You will have heard the horses in the yard, the feet on the stairs. The Governor of

Rome himself has been here. He has made clear that we must get to the end of this evil matter, and quickly. There can be no further delay. You each must speak the truth or it will be pulled from you.' He pauses to allow them to take this in. 'The Governor has stated that no exceptions will be made and no pity will be shown. We must have the truth, from all of you.' Still, silence reigns in the cells. Has he made himself clear enough? 'Tomorrow, you will be put to the question,' he says. Someone begins to weep. 'For some the sibyl, for others more extreme methods.'

'No!' a woman shouts.

Others take up the cry. 'Please God, have mercy on us!'

'We've told you all we know!'

'Please!'

More crying, more shouting, and it is like a terrible, rising dirge.

'Enough!' Stefano shouts, surprising himself with his anger. He does not want to hear it. He cannot. 'I have told you how it is. This is how the machinery of justice works. I am giving you a chance, an opportunity. Tomorrow morning, you may speak the truth by your own free will. After that, it is out of my hands.' Strictly speaking, at least, for it will not be his hands, but those of the guards, which will tighten the ropes and screws. 'Think on it carefully tonight. I must have the truth and I must have the name of the person who makes the poison. Give me that and you may be saved.'

Stefano turns from them and walks back towards the staircase.

'*You* won't be,' comes a low voice. He cannot recognise it. It seems neither male nor female.

He spins back round. 'Who speaks there?'

No answer. Stefano looks at the guard, but the guard merely shrugs. Does he really not know?

'I do what I am required to do,' Stefano says, as much to himself as to his hidden accuser. 'What the law requires me to do. It is not my soul which is in danger.'

As he climbs the stairs, Stefano tries to put the foulness of the air and the wretchedness of the sounds from his mind. Women are calling to one another, trying to comfort one another. Others are crying and wailing. Perhaps the Governor was right and it must be over with as soon as possible. He will speak to the guards tonight. They must start their horrible work first thing. He must have it over and done with so that he himself can breathe again.

43

Remedy for the nerves:
For the nerves over cooled, especially these are profitable, germander,
castoreum, the brain of a hare roasted, lesser centaury, root of St
Johns-wort, lavender, myrrh, pine kernels, dog fennel, primrose,
Italian spike, sage, and pitch-smelling trefoil.

Girolama

There must, Girolama thinks, be some way of stopping him,
some way of thwarting him, but what? Her preparations and
curses haven't been strong enough. Perhaps she's losing her
touch, or perhaps she deluded herself that she ever had such
powers and she's simply a foolish woman. She hurries about her
house, continuing with their preparations, snapping at anyone
who gets in her way: Cecca, the cat, Angelica. 'Mother, you're
as an angry as a jar full of bees.'

'Don't test me today, Angelica.' They don't see what she
sees, nor feel what she feels. In truth, she wouldn't want them
to, for it's as though the winter frost has crept into her soul.

Though she knows she shouldn't have done so, Girolama
went last night to the mirror, the spirit mirror, as she couldn't
bear to be kept in the dark as to what was going on in the
Tor di Nona. What she saw there, or in her own mind, has
made her wretched, for it was a looking glass full of pain. She
saw Vanna's face, La Sorda's, Maria's: the women who've

supported her for so long. She saw their torments, felt their fear growing like a monster in the dark. Should it be her there in that Tower, rather than them? For is this not mainly her doing? It's untypical for Girolama to have such ideas: she who's always focused on self-preservation. Perhaps she's growing feeble-minded with age.

'There's nothing else you can do for them,' Cecca tells her. 'What will be will be.'

Girolama wants to slap her. 'Cecca, don't talk to me. Go and make yourself useful elsewhere. Pack up the gardening tools.'

Surely there is something she can do. There has to be. She must find some way to use the nervous energy that sears through her or she will go mad, driven wild by the imaginings and the guilt that come to her whenever she's unoccupied. For many years she's managed to control her thoughts and memories, but now they rush upon her unawares, as though a dam or a sore has burst. She's even started to think of the men who've died, and God knows most of them deserve no pity. They are a rotten bunch of *bastardi*. Admittedly, there've been a few whose deaths she wouldn't have wanted (the sisters who poisoned their husbands for no better reason than dislike, the woman who claimed she needed the Aqua for her cruel father, but gave it to her stepson instead), but she never gave them the poison herself, did she? None of it can be pinned on her, not really, so why are these thoughts coming now? It occurs to her that they may not all be her own thoughts: they may be Vanna's seeping into hers. She thinks she can sense her friend's despair, though she's locked behind a series of stone walls over a mile away.

Then, for seemingly no reason at all, she remembers one of her final conversations with Giulia, when her stepmother was not far from the end.

'I sometimes think, Girolama, that I shouldn't have taught

you. That I should've carried on alone and left you to your own life.'

'Don't be ridiculous, *Madregna*. Why would you think that now?'

Giulia stroked her face, her fingers dry and papery, as though all moisture had been sucked from her body. 'Because it is a lot to ask of someone, and it can wear down the soul.'

'You're tired and talking nonsense. You've taught me almost everything I know and I don't regret that for a moment. Neither should you. You think me miserable? Mostly certainly I am not.'

Girolama wonders now if in fact Giulia was saying something else; if she was saying that Girolama had grown too hard, too angry, too careless of human life. Has she? Is that what Angelica also will become, after she herself is no more, or will the girl's good nature protect her? For an instant, Girolama is thankful that she is not Angelica's real mother. Perhaps the other woman's kinder character will provide what she herself cannot.

After another half hour of frantic preparations, she makes up her mind. Though she'd vowed not to take this route, for it's desperately risky, Girolama decides she must go and seek out someone she hasn't seen for years. Someone who may help them, or who may end it all.

She puts on her grey cape and pulls up the hood to hide her face and hair.

'Where are you going?' Angelica asks as she reaches the door. She could swear the girl's hearing was better than the cat.

'Out dancing in the Carnival. What do you think, girl? I'm off to try to save us.'

'Then I'm coming with you.'

'No, you're not. You're staying here and finishing our

preparations. If I'm not back by tomorrow morn, you and Cecca must leave without me.'

44

Stefano

All this pain has produced nothing, or at least nothing of great value. It is like trying to squeeze gold from a rock. Stefano is writing a report for the Governor to update him, but he cannot bear to recount the detail of who has been into the torture room and what their ordeal has produced. It is all recorded in the book of evidence should Baranzone or the judges who will hear the case care to see. Stefano will not be going back over the record himself, for it continues to replay in his own mind long after he has left the room. Lodovico stands next to him during the sessions reciting the paternoster or the miserere to measure the time for which the tortures may take place. There is surely an irony to using prayers to measure wickedness, even if it is a necessary evil. The women pray and shout and scream and beg as Lodovico mutters:

'Behold, I was shapen in wickedness: and in sin hath my mother conceived me. But lo, Thou requirest truth in the inward parts: and shalt make me to understand wisdom secretly.'

Only occasionally do the women give Stefano information,

and it is not the key evidence he seeks. It is not the identity of the poison-maker nor the location of her book of secrets. Marcello has insisted that he cannot sanction putting Vanna to the test, for he thinks her near death's door, and if she expires then they will have nothing. As for Maria and Laura, they could only be subjected to the sibyl, as Marcello warned him that at their age anything more would cripple or kill them, and despite Baranzone's easy instructions not to concern himself with such things, Stefano cannot bring himself to obey him. Now, though, having seen how Maria and Laura held up under the tortures, he thinks it unlikely that anything would break them in any event. Laura, he knows, has been given some very good reason not to relent: whatever she fears from the poison-maker (and the memory of her bloodied mouth disturbs him), it is more than the bodily pain that he himself can have inflicted. As for Maria, she seems to have a cloak of metal or some supernatural aura protecting her, but that surely is impossible and he must not give way to such thoughts.

His mind, though, is strained and confused. It is, he thinks, partly the sleep deprivation, partly the fear that he will fail, and partly the awfulness of his task. Stefano finds that he cannot hold his train of thought for long enough to make sense of the evidence before him. He goes through the lists he has compiled and that the officers have brought him, of midwives and female apothecaries, of Sicilian women in Rome. He feels sure there is information that is escaping him, that there are clues that have passed him by – they are like flies buzzing within his mind, but he cannot hit at them. It's as though he is flailing in the dark, reaching out from a nightmare. It does not help that his chest has worsened, sending shooting pains up to his brain with no warning at all, coating his skin in sweat. None of Marcello's remedies and poultices work and, in his state of exhaustion, Stefano thinks increasingly that it is not something physical that causes the pain, but something, or someone, external. Is it the central poison-maker? Does she seek to inflict back on him the pain he is causing to her accomplices? But he doesn't have a choice in that, he tells himself. He has been told, instructed, threatened. He has to use the tools with which the law provides him even if they sicken him, else he will be seen not to have fulfilled the role with which he was entrusted. Or saddled. Because yes, it seems with every day that passes that Lucia's prophecy was right and that this mission is not a privilege but a poisoned chalice, one whose venom is very real and very rich. Still Stefano does not know the exact ingredients that make up this Aqua and he deduces from the responses that the women give under torture that they do not know either. Maria, perhaps. She may know. But she will not give him anything except pain.

The name. That is what he needs more than anything: the name of the shadowy figure who has eluded him since the beginning, since that frightening journey into the dark labyrinth of the Colosseum. La Strolaga. La Profetessa. She is real, Stefano is sure of it now: not just the stuff of his infant imaginings, but a real woman who haunts him, who lurks beneath the earth, who he senses is very close.

As he considers his half-written report for Baranzone, Stefano realises that it will not do. He knows how the report will be received; indeed, he can imagine the Governor's face as he reads it, contorted with disapproval and contempt. Only three days remain of the ten that the Governor allotted him to conclude his investigation. Stefano knows what it is that he must do. It is Vanna who has already broken and who requires perhaps only a further nudge to give up the name she has been concealing. It irks him to prey upon the weak, but that is the task of the inquisitor, is it not? To strike at the most frail at the very point they are about to break? He thinks of the presiding

265

judge at the Governor's court and his relentless examination of witnesses, striking and striking at them until their defences are in tatters. That is how one gets at the truth and that is what he must now do.

Marcello, however, will not sanction it. When Stefano goes to speak to him in his room, he finds him hard-faced and intransigent. 'I refuse to authorise any form of harm to Vanna. It will kill her. This is on your own head, Stefano.'

'But, Marcello, you must see how things lie. You must see she is the last bulwark to the truth. And this is the law, Marcello. It is how the system operates.'

'Is that right?' He will not look at Stefano.

'Yes.' Stefano feels himself growing angry. 'Do not make me the villain in this, Marcello. I have consulted the legislation and, where there is authorisation to do so, torture must be employed even on those who are physically weak.'

'Whether or not it is the law, it is barbarous, and by enacting it, so are we, so are you.'

'The Governor has told us very clearly—'

'I don't care.' Marcello is staring at him, clear-eyed. 'I don't care what he has instructed us to do, nor what is written in some book of law. It is my soul and my conscience that are at stake here, and I do not authorise it. Override me if you wish, but I am not sanctioning what you're about to do.'

Stefano feels a rising tide of fury. Marcello is leaving him on his own, to be hung out to dry. 'So you refuse to do as I ask?'

'You have to account to God for your own actions, Stefano. I account to God for mine.' Marcello is standing, as if to leave.

'Where are you going?'

'Home, to my wife. Away from this place. You can manage without me from now on. My presence serves no purpose.'

Stefano's heart falls. 'We need a doctor here.' And more to the point, he needs a friend.

'Then get another one.' Still, Marcello will not look at him. 'I was appointed to investigate deaths, not to carry them out.' He takes his cloak from the hook on the wall.

'You think this is any easier for me?' Stefano asks, incredulous. 'You think that I relish such work?'

'I think,' Marcello says, fastening the brooch on his cloak, 'that you've lost sight of who you are, and what you wish to be. You are not Baranzone, or at least, not yet. Please, Stefano, stand aside.'

Stefano moves so that Marcello may make his way to the door. He watches him as he leaves the room. He does not move until the sound of his footsteps has died out.

★

Outside, mayhem. *Carnevale* is in full swing and the citizens of Rome, subjected for so long to the quarantine and drabness of the plague, have plunged into a licentiousness unknown in previous years. The Corso is a dark enchanted forest of foliage, flowers and paper streamers. Within it, masked figures roam, many carrying lighted tapers that stream into the night. The place is peopled by mock English sailors, Barbary pirates, giants on stilts, the whole cast of the *commedia dell'arte*. The rich are dressed as beggars, men are dressed as women, women are disguised as boys, boys are dressed as animals and mythological monsters.

As Stefano tries to make his way towards home, he is hit by darts and pellets made of *pozzolana* and plaster, and only narrowly evades the handfuls of flour and showers of water thrown from windows. It is gone nine o'clock at night, and the revellers, drunk with life and wine, have reached that stage of mild hysteria that precedes violence. People are dancing, clutching at one another, clambering up walls and shouting. Some wave their tapers, others try to blow them out, and flames streaming in such a dense crowd make Stefano nervous. It is as though the confusion of his own mind is mirrored in the nonsensical scenes before him. There comes a ringing of silver bells and Stefano must dart away from a decorated carriage being driven at great speed down the Corso, the plumes of its caparisoned horses waving as they trot. From atop it, three figures dressed as harlequins are throwing confetti down onto the crowds. It is like a mockery of his sister's wedding.

Worse is to come. In the Piazza del Popolo, a mock execution is being staged, with Pulcinella as the hangman and a masked man dressed as Colombina, Arlecchino's mistress, begging and pleading for mercy in a patched and torn dress. It seems a cruel lampooning of the real scenes playing out in the Tower and Stefano hurries past, not wanting to be any part of the charade. His mind is in such a state of agitation that it feels as if they have put on this spectacle to torment him. He even wonders if his brothers had some part in it all. He is in the midst of telling himself not to be so foolish, when someone grabs him by the arm. 'Look! It's a real judge! It's the one from the Tor di Nona!'

Faces turn towards him and the crowd moves closer in.

'Unhand me,' Stefano says, trying to pull away, but the man is not listening. Other people have pushed up towards Stefano and are now dragging him towards the masked Pulcinella.

'You must be the judge!' a woman screeches. 'You must be the judge and jury!'

'No, no,' Stefano protests, but no one hears or cares. The crowd are too carried away with their own merriment. He is pushed onto a wooden chair and held there as the mock trial plays out, the supposed witnesses pointing their fingers at the cowering Colombina and shrieking accusations. It is unclear to Stefano what specific crime she is supposed to have committed. The accusations are diffuse and tangled: witchcraft, sorcery, sexual lasciviousness, and, of course, poisoning. 'Tell the truth!' people shout at the character, who now kneels on the stones of the piazza, uncomfortably close to him.

'Please, Signore!' Colombina begs Stefano in her false woman's voice. 'Have mercy upon me!'

Stefano stares at Colombina's mask, transfixed. Does he know the man behind the mask? Does he know others in the crowd? Is this all some wicked game? His eyes search across their masked faces, but he can no longer tell whether he should trust his own mind. He only desperately wants to leave and return to the safety of his home.

'What's the verdict, Messer Judge?' Pulcinella demands, swinging the hangman's noose.

Stefano opens his mouth to speak, not knowing what to say, when he realises that it doesn't matter because the crowd are all chanting: 'Hang her! Hang Her! Make her pay!'

Men and women surge forward to surround Colombina, and Stefano uses the diversion to wrench free of his tormentors and scurry away, pushing his way through the thicket of bodies. He's aware of people laughing and pointing at him, but he keeps his head down and moves as swiftly as he can, so that by the time he reaches his house his chest is agony and cold sweat coats his face.

It takes him a moment to realise that the smell that fills his nostrils – of excrement and death – is coming from his own doorway. Stefano takes a step backwards. Once he is further from the door, he can see the shape of the cross which has been daubed across the paintwork. They have used some substance that gleams in the moonlight; that stinks. Is this a prank by some of the carnival miscreants, or is this something much darker?

He has heard of people creating mixtures from the bones of the dead and using them to anoint the doorways and windows of those they wish to curse. Is this what has happened here? For a moment, Stefano thinks he will retch, but he swallows it down. If someone is watching, he does not want them to see that their trick has affected him. Instead, he forces himself to approach the door, unlock it and walk in, steady and slow.

Only once he is in the darkened hallway does he allow himself to lean against the wall, pressing his face to the cool tiles. He has never felt so alone.

45

Anna

The men have come for Vanna and the prison is in uproar.

'You'll kill her, you know that?' Graziosa is shouting. 'She's already at death's door!'

'*Vergogna!*' shouts another woman. 'Shame on you for what you do!'

Banging on all the doors of all the cells. Feet stamping on the floor. It is a terrible, rising chorus of anger and pain, the frustrations and injustices of the past weeks, maybe of these women's whole lives, filling the stone room as a roar.

Though Anna's longing for her baby is an ache in her soul and in her milk-filled breasts, she thanks God the child has not been here with her in this hell-like place over the past few days. Anna thought she knew what torture looked like. She'd seen men whipped in the public squares and she'd seen them shambling through the streets with a kind of palsy, their limbs never recovered from the strappado. This, though, is something else. During the daytime: the unbolting of doors, the sounds of women begging, pleading, trying to resist the guards (there are two now) as they drag them out of their cells and up the stone stairs to the torture chamber. During the night, crying, coughing, wailing, or – much worse – silence. And now this: the taking of an old woman who has been growing steadily weaker so that she can now barely speak. 'I don't fear dying,' Vanna whispered to Anna earlier, 'but I do not want to be tortured. I won't be able to bear it. I won't be able to hold on to the secrets. I'd rather give them my life.'

Has Stefano truly sanctioned all this misery? During their interviews, he seemed to be struggling with his better nature. Perhaps he has managed to subdue it. Perhaps that is what power does. Anna saw it in Philippe's increasing need to control and kick her and had thought Stefano an entirely different kind of man, but maybe even good nature grows twisted when placed under certain pressures.

On most of these women, though, stress has acted differently. Through all their pain and misery, they have continued to support one another, calling to one another, telling each other to be strong. Maria, who has herself been subjected to the sibyl, continues to shout out encouragement to other women and to talk to Anna through the chink in the wall. She tells her she sees Aurelia and that she is thriving, that she will continue to cling on to life. She tells her that the woman Aurelia was placed with is kind and cares for her as best she can. Anna weeps with relief to hear this, for she believes that Maria knows. She tries to give Maria some comfort in return, and offers up prayers for her soul and her broken bones, but Anna knows herself to be a fraud, for she has spared herself the twist of the sibyl or the drop of the strappado by giving up some of her own secrets.

Laura has been brought into the prison now. Anna has seen her washing at the tap in the morning and the woman hissed at her: 'Was it you who named me, you bitch? Well, you will suffer for it, I promise you.'

Anna is both frightened at what Laura might do and racked with guilt at what she herself has done. She told Stefano almost nothing about her dark-haired midwife, thinking that was the best course. However, if she *had* told, would they be taking Vanna to the torture room now, or might she have been spared the agony? Vanna is the weakest physically and, they must have deduced, the prisoner most likely to snap.

'She's a frail old woman!' Camilla is shouting now. 'You can't do this.'

The banging continues, and the stamping, and the calling out of curses and pleas.

The guards, however, are untouched. 'Shut your mouths, you old witches. These are our orders and we'll carry them out. Save your shouting for the devil in hell.'

Beneath the dirge, Anna thinks she hears the sickening sound of them dragging Vanna up the stairs, her skirts slithering on the floor.

Will Vanna give Stefano the name he seeks, and the secrets that she's holding on to? Will that mark the end for all of them, even she who is supposedly saved? For Anna was given no guarantee, and, more than that, she fears that Stefano has lost his way entirely.

She returns to the cold floor and hugs her arms around herself. Milk leaks from her nipples, undrunk. Why would he hold to his word to one woman, when he is willing to kill another to get to what he wants?

46

Stefano

Girolama Spana. It isn't a name that surprises him. Rather, it seems almost as if Stefano already knew it, somewhere in the recesses of his mind.

He tries not to think about how this name was obtained (the winding of ropes around thumbs, the squeezing and crushing of bone, the tugging of the rope, the terrible snapping sound). In any case, he now has not only the poison-maker's name, but her address and the names of her two sons. What he still lacks is the recipe or the location of the book of secrets. He doesn't believe Vanna held anything back, for she seemed a woman entirely defeated. He must not dwell on how this was achieved, who achieved it. The screaming. He has instructed that another doctor must be brought in. He knows that her situation is grave and also that he will struggle to forgive himself if she dies, but what other choice did he have?

His focus must be on Girolama, the poison-maker. He must move forward now, and quickly, despite the worsening pain in his chest and the growing fog in his mind. He must finish this cursed task. Already, he has spoken to Maffeo and Bertuccio and they are set to accompany him to the woman's house to secure her arrest and confiscate her property. This is assuming that she has not already fled, but Stefano cannot contemplate that possibility. He must believe she is still within his grasp.

Just as they are about to set off, Lucia arrives at the Tower. It is the first time she has set foot within the prison and Stefano regards her with something approaching anger. She should not be here, in this domain of darkness. She is something quite apart from it. 'Sister, is something wrong?'

She takes down her hood. 'I wanted to see how you were,' she says quietly. 'I was worried, and I see now that I was right to be.'

'Really, Lucia, you have no need to worry, but I'm afraid you come at an inopportune time. We are about to make a key arrest.'

Lucia reaches up and touches his cheek. 'Little brother, you're not well.'

He flicks her hand aside, anxious to ensure no one sees her softness. 'Lucia,' he whispers, 'I'm nearly at the end of this thing. You must let me finish. I will visit you when I return.'

'Stefano, you've been avoiding me.'

'I've been very busy.'

'So I hear.' There is a hint of accusation in her tone.

Bertuccio and Maffeo approach. He nods to them: 'A moment, *ragazzi*.'

Lucia glances at the men, nervous, and admittedly they do look like murderers. 'Stefano,' she whispers, 'I must speak with you.'

'This is not the time.'

'Do you know what you're doing? Where you're going?'

He feels a flare of anger that she should doubt him at the

very moment he most needs her support. 'I know exactly what I'm doing and where I'm going: into the devil's lair.' He pulls his cloak tighter. 'The sooner I get it over with, the better.'

'But, Stefano—'

'Please, Lucia. Don't come here again.' He is about to say that it isn't a place for women, but then he realises that of course it is full of women. They are just not women like her.

The house, Vanna has told them, is on the Via della Lungara at the corner where it meets Via di San Francesco di Sales and Vicolo della Penitenza. They will know it from the small sign over the door which bears the shape of a lily.

They approach the house silently. Stefano hears only the crunch of their footsteps, the thump of his blood in his ears. Closer, he can now make out the picture. It is subtle, painted only a shade darker than the background. You have to look carefully to be able to see it, but is a marker all the same. Lilies, he knows, can be poisonous, despite seeming pure. Girolama is confirming, to those who know, that this is the house they seek.

They are now only a few steps away from the door. Stefano feels his stomach constrict, and his heart hammers against his ribs. Bertuccio meets his eye: a silent question. Stefano gives the nod.

Together, the two *sbirri* run forwards and kick the door to the ground.

There comes a shout from behind the collapsed doorframe and Stefano sees an old woman, grey-haired and bowed. This, he thinks, is not their poisoner. Maffeo quickly cuffs the woman to a chair. Whoever she is, they will deal with her later. Stefano pushes past them, moving through a *sala,* then a *camera,* then a kitchen, while Bertuccio runs upstairs, Maffeo into the loggia. 'There!' he shouts. 'Down there! I heard footsteps!'

Stefano runs to catch up with him and finds Maffeo in the cellar, turning this way and that. The room doesn't appear to lead anywhere. Bertuccio joins them. 'There's no door,' Maffeo says. 'No way out.'

Stefano is surveying the poorly lit room. Empty jars glint from the shelves. 'Yes, there is a way. There must be.' He opens a cupboard, which contains only old clothing, then feels along the walls for some secret opening, but his hands merely come away dusty. 'Pull that up,' he says to his men, pointing at the mat beneath them, but there is no hidden trapdoor concealed beneath, no entry point. What is it they're missing? 'You're sure, Maffeo, this is where you heard footsteps?'

'I think so,' Maffeo says. 'But it maybe some trick.'

They climb back up the stairs and Stefano sees that the room through which they've run is a workshop covered with the tools of an apothecary. He takes in the coppers lining the walls, the glass alembics and majolica pots. All the labels, though, are anodyne: comfrey, ginger, arrowroot. 'This is where you were standing when you heard footsteps?' he asks Maffeo.

'Yes, Maestro.'

Stefano takes a lamp and descends again to the cellar. He cannot allow himself to be outwitted.

He uses the lamp to cast light along the walls and floor, but still he sees nothing of value. For a long moment, Stefano stands motionless in the semi-darkness. Beneath him, he thinks he can hear the whispering of water and cannot help but imagine La Manalonga stretching her white hand from the well, reaching, reaching towards him. Something moves against his ankle and he almost shouts out, but it is only a cat. He follows it with his eyes. The cat noses at the cupboard door and climbs effortlessly in. Stefano waits a moment, then opens the cupboard door. He blinks. The cat has gone. How is that possible?

Stefano pushes at the back of the cupboard to test for some

hidden door, but there is no movement. He kneels down to push at the floor, but no, it is solid. Apparently this is a magical cat. For a moment, he stands, thinking. He remembers hearing of secret entrances that were used to escape during the Sack of Rome in the last century. He tries to recall everything he has been told on this. Is there a lever somewhere? But then how would a cat have operated it? It cannot be something complex, merely something he hasn't thought to try. Stefano bends down to the level of the cat. He runs his hand over the bottom of the back of the cupboard.

His fingers bush against a bump in the wall. He takes a breath. He presses.

A grating sound, and the wall begins to shift. It is not a wall, it is a door, and as it opens, a draught of cold, damp air reaches him, smelling of rotten leaves and things long dead. Carefully, Stefano moves into the cupboard and peers beyond the door, down into a gaping chasm. No doubt it is his exhaustion and his fear, but Stefano has the feeling of being at the mouth of a well, about to be pulled into its depths. He steadies himself and inhales the stagnant air. Holding the lamp before him, Stefano can make out stone steps leading downwards into greater darkness.

'Maestro?' Bertuccio's voice from above, then footsteps descending the stairs.

Stefano moves back into the room. In a low voice he says: 'There's a secret passageway of some sort. We must follow it, quietly and quickly. Bring lamps. Fast as you can.'

Once they have found and lit oil lamps, the three of them descend into the abyss beneath the closet, Stefano in the lead. The steps are damp and slippery. Girolama cannot, he thinks, have gone fast. After a minute or so, they reach a stone floor and, pointing the lanterns about, see that they are in a low tunnel. The men proceed along it in silence, all their attention focused on not tripping on the wet and uneven ground. Stefano thinks he can hear some noise ahead, but it may just be the dripping of water. The tunnel grows narrower, the air damper, thicker, and Stefano fears he will not be able to breathe. There is no real choice, though, but to go on. He cannot abandon the search at the very point he is about to catch the poisoner.

As he walks, Stefano wonders if Girolama moved to this house because she knew of the secret tunnel. Has she planned this for many years? From what he is learning of her, this seems possible – likely even. His father would applaud her efficiency.

A hand clasps his shoulder and he nearly drops the lantern, but it is only Bertuccio.

'What the devil is this place?' the officer whispers, his breath full of garlic.

'I'd guess it was built many years – maybe centuries – ago as an escape route. I've heard of many such places beneath Rome, Naples too, many built by the noble families. Never before, though, have I seen one.' There was a priest, he recalls, who published a book describing many of the strange tunnels, crevices and catacombs he'd discovered. Some built by the Romans, some even earlier than that.

'Well, I could have done without the experience,' Bertuccio mutters back. 'We're going deeper into the earth.'

He is right. The path is descending. Where in God's name is it taking them? They must have walked a mile already, or does it only seem so far because it's so airless and grim? As they walk, Stefano's imagination and exhaustion combine with the shadows from the lamps to create phantoms in the darkness: strange forms that loom from the walls and crawl along the path towards them. He thinks too of stories he has heard of underground labyrinths sprung with traps, of unsuspecting visitors dropped into caverns, or impaled on poisoned lances. He tells himself again and again to be rational and calm. This is simply an underground tunnel. He must continue step by step. Stefano is just repeating this when a black form brushes against him and his heart almost leaps from his chest, but it is, he realises, only Girolama's cat, apparently as happy here as it is above the earth. No doubt the place is full of rats.

The way grows narrower still, but begins to curve. Stefano's lamp illuminates a section of the wall and at first he thinks it must be some trick of the light or his mind, but no, it's a fragment of a fresco. Maffeo and Bertucci direct their lanterns at the walls, revealing what seem to be dragons: great winged beasts breathing fire at a small man brandishing a spear. They continue along the wall, their lights now showing a painting of a man kneeling in prayer, blood flowing from his neck.

'Sweet Mary,' Matteo says. 'What is this place?'

'It must be part of some ancient church or shrine,' Stefano says. He moves his lamp and sees a woman with wings: an angel. Her face is scrubbed out and featureless. He moves quickly on.

Further around the curved wall they come across what appear to be large lumps of stone. Moving closer, Stefano sees that they are ornately carved, one with a figure of a sphinx – head of a woman, haunches of a lion, wide wings of an eagle. It is a sarcophagus. This must be a crypt. He shudders, then stops abruptly.

A noise.

'D'you hear that?' Bertuccio whispers.

It was the crack of something – maybe a piece of wood – splitting.

'I say we move fast and catch her,' Bertuccio breathes in his ear. 'She isn't that far ahead. Let us go first, Maestro, and get this done.' Bertuccio pushes past him and for a moment Stefano feels the weakling he has always been made to seem, but of course this is their job: they're used to giving chase to criminals.

Bertuccio begins to run, holding his lamp before him, Maffeo behind. 'There!' he shouts. He must have caught sight of Girolama.

Stefano follows as best he can and is not far behind them when he hears a cry, then a terrifying crash that ricochets through the tunnel. Stefano races to catch up with them, his heart thumping in his chest, knowing it was a man's voice he heard, not Girolama's. He sees a shape on the ground and his stomach drops as he realises it is Bertuccio, prone, Maffeo hauling away the rocks that cover his legs and torso. *Lord have mercy.* Stefano crouches beside Bertuccio and sees the man's face is covered in blood and mud.

'Go, leave me,' Bertuccio manages. 'Catch her before she gets away.'

'Maffeo, stay with him,' Stefano directs, then moves on quickly, along the passage. He can hear Girolama's footsteps and, with the echo, it seems almost as if there are two people. She is not so far ahead that she will be able to escape him.

Stefano's breath is shallow in his aching chest and his heart feels that it will burst from his ribcage, but he knows he must reach her, the woman who has evaded him for so long. The path is leading upwards now, and here there are stairs, made not of stone this time, but wood. The tunnel lightens and he realises she must have opened the exit onto the street. He moves faster and faster, his lungs on fire, until he is pushing at a half-open door and fresh air is caressing his face. He squints into the light, searching her out, but he's emerged into a marketplace full of people.

For a moment Stefano looks about, his chest pounding, his eyes still blind in the sun. He sees no one running away and surely she was only a few paces in front of him. There is only a girl moving quickly, and he is not looking for a girl. He scours the crowd – women with baskets, priests in cassocks, a man with a barrel full of eels.

Then he sees her: dark eyes narrowed at him, dark hair pulled back into a bun. She is only a few steps away. Severe face, black clothing, upright bearing. She is not the woman he has imagined but it is her, all right. He is not quite sure how he knows.

When he approaches, she says: 'It would be better for you, Stefano Bracchi, if you left this place. Better for you if you hadn't found me.'

Her words chill him, but he says lightly, 'It is thoughtful of you, Donna Girolama, to consider my wellbeing, but I am arresting you. I am taking you to the Tor di Nona.'

'You make a poor choice,' she says.

'I don't think so,' he says.

He is relieved to see Maffeo is now with them and can apply the cuffs. He cannot bring himself to touch this woman.

47

That a woman may confess what she hath done:
Take a frog quick, and take away her tongue, and put it again into
the water and put the tongue unto a part of the heart of the woman
sleeping, which when she is asked, she will say the truth.

Girolama

They've put her in the cell named Purgatorio. If she wasn't so cold and so furious, Girolama would laugh. She wonders who's been locked in Inferno. By the sounds that come from the cells around her, she thinks it could be any one of the women who call out and cry. *Santo Cielo*, it's made her angrier than she has perhaps ever been: that these men should have shackled her women to cell walls, should have subjected them to tortures, justifying their actions no doubt by claims that they're doing the Lord's work and rooting out evil. There's nothing so simple as good and evil and anyone who's truly lived in the world knows that. Can they not see that *this*, this hell that they've created in the middle of the holiest city in the land, is itself a thing of evil? Women shut in dark enclosures like calves waiting for culling time.

Though she knows she'll be punished for it, she shouts to the other women, 'Have strength! They have no information save for what you give them. They don't have the right to harm you. They don't have the evidence to hang you.'

'Shut your trap!' the guard yells back, 'Or we'll shut it for you!'

'Girolama!' one of the women calls. She thinks it's Vanna, but her voice is cracked, different. What have they done to her?

'Girolama!' shouts another, louder. It is La Sorda. And though Girolama is pained to know her women are here, under lock and key, it is good to hear their voices and to know that they are close.

'Enough!' The voice, again, of the guard. 'Or your tongues'll be cut out of your mouths!'

A laugh, deep and throaty, that she recognises as Maria's. In the darkness, Girolama feels a smile growing on her face, she who rarely smiles. For she realises, as the laugh turns to a cough, that Maria is in the cell next to hers. She puts her hand to the stone wall. 'Maria,' she whispers. 'Maria.'

Some time in the early hours she is woken and dragged by a guard out of the hell cells and up into a large stone-walled room where candles are lit. In their glow, the judge's boyish face is a deathly grey. He is, she sees at once, exhausted, perhaps sick. When she last saw Stefano, he was flushed from running. Now he is candle-wax pale. He is a man who suffers, and rightly so, but somehow seeing that is true does not help her, for she also sees that the goodness that once existed in that face is hardening over, turning to something entirely different. But Lucifer, of course, was an angel before he was a devil. She will not allow herself to feel any pity for him. She has a finite supply of compassion and she will not waste it on a man so fortunate in life as him. He has made his own choices. She will save it for the women who have few choices and who need her. She will save it for Angelica.

It is the notary who speaks first, to read out her name and

some words in Latin. He is a stretched-out boy who makes her think of a plant, deprived of sunlight. Yet there is something beneath that blandness: a spark of something, she is not sure what.

'Girolama Spana,' Stefano says, 'you know why you're here.'

He has a fine voice, bigger than his frame. 'I know why you've thought fit to bring me here, yes. Do you know why you're here?'

Stefano, scowls. 'Yes, Donna Spana, I know what my purpose is. It's to end the many poisonings that have stained this city and to find the main poisoner. I know now that it is you.'

'Me? No, Signore, I make only cosmetics and women's remedies. Face waters and tonics and so on. You'll have found such things in my workshop, no doubt.' For she removed all save for the ingredients and equipments needed to produce the balms and eye drops and creams. She knows from his expression that he's found nothing else.

'You are directed to speak the truth. You are the chief poison-maker in an established poisoning ring that's been operating for years. You are the one who makes the Aqua. You provide it to your underlings who sell it on to other women.'

Girolama shrugs. 'You've seen my house, my belongings. I don't have the means to create poisons. Nor do I have the knowledge. I'm not a learned person like yourself. I had little schooling.'

'You came to Rome from Palermo.'

'I did.'

'You knew a woman called La Tofania.'

The name catches her at the back of the throat but Girolama makes an expression of confusion. 'No, I don't believe so.'

'You must have. How else did you know the recipe?'

'I don't know what recipe you're talking about, Signore.'

'You know perfectly well. The recipe for the Aqua di

Palermo, which you made into Aqua di Roma. The recipe written in Tofania's book of secrets.'

Ah, so he's learnt something, this Bracchi boy, but not everything. 'I left Palermo when I was nine years old, Signore, as the records will show. I was making cat's cradles, not poison.'

He frowns, realising his fine theory is punctured. 'Vanna de Grandis was quite clear that you were the poison-maker.'

'Yes, how is Vanna?' Girolama stares at him evenly. 'She's an old woman. Very frail. Her mind tends to wander. She'd be a reliable witness, do you think? You reckon the justices would believe her word, that was given, I assume, under torture?'

She watches his face and she thinks yes, you stinking pig, you had the poor woman tortured: no wonder she spoke at last.

'I think,' he says, 'that they'll see that you are the one at the centre of all this.'

'On the basis of the word of one woman alone? An old woman who's losing her wits? And tell me, Signore Bracchi, does Vanna say she has seen me making this poison?'

A pause. 'No,' he concedes. 'She says that you never allow anyone to see the recipe, nor watch you making it.'

'Ah,' Girolama smiles. 'So, in fact you have no eyewitness.'

'It matters little. She's seen you handing out the bottles. She has admitted to selling them herself.'

'Vanna has said the things you made her say, Signore, with your tools and your clever words. Once she's well, she will recant them.'

'No.' A note of anger has entered his voice. 'Her testimony will stand as evidence, as will the statements of the many people who admit to having bought poison from your women.'

She shrugs. 'What other supposed evidence do you have against me?'

'Your neighbours see people come and go. People of all classes.'

'To be sure they do. The face waters and cosmetics I provide are sought throughout Rome, including by the daughters of merchants and tradesmen, and ladies of the court. Ask them. Speak to my noble clients, why don't you?'

His face freezes and she knows she has him. He can go nowhere near the nobles.

'Yes,' she continues, 'I have many rich clients. They're very appreciative of what I offer them.' She glances at the scrawny notary whose hand hovers above the page. 'I wonder, Signore, that those who asked you to begin this inquiry didn't think to consider who might be buying these wares.'

'It is unwise for you, Donna Spana, to go down this route.'

She leans forward. 'And perhaps it's unwise for you, Messer Bracchi, to pursue this one.'

Girolama sees the tendons in his neck tense. 'I am investigating the most serious crimes at the request of the Pope himself. You cannot question my authority.'

Oh, yes, it's a fragile thing, this man's ego. She could shatter it in the palm of her hand. 'I don't question your authority, Signore,' she says quietly. 'I know who appointed you and why. I simply question whether you want to go there: whether you truly want to become the man known for crushing a horde of old women, misused wives, daughters and sisters who had nowhere else to turn.'

'Then you admit it? You admit you were selling poison to these women? That you were creating it?'

'I admit nothing, Signore. I confess *nothing*. But, since you tell me such poison exists and is used, I ask you to imagine the situation of a woman who lives through years of violence and degradation, who knows that her husband will kill her sooner or later. I ask you to imagine the life of a girl violated again and again by her own father who knows that her only escape is in the form of a bottle full of poison. Those are the buyers you're talking about, aren't you? Those are the stories the public will remember. You really want that all on you?'

Stefano, to his credit, does not look away from her, but holds her gaze. 'It *is* all on me,' he says, 'whether I want it to be, or not. I am the investigating magistrate, an officer of the Papal courts. My job is to uncover the crime and put forward the evidence. It is a role I must carry out, whether or not I believe the crime was justified in any particular case.'

Girolama is surprised. He's thought about it more than she anticipated. But he still hasn't seen how close to him it runs. 'And what happens then, Signore? After you've performed your humble role?'

'You know this, I think, Donna Spana. The matter proceeds to trial and the cases are determined by the Governor, together with the Congregation on Crime.'

'Ah, yes, the Governor Baranzone.' Girolama nods. She's heard of the judgments that man has passed down, the misery he has caused. She has heard of his deep hatred for women. 'You think him a fair man, do you? The man who requested this *inquisitio*? You think it a fair process that leaves the decision in the hands of the very man who started this investigation?'

A silence. In the grate, a log cracks open, spitting out a shower of fire. 'It is not for me to judge.'

'So you absolve yourself.' Girolama smiles.

'It is not I who am under investigation,' Stefano says, his voice growing louder. 'It is not I who stands accused of making and selling a poison that has killed perhaps hundreds of men!' He thumps the table before him and Girolama knows she's got to him, but she hasn't got close enough. He continues: 'I am giving you the opportunity to confess your evil of your own volition. If you don't do so now, then tomorrow you know what will happen.'

'Yes, I know.' Or least she can guess. The way things are

going, the state this man is in, he won't bother with the sibyl. They'll go straight for the strappado. 'Yet you accuse me of evil,' she says quietly.

He stares at her. 'I do nothing beyond the law. Nothing beyond what I have been commanded to do.'

She gives a choked laugh. Does he really think that will rescue him? 'How many, Signore, of your class have justified their actions in such a way? Do you think they've saved their souls through some book of law?'

'And you, Girolama Spana: do you think you've saved yourself from damnation by getting others to sell your wares? By refusing to acknowledge the many men you've killed?'

She blinks and they are there before her: the spectral horde of butchers and dyers and sieve-makers who've succumbed to her poison over the years. No, she thinks to herself. *No, I do not.* Not anymore. To Stefano she says only: 'You may torture me, Signore. You may do whatever you say the law allows you to do, whatever the Governor might have instructed you to do. But, in the end, you will hurt yourself more than you will me.'

'These are empty threats.' He speaks with apparent confidence, but Girolama sees beneath that.

'No, Signore. They're full to the brim. I will see you in the morning.'

The guard leads Girolama away from the large room and down the stairs. She has been watching him, this guard. She thinks she has the measure of this man: a lump of clay who has worked for years in this gloomy place, unregarded, and seeks a little hope, a little beauty. She waits until they are almost beneath the torch that burns on the wall, then taps him on the shoulder.

When the guard turns, she holds up the small item in her

hand so that it shines in the light of the flame. 'Yes,' she whispers. 'It's real.'

She holds it out for him to take. Will he?

48

Anna

It is the dead of night. A woman is shouting. 'You can come out! Your cell doors are open.'

Anna sits up, confused, straw in her hair. Is she dreaming?

'Hurry!' the woman continues, and Anna recognises the voice. 'We don't have much time to speak before the guard returns.'

It's her midwife, Anna thinks: the woman she now knows to be called Girolama. She is both pleased and horrified to hear her voice, for it means they have caught up with her at last.

Scuffling, footsteps on stone, some frantic. 'Can we get out?' someone is saying. 'Can we escape?'

'No.' Girolama again. 'The main doors are locked.'

In the pitch darkness, Anna pushes at her cell door and, miraculously, it opens. She moves into the room beyond, where a torch is burning, casting its flickering light over the other women and girls who are making their way out of their cells and towards one another. They're like white grubs reaching towards the light.

'*Mistress?*'

'Benedetta!' Anna embraces her, feels her maid's face against hers.

'How is this possible?'

'I don't know.' All around them, the other women are approaching one another, talking, holding each other's hands. 'The midwife must have bribed the guard, or tricked him, into letting us out here.'

Benedetta whispers: 'I've been praying and praying, for Aurelia, for us, that we'll be saved.'

'We will be. Stefano, the judge, he said the Governor had agreed it all. You mustn't worry.' But of course her maid worries. Anna worries too, every day, every hour. How does she know Stefano or the Governor will keep to their word, given the horrors they're inflicting in this place?

She looks about for Laura, but cannot see her. Close by, the woman she knows to be called Cecilia has her arms about her daughter, Teresa. Both are weeping. Anna notes, though, that the door to Vanna's cell has not opened. She is about to approach it when Girolama begins to speak.

'Listen,' she says into the darkness, 'for I may not get a chance to talk to you again.'

'Girolama!' says another woman, her voice strange, sing-song. It's the voice of someone who cannot properly hear.

'La Sorda, come here.' Girolama brings the stout woman close to her and La Sorda begins to laugh, as though Girolama being here is the funniest thing she has heard in weeks and, after all, perhaps it is.

'Who are you?' asks another woman. 'How did you get us out of our cells?'

'It doesn't matter who I am,' Girolama says. 'What matters is what I tell you.'

Muttering, whispering. 'You're the reason we're here!' a younger woman says.

'There's no time for that,' Girolama says sharply. 'You each made your own decisions. If we fight against each other then we will all lose. Now, you must understand that this judge, this Stefano Bracchi, he can only secure your convictions if you confess, or if there are two witnesses who speak against you, or some other key piece of evidence. Even then, there's no guarantee that the court will convict you. You must hold firm. You must stop speaking out against each other.'

'It's too late!' comes a voice. 'They know!'

Laura, Anna thinks. It is Laura. Anna shrinks back into the shadows.

'It isn't what they know, or think they know,' Girolama insists. 'It's what they can prove. They don't have the poison. They don't even know what it is. They don't have any proof that any man was killed by poison.'

A murmuring between the women. Is Girolama right, Anna wonders? But in her case, she has admitted to what she did. That itself is the evidence. Did she make the wrong decision?

'Some have already confessed, Girolama,' Maria says.

'I know that, Maria, because he has used everything in his armoury to turn us against each other. But where the confessions were under torture, they can be retracted.'

More murmuring, louder. 'But if we go back on what we've told them,' one woman says, 'then they'll torture us again! That's what the Holy Inquisition does!'

'Maybe,' Girolama says. 'Or maybe not. This judge is not so tough as he pretends.'

'He's a child!' That from La Sorda who begins, again, to laugh.

'Not anymore,' Anna says, daring to speak out. 'He's crushed his own humanity for this task, and he's determined to see it to its end.'

Girolama turns to look at Anna and her eyes seem very

black. Does she know Anna has spoken against Laura? Given them information about herself? 'He is determined yes, but troubled, and there's more, too, that you don't know. Assume nothing. Try everything.'

'Why should we listen to you,' a young woman says to Girolama, 'when it's because of you that we're here?'

'What's your name, girl?' Girolama asks.

The woman hesitates. 'Caterina,' she says at last. 'Caterina Nucci.'

'Caterina Nucci, it is in fact because of me that you're alive at all, if I remember rightly. You're the butcher's widow, aren't you?'

The woman doesn't answer her and Girolama nods. 'You can choose to listen, or not listen, it's all the same to me, but you've been kept in the dark here, not only in your cells, but as to the law. Soon they'll have to appoint an advocate for the poor. Don't give away anything else till then.'

'When will the guard return?' Maria asks.

'In a quarter hour. Maybe less.'

Maria approaches Girolama and begins to whisper to her. She leads Girolama to Vanna's cell. The stouter woman, La Sorda, follows, then Graziosa, then Laura. Minutes pass. When the women emerge, Anna notes that they are silent and that Girolama is stony-faced. Vanna, she thinks, is dying.

As they hear the boots of the guard returning, Girolama and her women embrace one another. Maria makes a sign over Girolama that Anna doesn't understand. It is almost as though she is blessing her.

49

Stefano

Does the devil protect this woman? Two hours in the strappado and Girolama has given him nothing. She has barely even cried out, though she should, by rights, be in agony. Stefano has left the torture room, unable to witness any longer the wrenching of sinew and bone. It is enough that Lodovico notes it down. Stefano now paces about in the prison courtyard, his heart thumping, his chest aching, his mind swirling with doubts. He has resorted to torturing women and he still has nothing to show for it. What kind of man has he become? Only two days remain until the deadline the Governor gave him, and though he has the poisoner, he does not have sufficient evidence to ensure her conviction.

When he returns to the room, Stefano tells the guard to cut her down, to leave her. He sees it will achieve nothing. Girolama is allowed to plunge to the floor, but her body is relaxed and even the drop does not seem, really, to damage her. It is as though she's drugged, though surely that is impossible. It must be something she has achieved with the strength of her mind.

Slowly, she gathers herself up from the ground and sits, resting her back against the wall. A thin streak of blood runs from her mouth. She licks at it, like a cat, and looks lazily at Stefano.

'I will have you convicted without your confession,' he says. 'I know, and God knows, what you have done.'

Girolama laughs – a strange, throaty sound, full of phlegm, or blood. 'Ah,' she says quietly, 'but do you know what you have done?'

He feels his jaw seize with anger. 'I have done nothing beyond the law. Nothing beyond what is necessary to extract the truth and get this matter to the judges.'

'Signore Bracchi, you can lie to everyone, including yourself, but you aren't going to fool me. You have no confession. You have no poison recipe. You have no one who claims to have seen me make this alleged poison. You have nothing except a group of old women whom you've tortured into saying they bought or sold poison. You don't even know what this sup- posed Aqua is.' Her words are strangely slurred. Is it the pain?

'Yes, I know it is arsenic, mixed with something else. I know it is the same recipe that killed in Palermo and which has now killed tens, maybe hundreds in Rome. You are responsible for each and every one of those deaths. Each and every one.'

There is more blood in the corner of her mouth. She spits it out. 'I have never poisoned a soul.'

The way she lingers on the word 'soul' gives him pause. What does she mean, exactly? Does she really exculpate herself from all these deaths? Does she not see them lined before her as she goes to sleep at night: all the men for whose deaths she's responsible? Perhaps not. Perhaps the only way someone could justify so much killing would be to stand apart from it and pretend it was nothing to do with them. Is that what he himself is doing? Standing apart from the actions in the torture chamber, when in fact what happens here is down to him?

At that very moment, a terrible pain pierces his chest, his heart. He feels something gripping at him with claws. Is it her? Is *she* doing this to him? Stefano knows he cannot let her see his suffering, but the fear grows on him so he cannot breathe and his heart is pounding so fast he begins to believe he will die. 'We are done here,' he mutters and retreats from the room, his hand over his chest. He sees Lodovico's eyes following him. He knows Girolama herself is watching him, no doubt gloating at her success.

Once in the corridor, Stefano stands, gasping for breath, shaking. He cannot attempt the staircase for the steps swim before his eyes. Dear God, what is happening to him? Is he dying?

'Signore?' It is Bertuccio. His hand is on Stefano's shoulder. 'What is it?'

'I am unwell, I think. I need to get away from this place.'

'I will take you at once. To where?'

It shames Stefano, but it is to his sister that he directs Bertuccio: she who looked after him through his sicknesses as a child. As Bertuccio's horse navigates the streets, Stefano lies in the cart, sweating, nauseous, the fear almost unbearable. Carnevale is still in full flow and he can hear the hooves of the Barbary horses that are being raced through the streets, the shouting of the crowds. By the time he reaches his father's house, he is calmer, but still shaken. Thank God it is Lucia and not his father who greets them. She hurries Stefano to her room where she sits him down on the bed and fetches water and linen and smooths the wet compress onto his forehead. Stefano stares at the small devotional images on the walls, the prie-dieux where she must say her prayers, the baby terracotta Jesus, the single stool, the plain, worn credenza. He has never seen this room before and, even in his own distress, he is saddened at how poorly she lives in a house as rich as his father's.

Only after a servant has brought spiced wine and several minutes have passed does Lucia speak. 'What happened, brother?'

He tells her: of how the pain and fear came on him in the interrogation room, like an eagle's claws ripping at his chest. 'It's her,' he whispers. 'She is doing this to me. Is that possible?'

Lucia regards him, continues smoothing his brow. 'Or it is you yourself doing this. You are terribly afraid, you are over-wrought.'

'I am being defeated, Lucia. This woman is no normal human. She is a sorceress. She is like a snake who slips from my grasp.'

'She is merely a woman, *fratellino*. A strong one, perhaps, but a woman of flesh and blood.'

'You haven't met her. You haven't seen how she behaves. Nothing seems to touch her. Even now, I can feel her claws ripping into me!' The pain is there again in his chest. He clenches his teeth against it.

Lucia watches him. 'Stefano, there would be no *vergogna* in stepping away from this case. You are unwell and I must insist—'

'No shame!' He laughs. 'Lucia, the shame would kill me.'

'No. This, *this*, is killing you.'

He shakes his head. 'I am so close, Lucia. I am a hair's breadth away from the truth. I must get to the bottom of this matter.'

Her eyes are very dark green today. They seem to shift in colour. 'Let someone else take on that task. Let it not be you who finds this truth. You have done enough to get there.'

'No, Lucia, it has to be me. Don't you see? If I were to abandon the case now that would be an admission of defeat, a recognition that I'm the weakling Father has always thought me. Imagine his disdain, his contempt, were I to resign now!'

She puts her finger to her lips. 'The servants. They listen

to everything in this house. But, Stefano, what Father thinks or wants is neither here nor there. He's always pushed us to be the children he believes would bring greatest honour to himself. He has little interest in your happiness or wellbeing, nor mine. He had none for Mother's either, though you won't remember how it was. He cares only about himself and always has. Do you not see that? Do you not see how he manipulates us all? But I care about you, Stefano, and you must not let fear of losing face push you beyond your limits. Let it be someone else who finishes this matter.'

When he does not reply, Lucia says, 'Stefano, are you listening to me?'

'Yes, Lucia, I am listening, and I am thinking.' He is thinking mainly about the first part of what she said. Could there be an answer within it? A way out of this quagmire? Stefano grasps at the idea like a drowning man clutching to a rope as the current pushes against him.

50

To avoid suffering the Question:
Swallow a note where the following is written in your own blood:
Aglas, Aglanos, Algadenas, Imperiequeritis, tria pendent corpora
ramis dis meus et gestas in medio et divina potestas dimeas clamator,
sed jestas ad astra levatur, or else Tel, Bel, Quel, Caro, Mon,
Aqua.

Girolama

The pain has now begun. Girolama has used up all the poppy ampoules she secreted in her dress and has no further remedies with which to numb herself. Even her charms seem to lose their effect. As they wear off, different parts of her body come back to life. The back first, then the shoulders, screaming out at what has been done to them, sending red hot pinpricks of pain up and down her spine. But she will heal, Girolama thinks, gritting her teeth. She must. She's surely not so badly damaged that she'll be crippled for life, as others are. Stefano might have hardened his soul to a certain extent, but he didn't have the fight in him to destroy her completely. She can tell that he's growing ill, both in mind and body: a darkness taking over. She should be pleased, but somehow she is not. It is merely a job half-done.

She knows she herself must remain strong and alert but, lying alone in her cell, the pain sparking along her nerves, the iron taste of blood in her mouth, Girolama feels herself growing delirious. Maria speaks to her through the wall, trying to keep her strong, but her old friend can't reach her. Nobody can. Wreaths of colour spiral in the dim light, like sprites come to dance before her. Are they spirits, or just mirages, caused by pain and poppy? She's reminded of the times when he, her first husband whom she will not name, locked her in the cellar, sometimes for days on end. Her mind would create friends in the darkness, familiars come to comfort her and to guard her against the monsters: the imagined ones that lurked in the dark and the real ones that populated the earth. The cellar was punishment, he said. For talking back, for defending herself against his blows. Ha! She punished him in the end, but my God, there was a long period in her life where she truly thought she was defeated. She was only sixteen when she married him and, though she'd experienced Ranchetti's violations, she hadn't realised that there are some men in this world for whom violence is a game and for whom girls' bodies and minds are testing grounds for cruelty and barbarity. She won't go there now. She refuses. It's taken her half a lifetime to heal as much as she has and to cleanse the images from her mind. She won't think of the things he did or why he did them, because she's beyond that now and he himself is long dead – the only man she's ever killed directly. The one who made her truly understand why that poison in a bottle was necessary.

Was it always needed, though? This is what she finds herself wondering as the visions whirl before her. Have some of the women to whom she sold the poison used it without proper cause? Maybe, yes. She hasn't always been as thorough as she should have been. Although there are many instances where she knows the woman had no other way out, there are some where she's later had cause to doubt whether the remedy was necessary. The laundresses, for example: the three sisters who all poisoned their husbands, or the lady who offered her gold. She should never have given in to them, but she'd reached a point where she didn't much care, where she'd heard so many stories of cruelty and degradation that she struggled to have sympathy for any man save for her own sons. She fears now that she did wrong and that, through her hand, too many have died. But this is the pain talking, and the exhaustion. This is no time for introspection. She must rally herself for whatever is coming next.

Girolama hears boots on the ground: the guard, returning. Then comes the sliding of bolts, the opening of the door. She pushes herself up to sitting and almost cries out with the pain, but she can't let them see how they've hurt her.

'You're wanted,' the man says. 'Upstairs.' He puts out a hand.

He's been gentler with her since she gave him the ruby, no doubt hoping she has more jewels with which she can bribe him. She takes his hand and he pulls her to standing.

In fact, she has no more rubies. She has only information.

When Girolama reaches the interrogation room, she sees that Stefano, though still ghastly pale, is bright-eyed. Horribly so. Perhaps it's the brightness of illness, but she fears it's the light of mania.

'Good day, Donna Spana. We have a visitor.'

Fear writhes in her belly.

'Are you not interested to know who it is?'

Girolama will not give him anything. She keeps her face a blank.

'It's a witness who has testified against you,' Stefano continues, mock cheerful. 'One who knows you well.'

Girolama feels the fear stretch from her stomach to her chest,

302

tentacles reaching into her heart. 'Is that so?' she says quietly. Although she thinks she knows who it is before the witness enters the room, the horror of it still makes her gasp.

The familiar, bow-legged gait, as though scuttling like a spider. Cecca moves into the room and takes the seat Stefano offers her. She does not look at Girolama. She looks instead at the floor.

Stefano says: 'Donna Cecca, please will you describe for me how you have seen your mistress making the poison?'

'Yes, Signore,' Cecca says dully. 'Like I said, I know she uses a quantity of arsenic—'

'Where did she procure this arsenic?'

'Padre Don Girolamo from San Pietro in Vincoli brought it to her: white, shiny stuff that looked like a hunk of white salt. He's dead now of the plague, but for many years he brought it to Girolama.'

'And once she has the arsenic, then what?'

'Then she takes the arsenic in a mortar and grinds it together with something else. She grinds it very fine. Then she fills a new water jar and adds the powder. She distils it until it's clear as water.'

Cecca could be reciting a recipe for milk pudding. Girolama's gaze remains on the woman's face. Behind them, she is aware of the notary scribbling in his book of evidence.

'How does she do that?' Stefano asks. 'How does she distil the liquid?'

'I don't know exactly the method. I know she covers the mouth of the jar with dough,' Cecca says, her voice still entirely without emotion, 'and seals it well so air can't escape. Then she puts it on the fire to simmer very slowly until the water level drops about an inch. That is all.'

'And then?'

'She lets it stand overnight, and then she pours it into these little glass vials that she has made, marked Manna of St Nicholas, so that people will think it is a pilgrim's oil and not a poison.'

'You are quite sure it is a poison?' he asks.

'Oh, yes. I've heard Girolama tell women so many times.'

'What does she tell them?'

'She tells them they must give the Aqua five or six drops at a time, either in wine or in pottage (because it doesn't spoil the taste), and if they continue to administer it, it will be fatal.'

Stefano turns his gaze to Girolama. 'So, you see, we have all the evidence we need. Now you must confess.'

Girolama opens her mouth. At first, no sound comes, then she manages: 'No. Cecca is lying, or mistaken. She has never seen me make any poison.' But of course she has, or at least she has seen part of the process. It is just that, after so many years, Girolama had come to regard Cecca as a fixture of the house, like a piece of furniture or an old boot. She hadn't judged her a risk. 'What she describes is me distilling a face water.'

Stefano smiles, a pale and ghastly smile like a rictus. 'I thought you might say as much, which is why I took the precaution of sending my man to your house to dig beneath the Seville orange tree.' Stefano stands up and goes to the door. 'Maffeo?' he calls.

Girolama stares at Cecca, who refuses to meet her eye. Please God let her not have told them anything of Angelica. If she has, may He strike her dead.

A man enters the room – one of the rough-looking *sbirri* officers who chased her through the tunnel. In his arms he holds a bundle of fabric. When he opens it on the table before Stefano, Girolama sees that it contains her clothbound book, and several of the glass vials. Soil spatters across the table. 'Proof enough, Signore Bracchi?'

'Oh, I'd say so,' Stefano answers.

'No,' Girolama rasps. 'This is no proof of anything, save that certain people are poisonous and weak and are best avoided.' Her eyes are still on Cecca. 'You will not have your confession, Messer Bracchi. This old woman's word wouldn't convince a soul, never mind a room full of learned men.'

Finally, Cecca looks at her: the woman whom she's known since she was a child. The woman Giulia trusted implicitly. What has caused her to betray Girolama after all these years?

As though in answer to this silent question, Cecca says, 'Didn't you always say crush, or be crushed, Girolama? I've no choice but to save myself now. I'm an old woman. I'm tired. I wish to live out the rest of my life in peace.'

And what of Angelica's life, Girolama wants to scream at her. What do you think will happen to that pretty young girl when she is left without a protector? 'Then you have forgotten what I am and what I can do,' Girolama whispers. 'You will not have peace if you speak further.'

'Yes, yes,' Cecca says, scornful. 'You with your curses and your potions, always thinking you were better than me, cleverer than me. I've paid your family enough in service over the years. I'll not go down with you now.'

Girolama is, in that instant, speechless. She, who is rarely shocked by anything, is left reeling: that this woman whom her stepmother provided with a living for year after year, this woman who's been at the heart of her home her whole life, should betray her with so apparently little thought. Simply for a quiet life.

Stefano picks up the book and moves closer to Girolama. 'You must confess now, Donna Spana. You have no choice. I have a witness. I have the recipe in my hand. I have the bottles. I have your women.'

You might have my women, Girolama thinks, but you do not have my girl. 'No, Signore Bracchi. You are wrong. You can't secure my conviction without my confession, and what you have in your hand?' She opens her own hand, showing her bare palm. 'In fact, it is nothing at all.'

51

Stefano

Stefano does not understand. His head aches as though a carriage has run him down. His vision is beginning to blur. He reads Girolama's book again and again and yes, there are unlawful recipes there, for abortificients and love potions and charms, many written in different hands. Perhaps one is Tofania's, for many of the papers are worn and old, the writing faded to silver. But there is no instruction on how to make the Aqua. There is no recipe for any poison at all. There is no mention of arsenic, or lead, or antimony or indeed any toxin that he can identify in a single one of the recipes. How can that possibly be?

Did Girolama remove the pages with the relevant recipes before burying the book, knowing that it would be found? Is there a different book, that he hasn't yet discovered, containing the more dangerous ingredients? Or has she used some *secreti leggieri*, such as an invisible ink? He holds the pages before the fire in case some secret writing may be revealed, but no, it seems there is nothing. How can she have tricked him again?

He turns the pages, some falling apart beneath his fingers, and resists the urge to tear them into tiny scraps. This is no book of secrets, he understands, but a book of lies and obfuscation.

As for Cecca and her account of Girolama making the poison, that too is a flimsy, inadequate thing. She did not know all of the ingredients her mistress used and she never saw her create the potion, only receive what she claims was arsenic, grind it down, and then, on a separate occasion, distil something into glass bottles. That may not be enough to secure a conviction, not without a confession, and Girolama will not confess.

He is due at the Vatican in two hours' time to report to the Governor and the Pope on the conclusion of his investigation. He knows he will be seen to have failed. Stefano prepares his arguments, he prepares his pleas and apologies. He tries to prepare himself mentally. Lodovico brings him food, but he has no appetite to eat it. He paces, reciting the arguments he will make, summarising the evidence he has, the work he has done. He knows it is not enough.

When the hour of the meeting approaches, Stefano washes his hands and face and sponges down his shirt and collar. He drinks a cup of wine to fortify himself. As he walks towards the Vatican he feels sweat trickling down his neck, though whether this is caused by nerves or sickness he is not sure. Either way, it does not matter, because he must complete this mission, come what may, and get this wretched thing over. He passes through the gardens of the Quirinal with their neat hedges dividing the walkways, and with their lines of statues blankly watching him. He has never entered the palace itself and, in his exhausted state, he finds it dreamlike, fantastical: a luxurious rabbit warren of dimly lit interconnected rooms populated by clerics, attendants and Swiss guards in their bright uniforms, walking here and there, talking in hushed tones. He is directed to a red-cloaked cardinal who leads him through this whisper-filled labyrinth of gold and marble until they reach a red-curtained room. By now, Stefano feels the fear prickling across his body and his heart races. Again, he rehearses the arguments he must make. He wipes the sweat from his forehead and takes a deep breath.

The chamber is crimson, like the dyer's stomach, the walls smothered in scarlet satin. The only light comes from large silver candles of dripping wax. At a long table two figures are seated: Baranzone is one. Pope Alexander VII is the other. Stefano has never before seen the Pope at close quarters and he is smaller and more fragile than he anticipated, swaddled in gold brocade and white ermine. Stefano bows deeply, kisses the ring of Saint Peter, and waits to be told he may rise.

'I have limited time.' Alexander's voice is high, slightly petulant. 'Please relate swiftly what your investigation has found.'

Stefano does so, trying to keep his focus on his words, not on the opulent and bizarre furnishings that surround him: a golden basket filled with wax fruit, a carved ebony writing desk, rows of gilt-edged books, a silvered reliquary in the shape of an arm which he imagines to be full of holy relics, a bed with a heavy red brocade canopy. He explains that, though Girolama has not confessed, and the recipe for the Aqua eludes him, he believes she has been making a slow-acting poison on a large scale. He has her ring of sellers. He has several women who have admitted buying the Aqua. He has a woman who has seen her putting the liquid into bottles.

'But no confession,' Baranzone observes.

Stefano feels his chest deflate. 'But no confession. I assure you I have tried all means.'

'Then I'm sure you will seek His Excellency's permission that the matter may proceed to the Congregation on Crime without a confession.' Baranzone's face is inscrutable.

Stefano had been preparing for verbal assault, not this. 'I ...

309

well, I admit I did not know such a thing was possible, but certainly if His Excellency is willing to consider such an option?' When Stefano looks at the Pope, he sees that he wears an expression of faint boredom.

Baranzone takes over, talking with confidence of how he is sure there are precedents for popes having allowed trials to proceed without confessions, of how during the witch trials the real witches were often the ones who held out and did not confess.

Alexander puts out his hand. 'I am not interested in the legal history of the issue. I am persuaded that this is a wicked woman whose case must be passed to the judges. Are there others who still refuse to confess?' He is addressing Stefano.

'Several, Your Excellency, though they have been put to the Question. There is one Maria Spinola, and—'

Alexander cuts him off. 'Wherever there is good evidence to suspect these women, their case must be considered by the Congregation on Crime, regardless of whether they have confessed. I will sign a Papal decree to that effect. After all, this is a particularly egregious scandal. Please ensure the matter moves to and through the tribunal quickly. Our reputation is already tarnished and it would do to have this matter concluded.'

Tarnished. Stefano looks at the silver candlesticks. Is that all, in fact, that matters? The surface?

Baranzone speaks: 'We assure you, Your Excellency, that the matter will now move to tribunal stage with all possible haste.' His eyes settle on Stefano. 'Bracchi here will instruct the *avvocato dei poveri*, the lawyer for the poor, and get all necessary papers sent to me and the Congregation on Crime forthwith. Will you not, Stefano?'

Stefano swallows. 'Yes, Monsignore.'

'Good,' Alexander says, pursing his little red mouth. 'Send the papers. I want the matter closed as soon as possible.'

The matter. It is as though the case does not involve tens of humans locked up in a tower, but merely a series of papers covering some bureaucratic inconvenience. 'For all of the women?' Stefano asks.

'Yes, of course,' Baranzone says sharply. 'The cases will be considered together. You heard His Excellency. All those whom there is reasonable evidence to suspect must now have their case transferred to the Congregation on Crime.'

But this is not the established procedure. This is not what the law permits. Perhaps it's the realisation that these men care nothing for the lives of the suspects and that the convictions are to be rushed through, or perhaps it is the lack of sleep, but Stefano finds himself saying: 'Your Excellency, you may wish to consider clemency for several of the women charged. Some of their circumstances were particularly awful.'

Baranzone frowns and Alexander waves this away. 'Perhaps, yes. The poor lawyer may put the applications in writing and I will consider them, but I have no time for this now. Simply pass the matter on as soon as possible.'

Stefano stares at them. 'I will need to take further evidence from our main witness, Cecca de Flores, the assistant of Girolama Spana.'

'Then do so today,' Baranzone says, standing up. 'In the meantime, I will inform the Assessor to the Congregation on Crime. Malvezzi has newly taken on the role.'

'Malvezzi?' He is the pompous man with whom Stefano was seated at Fioralisa's wedding. The harshest and most senior prosecutor of the lot.

'Yes. His appointment is timely as he is the right man for the job. He will be unmoved by attempts to pull at his heartstrings.'

When Stefano does not move, Baranzone says, 'Thank you, Stefano. That will be all. We are grateful for your work thus far.'

'We are,' Alexander says, without looking at him, 'but now we have other matters to discuss.'

Stefano bows to the Governor, bows deeper to the Pope, and backs out of the red-walled room.

Once outside of the chamber, Stefano loosens his collar. It is as though not enough air can get to his lungs. He supposes he should feel relief, even a sense of satisfaction, for the Pope has granted his application and indeed gone beyond it. Girolama's case will be considered, his investigation is at an end, and he has been thanked for what he has accomplished.

He does not feel any of these things, however. He feels a tightening, a sickness. What has he set in motion?

52

Against Melancholy:
Take one spoonful of gillyflowers, the weight of seven barley corns
of Beverstone, bruise it as fine as flour, and so put it into two
spoonfuls of syrup of gillyflowers, and take it four hours after supper,
or else four hours after dinner, this will cheer the heart.

Girolama

'All of the cases will be considered by the Congregation on
Crime in a week's time.' The clerk is standing outside Le Segrete,
reading from some document in his thin and reedy voice.

Standing alone in her cell, Girolama receives this knowledge
as a blow to the gut. It is worse than she'd anticipated, and she's
not exactly known for her optimism. All of the women are to
be prosecuted, all of them for murder, some for procuring and
selling poison. Not a single woman is to be freed, though the
clerk talks of an application for immunity. She guesses that
this is for Anna Conti, the only middle class woman among
them and therefore the only one worth saving, according to
the Papal courts. One lawyer is to be appointed to represent
all of the prisoners, even though there are over twenty people
in these cells. It is only through this man that the women may
speak, and in fact he will speak very little, but rather put his
representations in writing. All this the clerk reads to them in a
flat, expressionless tone.

313

Girolama leans against the damp wall, though her shoulders scream in pain. The despair is communal, universal. From the cells around her, she hears the other women moaning, swearing, praying.

'Mother!' comes a pained shout, and Girolama knows it is Teresa, the dyer's widow.

'Any words of advice for us now, Girolama?' another woman shouts, sarcastic. 'You said they couldn't try us without confessions!'

Girolama tries to rally herself. 'They've twisted the rules just as they've twisted our bodies,' she returns. 'But we're not defeated yet. There must still be a process and, for some of you, there may still be clemency. Use whatever you have. You hear me? Don't abandon hope.'

Hope. Admittedly it seems an impossible thing amid the wailing that surrounds her, but this is no time for self-pity. It never is, in Girolama's book, but certainly not now. This is time for action, even if her body wishes only to collapse.

'How long do we have?' another woman shouts. Girolama thinks it is Camilla, the innkeeper's wife. 'How long until we know our fates?'

The clerk says: 'The process begins on Monday. As to how long it takes, that is for the judges, but the matter is to be dealt with expeditiously.'

A few hours of court time for a bundle of lives. 'We must have a doctor,' Girolama says, 'for there are many women here suffering and one who is not far from death. You know this.' Girolama has looked into Vanna's eyes and knows she doesn't have long.

A pause. Evidently the man does not know what to say. 'I will pass on your request.'

Mocking laughter. Maria hisses. '*Non frega un cazzo*. They mean to kill us all anyway.'

'Tell Stefano Bracchi,' Girolama says, more loudly. 'Tell him what I said. Tell him Vanna is dying.'

'Good riddance!' Laura shouts. 'It's because of her that most of us are here!'

'Silence, Laura!' Girolama shouts, anger searing through her. 'It wasn't her who started this business, and she is now at her end.'

'Yes, it was *you* who started this business,' the woman shrieks back. 'It was you, Girolama Spana, and now we are all to be hanged!'

No doubt she is expected to counter this, but Girolama finds that she cannot. For, in a way, Laura is right. All these lives. All these deaths. They are hers.

It is Maria who speaks: 'You made your own choices, Laura, as did we all. Look to yourself and to the saints and spirits, not to Girolama.'

When the murmuring has died down, Girolama hears Maria's whisper through her wall. 'Your girl. She is safe. The secret is safe. That is what matters, Girolama.'

'For how long, though, *mia amica*? And she is so young.'

Cecca could still speak, or one of the others, in a last hour bid to save their lives. Then her legacy would be ended, her brightest light snuffed out. Even if Angelica has the recipe, she doesn't have its main ingredient. How will she procure it without Girolama's help? More than that: Girolama can't bear to think of Angelica left on her own. She is only fourteen years old in a city that crushes girls much older. If she herself is sentenced to death, who will there be to protect her?

53

Stefano

Stefano works as quickly as he can to prepare the papers that must now be passed to the Congregation on Crime. He has instructed the lawyer for the poor, though he knows he is saddling the man with an impossible task. He will have only a few days to prepare the cases of a prison-full of women. He will then face a pitiless prosecutor and a group of judges whose leader has already made up his mind.

Stefano brings in Cecca once more. Given the lack of confession from Girolama, the statement of the main witness is key. She regurgitates her evidence in the same dull voice she used before. Stefano understands why Girolama would not have suspected this woman of connivance or betrayal: she seems as drab as the colourless dress she wears, as faded as her greying hair. But clearly there is, beneath that, a selfishness. A strong sense of self-preservation. Is it possible that she has cultivated this mantle of dreariness as protection? Or is there just nothing there behind those colourless eyes?

He interrupts her repetitions to say, 'Donna Cecca, when did you first begin working for Donna Girolama?'

'Well, it was her stepmother I worked for first, of course, Giulia.'

'Giulia.' He thinks of the letter from Sicily. The young accomplice who fled Rome. 'Who was she? What was her full name?'

'Giulia Mangiardi, her name was. From Corleone.'

'When did you first start working for her?'

'I couldn't say. Many years ago. In Palermo.'

Stefano had not realised Cecca had commenced work for the family so long before. 'Donna Cecca, did you know of a woman there named La Tofania?'

'Yes, I knew her well enough.' Cecca still speaks without expression.

'She was an apothecary, was she?'

'Something like that. Tofania's husband, he'd been a *speziale*.'

Well. Stefano knows his focus must be on ending this case, but he needs to know how it began. 'Tofania taught Giulia how to make the Aqua, didn't she?'

'She might have, yes.'

'Well, she must have. That is how the recipe came to Rome.' Presumably in the book of secrets which remains hidden away.

The woman regards him but does not answer.

'Donna Cecca, were you in Palermo when Tofania was hanged?'

'Oh no, we were long gone.'

'We? You mean you, Giulia and Girolama?'

'Yes, though she was only young then. Giulia decided it was best to get out after there were some accusations made. That's how we came to Rome.'

Stefano wipes the sweat from his face with his handkerchief, vaguely wondering why he is always sweating. 'And Giulia began making the Aqua in Rome,' he says.

'Not immediately, no, but yes, eventually. For there were always women with a need of the liquid, you see.'

Yes, Stefano does see. 'She then taught the recipe to Girolama, her stepdaughter, so that she could continue her work. Is that right?'

Cecca wrinkles her nose. 'Yes. Giulia thought a lot of Girolama, and she was a bright enough girl, I suppose, but she turned after her first marriage.'

Turned. Like milk gone to curds. Stefano glances at Lodovico, who somehow is still writing. Although Stefano has limited time and scant energy, he says to Cecca: 'Why? What happened?'

Her eyes narrow ever so slightly. 'I think after all you've heard in here you can probably guess that yourself, Signore Bracchi.'

And yes, he finds that he can. He thinks of the deep scar on Camilla's wrist, the burn marks to her body. He thinks of Teresa imprisoned in her house, Anna Conti stabbed in the hand. He thinks of the stories other women have given him of brutality and degradation and suffering. 'What happened to Girolama's first husband?'

Cecca holds his gaze. After a time, she says: 'He died.'

Stefano considers this lethal recipe that has been passed from Tofania to Giulia, from Giulia to Girolama. To Cecca he says: 'Girolama has two sons.'

'Yes.'

'No daughter of her own?'

'No,' the woman says after a brief hesitation. 'No daughter of her own.'

Stefano nods. Continues his questions.

A half hour later they have finished the statement and Lodovico is cracking his knuckles. Stefano is bone-weary. He could almost fall asleep at his table. As Cecca stands, he says, 'Is there any other matter about which you think I should know? Any other woman of whom we haven't spoken?'

She considers. 'There is one, yes, since you ask. There was a lady that visited who lives on the Via del Corso. I don't know her first name, but I heard her tell Girolama she was the Lady Vitelleschi.'

Stefano looks up, now fully alert. *The Lady Vitelleschi*. 'You mean Sulpizia Vitelleschi?' The beautiful, raven-haired girl in green who attended Fioralisa's wedding. The friend of Agnese Aldobrandini, the Duca di Ceri's widow.

'Maybe,' Cecca says. 'I'm not sure. She was young. Very pretty. Fine skin.'

Stefano thinks of her sugar-loaf-white complexion. He thinks of La Sorda saying that Ceri's widow was introduced to the poisoner by a friend. He feels the sweat trickle from his brow down his cheek. 'What happened when this lady visited Girolama?'

'She told Girolama about her husband – said that he was arrogant and stinking and she couldn't live with him. Didn't sound too bad to me, all told, but Girolama sold her the Aqua. Clearly she wanted the woman's money.'

'You are quite sure that Girolama sold the Aqua to her?'

'Oh yes, I saw the bottle change hands.'

Stefano is so stunned it takes him a moment to realise that something in the room has changed. A silence. Lodovico is no longer scribbling. 'Lodovico,' he snaps, 'I'm sure you're tired, but please take down Donna Cecca's evidence.'

Lodovico's eyes slide from him, to the witness, back to the page. Slowly, he picks up his quill.

Stefano breathes out. 'Donna Cecca, please can you tell me exactly when this woman visited your mistress. Tell me everything from the start.'

★

319

After Cecca has been taken away, Stefano says: 'Lodovico, please can you go and ask the guard to fetch further wood for the fire?' When the young man doesn't stir, he says, 'Now.'

Reluctantly, the notary moves away from his desk and leaves the room. Once the door has shut behind him, Stefano moves to Lodovico's desk. He looks at the open page that bears to-day's date. There is no mention of Sulpizia. In the margin, Lodovico has been drawing pictures. A hangman. A group of stick figures. Stefano's heart begins to race. He turns the pages back, through the book of evidence, to find the testimony of La Sorda. His eyes run over the sentences, faster and faster. The Duca di Ceri is missing from the pages. So too is his widow. It is as if that whole section of their interview never took place.

A creaking sound as the door opens again. Lodovico has returned. He stands watching Stefano with baleful eyes.

'Lodovico, this is the book of evidence for the trial. It is an extremely important document.'

'Yes, Signore Bracchi.'

'Yet you have been deciding not to record within it the names of certain individuals.'

A pause. 'Not deciding exactly, no.'

'Not deciding?'

Lodovico runs his tongue over his lips. 'I've simply been doing as the Governor instructed me.'

Stefano feels a sinking sensation. 'What exactly did the Governor instruct you to do?'

Lodovico hesitates. 'He said that if the names of certain people were mentioned, that I was not to record that evidence.'

'Who are these certain people?'

Lodovico's eyes dart around the room as if someone else might leap out to rescue him. When they do not, he says, 'The Duca di Ceri and his widow, Agnese Aldobrandini. And Girolamo Mattei and his widow, Sulpizia Vitelleschi.'

Stefano thinks again of the young woman in the green dress. 'How did the Governor know about them?'

When the notary does not respond, Stefano stands and approaches.

'It was reported to him,' Lodovico says quickly, backing away. 'Some time ago.'

'When?' Stefano's mind is racing.

'I don't know. Long before he assigned me this role.'

And long before Stefano himself was appointed, no doubt. His skin prickles all over. 'How did the Governor know about these people? Who reported the matter to him?' He is still advancing on Lodovico.

'There was a letter, I recall,' the clerk stutters.

'Where is this letter?'

'I don't know!'

Stefano seizes the clerk by his collar.

'I don't know, I tell you,' Lodovico says, shaking. 'I never saw it again. For all I know, it's been destroyed.'

'Because Baranzone wanted the evidence of any noble involvement eliminated.'

'He said it was important the killing was stopped, but not in a way that would be damaging.'

Stefano lets go of the notary and moves away from him. His fight is not with Lodovico. It is with Baranzone. The man must have known months ago that two noblewomen had poisoned their husbands. *That* is why he initiated the investigation. That is why he bothered to delve into the death of a common dyer.

Stefano stares from the window at the grey Tiber. What can he, Stefano, do about this? He is now a fundamental part of the system. He has made himself a part of the injustice it perpetrates. Can he shout from the top of the Tower that in fact it was the deeds of nobles that sparked this investigation? Can he tell everyone that, though it is only poor women who languish in the prison, there are at least two noblewomen (one in a convent, one in a palazzo) who are just as guilty, perhaps more? No, of course he can't, for he will bring the whole thing crashing down about his pounding head. He must finish preparing the papers. He must get to the end of this wretched mission.

A banging on the door to the interrogation room and the door opens. It is the slab-faced guard.

'Yes?'

'This woman,' the guard says, gesturing to the space behind him. 'She insisted I bring her here. She says it's important.'

Stefano hopes for an instant that it will be Girolama, but of course it is it not. It takes him a moment to recognise the woman who steps forward, but it is Cecilia, the mother-in-law of the dyer. The woman who fled from Rome with her daughter, Teresa.

'Donna Cecilia, I have only a few moments. Whatever it is you wish to tell me, you must do so quickly.'

She walks all the way up to his desk. 'I wish to confess.'

Stefano now looks at her properly, takes in her determined expression. 'You wish to confess.'

'Yes.'

He frowns briefly, then turns to the notary, who still looks as though he expects Stefano to hit him. 'Lodovico, please take this down in the book of evidence.'

'Yes, Signore.' He quickly seats himself at his desk and dips his quill in ink.

'Well, Donna Cecilia,' Stefano says. 'You admit to poisoning the dyer?'

'I do. I confess to buying the poison from Maria Spinola. I gave it to my daughter, Teresa, and told her it was a special saint's oil for healing. I said she was to use it on her husband to cure him.'

322

Stefano's tired eyes remain on hers. 'You are saying that Teresa had no idea that the liquid in the bottle was poison?'

'Yes, Signore Bracchi. That is exactly what I'm saying.'

He licks his lips, which are uncommonly dry. He could ask her how Teresa could possibly have been ignorant of the fact she was poisoning her husband, or how Cecilia could feasibly have duped her daughter in such a way. Instead he says: 'Why did you poison him?'

'Because I believed that, when he came out of prison, he would kill Teresa. He'd threatened to do so several times and I couldn't just stand by and watch him do it. She is my daughter. She is my everything.' Her voice cracks.

Stefano nods. 'He threatened you too, did he not?'

'He threatened to slash my face. He threatened to deflower my younger daughter. I believed him capable of doing all these things. But Signore Bracchi: Teresa did not know what I intended. She had no hand in any of this.'

Stefano scratches his head. 'Donna Cecilia, you understand, don't you, what your confession means? You understand what will happen?'

'Yes, Signore Bracchi. I know what will happen.' Her eyes gleam with tears. 'I am begging you to release my daughter. I am begging you to let her go free. Please, Signore. I believe you are a good man. I love her more than life itself.'

For a long time Stefano says nothing, merely stares at his hands.

'I will do what I can, Donna Cecilia.'

Once Cecilia has gone, Stefano works methodically, then desperately, hour after hour after hour. He rejects the idea of sleep, as sleep does not come these days, merely thoughts he doesn't wish to contemplate. Instead, he remains at his desk throughout the night, the fire burning, the tallow candles giving off their animal reek, checking the copies that have been made of the record of evidence, and writing letters to the poor lawyer, letters to the Assessor. His hand aches, as do his shoulders, and the pain in his chest is now almost constant, but the pain is good for him. The pain is punishment for his folly. The pain is an echo of the pain he's wrought on the bodies of impoverished women. He drinks wine to dull the ache, to limited effect. In the morning, Lodovico brings him food, but he can eat little of it. He simply wants to get to the end.

By the time Stefano has finished his letter to Baranzone and is trying to read it through, he realises that the words have lifted off the parchment and are floating somewhere beyond it. He blinks. He is too tired. He is, as Lucia recognised, ill. Indeed, he has begun to cough. The letter will have to do. He sprinkles on sand to blot the ink and waves the parchment in the air. Then he pushes a stick of hot red sealing wax onto the document, and imprints it with his signet ring. He tells Lodovico that he can do no more. He must take the papers to the judges.

'Is that all, Signore?'

'One more thing, Lodovico. Teresa Verzellina. She should not be charged with murder. I have written the letter.'

'Not charged, Signore Bracchi?'

'Yes, Lodovico. You heard her mother, Cecilia, earlier. She confessed to poisoning the dyer. She said her daughter had no hand in it. There is now no reasonable evidence against her.'

He stares the notary in the eye, daring the young man to challenge him. He does not. Perhaps he understands. They can save one soul among many.

'Now I am going to my lodgings to rest.'

Stefano returns to his house, to his narrow bedroom where the walls seem to sway. He finds he is desperately thirsty and drinks from the ewer of water. It tastes dusty. He is so exhausted he can barely remove his boots. He lies on top of the blankets and closes his red-raw eyes. He falls, down and down, through the bed, into a well, fathoms deep. When he reaches the bottom it is soft, sludgy, a mire of putrid matter that sucks at his hands and toes. The witch La Manalonga is there, as he knew she would be, etiolated and white like a worm. But her body is mangled, the long arms broken and malformed. She holds them up to him and he sees that the fingers are smashed and splayed as though from the sibyl. 'You did this,' she hisses. 'You.'

He wakes and finds his entire body is covered in sweat. He drinks more water but it is not enough. Has he been poisoned? Could that be it? But he has a fever, he realises, and Marcello told him fever is not a sign of poisoning. No, he is simply ill. There is a familiarity to it. He closes his eyes again. He falls again. The well becomes a tunnel and he is chasing Girolama through it, through sewers and tunnels that warp and twist.

Something is touching him. It is La Manalonga, reaching out from the well, her fingers damp.

No, it is Lucia. She is holding a cup to his lips and the water is cool and good. 'You are very unwell, little brother.'

'How are you here?'

'I knew something was wrong. I came to find you.'

'We need to find *her*.'

'Who, Stefano?'

'Girolama. The poisoner.'

'But you have found her, Stefano. She is in the Tower, remember? Here, drink a little more.' Lucia smooths a wet compress on his brow. It is as though he is a child again. He feels the same vulnerability, the same fear.

'She is still winning, Lucia. It is she who makes me ill.' Because yes, that is what is happening, he sees that now. She may be locked in the Tower, but Girolama means to kill him.

'No, Stefano. This is the fever that speaks. Lie back. Hush.'

He obeys his sister. He does not have the strength to do otherwise. He cannot even keep his eyes open. A weight falls upon him, pressing him down. He can't move even his lips. It is her. It is Girolama. She is sucking the life from him.

Some time later – he does not know if it is hours or days – he wakes in the red-walled chamber of the Vatican, but it is dark and hot as hell and his teeth are rattling in his skull. It's as though his very blood is on fire. Is he in the inferno? At the centre of the earth? Have the devils dragged him here? Stefano has never felt such heat and horror. It is as though the flames are not only around him but inside of him, burning away at his entrails.

'I'm on fire,' he tries to tell Lucia, who is somehow still there, and he sees from the fear in her face that he is right.

His brothers seem to be here too with them, in hell. Well, that is only fitting.

Later, he hears the voice of his friend. Marcello. No, not friend. He'd hoped that it would be so, but in the end, no. It was too much to ask. Stefano tries to tell him about how the whole venture has been a lie, how the Governor knew at the beginning that the Duca di Ceri had been poisoned, that he knew about Sulpizia. They have been drawn into a fraud.

Marcello tells him to quieten down. He tells him he needs to rest. He has brought some medicines that will help him. 'I understand,' Marcello says. 'I hear you, Stefano, truly I do, but others will hear you too.'

The medicines do not help. How can they, when what is being done to Stefano's body is the work not of nature, but of the blackest sorcery? His blood boils, yet he shivers. He eats nothing, yet he vomits. Within his gut the demons get to work with their red hot pincers and their pokers.

The days and nights blur. It is always dark. Waves of heat wash over him, waves of horror, waves of icy water. Occasionally he comes far enough out of his anguish that he may open his eyes and see the outline of objects in his room: the bed, the desk, the shutters: a line of light around a rectangle. He sees his sister or Marcello, sitting by his side. At those times he tries to fix his gaze on them, to remain in the room and hold off from sliding back into the abyss.

'Stay with me,' he hears Lucia say, but he cannot, for *she* is come with her long white arms to drag him down the slippery well, through the spiralling circles of hell.

54

Anna

Four days remain until the judges convene; four days until they determine whether the women are to live or die. Anna feels it as a growing tightness in her chest, a surging sickness in her stomach. Even Maria is truly frightened now, though she expresses it in anger and curses. Vanna is barely conscious. Anna talks to her anyway.

The lawyer for the poor has come to the Tor di Nona to explain the legal procedure. Anna meets him in the Tower's visitors' room, which is blessedly sweet-scented and airy compared to her stinking cell, the straw of which hasn't been changed since she arrived. She is conscious of how she must look and smell, of sour milk and sweat, but this is no time for vanity. This is the one meeting that they will have before the trial and she must concentrate on the matter of surviving.

The poor lawyer is explaining the procedure at the *processo*. It is entirely in keeping with Anna's experience that a small group of men should be deciding the fates of a tower-full of women, yet the reality of it still takes her breath away. None of the women, the lawyer tells her, are to be produced to the Congregation on Crime. They will not give evidence. They will not even get to hear what is said against them. They must remain in the squalor of Le Segrete while the Assessor lays out the case against them, and he – this faintly ridiculous-looking man in a black doublet and cap – will make short arguments to a row of judges who sit in a closed room.

'The Governor will lead the proceedings,' the lawyer says in his nasal voice, 'and he is clearly determined that the entire trial will be finished within the allotted two days. Regrettably, this means that each defendant will be allowed only a sliver of time, but I am preparing myself as best I can, and obviously in your case immunity has more or less already been agreed.'

'What do you mean "more or less"?' Anna says sharply. 'Surely it was agreed. That was what Stefano Bracchi said: that the Governor had agreed with respect to both myself and Benedetta.'

The man rubs his long nose. 'I believe what he would have said is that he would ask the Governor to apply for immunity to His Excellency the Pope, and I am almost certain that he would have made such a request, so you must not worry in that regard.'

So much hangs on that word 'almost'. 'Well, can you speak with Signore Bracchi? No doubt he can confirm the state of affairs.'

More rubbing of the nose. 'Unfortunately, Stefano Bracchi is indisposed.'

'Indisposed?'

'That is all I was told,' the lawyer says. 'But I repeat that you must not trouble yourself. Now, let me confirm a few matters with you, Signora Conti.'

Anna answers the lawyer as best she can, but agitation is growing in her mind. What has happened to Stefano? Though he was no friend, and although his nature seemed to be coarsening, he was at least recognisably human. She knew when she met him that he understood something of her plight, even if he did not acknowledge it, even if he suppressed his own pity. What have they done with him? Is he in disgrace? Has something terrible happened?

What now will happen to their agreement? Will it still stand?

The waiting is itself a form of torture. The women continue to shout to one another and pray, during both day and night for no one really sleeps any longer. Sometimes they sing: traditional songs from Rome, folk songs from Sicily. Anything to try to lift the spirits. But it is hard to find hope and strength in conditions as bleak as at these.

On the day that the *processo* begins, Anna paces up and down, up and down in her cell like a caged tiger, guessing at what might be happening within that closed court. Around her she can hear women praying. Maria is uttering some kind of incantation and Anna dreads to think what it is, but she cannot truly blame Maria for trying anything at this stage. The bells for five o'clock come, then the evening draws on, yet they hear nothing from the poor lawyer, nothing from the guards or the notary, nothing from anyone, and the waiting is almost worse than anything. She cannot bear not to know what has been decided.

At last the notary comes. He says that no decisions have been made and that the sentences will not be announced until the following week.

A collective groan goes up, of despair and anger and frustration.

'Another week?' Girolama shouts. 'You're making us wait another week?'

'What did they say?' someone else calls. 'What did they say in that room?'

'I cannot tell you,' the notary replies.

Yelling and cursing. Howls of rage. 'How can we be told nothing at all?'

'That is the procedure,' the notary says blandly. 'That is all I am allowed to say.'

Hissing and jeering from the cells.

'I will, however, now read a list of the women whose cases are to be heard tomorrow.' In the same, toneless voice, he proceeds to recite the names of the women whose lives are to be held in the balance the following day.

'Caterina Nucci

Elena Contarini

Maddalena Ciampella

Francesca Laurenti Giuli

'Benedetta Merlini...'

The air around Anna seems to thicken. It is so dense she cannot properly breathe.

'No!' she whispers. 'No, no, no. He told me she would have immunity. He promised!'

But of course Stefano did not promise. He specifically did not promise. He said he would ensure the Governor made the application for immunity to the Pope. Either the Governor failed to do so, or the Pope refused the application. Anna swallows down the bile that rises in her gullet and pushes herself up from the floor. There is no time for despair.

Anna hammers on the cell door. 'Guard!' She will have to bribe him to get a message out. She must be able to get to the money that was taken from her. She must be able to reach Stefano, to make him help, to do anything at all. She cannot lose the woman who has stood by her throughout, who held her hand in the darkness.

55

Stefano

Stefano is dreaming. He dreams of the two-headed calf that Marcello told him was pulled from the Tiber: the beast Baranzone instructed him to anatomise to discover if it was some trick or omen. No, Marcello tells the Governor, this is no trick. It is simply a quirk of Nature. She creates wonderful and horrifying things.

The Governor will not believe him. He is adamant it is a work of sorcery. He wants the heads severed, and that is bad enough, but when Stefano looks back at the calf he realises that its heads are those of women, and they are still alive, their mouths gaping. *No,* he tries to shout. *No!*

'Stefano,' Marcello says. 'Can you hear me?'

Marcello is there, it seems, not just in his dream, but in his sickroom, as he often is. The fact of this surprises Stefano. He thought the doctor had given up on him. Stefano tries to raise his head, but he has no energy still. 'Marcello, it's all been a lie,' he tries to tell him, but his throat is parched and his tongue is like a piece of rotten meat, heavy in his mouth. All he produces is a faint whisper. He's never been so aware of the fragility of his body, or indeed his brain, which won't comply with what he wants.

'Stefano, listen to me,' Marcello continues. 'We require your mind and your mettle. We must support the poor lawyer in the applications for clemency.'

Screaming, high like a mosquito's whine. Marcello is saying something else, but shrieking sounds drown him out and his face slides out of view.

Stefano is back in the world of the dream where the two-headed calf woman opens her mouths and screams at him to save her.

Some hours later, or maybe it is minutes, he resurfaces, more fully this time, and he can hear Marcello and Lucia talking about him. Stefano doesn't have the energy to respond to them, or even to keep his eyes open. The air is thick with burnt rosemary and candle wax.

'I should have recognised it was a recurrence of the scrofula. I shouldn't have left him.'

'He was impossible,' Lucia is saying calmly. 'Even if you'd told Stefano to take to his bed, he wouldn't have done it.'

Stefano hears the scrape of the chair as Marcello moves closer to his bed. 'My friend,' he says, 'I need you to listen to me. I need you to recover. There is important work for you to do. There is no sorcery, no magic. There is only a childhood disease that has returned now because your constitution was weakened.'

He tries to focus. 'The curse,' he mutters.

'Stefano, if the mind believes that the body is cursed, then it will continue to attack itself. If anyone is punishing and tormenting you it is you, Stefano. Yourself. You must stop. You must allow your body to recover.'

He opens his eyes. 'Why?'

'Because you are needed, Stefano, because you must help me tame this monster we've helped to create.'

Stefano's eyes close again. He tries to hang on to what Marcello is telling him, of the Congregation on Crime, a letter from Anna Conti. 'They mean to hang all of the women save for her, Stefano. Even the maid who was to have immunity.'

Stefano struggles to stay above the surface. 'That can't be.'

'But it can, Stefano. That is what is happening. The Governor and the Assessor and the other judges have decided to make an example of these women and string them up for all the city to see. But you and I both know that many of those women – and some of them are little more than girls – did what they did in desperation. Because they had no real choice.'

Stefano can hear Lucia praying, he can sense her leaning forward over him. He wants so much to reach out to her, but he cannot move his limbs, and he is falling again, down and down. He is slithering into the well.

'You are needed and you are loved, Stefano.'

The darkness is covering him, choking him, pushing him down. He is like a drugged man, drowning.

56

An ointment for the ache in the bones:
Take the juice of sage, chamomile and rue, of each a like much, and
mix them with Oil of Exceter.

Girolama

The doctor has returned. He works on resetting the bone in Girolama's shoulder so that it may move more freely. The pain is excruciating but it distracts, at least, from her fear about Angelica, about what is to come. The court is to announce the sentences on Monday and the cells are so full of terror that it is like a new scent on the air.

'There,' Marcello says. 'Your shoulder will begin to improve now, I hope.'

She regards him: his dark brows and earnest eyes. 'It is a peculiar thing to be healing women who, in a few days' time, are almost certain to be condemned to death. Why did you come back, Dottore?'

He busies himself with the bandages. At length, he says, 'In part, because I have a favour to ask.'

Despite the pain, Girolama laughs, because really it is impossible not to. 'A favour,' she says. 'A favour! After everything that's been done in this place?'

The man has the decency to look chastened. 'It will work in your favour also, Donna Girolama.'

335

Girolama wipes her eyes with her one good hand. 'Go on, then. Tell me: what is this favour?'

The doctor hesitates. The words, when they come, are stilted as though they have been rehearsed. 'I need to ask you to cease using whatever magic you are using against Stefano. I need him to believe you have lifted any curse you placed on him.'

Girolama smiles and feels the chapped skin of her lips cracking. 'Surely you don't believe me capable of such things, Dottore. Us women are weak vessels, aren't we, according to you medical men? Our humours too cold to achieve power over any man. And curses? They're not possible, not outside of the Church. Isn't that what the Papal Court tells us?'

The doctor looks away. 'Donna Spana, Stefano is extremely ill. He may die. It is only he who may be able to dissuade the Governor from passing the death sentence on all.'

Girolama's face falls. So, it's as bad as she thought. She tries to swallow and it's as though there's a lump of chalk in her throat. 'Why would the man who investigated this case, who had us all dragged in here, ask the Governor to show mercy to the very prisoners he locked up?'

Marcello meets Girolama's eye. 'Because Stefano is not what he has been pretending to be,' he says. 'He doesn't want all these women do die. He understands why, in certain cases, women acted as they did.'

Girolama waits. 'And you, Dottore? Do you understand?'

'I understand that there are things I've never experienced, nor am likely to. I understand that there may be pain and terror for which there seems to be no other remedy.'

She blinks. 'Sometimes, yes.' Girolama thinks again of the three grasping sisters, of the noblewoman with her handful of gold. After a moment she says, 'You believe that Stefano will be able to make a difference, even now?'

'Truthfully, I don't know, but he's the only one who stands

a chance. He's the only person who knows what Baranzone originally agreed to, and at the moment he can do nothing. He can't even sit up in bed. If I can tell him that you've agreed to lift the curse, he may begin to make a recovery.'

Girolama looks levelly at the doctor. Yes, it may indeed work in her favour. 'Then tell Stefano Bracchi that I lifted that curse some days ago. Tell him I must speak with him. Tell him that he has work to do.'

The doctor frowns. 'You had already lifted it?'

'Yes.' She will not explain why. 'Now, in return, I have a favour to ask of you,' Girolama says. 'Vanna de Grandis. She is extremely ill.'

'I know that. I've done what I—'

'Dottore, I must see her myself. She's been my friend for many years.'

The doctor considers this. 'It isn't permitted, of course.'

'No. Nor, I suspect, is visiting a prisoner to ask she take pity on her prosecutor.'

He gives a half-smile. 'I suspect you are right in that.'

The doctor leads Girolama from her cell, across the stone floor, to Vanna's tiny chamber. The guard watches them without much interest. He is too drunk, and too sick of this place, she guesses, to care any longer what happens in it.

The smell in the room is rank: of sickness and neglect. Girolama moves slowly towards the pallet on the floor and bends to a crouch, though her body screams against it. She smooths her hand over Vanna's face, which has sunk in on the bones of her skull. The skin is clammy and cold.

'You are here,' Vanna says, without surprise.

'Yes, I'm here.' She can hear Vanna's breath wheezing in her chest.

After a time Vanna says: 'It's my fault, Girolama. All this.'

Her voice is hoarse. 'I was frightened. I thought he'd take my daughter.'

Girolama exhales. Maybe a younger version of herself would have reprimanded Vanna for her gullibility, but she isn't that woman anymore. She has too many of her own demons. It is only Cecca whom she blames, a viper in her house, who sold her secrets without a second thought, not caring what it meant for Angelica or for the continuation of Giulia's legacy. 'Vanna, he'd have broken someone else if not you, and you kept the biggest secret back, didn't you? It wasn't only your own daughter you protected, so let's have none of this talk of fault.' She puts her hands over Vanna's. She tries to transfer some of her remaining strength.

After a minute, Girolama stands again, each movement of her body an effort, and says to Marcello: 'Please bring me a basin, water and clean clothes.'

'Very well.'

'And some sage.'

'Sage?'

'Yes. It's good for sore throats. I'm surprised you didn't know, Dottore.'

It isn't for a medicine, though. They are beyond that. She means to burn it for a spell. Girolama is no longer certain that her magic works, but it's worth one last try.

57

Stefano

'Good God, man, you look awful.'

As do you, Stefano thinks, for Baranzone has grown more corpulent since he last saw him, as though all this cruelty and mendacity have fattened him. His desk now seems too small, his chair too fragile, for his frame. 'I feel better than I appear,' Stefano lies. 'Dottor Marcello has worked his cure.'

'I'm pleased to hear that, but you should concentrate on making a full recovery. You are not needed here.'

Stefano licks his lips. 'It is kind of you, Monsignore, to consider my health, but I assure you I am well enough to be here, and indeed I think it important that I am.'

The Governor's smile vanishes. 'Why is that, Bracchi?'

Stefano is not offered a seat, but he takes one. In truth, he has not the strength to stand. 'I understand that the Congregation on Crime is minded to sentence all of the prisoners to death.'

Baranzone's eyes narrow. 'No, not all.'

Stefano smiles. 'Almost all. Not Anna Conti, the only woman of middling class.'

A pause. 'Where did you hear this?'

'From the poor lawyer. And from Anna Conti herself. She wrote to me.'

He raises an eyebrow. 'Did she, indeed?'

Stefano says: 'Her maid, Benedetta. You will recall that you told me that I might offer immunity for her also. That is what I did.'

Baranzone scratches his chin and sits back in his chair. 'I told you, Stefano, to do whatever you thought necessary to obtain important information.'

'Yet not hold to what we had promised? That seems a little underhand, does it not? We, who are supposed to uphold justice?'

The Governor's face is stony, ugly. 'You are accusing me of being underhand?'

'I am saying, Monsignore, that we would do well to keep to what we have promised, or it looks amiss, and it may lead to people looking more carefully into how and why this investigation was initiated.'

Baranzone draws himself up in his chair. 'What do you mean by that?' His voice is icy.

You bastard, Stefano thinks. You lying, conceited *carogna*. 'I mean that if you wish to ensure the names of nobles remain out of the book of evidence then you would do well to reconsider, Governor Baranzone.'

'You threaten me?'

'No, no,' Stefano says, calmly, 'I merely ask that you consider the full state of affairs. Anna Conti gave her confession on the basis that not only she, but her maid Benedetta Merlini, would be immune from prosecution. If you continue with the proposed course of action, I have little doubt that Signora Conti will make her displeasure public. She is an intelligent woman with some status. Then, when I am asked to confirm the conversation I had with her, I will have no choice but to confirm that I did indeed agree that you would apply for immunity, and that you agreed to make that application to the Pope.' He pauses, then says lightly: 'I am assuming no application was made to His Excellency?'

No answer. Stefano was right: Baranzone never had any intention of applying to Pope Alexander for immunity for some maidservant. He merely said it to get Stefano to do what he wanted.

'Is that all?' Baranzone says, his hatred thinly concealed.

'In fact, no, it isn't.' Stefano places a set of papers on the Governor's desk. 'These are copies of the petitions for clemency that were drafted by the lawyer for the poor. I understand that the originals were delivered to you but have not received any response. Since I am now recovered, I've taken the liberty of going through them and considering them.'

'That was not your role.'

Stefano meets his eye. 'I am still the investigating magistrate. I am the only one who has seen all the evidence, heard all of the witnesses. It is always the role of the inquisitor to consider the petitions, and so I have done in this case.' Stefano speaks quickly, not allowing Baranzone to interrupt. 'Camilla Capella, the innkeeper's wife. Hers was the case of most egregious cruelty I have seen, and a child was also involved. His Excellency will wish to consider clemency in her case. Teresa Verzellina, the dyer's wife: her mother gave a confession to the effect that she alone was responsible for his death. Teresa should be granted clemency. I had in fact asked that she not be charged at all. Vanna de Grandis was the first woman to give state's evidence. Without her, the prosecution of the other poisoners would not have been possible. She is also in the balance between life and death. It is politic that she should be spared.' So he goes on, running his fingers over the lines he has written.

'Poison,' Baranzone says over him, 'is the most insidious of evils. The most sly. Unlike a knife to the throat or a shot to the heart, a poisoning allows the subject no means of putting up a fight. We can show no mercy to these women.'

Stefano considers. Yes, it is insidious, silent. The Aqua was transparent, odourless. That was the only means these women had given their weakness compared to their husbands, fathers, brothers. Did that mean it was evil? He is not sure. He says: 'There is always room for mercy, Governor. Always. I am asking that you present these arguments to Pope Alexander.'

Baranzone exhales. 'I will pass him the papers, as I always do.'

'He doesn't read the papers, Governor. You know that. He isn't interested. He will agree with whatever is recommended to him. I am asking you to support my recommendations.'

Baranzone is staring intently at him. 'These women are dangerous, Stefano. Do you not see that?'

'Yet not the other, richer women? Not young women who happen to have titles and money? Does that somehow render them anodyne?'

The Governor regards him with cold eyes. 'One is locked in a convent, the other is safely married.'

Of course, Stefano thinks. Even upper class women must be imprisoned in some way. 'Safely?' he says quietly. 'Was Sulpizia not married before?'

'You do not understand how this world works, Stefano.'

'I understand, Monsignore, how this society works, but that does not mean I have to like it.' He holds the Governor's gaze. 'I ask you again to support my arguments. Not all of the women have to die in order for your point to be made. Indeed, is it not more likely that the public will consider it a fair court that punishes the worst offenders, but dispenses mercy to those who've suffered most?'

'You're a diplomat now, are you, as well as a lawyer?'

Baranzone's tone is mocking. 'I will consider your little speech, Stefano, but really it is too late. The Congregation announces the sentences tomorrow. The die is already cast.'

Stefano stands, his entire body aching. 'Then I would suggest, Governor, that if you wish to ensure that the names of nobles remain obscured, you should convene a meeting at once.'

58

To know if a man shall live or die:
Take the sick man's water and let a woman drop there in her milk,
and if it mingle with the water he shall die, and if it swim above
the water he shall live.

Girolama

Girolama knows she dreamt of Giulia, for her lined, clever face is before her as she opens her eyes onto the gloomy cell. She wishes she could return to the dream and keep hold of her stepmother for a little longer. How she wishes she could talk to her, to ask, *Was what we did always right? Did I, grown jaded and careless, cause suffering to innocent people?* She needs her guidance, for though Girolama turns the situation in her mind like a crystal so that she may see all angles, there seems no correct way forward.

But there can be no more reflecting and ruminating for today is the day of the sentencing, and they are all to be dragged before the Congregation on Crime to hear how the judges have valued their lives. Girolama already knows what her sentence will be, though she doesn't know the exact method they'll devise for her. She thinks of Tofania, dropped in a sack from a roof, and for a moment she closes her eyes, clenches her fists, sending pains shooting up her arms. Whatever they can invent, it won't be worse than the things that were done to her when she was but a girl. It won't be worse than what many women endure day after day, year after year. And also, there is nothing definite in this life.

Coughing and muttering from the other cells as the women rise and ready themselves. Girolama puts her hand against the wall and knows that, on the other side, Maria is doing the same. Courage. They must have courage. They must not simper and cry as the judges want. They must keep their feelings locked inside and give them nothing at all.

It is a shock to face daylight after so many weeks in near darkness. As the women are led out of Le Segrete and into the main prison with its long windows, they cower like cave-dwelling lizards brought for the first time into the day. They can't put their hands up to cover their faces, as they are shackled. They must bend their heads and squint.

To Girolama, though, this light seems a marvel. It must be March now and, as they make their way through the vaulted passage, she can feel the spring breeze brushing against her skin, fresh and glorious. She wonders how her plants are growing, and if Angelica has been tending them well. Her clever girl. They pass through a portcullis, then they are in the prison courtyard where she breathes in the air, a miracle after the stink of the cells. She can hear the sounds of the city just outside: the shouts and hooves and the roll of wheels, the background shush of the Tiber, the slap of waves on boats. She thinks: I cannot leave all this behind. I cannot leave Angelica. I want so much to live. The force of this surprises her.

They are taken then to the *Sala di Tribunale*, which is in a separate building. To prove some kind of point or merely to display his own power, the Governor has declared that, on this occasion, the sentences will be read in public. There are therefore many people here, not just black-robed lawyers,

345

but regular folk, drawn to this disaster like crows to the smell of carrion. The air is a mixture of stale body odour and rich perfumes: musk and ambergris, frangipani and rose. Though most in the gallery are men, a handful are women, dressed in their finery for the occasion. Some whisper, others point. The prisoners stare back at them, some resignedly, some with hatred. 'Who are these people to judge us?' Maria mutters. 'Have they nothing better to do with their days than pester poor old women?'

But of course they are not just poor old women. If they were, no one would be here to watch. They've exercised some power in a city where women, particularly old women, are to keep silent and keep to their place. That's why they are a fascinating, horrifying spectacle. That's why these spectators have turned out to gawp.

It doesn't take them long to deduce that she, Girolama, is the main attraction, or the main villain, and there is hissing, gesturing and murmuring as she makes her way to the long seat at the front of the court.

'Poisoner!' someone shouts. 'String her up!'

'But she's a heroine!' a woman cries.

The Governor, however, has appeared, and has no time for their theatrics. 'I remind members of the public in the gallery that this is not some show. This is a serious matter of law and order and you would all do well to remain quiet.'

His voice is large and rich: the voice of a man who believes himself significant, who is used to being listened to. Girolama knows, though, that for all his blubber, the soul of this man is paper-thin and that, running beneath his velvet voice is a dark, corrosive liquid.

Where is Stefano Bracchi? Girolama peers about the court, but she cannot see him. Is he still too sick to stand? Have they kept him from the court? And where is Cecca? She must still be within the Tower, but no doubt kept well away from Le Segrete lest Girolama tear her to pieces.

Her eyes rest on a girl who is smiling at her. Angelica. Her heart almost bursts with joy and grief combined, but she contorts her face into a frown. The girl should not be here, in this place. It's too dangerous by far. Nevertheless, she is moved to see the child more than she dares admit to herself.

The other judges have shuffled into their seats: old men with paper-white or wine-reddened faces and ridiculous, wispy beards. She knows what to expect from this collection of corpses and it will not be anything pleasant, nor original.

La Sorda says, too loud, 'Is this the best they could muster? They look half-dead already.'

Girolama suppresses a smile. La Sorda. Bless her rounded cheeks and huge heart. She must know she's likely to be sentenced to death, yet still she retains her spirit.

The Governor stands. 'The court, having heard the evidence and the arguments made for the prisoners, and having considered the petitions for clemency and applications for immunity, now issues the following judgment.' He pauses for effect and Girolama feels herself holding her breath. Please God, let some of them be spared. Let Stefano have achieved something of what Marcello said he would attempt.

Baranzone says: 'The crimes of which these women stand accused are the most egregious of all crimes. This ring of women, headed by one Girolama Spana from Palermo, has brewed and sold a deadly poison that has killed untold numbers of victims. The Aqua, being transparent and odourless, and being administered slowly in the victims' food, did not allow the subjects any means of defence. It cheated doctors, relatives, and the Papal court. It could not, however, fool God. The principal at the heart of this conspiracy is Spana, but she has been aided by a web of women, mainly widows, who've distributed the poison throughout Rome. The buyers of the Aqua were mainly women also, obtaining the poison in order to murder their unsuspecting husbands, brothers, fathers, lovers. It has amounted to a poisoning plague and it will now be purged from Italy.'

Girolama stares at this monster of a man, this man who's lived a life of privilege and power. Why does he think he has the authority to bring judgment on them? What does he know of their world?

'However,' the Governor continues, 'we are a just and merciful court and His Excellency is a bountiful and considerate Pope. In some, exceptional, cases, we are therefore willing to show leniency.'

There is murmuring from the gallery. The prisoners stare at one another, silent.

The Governor puffs himself up even further. 'Firstly, Camilla Capella. Though guilty of purchasing poison to kill her husband, innkeeper Andrea Borelli, she will be exiled rather than hanged due to her youth and the extreme nature of her suffering. She is to leave Rome with immediate effect, never to return.'

A cry. Camilla is staring at a man on the other side of the court who now stands, his hand outstretched as if to try to touch her. This must be her husband.

The Governor goes on: 'Benedetta Merlini, though guilty of assisting her mistress to purchase the poison that killed the painter Philippe Imbert, will be spared the death sentence in light of her mistress's confession. She will, however, be required to stand beneath the gallows and watch as the other prisoners are hanged, then exiled from the Papal States for life.'

Benedetta has dropped to the ground. She is weeping.

'Cecilia La Sorda, there being no evidence to prove that she sold poison to any specific woman, will also stand beneath the gallows, then will be flogged through the streets and banished from the Papal States for life.'

Girolama's lips twitch towards a smile. Clever La Sorda. They can flog her generous behind all they like, but what matters is that she will live.

The names of other women are read, those who have warranted mercy, those who have not. 'Teresa Verzellina, though she administered the Aqua to her husband, Giovanni Beltrammi, The Dyer at the Elm, did not know that the bottle her mother gave her was poison. So much has Cecilia Verzellina confessed and will thus be hanged. Her daughter will be spared, but exiled from Rome and the Papal States.'

Silence, then a howl, as though from some animal snared by a trap. Teresa, tall, beautiful, wild-eyed is trying to rush towards Cecilia. 'What have you done, Mother? What have you done?'

The Governor is still talking. He is reading the names of various other buyers of poison who are to be exiled or flogged, or both. Then he says: 'The following prisoners are to be put to death by hanging before the gaze of the people of Rome.' He pauses for effect. Girolama looks at Angelica, whose eyes are fixed on the Governor's face. The girl must know what's coming.

Finally he speaks: 'Girolama Spana, Maria Spinola, Vanna de Grandis, Graziosa Farina, Laura Crispoldi, Cecilia Verzellina.'

Shouting from the gallery, wailing from Teresa. The rest of the women make no sound at all.

Girolama swallows down the bile that rises to her throat, the sob that is building in her chest. She'd known it would be so, but, still, to hear it is an iron fist crushing her to the ground. Though she cannot stretch out her hand to Maria or Graziosa, she can move a little closer to them. She can breathe in the air they breathe.

349

'They could have spared Vanna,' Graziosa whispers. 'She's near to death as it is. That is why they've left her in her cell.'

Laura is looking at the ground, her expression confused. Had she expected anything else?

The Governor continues: 'By their acts, Girolama Spana and her associates lured hapless wives into the monstrous crime of mariticide, daughters into parricide, sisters into fratricide. Once the maker and the purveyors of the diabolical poison are extinguished, Rome can breathe – and eat – safely again. The hangings will therefore take place a week hence. No further appeals for mercy or clemency will be heard.'

Girolama looks at the faces of her women. She thinks of Vanna lying on her pallet in the dark. In her mind, the crystal turns and turns again. All of these lives. They are to be lost at least partly because of her. She wants to save every one, but she knows it cannot be done. Even La Sorda, the sole survivor, is banished forever from Rome. Can she take Angelica with her, and protect her, or will she be taken from the city tonight? Can either of them procure the arsenic and continue the line? It now seems such a thin, insubstantial thing.

Girolama searches out Angelica in the crowd. The girl is no longer smiling, of course, but she is not crying. Their eyes lock and Girolama tries to convey to her what is in her mind.

59

Stefano

The knocking of hammers, the sawing of wood, the occasional whistle or shout. At the mouth of the Via Della Corda they are building a tall, many-beamed gallows: the largest anyone can remember having seen. In the houses that surround it money is changing hands – six to thirty *scudi* for a place at one of the windows that face the Campo de' Fiori: the best seats in Rome. The mood, though, is mixed and changeable. While some think this is a spectacle of justice, others wonder how it is that the only time a woman exercises power in this city, whatever power is available to her, she has her neck stretched before a crowd. All want to see, however. This is history being made.

The *avvisi* and pamphlets talk of how, in the Tower, the confessors make little progress with their charges. The women are not for confessing, regardless of the verdict. Do they think that they might, at the last minute, be reprieved? Girolama Spana, the gazetteers say, shouts and spits and refuses to acknowledge anything. There's something to be said for her continued resistance, many think, but does she really want to go to hell? Surely that's what will happen to her, to all of the women, if they refuse to confess their sins, and people have learnt enough about hell (from the pulpits and preachers, and from the images printed and painted across this city) to know that it means unending and unutterable torment. Does Girolama think the devils down there will welcome her as one of their own?

When the day of the executions comes, the crowd in the Campo de' Fiori is immense, but muted. People have climbed on top of the carriages that were allowed into the piazza. Others have clambered onto the roofs that face the gallows. Every single window is full. On the ground, all of the surrounding streets – the Via di Ripetta, the Strada Pauline and the Corso itself – are entirely blocked with spectators.

Stefano, seated with the Governor on a stage for the officials, would prefer if the crowd were shouting and rowdy, as they often are at executions, but no, they are deathly quiet, watching. Stefano watches too, for it is out of his hands now. There is nothing more he can do.

First comes the procession of priests carrying a large silver crucifix hung with a black curtain. Next, come the members of the *Confraternita della Miseracordia* robed in long black gowns and wearing masks with only slits for eyeholes. Those in front carry lighted torches, those behind shoulder between them five coffins shrouded in black cloth. Immediately after them, walk the executioner and his two assistants, dressed in scarlet coats.

The acrid stench of thousands of bodies rises to Stefano's nostrils and for a moment he thinks he will retch.

'Why the long face?' Vincenzo asked him earlier, for both his brothers are here, their father too, even his little sister, Fioralisa. 'You look like one of your beloved horses. Surely this is your moment of victory. You've done it. You've brought the villains to justice.'

Has he? Are these women, who are now being brought along in prison tumbrils, villains? Graziosa Farina is taken from the carts first, a comforter on either side of her, a noose already draped about her neck. Shorn of her dyed red hair she looks even tinier and, in her black dress, she puts Stefano in mind of the bird in the box that was left for him, that has perched ever since in his mind. Next is Maria Spinola, white-eyed Maria, supporting Vanna, who is now as bent as a shepherd's crook. Then comes Lauraccia, who mostly keeps her head down, but now and again shoots looks of spite at members of the crowd.

'Here they are,' the Governor says, his voice acidic. 'Satan's decrepit servants.'

Last in the group is Cecilia. Her gait remains upright and dignified, her head covered with a shawl. Despite Cecilia's claims, Stefano suspects Teresa knew full well what medicine she was feeding her husband. But Cecilia told him she loves her daughter more than life, and here she is, proving it.

Stefano glances back at his father, who sits behind him on one of the rows of seats that have been built for the occasion. Would he give his life for any of his children? All of them? No.

His father, sensing he is watched, looks back. 'So, these were your adversaries, were they, Stefano? I'm surprised it took you so long to break them. They look like a flock of crows.' He is smiling, but his eyes are cold.

Stefano turns back to face the gallows. It's plain to him in that moment that, no matter what he achieves, his father will always strive to make him feel inadequate. He could be the most esteemed judge in all of Italy, he could be the Governor of Rome himself, but still his father would attempt to make him feel small, a failure. It is just as Lucia said and it is nothing to do with him, what he has done, who he is. It is to do with his father and whatever has formed him. What was it Girolama said? Some people are poisonous. One does best to avoid them.

La Sorda is brought out next. She somehow still walks like a woman on her way to market, not to the gallows to see her friends die. Not so Benedetta, Anna Conti's maid, who already has her hands to her face. The guards position them beneath the gallows, where the other women are being prepared for death, blindfolds tied around their heads.

Stefano realises that Anna Conti is there, near the front, with the common people. She is reaching her hand out towards Benedetta. She is telling her maid, *I am here.*

'They have all confessed now,' the Governor tells those around him loudly. 'All save Girolama Spana. May she burn in the fires of hell.'

And then they bring her, shrouded, several masked confessors about her.

'There she is.' The Governor stands, no doubt to ensure his voice is better heard. 'The origin of all this evil. Thank God that she is finally brought to justice. She seems a broken woman. Look! She can barely stand. So much for her terrible powers!'

Others murmur in agreement, but Stefano remains silent. He has nothing to say to this man and he not sure, in any event, that he could speak. His throat is knotted with fear.

The comforters are kneeling beside the women, holding up silver crosses and images, praying for them. Some people in the crowd are wailing.

As he watches the women at the scaffold, Stefano replays in his mind his final meeting with Girolama shortly before the sentencing. They are in the room at the Tower where he carried out all the interrogations. He asks her: 'Will you not confess? Will you not acknowledge the wrongs you've committed? Surely you wish for absolution.'

'Ah,' she says, 'absolution.' She is looking out of the window, at the Tiber. 'What about you, Signore Bracchi: what is the state of your soul? Do you think God approves of what you've done?'

'I too will be going to confession, Donna Spana,' he says quietly. 'I don't pretend to know the Lord's plan. I acted as I thought right.' For do we not almost always think, in the moment, that we do right, and only after form a different conclusion?

She smiles. 'As did many of the women who'll now be hanged or banished from their homes forever. They acted as they felt they had to do to escape no imagined inferno, but a living, breathing hell. Reflect on the women in your life, Signore Bracchi. You think they applaud your achievement?'

He is still so tired, down to his bones. 'This is not about me, Donna Spana. This is not my time. I am asking you to confess.'

'And I am asking you to consider my question properly.' Girolama is no longer smiling. Her eyes are very dark and still. 'I am asking you to think of the women in your life. I am asking you, in fact, to think of the woman you love most in all the world.'

It takes Stefano a moment to understand what she is saying and he feels a constriction of his chest. 'Why?'

She waits, the silence stretching out like the string of an archer's bow. 'Many years ago, Lucia came to me.'

No, Stefano thinks. *No.*

'She showed me some of the marks on her body, told me a little of what he did.'

Stefano feels that he is slipping, falling, back down into the darkness.

'Lucia didn't really need to tell me, though, because I could see, as soon as I saw your sister, what her life was. Yet you yourself saw none of it.'

'What are you saying?' Stefano's world is folding in on itself. 'Why are you saying this?'

Girolama continues: 'I recognised it because I'd been there myself, as a girl, and I had no wish for her to suffer likewise. That's why I sold her the Aqua.'

Stefano is dredging from his memory an image of Lucia's husband: a neat, grey-haired man with an unremarkable face. He never thought. He never guessed. How? *How* did he not see? He thinks of Lucia, generous Lucia, who has always given him everything. Why, in God's name, did she not tell him? Or did he not hear what she was trying to say? Did he not see what was before his eyes? Stefano wants in that moment to kill the man. But of course he is already dead.

Girolama is looking at him, her gaze not unkind. 'Now you understand.'

Stefano is remembering his conversation with his sister on Fioralisa's wedding day. *One cannot assume happiness, Stefano.* He is thinking of how Lucia tried to persuade him to step down from this role. He is thinking of the times during her marriage when she could not ride and claimed it was for women's reasons. His hands are over his face.

'I will offer you a deal, Signore Bracchi: my silence for the lives of my women.'

Stefano tries to concentrate, to rationalise, but his mind is a scatter of images and imaginings. He knows, though, what will happen if this story becomes known: it will destroy Lucia, him, all of them. It will bring everything crashing down. He tries to breathe slowly, think logically. There must be a solution. Surely there must.

As if she knows his thoughts, she says, 'Lest you think there's some way out, be assured that I'm not the only one who knows about your sister, who knows the details well. They're also recorded in a book: the date she bought the Aqua, the quantity, the reason. I don't want to harm your sister, but if I go to the gallows, I promise you that her secret will be brought into the light.'

Stefano does not doubt what she says. Girolama is methodical in a way that his father would no doubt admire. She has planned everything, foreseen everything. 'This is why you didn't flee Rome months ago,' he says. 'You knew you had the highest trump card and you've waited until the end to play it.'

Girolama shrugs. 'Lives are not cards.'

He snorts. 'Yet you've treated many as though they were. Whole decks have been knocked from the table. How many men have died?'

She chews her lip. 'I don't pretend to goodness, Signore. I have my own regrets, but they'll get me nowhere now. What matters is the way forward.'

Stefano shakes his head. He is thinking that, if this is a game of Tarocco, he himself is the Fool. 'Even if I were to agree, there is no way this thing you propose could be done. You must know that yourself. What? Am I simply to allow you and your accomplices to leave the Tower? To stage some kind of mass escape? There would be uproar, an enquiry, a prolonged search. My part in it would be immediately known. You and your women would almost certainly be found. What you ask: it is impossible.'

For a long time she is silent. Finally, she says: 'Then a compromise. My life alone.'

'It is still impossible.'

'Difficult, yes, but not impossible.' Her tone is one of sadness.

He shakes his head. 'You would leave all your women and be the sole survivor?'

She frowns. 'If that is the way it has to be, then yes. I have my reasons.'

'What reasons?'

'Partly the same reason that you will do as I ask, Stefano Bracchi. To protect the girl I love most.'

Stefano blinks. Who does she mean? He recalls Cecca saying, 'No daughter of her own.' He sees a girl, running through a marketplace.

'I don't see how, even if I were to agree, this thing could ever be achieved.'

'It will be risky, yes, but it can be done. I've thought it through. This is how it will happen.'

A shout from someone in the crowd brings Stefano back to the moment. His eyes return to the shrouded figure who now approaches the scaffold. The figure that cannot stand unaided. This is nothing to do with fear or sickness. It is because she is drugged with poppy and mandragora, and her mouth is stuffed with a rag. The maid who betrayed Girolama. Stefano's stomach convulses with dread. Will they get away with this? Is he really going to allow it to happen? What other choice does he have?

At least, he tells himself, this woman is not entirely innocent, not entirely good. She helped Girolama for years, and helped her stepmother, Giulia, before that. She knew what they were doing. She betrayed Girolama only to save herself. Still, he is condemning the wrong person to death. It is costing him heavily, both in terms of his soul and in the gold with which he's bribed the man who cuts down and buries the bodies. As Marcello said, our bodies give up secrets after our deaths that we have maintained in life. This one must be a closed book.

'Tell me,' Stefano said to Girolama after they'd discussed her devil's bargain. 'Where is the book of secrets with the recipe for the Aqua?'

'Burnt. Long ago. Tofania realised it was too dangerous for the poison recipe to be written down. The book could have got into the hands of the authorities. It could have got into the hands of anyone. No, she and Giulia learnt the recipe for the Aqua and the other key poisons by heart. When it was time, Giulia taught them to me. The secrets?' she tapped her head. 'They are here.'

Watching Cecca now as she is led to the stage, Stefano wonders if that is true. He can have no way of knowing. Maybe that's what all this has taught him: that one cannot know anything truly, definitively, even oneself. There are, after all, dark fragments within his mind that he hadn't known were there. How, then, can he claim to know or judge the actions of anyone else? He is sitting before a spectacle of death that he himself has helped to create.

The hangman approaches Cecca. A comforter stands next to her, chanting prayers, holding up a picture of Christ. Executioner and saviour side by side.

Perhaps, Stefano thinks, there is no clear dividing line between a good person and a bad one, between what is good and what is evil: the barricade between is nebulous, porous, as thin as the gossamer that his sister's silkworms weave.

The executioner tightens the noose around Cecca's neck. He takes a step back.

Stefano could still stop this. He could stand up, he could shout. But of course he does no such thing.

The executioner raises his arm to indicate that the moment has come and, as he does so, hands fly to mouths, to chests, to cover children's eyes. There is, they understand, to be no last-minute reprieve, no miracle, no intervention by God or the devil to stop this taking of life. Some members of the audience begin to wail, but most of the crowd is silent.

The executioner's assistants move closer to the hooded women, ready to push them off. Graziosa, Maria, Vanna, Laura, Cecilia, and the woman everyone believes is Girolama.

Beneath the gallows, Benedetta and La Sorda stand, hand in hand, waiting.

There is a collective holding of breath, a slowing of blood and of time; a complete and terrible stillness.

Then comes the jolt of the ropes, a gasp, a cry, and the women step out into the air.

60

To refresh the spirit:
Take sea wormwood, spearmint, betony, marjoram, rosemary,
balme, borage, savory of each alike quantity, as much as your still
will hold. On the top of the herbs, 2 ounces of beaten cinnamon and
so distil as much water as you can, and keep it all together. Take
8 or 10 or 12 grains of prepared pearls in one or 2 spoonfuls of the
water in the morning fasting. You may take it a week together or as
of oft as you please it strengthen the whole body.

The swifts are returning to Rome. They dart between laundry
lines, swoop after insects, and nest in the eaves of the houses.
The pilgrims are arriving too, thousands of them swarming in
through the gates in preparation for Holy Week: to be in the
city of God when Christ rises again.

Amid these arrivals, Benedetta is preparing to leave. Anna's
maid – her friend – is to go to Venice to live with her family
and find some means of existing. They do not know when, if
ever, she'll be allowed to return. That will depend on the clemency of the Pope, a man who barely knows of their existence.
The sadness of it is sometimes so large that Anna feels she will
choke on it, but it is better than the others' fates. They have
not discussed what it means that they have survived, while so
many of the women who surrounded them are dead. It doesn't
seem possible for Anna to voice it, except in her own prayers.
She still thinks every day of Maria and Vanna, of Girolama and

Laura. She still hears their voices when she sleeps at night, like whispers through the wall.

Aurelia, though, has clung onto life just as she has from the very beginning, and just as Maria told her she would. Now, while the baby sleeps in her crib, Anna is slicing vegetables and herbs from the garden for a *minestra* while, on the *madia*, Benedetta is cutting out tiny pasta stars. This will be their final meal together.

'Family is family,' Benedetta is saying. 'They'll put me up, like it or not, until I'm back on my own two feet.'

Anna tips the herbs into the pan. Going to her own family is not an option. Her mother has made that clear. She too will have to find a way forward and that is frightening, but it is also liberating.

'You'll find work quickly, I know you will,' she tells Benedetta. 'God willing, I'll visit you when Aurelia is older. See what you've made of yourself.'

★

The colours too are returning to Rome: the green of vines and leaves on trees, the gold of sunlight on stone and travertine, the washed blue of the sky.

Angelica and Girolama are in the garden where purple sweet pea blooms. Girolama, her head shrouded in a shawl, is pleased to see that the calendula are already reviving, the iris flowering. Such life lifts her soul which has lately been plunged into darkness. So many of those closest to her dead, and for selling the poison that she herself made. Should she have gone with them, since she couldn't save them? Was she wrong to forfeit Cecca's life to preserve her own, even if the woman betrayed her? These aren't questions to which she knows the answers. Her views wax and wane like the moon. When she looks at

Angelica, she is glad, however, that her girl is not in this world alone. That she stands a chance at life.

They are uprooting some of the plants and taking clippings from others, the strongest ones, the ones that have survived the frost, the rain, the lack of care, for plants grown from these are the most likely to survive. Girolama will have to replant her garden in another city.

'Will they last the journey?' Angelica asks.

'Not all, but some. They'll take root again elsewhere, if we help them.'

'What about us? You think we'll take root?'

'Oh, I should think so. La Sorda will be with us, who always finds friends and customers. We'll set up again, find a new supplier and recruit new women.' Not as good, perhaps, not as faithful and clever as Vanna, Maria and little Graziosa, nor as wily as Laura. 'What we provide will always be needed,' she says. At least until a woman's life is properly valued, and Girolama can't see that happening any time soon. So many killed every day. It was what Tofania recognised, and Giulia. It's what Girolama herself has always known. She'll be more careful now, though, with the secret she was given, with that power sealed in a small glass bottle.

'What if they all die?' Angelica asks, and it takes Girolama a moment to realise she is talking about the plants.

'Then we start afresh. Giulia started here with nothing, and look what she managed to create.'

What matters is that the line continues, and that the secrets are never lost.

★

Stefano leaves Rome at the Porta San Pancrazio, passing the verdant vineyards and lush gardens of the nobles, then crossing untended open land. Lucia's convent lies some miles to the south and it is a journey he already knows well. Each time he rides it he thinks of what he has unlearnt and learnt, what he has saved and lost, what is written down and what remains off the page. He remembers Girolama's book with its silvery lines written and amended by different hands. The recipe for each of us, he thinks, is like that: concocted from what we're taught, what happens to us, and the choices we make, all stirred in the pot together.

He spurs Damigella faster and faster until they are galloping across the countryside, the landscape a blur, the wind hard in his face, cleansing away everything, even thought, even his sense of self.

There is just the wind, the smell of spring, and the movement of the horse.

They are a tiny spot moving across a vast expanse of earth.

On they go, and on.

Historical Note

This is a work of fiction. I have used within it many of the facts that appear in the historical record, but of course that record is itself incomplete and biased, having been composed by the legal authorities and by the *avvisi* and gazetteers of the time. The only record we have of the women's voices is in the notary's document, which of course he transcribed and, as Philippea Feci points out in her article 'Trame di donne all'indomani della peste romana del 1656', the whole poisoning inquisition has to be seen in the context of a society that was fixated on plague and contagion, and in curtailing subversive activities. Much of what people will have heard of the so-called Aqua Tofana case was in fact invented in the nineteenth century, including the figure of Giulia Tofana who seems to be an amalgamation of several characters. The real name of Girolama Spana's stepmother was Giulia Mangiardi, and she may or may not have been the daughter of Tofania di Adamo from Palermo.

In some instances I have intentionally diverged from the record that exists in order to create a more satisfying and intelligible story. There were more than thirty defendants in the original case, and I obviously have not been able to make them all characters in the book, but rather have selected a few of the women's stories to represent the whole. It seems Giovanna de

Grandis ('Vanna') and Maria Spinola also knew the recipe for the Aqua, but I have changed this so that only Girolama Spana, the key poisoner, is aware of the deadly formula. Vanna in fact (and somewhat inexplicably) confessed fairly early on in the *inquisitio* process, giving Stefano Bracchi the names of many of the other players, but I have trickled out the flow of information within the investigation process to make it fit more to the mystery genre. It is true, however, that Girolama Spana tied Stefano Bracchi in knots and refused to confess until the very last moment. She was evidently a tough and intelligent woman. As for Stefano, although I know he existed and carried out the role of inquisitor at the request of Baranzone, the Governor of Rome, I have been able to find out almost nothing of the real man, so have felt free to invent. There would have been a doctor who examined the prisoners, but I do not know who he was, so Marcello is entirely my invention. Similarly, although I know that there was an orphan living in Girolama's house, I know nothing about them. Angelica is therefore a figment of my imagination.

Regarding the outcome of the legal process, Cecilia Verzellina was not executed at the same time as the other women, but some months later, after she was caught in Naples. Similarly, La Sorda was not caught until 1660. As for Girolama Spana, so far as we're aware, she was in fact hanged with the other women at the gallows in the Campo de' Fiori, survived by the servant who betrayed her. The reader will have to forgive me for letting her live in my version. I couldn't bring myself to kill her.

I have also altered some of the names to avoid confusion: Giovanna de Grandis is 'Vanna' to avoid being mixed up with Girolama and Giulia. Anna Conti's real name was Anna Maria Conti, but I changed this to avoid confusion with Maria Spinola. Similarly, I renamed Anna Maria Aldobrandini

'Agnese' Aldobrandini as there were too many Annas and Marias and early readers ended up in a pickle. I renamed Simon Imbert 'Philippe' Imbert, as it was, frankly, difficult to envisage a Simon as a villain.

For a detailed account of the real prosecution, Craig Monson's *Black Widows of the Eternal City* provides a fascinating read.

References for Recipes and Spells Featured in Girolama's chapters

Many thanks to The Esoteric Archives, Llewellyn, the Wellcome Collection, and the Text Generation Partnership for their permission to quote from the relevant works.

Chapter 5: From A Choice Manual of Rare and Select Secrets in Physick and Chyrurgery by Countess Elizabeth Grey of Kent, 1662

Chapter 9: From The True Preserver and Restorer of Health being a choice collection of select and experienced remedies for all distempers by George Hartman, 1682.

Chapter 13: From A Choice Manual of Rare and Select Secrets, as above.

Chapter 17: From Natural Magick by Giambattista della Porta, 1558.

Chapter 20: From I Segreti della Isabella Cortese, 1662 (my translation).

Chapter 29: From The Key of Solomon – *Clavicula Salomonis* – Edited by S. Liddell MacGregor Mathers, Revised by Joseph H. Peterson.

Chapter 32: From The Book of Oberon: A Sourcebook of Elizabethan Magic, edited by Daniel Harms, James R Clark, Joseph H Peterson.

Chapter 38: From A Choice Manual, see above.

Chapter 43: From Medicaments for the Poor: or, Physick for the Common People, Nicholas Culpeper, 1656.

Chapter 47: From The Book of Secrets of Albertus Magnus: Of the Virtues of Herbs, Stones, and Certain Beasts, Also a Book of the Marvels of the World, 1502.

Chapter 50: From The Grimoire of Honorius, 1670.

Chapter 52: From A Choice Manual, see above.

Chapter 56: From Natura Exenterata: or Nature Unbowelled by Lady Alathea Talbot, 1655.

Chapter 58: From Nature Exenerata, see above.

Chapter 60: From Receits of Phisick and Chirurgery, Lady Ayscough Booke, 1692 (MS1026)

Anna loves to hear from readers, so do say hello on social media, or send a message via her website.

http://annamazzola.com
https://twitter.com/Anna_Mazz
https://bsky.app/profile/annamazz.bsky.social
https://www.facebook.com/AnnaMazzolaWriter/
https://www.instagram.com/annamazzolawriter/

Acknowledgements

Firstly, thank you to all the readers, reviewers, booksellers, bloggers and librarians who have supported my books. I wouldn't be able to keep writing without you.

Thank you to my superstar agent, Juliet Mushens, and all the team at Mushens Ent (Rachel, Alba, Kiya, Catriona, Emma and Seth) for their continuing support and vitality. My talented editor, Charlotte Mursell, helped me make this a much stronger book, so big thank you to her and all the team at Orion, including Frankie Banks, Hennah Sandhu, Snigdha Koirala, and Sally Partington, copyeditor of dreams. Thank you to Andrew Davis for another stunning cover.

Many people have helped me with elements of the research for *The Book of Secrets*, and I have been repeatedly taken back by the generosity of the academics and professionals to whom I've reached out. Where I've got things wrong, this is entirely my fault and not theirs. Thank you to Professor Craig A Monson, Professor Thomas V Cohen and Professor Elizabeth Cohen, Daniel Harms and Joseph H Peterson of the Esoteric Archives, Tom Knox, head gardener at Alnwick Poison Garden, the brilliant staff at the British Library, Professor Jill Burke, Dr Melissa Reynolds, Joyce Froome, Assistant Curator at Boscastle

Witchcraft Museum, Professor Stuart Carroll, Professor David Gentilcore, Dr Tom Wedgwood, Dr Gargi Patel, Sally Rendel, and Matthew Plamkin.

Thank you to my writer friends for their ongoing support and in particular to the following for their help with thinking about and formulating this book, and/or listening to me complain about it: Abir Mukherjee, Laura Shepherd-Robinson, Tammy Cohen, Marianne Levy and all at North London Writers, The Ladykillers, and of course Colin Scott.

My colleagues at the Centre for Women's Justice do an incredible job of pushing for state accountability for violence against women and girls. When I began reading the Spana prosecution notes, I realised that many of the accounts from 17th century witnesses were all too similar to the accounts we hear from survivors now, and though our justice system is some way from that of early modern Italy, we still have a very long distance to travel. To learn more about the CWJ's work and to support them, see https://www.centreforwomensjustice.org.uk

Lastly, thank you to my wonderful family who continue to put up with my nonsense and to support me every step of the way. I know how lucky I am. In particular, thank you to Jake, Iris, Edward and my writing assistant, Obsidian, aka Sid.

Credits

Anna Mazzola and Orion Fiction would like to thank everyone at Orion who worked on the publication of *The Book of Secrets* in the UK.

Editorial
Charlotte Mursell
Snigdha Koirala

Copy editor
Sally Partington

Proof reader
Linda Joyce

Audio
Paul Stark
Jake Alderson

Contracts
Dan Herron
Ellie Bowker

Design
Tomás Almeida
Joanna Ridley
Andrew Davis

Editorial Management
Charlie Panayiotou
Jane Hughes
Bartley Shaw

Finance
Jasdip Nandra
Nick Gibson
Sue Baker

Marketing
Hennah Sandhu

Publicity
Frankie Banks

Production
Ruth Sharvell

Sales
Jen Wilson
Esther Waters

Victoria Laws
Toluwalope Ayo-Ajala
Rachael Hum
Ellie Kyrke-Smith
Georgina Cutler

Operations
Jo Jacobs